# SWORN SWORD

James Aitcheson

**WINDSOR**
**PARAGON**

First published 2011
by Preface Publishing
This Large Print edition published 2011
by AudioGO Ltd
by arrangement with
The Random House Group Ltd

Hardcover  ISBN: 978 1 445 85934 7
Softcover    ISBN: 978 1 445 85935 4

British Library Cataloguing in Publication Data available

Printed and bound in Great Britain by
MPG Books Group Limited

To my parents

# CONTENTS

# LIST OF PLACE-NAMES

To add to the historical authenticity of the setting, I have chosen throughout the novel to use contemporary names for the locations involved, as recorded in charters, chronicles and Domesday Book (1086). For British locations my main sources have been *A Dictionary of British Place-Names* (OUP: Oxford, 2003) and *A Dictionary of London Place-Names* (OUP: Oxford, 2004), both compiled by A. D. Mills.

| | |
|---|---|
| Alchebarge | Alkborough, Lincolnshire |
| Alclit | Bishop Auckland, County Durham |
| Aldwic | Aldwych, Greater London |
| Aleth | Saint-Malo, France |
| Bebbanburh | Bamburgh, Northumberland |
| Bisceopesgeat | Bishopsgate, Greater London |
| Cadum | Caen, France |
| Ceap | Cheapside, Greater London |
| Commines | Comines, France/Belgium |
| Cosnonis | River Couesnon, France |
| Dinant | Dinan, France |
| Drachs | Drax, North Yorkshire |
| Dunholm | Durham |
| Earninga stræt | Ermine Street |
| Eoferwic | York |
| Execestre | Exeter, Devon |
| Gand | Ghent, Belgium |
| Haltland | Shetland |

| | |
|---|---|
| Hæstinges | Hastings, East Sussex |
| Humbre | Humber Estuary |
| Kopparigat | Coppergate, York |
| Lincolia | Lincoln |
| Lincoliascir | Lincolnshire |
| Lundene | London |
| Orkaneya | Orkney |
| Ovretune | Overton, Hampshire |
| Oxeneford | Oxford |
| Reddinges | Reading, Berkshire |
| Rudum | Rouen, France |
| Searobyrg | Old Sarum, Wiltshire |
| Silcestre | Silchester, Hampshire |
| Stanes | Staines, Surrey |
| Stanford | Stamford, Lincolnshire |
| Stybbanhythe | Stepney, Greater London |
| Sudwerca | Southwark, Greater London |
| Suthferebi | South Ferriby, Lincolnshire |
| Temes | River Thames |
| Trente | River Trent |
| Use | River Ouse |
| Walebroc | Walbrook, Greater London |
| Waltham | Waltham Abbey, Essex |
| Wæclinga stræt | Watling Street, Greater London |
| Wærwic | Warwick |
| Westmynstre | Westminster, Greater London |
| Wiire | River Wear |
| Wiltune | Wilton, Wiltshire |
| Wincestre | Winchester, Hampshire |

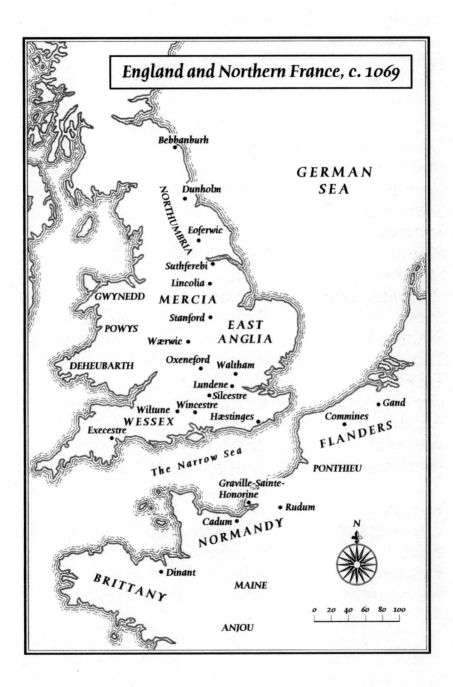

England and Northern France, c. 1069

# CHAPTER ONE

The first drops of rain began to fall, as hard as hammers and as cold as steel against my cheek. My mail hung heavily upon my shoulders, and my back and arse were aching. We had risen at first light and had spent much of the day in the saddle, and now night lay once more like a blanket across the wooded hills.

Our mounts' hooves made hardly a sound against the damp earth as we pressed on up the slope. The path we followed was narrow, little more than a deer track, and so we rode in single file with the trees close on either side. Leafless branches brushed against my arm; some I had to fend away from my face. Above, the slender crescent of the moon struggled to make itself shown, casting its cold light down upon us. The clouds were rolling in and the rain began to come down more heavily, pattering upon the ground. I pulled the hood of my cloak up over my head.

There were five of us that night: all of us men who had served our lord for several years, oath-sworn and loyal knights of his own household. These were men I knew well, alongside whom I had fought more times than I cared to remember. These were men who had been there in the great battle at Hæstinges, and who had survived.

And I was the one who led them. I, Tancred a Dinant.

It was the twenty-eighth day of the month of January, in the one thousand and sixty-ninth year since our Lord's Incarnation. And this was the third winter to have passed since the invasion: since we had first mustered on the other side of the Narrow Sea, boarded ships and made the crossing on the autumn tide. The third winter since Duke Guillaume had led our army to victory over the oath-breaker and usurper, Harold son of Godwine, at Hæstinges, and was received into Westmynstre church and crowned as rightful king of the English.

And now we were at Dunholm, and further north than any of us had been before: in Northumbria, of all the provinces of the kingdom of England the only one which after two years and more still refused to submit.

I glanced back over my shoulder, making sure that none were lagging behind, casting my gaze over each one of them in turn. In my tracks rode Fulcher fitz Jean, heavy-set and broad of shoulder. Following him was Ivo de Sartilly, a man as quick with his tongue as he was with his sword, then Gérard de Tillières, reticent yet always reliable. And bringing up the very end of the line, almost lost in the shadow of the night, the tall and rangy figure of Eudo de Ryes, whom I had known longer and trusted more than any other in Lord Robert's household.

Beneath their cloaks their shoulders hung low. They all held lances, but rather than pointing to the sky as they should have been, ready to couch under the arm for the charge, they were turned down towards the ground. None of them, I knew, wanted to be out on such a night. Each would rather have been indoors by the blazing hearth-fire with his pitcher of ale or wine, or down in the town with the rest of the army, joining in the plunder. As too would I.

2

'Tancred?' Eudo called.

I turned my mount slowly around to face him, bringing the rest of the knights to a halt. 'What is it?' I asked.

'We've been searching since nightfall and seen no one. How long are we to stay out?'

'Until our balls freeze,' Fulcher muttered behind me.

I ignored him. 'Until daybreak if we have to,' I replied.

'They won't come,' Eudo said. 'The Northumbrians are cowards. They haven't fought us yet and they won't fight us now.'

They had not; that much at least was true. Word of our advance had clearly gone before us, for everywhere we had marched north of Eoferwic we had seen villages and farms deserted, people fleeing with their livestock, driving them up into the hills and the woods. When finally we reached Dunholm and passed through its gates just before sunset earlier that night, we had found the town all but empty. Only the bishop of the town and his staff had been left, guarding the relics of their saint, Cuthbert, who resided in the church. The townsmen, they said, had fled into the woods.

And yet there was something about the ease of our victory that had made Lord Robert uncertain, and that was why he had sent the five of us, as he had sent others, to search for any sign of the enemy nearby.

'We keep looking,' I said firmly. 'Whether or not our balls freeze.'

In truth I didn't think we would find anyone tonight, for these were people who would never before have seen a Norman army. Naturally they

3

would have heard of how we had crushed the usurper at Hæstinges, but they could not have witnessed it themselves. They had not felt the might of the mounted charge which had won us that battle and so many others since. But now at last we had come in force: a host of two thousand men come to claim what was the king's by right. They would have seen our banners, our horses, our mail glinting in the low winter sun, and they would have known that there was no hope of standing against us. And so they had fled, leaving us the town.

So it seemed to me, at least. But what I thought didn't matter, for the decision was not mine to make. Rather it belonged to our lord, Robert de Commines, by the king's edict the new Earl of Northumbria, and the man charged with subduing this quarrelsome province. Of course Eudo and the others knew this, but they were tired and all they wanted was to rest. We had been on the road so long: it was nearly two weeks since we had left Lundene. Two weeks which we had spent riding and marching through rain and sleet and snow, over unfamiliar country, across marshes and hills that seemed to go on without end.

We carried on up the slope until we had come to its brow and could look down upon the land in every direction: upon the wooded hills to the north and the open fields to the south. The moon was partly hidden behind a cloud and I could see almost nothing but the rise and fall of the earth. Certainly there was no hint of firelight or spearpoints, or anything else that would have betrayed the enemy. The wind buffeted at my cheeks and the rain continued to fall, though far to the north and east, near to where the land met the German Sea, I saw clear skies glittering with stars and I hoped that the weather would soon ease.

I checked Rollo, my horse, and swung down from the saddle, patting him on the neck.

'We'll rest here awhile,' I said. I thrust the end of my lance into the sodden ground, leaving the head to point towards the sky, while beneath it the damp pennon limply displayed the hawk that was Lord Robert's device. I lifted my shield from where it hung by its long guige strap across my back, and rested it against the trunk of a tree. It bore the same emblem: a black symbol upon a white field; the bird in flight with talons extended, as if descending for the kill.

There was not much forage to be had here, and so I dug a brace of carrots out from my saddlebag to give to Rollo. He had kept going without complaint all day, and I would have liked to have offered him more, but for now it was all I had.

The others said nothing as they too dismounted and began to pace about, feeling the use of their legs once more. Eudo rubbed at the lower part of his back, doubtless nursing some twinge from spending so long in the saddle.

To the east the clouds were beginning to break, and I could spy the silver-flecked ribbon of the river Wiire as it wove about the town of Dunholm. A narrow promontory jutted out to the south, atop which stood the fastness: a palisade surrounding a small huddle of buildings; shadows against the half-lit clouds. The promontory was sided by steep bluffs and the river coiled about them, enclosing the fastness on three sides. Thin spires of smoke rose gently from the thatch of the mead-hall there:

threads of white lit by the moon.

Below the fastness lay the town. There the rest of our army would be out in the streets: half a thousand knights like ourselves, the household warriors of the lords heading this expedition; seven hundred spearmen; and another three hundred archers. And of course there were the scores upon scores of others who attended on such an army: armourers, swordsmiths, leech-doctors and others. Many of those would be there too: close to two thousand men revelling in the spoils of war, the capture of Dunholm, the conquest of Northumbria.

It was perhaps something of a risk to allow those men to go plundering when there was a chance that the enemy still lurked, but the truth was that they had been waiting the whole march for the promise of booty. It mattered less for knights like ourselves, for we were paid well enough by our lord, but the spearmen fought out of obligation: most were drawn from the fields of their lords' estates and so this was their only hope of reward. For Robert to deny them it now would be to turn them against him, and that he could not afford to do. Already there was discontent amongst the other nobles, some of whom were reckoned to have felt (though none had said openly) that they were more deserving and that the honour of the earldom should have gone to them, to a Norman rather than a Fleming, as Robert was. But many were the men who had come over in the last two years who were Normans only by allegiance, rather than by birth. I myself hailed from the town of Dinant in Brittany, though it was some years since I was last there; Fulcher was Burgundian, while others came from Anjou or even Aquitaine. But in England that should not have mattered, for in England we were all Frenchmen, bound together by oaths and by a common tongue.

Besides, Lord Robert was one of the men closest to King Guillaume, having served him for more than ten years, since the battle at Varaville. I found it odd to say the least that a man who had served loyally and for so long should be resented so vehemently. On the other hand these times were not as settled as once they had been, and there were many, I knew, who would look only for their own advancement rather than the good of the realm.

'It was on a night like this that we took Mayenne five years ago,' Gérard said suddenly. 'Do you remember?'

I had fought in so many battles that most of them had blurred in my memory, but I recalled that campaign. It had been a protracted one, extending late into the autumn, perhaps even into the early part of the winter. I knew because I could picture the sacks of newly harvested grain we had captured on our raids, and I could see the leaves turning brown and falling from the trees in the countryside all about. Yet, strangely, of the battle for the town itself no images came to mind.

'I remember,' Eudo said. 'It was in November; the last town to fall on that campaign. The rebels had retreated and were holding out within its walls.'

'That's right,' said Gérard. 'They expected a long siege, but Duke Guillaume knew they were well supplied.' He took a bite from his loaf, then wiped a grimy sleeve across his mouth. 'We on the other

7

hand had over four thousand mouths to feed, but it was nearing winter and the countryside lay barren—'

'And so we had no choice but to attack,' Eudo said. A smile broke out across his thin face. 'Yes, I remember. We attacked that night, so quickly that we had overrun the town even before their lord had dressed for battle.' He laughed and looked up at the rest of us.

I shook my head; five years was a long time. Back then I would have been but twenty summers old and, like all youths, my head was probably full of ideas of glory and plunder. I had craved the kill; not once had I paused to consider the details of who we fought or why, only that it had to be done.

Beside me, Fulcher yawned and shrugged his shoulders inside his cloak. 'What I'd give to be with my woman right now.'

'I thought you left her back in Lundene,' I said.

'That's what I mean,' he replied. He took a draught from his waterskin. 'I say let the Northumbrians keep their worthless corner of the country. There's nothing in this land but hills and trees and sheep.' He gave a laugh, but it seemed to me that there was little humour in it. 'And rain.'

'It's King Guillaume's by right,' I reminded him. 'And Lord Robert's, too, now that he's been made earl.'

'Which means we'll never be rid of the place.'

'You'll see your woman soon enough,' I said, growing tired of these complaints.

'That's easy enough to say, when your Oswynn is waiting for you back in Dunholm,' Ivo put in.

'If there isn't another man taking care of her instead,' Eudo added, smirking.

8

Had I been more awake I might have been able to think of some retort, but instead I simply glared at him. I was not young or foolish enough to think that I loved Oswynn, or that she loved me; she was English and knew hardly a word of French or Breton, and I was French and knew almost none of English. But she was my woman all the same and I prayed to God that she was safe. Perhaps Eudo had been speaking in jest, but on a night such as this, when wine and mead flowed freely, I knew how high men's spirits could run, how hard it was for them to control their lusts. There were few enough women to be had as it was: only those who had come northwards with the army. Soldiers' wives and camp-followers. Women like Oswynn.

There was a kind of wild beauty in the way she always wore her hair unbound, in the way her eyes appeared dark and yet inviting, that drew the stares of men wherever we went. More than once before, it had been only the threat of my blade meeting their necks that had kept them away. I did not like to leave her on her own, and for that reason I had paid Ernost and Mauger, another two of the men from my conroi, to stay away from the plunder and to keep guard over the house I had taken for us. Both were fearsome fighters, men who had been at my side at Hæstinges, and there were few, I was sure, who would try to defy them. But even so, I would be glad when the morning came, when I could get back to her.

I swallowed my last mouthful of bread, laced up my saddlebag and looped the shield-strap back over my head. 'Mount up,' I said to the rest of them as I climbed up on to Rollo's back and freed the haft of my lance from the earth. 'We move on.'

9

The track continued to the west. There had been high winds recently and on several occasions we had to negotiate around trees that had fallen across the way. More than once the path itself seemed to disappear and we had to turn back until we found it again. To venture into the heart of the woods in the dark was to risk getting lost, for we did not know this country.

But the enemy would. They would know to stay away from the paths; they would probably travel in small groups rather than together. They could be less than a hundred paces from us and still we might pass them by.

I felt an angry heat rise up inside me. Our presence out in these woods was as much use as a cart without wheels: Robert had sent us out only so the other lords might see that he was being vigilant. And yet if we returned before dawn without having seen anything of the enemy, then we would have defied his orders and failed in our duty to him.

I gritted my teeth and we rode on in silence. I had been with Robert since my fourteenth year, when he was little older than I was now, and in that time I had come to know him as a generous lord, who afforded his men good treatment and rewarded them well, too, often with gifts of silver or arms or even horses. Indeed it was from him that I had received Rollo, the destrier I rode: a strong mount of constant temper who had seen me through several campaigns and many battles. To his longest-serving and most loyal retainers, moreover, Lord Robert gave land, and I, as one of the men who had led his conrois into battle, as someone who had saved his life on more than one occasion, would soon be one of those. I was patient, as one had to be, and grateful for what he had given me, and rarely in those years had I found cause to resent him. But now, as I imagined him with the rest of the lords, sitting by the hearth in the mead-hall up in the fastness, while we were here—

I was broken from my thoughts by the sound of church bells ringing out from the east.

'What's that?' Eudo said.

There was no pattern to it, no rhythm, just a clash of different notes. It came from across the river, from the direction of the town, and I frowned, for my first thought was that some drunken men had taken to violating the church. And then, as suddenly as it had begun, it stopped.

I pulled on the reins and Rollo slowed to a halt. He whickered, his breath misting in the frigid air. The night was quiet and all I could hear was the soft patter of raindrops upon the earth, and the branches whistling and creaking as the wind began to gust. But then the chiming came again: a long, dull tolling that seemed to resound off the distant hills.

Sickness clawed at my stomach. I had heard bells like those before.

'We have to get back to the town,' I said. I turned my mount about, and then, because I was not sure whether the rest had heard me, shouted: 'We have to get back!'

I dug my heels into Rollo's flanks. He reared up; I leant forwards as he came back to earth and we took off up the hill, back along the way we had come. Hooves pounded; the ground thundered. I spurred him on, faster, not looking behind to see if

11

the others were following. The rain lashed down harder, driving through my mail, plastering my tunic and braies against my skin. Trees flashed past on either side and still I looked to the east, towards the river, trying to see beyond them to the promontory and to Dunholm, but through the mass of trunks and branches I could see nothing.

A war-horn sounded out across the hills: two sharp blasts that pierced the night air. A signal to rally.

Suddenly the ground fell away and I was racing down the hill towards the river. I neared the edge of the trees; the three stone arches of the bridge came into sight. The wind tugged at my cloak as it swept down from the north, and carried on that wind came a faintly rippling beat: the sound made when a hundred spear-hafts drummed against a hundred shield-rims. A sound I knew only too well. It was one I had first heard at Hæstinges, when I had stood at the bottom of the hill and gazed up at all those thousands of Englishmen lined with their shields and their weapons along its crest, each one ready for us to charge up towards them, each one taunting us to come and die on their blades.

It was the sound of the battle-thunder, meant to intimidate, and even after all my years of fighting it still did. My heart thumped in time with the beat.

For Lord Robert had been right, and the Northumbrians had come.

# CHAPTER TWO

We galloped down towards the bridge, leaving the woods behind us. I looked out across the river towards the town: a crowd of timber and thatch buildings interwoven by narrow streets, with the tower of St Cuthbert's church rising tall above them. Orange light flickered across its stone face and, in the distance, I could see flames amidst the houses. They licked at the sky, sending up great plumes of black smoke, together with still-glowing ashes which lit up the starless night. Again I heard shouts, although these were no longer shouts of joy but cries of pain, the screams of slaughter. And over those voices, almost drowning them out, came the drumming, steady and ceaseless.

Eudo cursed as he drew up beside me, and I realised I had come to a halt.

Underneath my helmet my brow was covered in sweat. A drop trickled down in front of my eyes; I wiped it away as I reached down my shirt and pulled out the little silver cross which hung around my neck day and night.

'Christ be my shield,' I said, and I kissed it, as I always did before battle, before tucking it back under my shirt. Whatever lay ahead, I trusted that God would see me through safely.

'Watch your flanks; don't rush ahead or dawdle behind,' I shouted to the others. 'Stay together; stay with me!' I raised my ventail up over my throat and chin, hooking the chain flap into place, and passed my forearm through my shield's leather brases, gripping the topmost cross in my hand.

13

I kicked on, controlling Rollo now with my legs alone. Iron clattered against stone as we rode across the bridge, over the fast-flowing Wiire and on to the rutted street which passed below the bluffs and the fastness's high palisade. Gobs of mud flew up as I splashed through a long puddle, spattering over my hauberk and my face, but I did not care. Houses streaked past on either side. We were going into the wind and the raindrops were hard as hailstones as they smacked into my chest and my cheeks, but my heart was pounding and all I could think about was riding harder, harder.

And then I saw them, a hundred paces ahead: a host of shadows rushing on foot through the darkened streets, spearpoints and axe-blades glinting in the light of their torches, round shields upon their forearms, long hair flailing behind them as they ran. Beyond them stood a line of Normans, a mere dozen men without mail or helmets, armed only with spears, and the enemy, two score and more, were charging towards them.

'On!' I shouted to the rest of my men, and I lowered my lance before me, gripping it tightly in my hand. 'For King Guillaume and Normandy!' The white pennon whipped up with the passing air, wrapping around the haft.

We fell upon the enemy like the hawks we bore on our shields, swooping down on their rear almost before they knew that we were there. I drove my lance into an Englishman's back, letting it go as he fell forward, then I drew my sword as another half turned to face me. I cut the blade down hard across his chest and blood sprayed forth, but I was already riding on through, not looking behind to see whether he was dead, for I had seen my next

14

victim. He screamed as he came at my right, his face red with anger, his hair flying from beneath the rim of his helmet, his spear held before him. He thrust it forward and I fended it away with my sword. As he overbalanced, I struck down hard across the back of his neck, ripping through flesh and through bone, and he went down. To my left an axe bore down on my flank, but I took its brunt on my shield, and while its wielder struggled to recover for his next attack, I smashed the iron boss into his face. He staggered back, his face streaming with crimson, just as Eudo came forward and slashed across his throat. The Englishman had no time even to let out a cry as his eyes widened and he sank to his knees.

The rest, seeing the danger from their rear, were beginning to turn, but we were amongst them now and they were in disarray. The battle calm was upon me and time itself seemed to slow, each heartbeart a fresh surge of vigour through my veins as we tore into their lines.

'Kill them!' I roared, and my cry was taken up by some of the Normans on foot.

'Kill them!' they shouted, the few of them that they were, and they pushed their shield-wall forward, driving into the dwindling English ranks.

When a line breaks it is almost never a gradual thing but rather happens all at once, and it was no different then. Pressed from both front and rear, the enemy crumbled, and suddenly on all sides there were men fleeing. One stumbled back into the path of my sword, and he was dead before he hit the ground. Another tried to raise his spear to defend himself, but he was too slow and my blade tore into his throat. Yet another tripped as he ran,

15

falling face down into the mud, and he was struggling to get to his feet when Ivo rode him down, his mount's hooves trampling across the man's back, crushing his skull.

The Northumbrians were running now. Gérard and Fulcher were pursuing them, but we were few and I did not want us to get separated from one another, in case there were more of them on their way.

'To me!' I called, sheathing my sword and going to recover my lance, which still protruded from the back of the first man I had killed. It took some effort to pull it out: I had driven it deep through his torso, but I twisted the head about and eventually it came free. The head and top part of the shaft were streaked with his blood, and where before the pennon had been white, it was now pink.

Gérard and Fulcher rode back to rejoin us, and we were five once more. Four of the dozen spearmen lay dead in the street, but there was no time then to feel sorry for them. I rode up to those who remained. Some leant on the top edges of their shields while they recovered their breath; others staggered about amongst the corpses, retching by the side of the street, and I supposed those ones were drunk. If they were, it was something of a miracle that they were still alive.

'Where's Earl Robert?' I asked those who looked the most sober, but they looked blankly at each other.

'We don't know, lord,' said one. His eyes were bleary and he smelt of cattle dung.

I was about to correct him, for I was not a lord, but evidently he had seen the flag attached to my lance and it was easier to let him assume that I was. I let it pass.

'Go back up the hill,' I told them. 'Back to the fastness.' I did not know where the earl would be rallying his men, but eight warriors on foot were unlikely to accomplish much here on their own.

A flash of silver caught my eye further along the street and I saw a conroi of knights—at least a dozen, perhaps as many as twenty—charging down the road from the stronghold, towards the town square. I couldn't see any banner, but a few were carrying torches and the flame streaked behind them as they galloped past.

'Go,' I said again to the spearmen, then I waved to Eudo and the others to follow me, and we rode on.

The road was strewn with corpses both Norman and English, but far more of them were Norman; this I could tell because their hair, rather than running long and loose, was cut short at the back in the French fashion. There were corpses with spears through their chests, corpses missing arms and some missing heads. One lay sprawled forward, his face deep in the mud, a great gash across the back of his neck.

The road branched to the left, down the hill towards the north, and we turned to follow the conroi I had seen, which was some way ahead of us, already passing the tower of the church, disappearing around the bend that led down to the square. One of the lords had joined them from somewhere, for I saw a banner flying over their heads, though I did not recognise the colours: two thin green stripes on a red background.

'With me,' I said. I noticed Ivo was beginning to

17

lag behind, and thought he shouldn't be tiring so quickly, but then I saw that he was clutching one hand to his side, close to his waist, and I realised that he had been struck.

'Onwards,' I told the other three as I slowed Rollo and trotted back towards Ivo.

His teeth were clenched tight and he had a pained expression on his face. 'I'm not hurt,' he gasped. 'Go with them.'

'Let me see,' I said as I prised away his fingers. His mail was wet with crimson; beneath it, his tunic was similarly stained, and there was a round, open wound where a spear had pierced his skin. It looked deep, and I only hoped that it had not penetrated his gut.

'Get back to the fastness,' I told him. 'Find someone who can help you.'

'It's nothing,' he said, shaking his head. 'I can still fight.'

'Don't be a fool,' I said, more harshly than I had meant, perhaps, but it was plain that he was going to be of little use in the fighting that was sure to come.

He bowed his head feebly, but did not argue as he tugged on his reins to turn back up towards the stronghold.

'Go,' I said, slapping his horse on the rump to start it moving, and slowly he began to ride back up the hill. I did not wait to make sure he was gone, but wheeled around to follow the others, who had already disappeared from sight, beyond the bend in the street. On either side of me Normans were fleeing back up the hill, some staggering, some managing to run, and there were some too on horseback, although they had no mail or weapons with them.

'Back to the fastness,' I shouted to them all. Silently I cursed at how we could have been caught so unprepared. I thought of Oswynn and I inhaled deeply, praying to God that Mauger and Ernost had taken her to safety.

The wind rushed past and the ground disappeared beneath Rollo's hooves. On my right the church tower rose up, tall and dark, though its bell was no longer tolling. The street turned sharply to the left, and all of a sudden the marketplace was before me and I was charging at full gallop towards the enemy. For the square was filled with men: Normans and English running amongst each other, shields clashing against shields, all in disorder.

A horse screamed in pain, and I watched as its rider was toppled from the saddle, still desperately clinging to the reins as he hit the ground. The animal teetered on its hind legs, and the knight, with one foot caught in the stirrup, was kicking, struggling to get away. He was still shouting when the hooves came down on his face.

I looked for Eudo and the others, but in the darkness and amidst so many men and horses I could not see them. In the very centre of the mêlée the hawk banner flew high, and I searched for Lord Robert amongst his knights. At first it seemed he was not there, and I felt my heart race, but then he lifted his head, shouting as he drove his sword through an Englishman's chest, and I saw the red strips of cloth attached to his helmet: the tail that signified that he was the earl. There were ten knights with him, and a great many spearmen as well, but the Northumbrians must

19

have recognised who he was, for they were throwing most of their numbers into that part of the battle and were already beginning to surround him.

'For Lord Robert and King Guillaume!' I roared as I charged to his banner.

A sole Northumbrian, separated from the rest of his kinsmen, came at me from the front, throwing the full weight of his body behind his spearhead; I cut to the right and took the blow on my shield, striking the weapon away so hard that the haft slipped from his grip. I followed through before he could get out of the way, bringing the boss down on top of his bare head, and he fell to the ground.

More of the enemy had seen me coming and quickly they turned to face me, away from Robert and his men, bringing their shields together, overlapping them to form a wall. They began to level their spears, but they were few in number and so I spurred Rollo on, trusting in him not to falter, not to panic. I raised my shield to cover his flank, ploughing onwards, ducking my head and closing my eyes tight, and then I heard the snap of ashen shafts and the clatter of limewood shields upon the stones and I knew I was through. I looked up to the sight of splinters flying and Englishmen fleeing around me, and then I was amongst them, cleaving with my blade: tearing through leather, through mail and through flesh; making space for anyone who might be behind me to follow.

'For King Guillaume!' came a cry, and I recognised the voice as belonging to Lord Robert. I looked to my right and he was there by my side, pressing forward through the Northumbrian ranks, his helmet-tail flailing behind him, his teeth gritted in determination as he brought his blade down, shattering the rim of an enemy's shield. 'For Normandy!' he yelled.

The enemy clustered close around us, thrusting forward with their spears, but then a war-horn blasted out and suddenly most of their kinsmen were falling back to form a new shield-wall further down the marketplace, leaving these few without support. The rest of Robert's knights were with us now, and the English must have realised how exposed they were, for fear took hold of them and all at once they fled.

I was about to give chase when Robert shouted out: 'Hold back!'

I looked behind me and understood why, for there were barely twenty knights under his banner and he could not chance to lose any of us. More spearmen had arrived to fill out our ranks; and, down the road from the fastness, I saw banners of all designs, banners in red and white, green and blue, and riding beneath them were men in mail hauberks, men with helmets and swords, coming to join us. For a moment I breathed more easily, but only for a moment, because at the same time the English were gathering, marching up the hill from the town gates, and once more they were banging their weapons against their shields, all of them roaring with one voice.

'*Ut*,' they chanted, like animals; like the hounds of hell. '*Ut, ut, ut!*'

A shiver ran through me; never since Hæstinges had I seen so many Englishmen bearing arms together, ready for battle, baying for our blood. There were hundreds of them under a purple-and-yellow-striped banner, and for every beat of my

21

heart, dozens more were joining them in their long shield-wall.

One knight charged forward from our line, his ventail still undone and flapping away. Perhaps he thought we would all be behind him, or perhaps anger had simply taken hold of him, but he rode hard and he rode alone, straight for the enemy's bristling spears. He lifted his lance high above his head and hurled it into their ranks, and then drew his sword, preparing to meet their wall, when a spear flew out of the sky, catching him in the throat. His sword fell from his hand as he tumbled from his mount, and I saw his neck snap back as he struck the ground.

The enemy whooped with delight, and the battle-thunder grew louder, faster. '*Ut! Ut! Ut!*'

Rollo fidgeted with his feet and I rubbed his neck to keep him calm. Around me men exchanged uncertain glances.

'Hold back!' Lord Robert shouted as he rode along in front of our forces, signalling to the rest of the lords who had gathered with their men and their banners. 'Hold back!'

I realised I was still holding my sword and sheathed it again, looking around the rest of Robert's men to see if there were any faces I recognised. The earl had nearly one hundred knights in his employ and I was not familiar with them all, but I saw several men who normally rode within my conroi and I called them to me. There were ten of them in all: Rualon, the sole other Breton apart from myself; Hedo, who had the broken nose; and several whose names I could not at that time recall. All of them appeared tired, but so far as I could see, none had been injured.

Ten, when there ought to have been nearly thirty. I spotted Eudo and the other two, who had seen the hawk banner and were riding back towards us. The three of them brought our number to fourteen—myself included—but even so that was only half of my conroi.

'Where are the rest?' I demanded.

The men bowed their heads and refused to meet my eyes. I knew what that meant. A lump rose up in my throat, but I knew I couldn't think of such things now; that would have to come later, after we had secured victory.

For now the English remained where they were, standing, taunting, no more inclined to attack than we were, it seemed. They were waiting for us to come to them, just as we waited for them to come to us, both sides separated by little more than fifty paces.

Lord Robert returned to us, untying his chin-strap and removing his helmet. His face was weathered from the years we had spent in Italy; his hair, while not as long and loose as the Englishmen were accustomed to wearing it, was certainly not cut in the short style fashionable in France. And unlike the Norman lords who usually went clean-shaven, Robert was possessed of a full but well-trimmed beard, which he often stroked when deep in thought. This he did now while he surveyed his men.

Including those who had this moment arrived from the fastness, I guessed that we had fewer than four hundred in that square—too few given that we had come to Dunholm with a thousand and a half. Most of those men were spearmen and horsemen, but there were some archers too, busily loosing

23

volley after volley into the English ranks, though it seemed to me they were only wasting their arrows; most of the enemy had shields and few of the missiles got through.

Lord Robert rode towards me. His hauberk was spattered with English blood, his eyes were bloodshot and he bore a bright cut across his cheek.

'Tancred,' he said.

He extended a hand and I clasped it in my own. 'My lord,' I replied.

'They were waiting for us,' he said through gritted teeth. 'As I said they would be.'

'They were.' I would have liked to know how they had managed to break into the town, where so many men had come from, but it seemed to me pointless to be asking then, when they were standing but fifty paces from us. It looked as if the whole of Northumbria had gathered to drive us out from Dunholm. I glanced back at our small host arrayed below the church, their anxiety almost palpable in the air. My spirits fell, for I knew that we could not hope to drive the enemy off.

'We have to fall back to the fastness while we still can,' I said to Robert.

He came closer, lowering his voice so that the others around us could not hear. 'If we do that, we hand them the town,' he said. 'We don't have supplies to withstand a siege. We must fight them now.'

'We don't have the numbers, lord,' I said. 'If we retreat we can gather our strength, sally out on our own terms.'

'No,' Robert said, and his dark eyes bored into me. 'They fear us, Tancred. See how reluctant they are to attack! We will defeat them tonight and we will defeat them here.'

'They haven't attacked because all they need do is hold us here,' I pointed out. 'The rest will come around the side streets.' And I told him how we had come upon a group of them close by the bridge. 'They'll return, and when they do it will be in greater numbers than before. When that happens, we'll be trapped here with no hope of retreat.'

He remained silent. The English continued to bang their shields; some of the Norman lords were doing the same as they tried to encourage their men.

'Take thirty knights, then,' he said at last. 'Try to head the enemy off.' He began to marshal a dozen or so of his men to go with me as he retied his helmet-strap under his chin.

I swallowed, for I knew if we became cut off from the main army, then we were all dead men. But the order had been given and I could not refuse.

'Give me forty,' I called after him.

He looked back at me. For a moment he hesitated, as if uncertain what to do, but then he nodded and gave the signal for ten more of his men to follow me.

'If you can't head them off, then we'll have to retreat,' he said. His lips were solemn and his eyes had the look of one who was beginning to see only failure ahead of him; a look that, in twelve years of campaigning, I had never seen him wear. This was the man who had led us at Varaville and at Hæstinges, who had rallied us when all had seemed lost, whose temperament never wavered, whose prowess at arms was bettered by none—and

25

yet I saw his despair. A sudden chill came over me.

He rode back to the head of his men. Breathing deeply, I raised my lance and waved the pennon so that the whole of my conroi could see me. There were men of all ages: some young and fresh-faced, who had only recently sworn their oaths to Robert; others who had served him since before the invasion, who were nearly as old as myself.

'Stay close to me,' I said to them. 'Keep in mind always that the strength of the charge is in weight of numbers. Watch your flanks; don't lose sight of the men beside you.'

I checked to see who was behind me, and was relieved to find Eudo and Fulcher and Gérard, though none of them were looking at me then; their eyes were either closed or fixed on the ground. Perhaps they were thinking over the instructions I had just given, or perhaps they were imagining the charge and what they would do when we met the English line.

I glanced once more towards Robert, who was speaking now with one of the other lords, his face red as he gestured wildly at some of the men further along our line. I swallowed once more, but as I lifted the hawk pennon high above my head, all my doubts fell away. For I knew that in twelve years of fighting I had faced worse circumstances than this, and had made it through. As long as we kept faith in our sword-arms, we would yet prevail.

'For Normandy,' I shouted.

My heart pounded as hard as Rollo's hooves as we climbed back past the church and on around the bend, towards the western side of the town. That was where the enemy would be coming from, if they were coming at all, for the approach to the promontory was less steep there than it was on the eastern side. We passed the place where we had fought our skirmish earlier, though the road was now empty.

'This way!' I said, as I cut to the right, down a street so narrow that three of us could barely ride abreast, between houses on one side and wattle-work fencing on the other. I caught a glimpse of the river to our left, a ribbon of deepest black weaving beneath the trees.

Then the houses came to an end and we came out on to a field of furrowed earth, some thirty paces in width and perhaps two or three times as long. And there, at the far end, from out of the midst of the houses, were Normans fleeing towards us, scores of them on horseback and on foot. Behind them, roaring, running forward with torches bobbing and weapons drawn, came the enemy.

## CHAPTER THREE

I lowered my lance, gripping it firmly in my right hand just as I clutched at the brases of my shield in my left.

'On!' I called to my conroi. 'For St Ouen, Lord Robert and King Guillaume!'

'For King Guillaume!' they returned the cry, and we were racing across the field, scores of hooves trampling down the furrows, kicking up mud and stones. Beside me rode Eudo and Fulcher and Gérard, knee to knee, with three more on either flank, so that there were ten of us in that first line,

27

leading the charge. A few on our right were beginning to draw ahead, and I shouted to them to keep formation, though how many could have heard, above the thunder of hooves and wind buffeting in their faces, I did not know.

The fleeing Normans scattered from our path. The enemy were behind them still, a tide of men rushing forth to meet us, but we drove on, and then we were among them, crashing our lances into their shields and their faces, riding over their bodies as they fell. The rest of the conroi were behind us as we tore into their ranks, beating down with our swords, and the screams of the dying filled the air.

'*Godemite,*' one of the enemy shouted, raising his spearpoint with its scarlet pennon high into the air. '*Godemite!*'

Unlike the rest who went without armour, or at best with only a leather jerkin, he wore mail. His sword-hilt was inlaid with gold, and I took him for a thegn—one of the English leaders—for he was rallying his men to him, until seemingly without any signal being given they began running at us, their spears levelled forwards. So eager were they to die, however, that they came not all at once with shields overlapping, but rather in ragged fashion.

I charged on with Eudo and Gérard and the rest beside me, cleaving, battering the enemy down, until the thegn himself stood before me. His teeth were gritted and his face was red as he aimed his spearpoint at Rollo's neck, but I swerved right and it hammered into my shield instead, sending a shudder up through my shoulder and knocking me backwards against the cantle. I gripped Rollo tight with my legs, determined not to fall.

He drew his gilded sword and made to attack again, but before he could, Eudo had come around by his flank and was slashing across the man's unprotected forearm, through the bone, severing the hand which remained still gripped around the sword-hilt. The man screamed and stumbled back, clutching at the bloody stump, but in doing so he brought his shield out of position, and his head was exposed.

I saw the opening and smashed my sword down into the thegn's face. His head jerked back, his long moustache soaked in blood; the nasal-guard of his helmet had taken the brunt of the blow and still he lived, though not for long. Eudo sliced across his chest, penetrating the links of his hauberk to the flesh beneath. Gasping, the man took another step back, looking down at his breast as he pressed his one remaining hand tight against the mail. Blood spilt through his fingers; his eyes glazed over and his lips moved, but no sound came out; and then he collapsed.

No sooner had he done so than he was forgotten, for I was moving on: parrying, thrusting, carving a path through the enemy until there was space around me. I checked to see that the rest of my conroi were with me still, and most were, but not all. Several horses lay dead on the ground, their riders beside them, and among those who had fallen I saw the face of my countryman, Rualon.

I had no time for reflection, however. Over the enemy's heads, to my left and close to the river, I glimpsed a white shield with a black hawk upon its face. Its owner, robust and barrel-chested, was fighting on foot and his free hand wielded a long spear: a spear which carried a pennon the same as mine. He had his helmet on and his ventail up, but I could just see the scar below his eye which he had borne ever since Hæstinges, and I recognised him straightaway.

'Wace!' I called, hoping to catch his attention, but above the noise of swords clashing upon shields and mail he could not have heard me. I raised my sword aloft. 'With me,' I said to my men. 'With me!'

Apart from Lord Robert himself, I knew of few men more skilled with a sword than Wace. He'd been in Robert's employ even longer than I, had fought in the same battles, and, like me, was in charge of a full conroi of his household knights. Except that now there were but six or seven men with him. Three were knights, for they wore mail and helmets. One had lost his shield and was fighting with a spear in either hand, another with two swords. Together they were being pressed back into a tight ring as the English closed on them from all sides.

'On! On!'

Northumbrians fled before me, and my sword felt light in my hand as I brought it down, again, again, again. I no longer knew how many I had killed, for all I could see were those ahead, and I knew I had to get to Wace. He stabbed his spear up under the shield of the man in front of him, into his groin, but no sooner had that corpse fallen to the ground than another man had stepped over it to fill the gap, eager for blood. On the other side, the Norman with the two swords pressed his advantage, coming out of the ring against his comrades' warnings, raining blows on the shields before him, hacking so hard that the hide fell away

30

from the wood. He forced his way through their wall, striking out left and right, and several of them died before a spear pierced his chest.

Wace looked up and saw me. He shouted something that I could not hear, but it did not matter, because the enemy were beneath me and my blade was singing with the joy of battle, gleaming in the torchlight as it struck and struck again. And I was reminded of the end of the day at Hæstinges, when the last of the English tried to hold us off, even though the battle was by then already won, and the man they called their king lay dead on the field. I recalled how we had pursued them as they fled the mêlée, and suddenly I was there again, riding the enemy down, losing myself to the will of my sword, arcing it down, slicing it across their throats.

'For Lord Robert!' I cried. 'For Lord Robert!'

I looked about for my next kill, but the enemy were running back to their ranks, where hundreds more, it seemed, were slowly advancing, shouting as they came: *'Ut! Ut! Ut!'*

Wace stood, breathing hard, while the three men that remained of his group rallied around him. The shaft of his spear had cracked, lodged in the chest of one of several Northumbrian bodies littering the earth in front of him. The pennon, soaked with blood, was torn to shreds. He looked, half squinting, up at me. The same blow that had given him his scar at Hæstinges had also crippled his eye, and though he could still see almost as well as before, he had never been able to open it fully since.

'You took your time,' he said, which was exactly the kind of remark I would have expected from

31

him. He had a voice like gravel: rough and sharp.

'We have to get back,' I told him, ignoring his lack of gratitude. 'We must get back to the fastness.'

I glanced about at the rest of my conroi, who were staring at the massed ranks of English spears bearing down on them. Some of them were already turning, breaking off, riding back the way we had come.

Sheathing my sword, I waved towards the promontory and the palisade wall ringing its crest. 'Retreat!'

Several horses had lost their riders and had bolted away from the fighting, down towards the river's edge. Already Wace and his men were making for them, though some seemed reluctant to take another rider and were taking flight again, a few lashing out with their hind legs at any who approached.

A horn blew again, and it seemed to me that the sound was coming from close to the church, the tower of which I could see even now, rising above the roofs of the houses. Embers blew on the wind, some of them landing on the thatch and starting to set it alight; from further to the north came a long cloud of black smoke which billowed in my face, obscuring the way ahead and causing me to choke, but I could hear the cries of the enemy behind me and I knew I had to keep riding. The furrows ran the length of the field, and I followed them until the path between the houses came into sight. Rollo was slowing, and I knew he must be tiring, but I could not let him rest yet.

As we came up the steep slope towards the fastness I heard the clash of swords ahead in the main street; we came out just as two Englishmen were finished on the spears of a group of knights. And among those knights I recognised the square face of Mauger: one of the two I had left to protect Oswynn, who was not with him—

'Mauger!' I called, trying to make myself heard above the clash of steel, the cries which were coming from the marketplace, the drumming of hooves.

He looked up, tugging on the reins so as to face me. 'Tancred—' he began.

'Where is she?' I cut him off, glancing about to make sure that I hadn't missed her. But my eyes had not deceived me. She wasn't there. 'Where is she?'

'I'm sorry,' he said, and I saw the lump in his throat as he swallowed.

'What?' I stared at him, urging him to go on, my gut already wrenching as he opened his mouth and I sensed what he was about to say, though I did not want to believe it. 'Where is she?'

He looked down towards the ground. 'I'm sorry,' he said again. 'The enemy—they came upon us without warning while we were riding back to the stronghold . . .'

'No,' I said. I felt suddenly cold, as if my very soul had flown from my body. Words stuck in my throat, the breath torn from my chest. 'It can't be.' I saw her face before me, her black hair running wild as she glared at me with her dark eyes, cursing in her English tongue.

'I'm sorry,' Mauger said.

'No,' I repeated. 'She's not dead. She's not.' I stared into his eyes, willing him to deny it, but I saw only his guilt. Guilt because he had failed me.

33

I wanted to strike him for that failure, strike him from his horse to the street below, except that all the strength had left my limbs and I could not have done so even had I tried.

I heard Wace's voice behind me, ordering the retreat, and the horn blowing from the direction of the marketplace, and the shouts of all those men, cheering, screaming, chanting, dying. Around me the smoke was growing thicker and blacker, swirling in my face, stinging my eyes. Sparks lifted into the air like a scattering of stars, flaring momentarily before one by one their lives were extinguished and they disappeared, swallowed up by the night.

Men rushed past me, on horse and on foot, and I heard their cries but knew not what they were saying as I sat frozen to the saddle. Behind me the drumming was closer and I imagined all those Northumbrians marching towards us, with nothing but murder in their hearts—

And I knew that Mauger was not the one to blame.

I yanked hard on the reins and Rollo reared up, but I no longer cared, for I had but one thing in mind.

'Tancred!' Mauger said, but I pretended not to hear as I turned back down the way between the houses, pressing my heels in harder than before, drawing every last fraction of speed from Rollo's legs.

I pulled my sword free of its scabbard, flourishing it high above my head, just as the smoke cleared and then without warning the English were rushing towards me. I crashed into their first line before they could even come together and form their shield-wall: roaring, swearing death upon them all; slashing, scything, cleaving with my blade; and I was shouting in anger, shouting without words, shouting so that my voice would be the last thing they heard before I sent them all to hell.

There were others with me now as I tore into the enemy, but in truth I didn't care whether or not they were there, for the bloodlust was upon me and there was nothing that could stop me. I heaved my sword up and across the back of a Northumbrian's helm, and he fell under Rollo's hooves. Straightaway I was turning, lifting for another stroke, using the full weight of the weapon to batter down another's shield before drawing the point across his throat and up under his chin.

Beside me, a horse rose up on its hind legs; its front feet pawed at the air and the whites of its eyes gleamed in the darkness, before one of the Englishmen plunged his spear deep into the animal's belly. It thrashed wildly, screaming in pain, and its rider was suddenly thrown from the saddle. The breath caught in my chest as I saw that it was Fulcher, but I was too far away to do anything. He was struggling to get to his feet when the same spearman thrust the point down, through his broad chest into his heart.

'Fulcher!' I shouted, and gritted my teeth, putting all of my strength into my sword-arm as I swung—

There was a flash of steel from below and pain seared down my lower leg. I clung on to Rollo's neck even as I backhanded my blade across the chest of the one who had struck me, screaming to God and the saints, as the full agony overtook me.

35

'Get back,' someone said, and I realised it was Wace's voice. Fire reflected in his sword as he brought it to bear upon the enemy. 'Get back!'

It took me a moment to realise that he was shouting at me and not at the English, but in that moment the bloodlust faded and suddenly I found myself in the midst of more spears than I could count, with only Wace by my side. I looked to my left just as Gérard was dragged from his mount, and I sat rooted to my stirrups while the English set upon him with swords and knives and spears. Still he struggled, fending off the blows with his shield, until one of the enemy, taller than the rest, came forward with a long-handled axe and brought it down upon Gérard's chest.

'Go,' Wace was shouting.

Sweat poured down off my brow into my face, mingling with my tears. I didn't care whether I lived or died; all I wanted was to strike down the man who had killed Gérard. I charged forward before he could lift the weapon for another swing, turning my sword-hilt in my hand so that I held it instead more like a dagger. His eyes widened as he saw me coming, and he dropped the axe as he ducked to one side, but he was too slow and too tall and I was able to stab down, driving into his back so hard that the blade stuck as I tried to pull it free. The hilt was slick with the spilt blood of my foes and my own sweat, and I felt my hand slipping. I struggled to clutch on to it but my fingers found only air, and then I saw it falling behind me, tumbling point over hilt, glinting with the light of so many torches, before it thudded into the ground and fear overtook me.

Spears thrust up at me from my right and I leant

36

back in the saddle, away from them, even as a forest of steel pressed in from my left; I could not see an end to the enemy. I clung to Rollo's neck, keeping my shield by his flank, taking each blow that came. The dark shadows of the houses rose tall to either side.

'Go,' Wace said, alongside my exposed flank. 'Faster; ride harder!' His sword flashed and the enemy fell before us, and I was riding onwards, onwards, onwards.

And then we were past them and on the main street once again, except that the way to the stronghold was blocked and the enemy were streaming through the alleys with fire and steel in their hands, hacking down those few who remained. There were corpses everywhere and the earth was stained crimson. Above us, behind the palisade which crowned the promontory, the mead-hall was burning; great flames writhed up towards the clouds above, twisting around each other, quickly breaking out across the whole of the thatch as the wind gusted down from the north.

'We need to find Lord Robert,' I breathed, wiping my hand across my face, as if that might somehow dispel everything I saw before me. A fresh surge of pain coursed through my leg, but I bit it back. 'We need to find Eudo.'

'Not now,' Wace said, and he tore the reins from my grasp, tugging Rollo away, towards the river and the bridge. For the enemy had spotted us and they were running towards us, sensing more blood. I sat frozen in the saddle, my whole body numb as I stared at them, scarce believing what was happening. I had no sword, the rim of my shield had split, my mount was almost spent, and I knew that all was lost.

'Ride,' Wace said, already spurring his horse on down the slope towards the bridge.

I looked back at the town, at the hordes of Englishmen who were giving chase, at the few Normans in the distance, still fighting desperately on. I heard the cries that came from the fastness, the scrape of steel upon mail, the roars of victory from the enemy, and the battle-thunder, which was louder than ever. A plume of smoke blew in front of me, blocking my sight, and then at last I turned, following Wace as he raced down towards the river. Hooves sounded hollow against stone as we passed across the bridge, over the cold black waters.

'On,' I told Rollo.

The cries still filled my ears but I did not look back, watching only where my mount placed his tired feet as we climbed up amongst the trees. Rain began to spit upon us once more, and as the drops grew heavier, slowly the noises from the town started to fade.

'On,' I whispered, to none but myself. The water ran off my nasal-guard, seeping inside my mail and my tunic, and the darkness closed in around us as we rode deeper into the woods, into the night.

## CHAPTER FOUR

We did not stop until dawn. The woods were dense, the hills steep and the paths treacherous, but we pressed on nonetheless. The more miles we could put between ourselves and the enemy, the better. I didn't know whether they might send riders out to chase down those who had fled, but I had no wish to find out.

The whole sky was covered in cloud; no stars or moon could be seen. Still the rain fell, the drops bouncing off my helmet. Underneath I was soaked through, my tunic, shirt and braies all clinging to my skin as water mingled with sweat. My calf felt as though it were aflame, while each gust of wind was like a lance through my back. My cloak offered no protection, hanging damp and heavy around me, stained with the blood of my foes and some that might have been my own; I could not tell, and in truth I did not care. None of it mattered, for the battle had been lost, and Oswynn was dead.

If only I hadn't left her. I should have stayed, or else taken her with us, for then she would have been safe. As I had ridden away to join the others I had not even looked back. But then I couldn't have known that by leaving her there, I would be leaving her to her death.

I couldn't have known, I kept telling myself, repeating the words over and over in my head. I couldn't have known.

I felt tears welling up inside but tried to hold them back. I should have left her in the south. Instead, by bringing her to this godforsaken place, I had failed her, just as I had failed Fulcher and Gérard. I had known those two for so many years; together we had fought through so much, away from the field of battle as well as on it.

I closed my eyes. Gérard, Fulcher, Oswynn: all of them now dead. And I was the one who, through my foolishness, had killed them.

I swallowed, wiping a hand across my eyes, brushing away the moisture that I could feel forming. I wondered what had happened to Eudo and Mauger, Ivo and Hedo and all the rest of my conroi, and prayed that they too had managed to get away: that they and Lord Robert were all safe.

Beneath me Rollo was tiring: each step seemed slower, each breath more laboured than the one before. I knew how he felt. My own eyes were growing heavy, and my limbs were tiring, but I knew we had to keep going. Several times I heard a war-horn in the distance, its blast long and deep as it cut through the night, though whether it was theirs or ours, I could not tell. All I could do was keep riding, urging Rollo on, digging my heels in every time he slowed.

Ahead, Wace picked his way through the trees. In the darkness the deer-tracks were difficult to follow, forking and then forking again, often seeming to double back upon themselves. We had left the better-trodden paths behind us, which meant that if the enemy were in pursuit, there was less chance of them overtaking us. But I was not sure whether we were even riding in the right direction; the woods looked the same no matter which way I turned. All we knew was that the wind had been blowing from the north earlier, and so we kept it at our backs as much as we could, striking out south, in the direction of Eoferwic.

For if there were any others who had managed to get out of Dunholm, that was where we would find them. The city of Eoferwic, captured from the English the previous summer and since entrusted to Guillaume Malet, one of the most powerful lords in Normandy, and held in high esteem by the king. But it was at least three days' ride away, and probably more if we kept off the main tracks, since the country was not known to us. The old Roman way, if we could find it, would be dangerous, though certainly quicker. That was the route we had taken on our march here, an army of nearly two thousand men under Lord Robert. I wondered what remained of that army now.

Shortly we came upon a clearing where a great oak had once stood, though now it was fallen: a victim of the recent winds, perhaps. At one end its splintered branches splayed out across the ground. At the other, its roots, clogged with dirt, hung over the rough pit where they had been ripped from the earth.

From somewhere in the distance came a shout and I froze, bringing Rollo to a halt. I turned, feeling myself tense, reaching for my sword-hilt, until I realised it wasn't there. The voice had come from off to our right, but amidst the trees I could see nothing. I looked to Wace, but he did not appear to have heard, for he was riding on ahead.

'Wace,' I said, keeping my voice low.

He brought his horse to a stop. There was an impatient look in his eyes, but then again Wace rarely had much patience for anyone. His jaw was clenched, his ventail unhooked and hanging from the side of his coif.

'What?' he asked.

'I heard someone,' I said, gesturing in the direction that the shout had come from.

His face turned stern as he looked out through the trees. Around us the rain carried on falling. Otherwise all was quiet.

'You're mistaken,' he said, and spurred his mount onwards again.

But then the same voices came again, two of

41

them at least, calling to each other in words I did not understand, but which sounded like English. They could not have been far away, either; a couple of hundred paces at most, and probably less: sound did not carry far in the woods. Had they been following our trail?

Wace glanced at me over his shoulder, no doubt thinking the same thing. 'Come on,' he said as he made for the other side of the clearing. The track we had been following turned to the east here, back towards the river Wiire, but he was heading west, into the heart of the wood.

I pressed my heels in and Rollo started forward, moving quickly into a trot. I patted him on the side of his neck. He had worked hard already this night, but he could not rest yet.

We left the clearing behind us, pushing on through the trees. A layer of leaves and pine needles covered the ground, muffling the sound of our horses' hooves. More than once a branch scraped against my wounded calf. I winced at the pain, but I could not think about it as we kept on going.

I heard the same voices again, behind us, laughing and calling to one another. I glanced over my shoulder, finding it difficult at first to make much out, but then I glimpsed the fallen oak, and beside it shadowy figures on horseback. Three of them in all. I held my breath as I watched them, not wanting to make any sound that might give us away. They dismounted and, still talking, staggered about the clearing. One of them began to sing, another joined in, and then they began to dance about in drunken fashion.

'*Sige!*' they shouted, almost as one, though

whether it was meant for us to hear or not, I could not be sure. *'God us sige forgeaf!'*

I realised that Wace was already some way ahead of me, and kicked on again to catch him up. Branches crunched under Rollo's hooves, and I hoped that they would not hear us, but the laughter and singing continued and I took that as a good sign. As we approached the top of the rise, gradually the shouts began to fade, and the next time I glanced back, the three figures were gone.

*      *      *

There was no more sign of the enemy that night, and for that I thanked God. Several times one of us thought we had heard a sound, but it could only have been an animal, or the wind in the pine branches, for we never saw anything.

We continued west for some while, until we had put enough distance between ourselves and the Englishmen to feel safe. Then we turned to the south once more, or at least what we thought was south. It was becoming harder to tell; the wind was easing, and without the moon or the stars to guide us, we could only strike out and hope for the best.

Before long we came once more to the banks of what must have been the river Wiire. The waters were fast and black as pitch, tumbling and frothing over rocks so jagged they seemed to me like the teeth of some immense beast. There was no chance of us being able to ford it, and so we had no choice but to carry on following it upstream, keeping to the trees as much as possible, in case anyone was watching from the opposite shore.

The first bridge we passed had fallen into ruin,

its two stone piers all that remained; another we found in better repair, but the country on the other side lay open, and even in the dark we judged it better to stay in the cover of the woods. It could have been as much as an hour, and perhaps even more, before at last we came upon one we could cross. Beyond it on the other bank the woods continued, and it seemed that they were even thicker than before, if that were possible. The land rose steeply here, the paths slippery with mud and loose stones, and we had to dismount to lead the horses up it, or else risk falling and breaking our own necks as well as theirs.

I staggered up after Wace, my leg paining me more and more with every step. But I knew that if I stopped to rest I would not want to move again, and so I forced myself to carry on, trying to put my weight on my good leg. Behind me, Rollo followed meekly, his head bowed low. I trudged on, concentrating on placing one foot ahead of the other, hardly daring to look towards the summit, but before long I was falling behind again.

'Don't stop,' Wace called back down to me. He was perhaps twenty paces ahead, already close to the top of the rise. 'We need to keep going.'

'It's my leg,' I said, grimacing as another bolt of pain shot through the wound.

He left his horse and descended the path once again, taking care over the many roots and stones protruding from the ground.

'I hadn't realised,' he said when he reached me. 'Is it bad?'

'I don't know,' I said, shaking my head. 'I was struck during the battle. It wasn't so bad while we were riding.'

44

He knelt down to examine it, and I watched the expression on his face, though it revealed nothing. 'It's hard to see,' he said. 'But we can't stop here. It's not much further to the top. Then we can ride again.'

He placed his arm around my back and under my shoulder, helping me as I limped up the slope. While I regained my breath he went back down for Rollo. I waited, gazing up towards the skies, which were beginning to clear. The rain was easing, now little more than a drizzle.

Soon, though, we were back in the saddle. Even as far as we had come, we could not afford to stop, and so we rode on through the darkness, hour after hour. I had almost begun to think that this night would never end, when at last the skies began to lighten, and as the first rays of sunlight began to break over the horizon, we found ourselves atop a ridge on the edge of the woods. Open country lay to the south, wide and flat all the way as far as I could see, until in the very distance the horizon was lost in the haze. A spire of smoke rose from a farmstead, a small black dot on the plain: the only sign of life.

'We should rest here,' I said. 'It's sheltered, and we'll be able to see anyone coming.'

'From the south, maybe,' Wace replied, his expression stern. 'It's those coming from the north I'm worried about.'

But it was not as if we had much choice, for the horses were spent: we had ridden them hard all the way from the battle, and they would surely not be able to go on much longer, even if we ourselves wanted to. And I could see the tiredness in Wace's eyes—both his good one and the other—as much

45

as I felt it in my own.

Not far off I could hear the trickling of a small stream, and we led our mounts to it. We unsaddled them and let them drink before tying the reins to a nearby birch, where there was enough grass around for them to eat: although if they felt anything like I did, they would not be hungry.

I lay down upon the soft earth, doing my best to ignore the pain. A gust of wind rustled the branches and I shivered, pulling my cloak closer, though it did not offer much protection. Only the night before last I had been sharing my tent with Oswynn, feeling the warmth of her embrace, the tenderness of her touch, and all had been as it should be.

The wind gusted again. I closed my eyes, seeing her face rise before me, and as I lay there on the damp ground, at last the tears began to flow. My breath came in stutters, catching in my chest, pulling at my heart, and my mind was filled with thoughts of her as I told myself over and over: I could not have known.

But none of it helped. For she was dead, and I had killed her.

\*       \*       \*

I slept after that, though it could not have been for long, for the sun was not yet at its highest when I woke, almost blinded by its brightness. Birds chirped in the trees about me; in the distance I could hear the bleating of sheep. The frost had since melted, and now the plains were a patchwork of green and brown. My eyes were sore and there was a dull ache in my head. For a moment I lay

46

still, unsure where I was, until suddenly it all returned to me.

I blinked and tried to sit up, though straightaway I regretted it as agony gripped my leg, and I cursed out loud. There was no one about to hear me. Wace was not to be seen, though he had left his shield behind. Lord Robert's hawk looked as though it had seen better days; there were several long scratches across it that would need repainting. Nonetheless, it was in better condition than mine, which rested beside me, its top edge split, the leather strips around its edge hacked away, the wooden planks beneath cracked. It would not last much longer.

Wace's horse was still there, too, which meant that he could not have gone far. I watched the animal and he watched me back, his bay coat glistening in what sunlight reached through the branches. Beside him Rollo lay on his side, asleep.

I shifted, trying to get more comfortable. I was still wearing my hauberk and chausses, though I had removed my helmet. Resting while in mail was never easy, but I didn't want to be unprepared in case the enemy should happen upon us.

My leg continued to throb, worse even than it had just a few hours ago. I bent down and saw what I had missed earlier: the blow had gone past the mail of my chausses, tearing through the calf-straps, as well as through my braies, which were stained a deep red. And beneath it all was the cut itself, about a hand's span in length, beginning slightly above my ankle and ending just short of my knee-joint. I touched at it lightly, wincing at the tenderness of the flesh. My fingers came away smeared with blood. It did not look deep—

47

whatever had struck me, only its point could have broken the skin—and for that at least I was thankful. But it was still a serious wound.

I heard a chink of mail behind me, and turned to see Wace emerging from the woods, a leather wineskin in hand.

'You're awake,' he said.

He didn't look as though he had rested at all; his eyes were every bit as red as they had been at dawn. 'Have you slept?' I asked.

He shook his head and tossed me the flask; it was heavier than I expected and I almost fumbled it. 'One of us had to keep watch,' he said. 'You looked as if you needed the rest more than I.'

I took out the stopper and lifted the wineskin to my lips. It was icy cold, and I nearly choked, the water streaming down my chin, splashing over my cloak and my hauberk, but I did not care. It was the first moisture to pass my lips in a long time, and I drank deeply.

I held the bottle out to him but he shook his head, and so I put it to one side while I set about removing my chausses. They were attached to my belt by means of leather braces, and I untied them before undoing the unsevered laces. That done, I rolled up the leg of my braies up to my knee, and began to splash some of the water from the flask over the wound, biting back the sudden sting. As a youth I had spent some years in a monastery, where the infirmarian had taught me the importance of keeping a wound clean.

He had been a quiet, ancient man, I remembered, with a rough fringe of snowy hair around his tonsure, and sad eyes which told of many hardships witnessed but never mentioned.

Of all the monks there he was one of the few I took to, and his was the only teaching that stuck in my mind. It had probably saved my life more than once over the years.

I wiped the half-dried blood from around the cut, revealing a great crimson gash, about one-third the width of my fingernail.

Wace inhaled sharply. 'That doesn't look good.'

'It looks worse than it feels,' I said, though I was not sure that I meant it. I swallowed, and changed the subject. 'Where do you think we are?'

'We passed a village a little before dawn,' he replied, still gazing at the wound. 'If that was Alclit then it means we can't be far from the old road.'

Alclit was one of the places we had passed on our march; we had learnt the name after our scouts had captured one of the families trying to flee. They had been some of the last to leave; most of the rest had gone by then, disappeared into the hills and the forests. The tears of the wife came back to me now, her husband's terrified silence also. In particular I recalled the wide, uncomprehending eyes of the children, too frightened to speak or even to cry. But once they had given us the answers we needed, Lord Robert set them all free, even giving them horses and supplies so that they could ride on ahead and tell their countrymen of the size and strength of our army, in the hope that they would surrender without a fight. We hadn't imagined that they would be already lying in wait, like a pack of wolves preparing to ambush their prey. None of us had.

Wace looked up, over the fields to the south. 'I confess, though, I don't recognise the land.'

'Neither do I.' I drew my knife out from its sheath and began to cut a strip from the hem of my cloak. The wool was thick, but my blade was sharp, and soon I had enough to wrap around my calf, tying it firm to try to close the wound. It was as much as I could do, until we got back to Eoferwic at least. It was a good thing that we had horses, for I couldn't have walked on it for long without opening the gash further.

'I'll try to get some rest, if you don't mind,' said Wace.

'I'll keep watch,' I replied, as he paced about, testing the ground with his feet, searching for a place where it was least damp. Then he lay down, facing away from the sun, his cloak wrapped around him like a blanket. The next time I looked in his direction, he was soundly asleep.

I sat leaning back against one of the birch trees as the morning passed. Tiredness still gripped me, but even had I not been keeping watch, I wouldn't have felt able to sleep. The wind had stilled; the branches above my head were motionless. Clouds began to gather and the land became a patchwork of light and dark.

The jangle of a horse harness from within the woods made me sit up. I looked at Wace, but he was still asleep. I nudged his side and he woke with a start, his hand straightaway leaping to his scabbard, fumbling for his sword-hilt.

'Someone's coming,' I said.

He saw me then and paused, his eyes wide and bloodshot, until at last recognition seemed to come and he scrambled to his feet. 'Where?'

I got up, too quickly: fire shot through my calf and I stumbled, but managed to stay on my feet as

I gestured back up the track. It sounded like just one rider, though I could not be sure. Our horses were about twenty paces away, a short distance inside the woods where they would be hidden from the plains below. We might make it to them before the enemy was upon us, though we would surely be noticed if we tried to ride away.

I half ran, half limped forward, following Wace towards the animals, who were both awake now, though they did not seem to have sensed anything amiss. We were just in time, as suddenly I heard hooves and then a rider came into view. There was just one, his mount at no more than a walk as he made his way through the trees.

An earthen bank lay between us and the path, and we hid behind it. As long as the rider did not look in our direction, he wouldn't spot the horses and we would be safe. But then I thought: What if he did? We were two against one, and providing that he did not have any friends riding just behind him, we ought to be able to win if it came to a fight.

The man was tall and long-limbed, with a brown cloak wrapped around drooping shoulders, and a helmet covering his head. Sunlight burst through the clouds and Wace crouched down, further out of sight, but at that moment I saw the rider's face, and a rush of joy came over me.

'It's Eudo,' I said to Wace, and then standing once more, waving out, I called, 'Eudo!'

The rider came to a halt. He searched around, and as I stumbled forward through the leaves and the branches, he saw me. There was mud in his hair, there were scratches upon his thin face, and his eyes were red-rimmed from tiredness, but it was clearly him.

'Tancred?' he asked, as if he did not quite believe it. He slid down from the saddle, laughing, threw his arms about me and embraced me like a brother. 'You made it out alive.'

'We did,' I said, and gestured at Wace, who was not far behind me.

'Wace!' Eudo shouted.

'It's good to see you,' Wace said, smiling.

'And you,' Eudo replied, and I thought I spotted moisture in his eyes as he stood back. 'I never thought I would see either of you again—after what happened . . .'

But he could not finish, as suddenly the tears began to brim over.

'What about the others?' I asked, glancing back up the path in search of more of our conroi. 'Are any of the others behind you? Mauger, Ivo, Hedo?'

He shook his head. 'I don't know,' he answered. 'I don't know.'

'And Lord Robert?' said Wace. 'What about Lord Robert?'

Eudo simply stared at him, and then at me, open-mouthed. Dark shadows lay beneath his eyes. A cloud came across the sun; from the north the wind blew and around us I heard the trees themselves shiver.

'Lord Robert . . .' he said. His voice trembled, seeming suddenly distant, as if it were no longer his own. 'Lord Robert is dead.'

52

# CHAPTER FIVE

I stared at Eudo, scarce understanding what he was saying. It could not be true. I had been with Robert in the square at Dunholm only hours before. I had spoken to him. I had clasped his hand.

The pictures whirled through my mind. It seemed to me I was stuck in some terror of a dream, and I needed desperately to wake up, but of course I could not.

First Oswynn, and now Lord Robert. The man I had served half my lifetime: since I had first taken up arms in my youth. I remembered that look of unspoken despair on his face as he had sent me from the square at Dunholm. And I saw again those eyes, hollow and lost, as if he had somehow known that defeat was at hand, that his own end was near.

I would have liked to say that the words stuck in my throat, but that would have been false, for in truth no words existed for a moment like this. My mouth was dry, the air gone from my chest. I felt myself sit down upon the ground, though I did not recall having willed my body to do so. I expected tears to follow, but strangely they did not, nor could I summon them. Instead I just felt numb. It was too much to take in.

I had sworn my life to Lord Robert's service. By solemn oath I had pledged both my sword and my shield in his defence. Still I remembered that spring morning at Commines many years ago: clear and warm it had been, with the blossom on the apple trees in the orchard and the smell of earth on the breeze. It was on that morning that I'd made my pledge and he had accepted me as one of his household knights: taken me, as he had taken Eudo and Wace not long before, into his conroi, his closest circle of men. And now that pledge lay in tatters; the oath that I had sworn to him was broken. I had not been there to protect him, and now he lay dead.

Wace's head was buried in his hands, his face red, weeping, while Eudo sat upon a rock, staring in silence down at the ground. I could not recall having ever seen either of them like this before.

'What happened?' I asked.

'What does it matter?' Wace said, and amidst his tears there was anger in his eyes.

'I want to know,' I replied.

Eudo wiped a hand across his face. 'I only saw from a distance,' he said. 'You remember I became separated from you?'

I did. In fact, the last I had seen of him was when we had cut down the thegn with the gilded sword. After that everything had been thrown into confusion. I no longer remembered who had been with me when we came to Wace's aid, only that that was when the battle had turned against us.

'I didn't know where you were,' Eudo went on, 'but I heard the horns sounding the retreat from the square, saw our banners heading back towards the stronghold. The English were pressing up the hill; there was fighting in every street. I joined with another conroi and we tried to push through to rejoin the rest of the army, but the enemy were too many and it was all we could do to hold them back.'

He turned his head down towards the earth, his eyes closed. 'I looked up to the fastness and saw the hawk banner being pushed back. The English had broken through the gates. They had Robert all but surrounded, with the mead-hall at his rear. He retreated inside—it was the only place left to go . . .'

He covered his face with his hands, and I saw him tremble.

'What?' I asked.

He glanced at Wace, and then at me, his eyes full of apology. 'Then they set the torch to it. The building went up so quickly; he could not have got out.' He bowed his head again. 'After that I fled. Men were dying everywhere; the English had won. There was nothing left to fight for.'

That was when I recalled that I too had seen the mead-hall in flames, the blaze sweeping through its thatch, the smoke rising thick and black. I had not thought anything of it at the time; that Lord Robert could have been there had not crossed my mind. But then Eudo must have had better sight of it. He had seen it all happen, and yet been powerless to do anything to stop it.

How much longer we stayed there I did not know. Nothing more was said as each of us sat, heads turned down, lost in his own grief. Above, the skies were growing grey and dark. It looked as though more rain was to come.

'Come on,' Wace said eventually, rising. 'Let's get away from the path.'

We led Eudo with his mount back to where we had tied our horses. I gestured for him to go ahead of me and struggled on behind. My leg was agony to walk on: already it seemed worse than when I had woken.

'You're wounded,' Eudo said, when he saw that I was limping. He glanced down at my calf, at my blood-stained braies and the crude bandage I had made.

'It's not bad,' I said, grimacing despite myself. 'I'll be fine until we can get back to Eoferwic.'

I saw the doubt in his eyes, but he said nothing. We settled down behind the earth bank close to our horses. Eudo found some nuts and damp bread which he had in his cloak pocket and we shared them out. It was the only food any of us had.

'We should shelter through the day, travel by night,' Wace said, when we had all finished. 'If the enemy are still marching, we're less likely to be spotted that way.'

I nodded in agreement. With any luck we would be in Eoferwic within a couple of nights. I only hoped that my wound did not get any worse in that time.

After that, each of us took it in turns to keep watch while the others slept. Since I had already rested some that morning, I offered to go first, and neither Eudo nor Wace objected. My eyes stabbed with heaviness but I knew I could not sleep, for fear of what my dreams might bring.

I thought back to the day I had met Lord Robert, when he had been as old as I was now, and I was but a boy in my fourteenth summer. It had not been all that long since I had left the monastery—a few days at most—and I was travelling I did not know where, free but hungry, walking alone. All I knew was that I wanted never to return.

Already it had been a hot summer, I remembered, though it was still only June. I had not found a spring in more than a day and all the streams were dry to their beds. Where I could, I had kept to the woods, since there I was protected from the heat of the sun; but as evening drew on I suddenly came upon a winding river: a river I later learnt was the Cosnonis, which marked the boundary between Brittany and Normandy. Between its banks and the edge of the woods a number of tents had been erected around a campfire, beside which half a dozen men were practising with swords and shields, stepping deftly forward and back in time with every stroke, ducking and turning before thrusting again.

Their blades flashed brightly in the late sun; the scrape of steel against steel rang out as they clashed. I crouched behind a bush and for a while I simply watched them, almost forgetting my thirst and my empty stomach. I had never seen such a thing before. It was like a dance: each movement, each swing, each parry all carefully considered and yet it seemed at the same time instinctive.

Eventually, though, my hunger had got the better of me, and I realised that if these men meant to stay the night here, they must have food. I moved back amongst the trees, around the back of their camp. There were more men sitting by the fire, passing bread around and speaking in what sounded like French, a tongue which at that time I only half knew. All had beards and wore their hair long, which took me aback a little, having spent so long in the company of monks, with their tonsured heads and clean-shaven chins. One of them was dressed in a mail coat, polished and gleaming, and had silver rings on his fingers. He must be their lord, I thought. His shield he had across his knees, using it like a table from which to eat; on its white face was painted a black hawk.

Had I been thinking more clearly, I would have understood that these were fighting men—men I would do well not to cross. But at that moment my stomach was all that I cared about, as the smell of roasting meat drifted on the breeze. And so, taking care not to stumble or to tread on any twigs, I carried on. One tent on the other side of the camp stood slightly further back from the rest, and I chose this as my target.

Closer to the river, a handful of boys were running at each other with wooden swords and wicker shields. They looked to be the same age as me, or perhaps a little older—it was difficult to tell from so far away. One, taller than the others, seemed to be fending off two by himself. I paid them no mind; they seemed too involved in what they were doing to notice me. Keeping low, watching to make sure that none of the men by the fire had seen me, I made my way out of the cover of the trees, towards the tent. It was made from several hides stitched together and stretched over wooden poles, and was probably large enough to fit two men comfortably. Leather ties hung from the flaps that made the opening, but they were not fastened and so I slipped inside.

The heat was the first thing that struck me; the second was the darkness. I fumbled about while my eyes adjusted, searching for something that I might be able to eat or drink. Linen blankets were laid out over the grass; a rolled-up tunic made for a pillow at one end. Beside the tunic lay a pouch with some silver coins inside. I pocketed a few, thinking that they might be useful later, before in the corner I spied a leather bottle. Without thinking I removed the stopper and began to gulp it down, and straightaway began to splutter, sending scarlet droplets everywhere. Instead of water I had found wine, and far stronger wine than any I had ever tasted.

I replaced the stopper and hurriedly put the bottle back where I had found it, hoping I had not made too much noise. There was nothing else of use here in any case; I would have to try another tent. I turned to go, but at that moment the flaps were pulled aside and the evening light flooded in. A dark figure stood before me. The sun was behind him, dazzling me with its brilliance, and I shielded my eyes. It was the tall boy I had seen by the river.

'Who are you?' he said in French, his eyes narrowing. His hair was dark, cut short on the top and shaved at the back like mine. He had thin lips and a keen stare.

I was still on my hands and knees. I looked up at him, too fearful to say anything. My mind was whirling: what would these men do to me now that they had caught me?

'Folcard!' the boy called in the direction, I guessed, of the men at the campfire. 'There's a thief in your—'

He had not the time to finish, for I was scrambling to my feet, my head down like a bull's as I barrelled into his lower half. He went down, and I was half running, half stumbling past, seeing the safety of the woods before me, when all of a sudden I felt him grab first my tunic and then my leg. I heard cloth rip and found myself falling too. The wind was knocked from my chest as I hit the ground. I struggled to get free, flailing my leg, trying to kick him away, but he held on, and then somehow he was on top of me, one hand pressed down on my collarbone, the other raised high.

I saw the blow coming and turned my head to one side. His hand connected with the side of my face and I felt the impact jar through my jaw. He sat back, getting ready to deliver another strike, but I rose up, grabbing him around the waist and wrestling him from me. He lashed out, missing my head, and I slammed my fist into his nose. He reeled back, crying out as he put a hand to his face. Blood, thick and dark, dripped through his fingers.

I had never struck anyone before, let alone drawn blood. I stared at him, not knowing what to do. My heart was beating fast; a rush of excitement came over me. Then I heard voices and looked up. The men from the fire were running towards me, some with swords drawn. Their legs were longer than mine and I knew that for all my speed, I could not outrun them. I stood in my torn tunic, frozen to the spot as they approached and began to spread out, surrounding me.

'You,' said the one I had taken for their lord. 'What's your name, boy?'

His voice was deep, his face stern. He was not all that tall, but there was something about his manner that nevertheless commanded respect.

'My name is Tancred,' I replied nervously. The words felt awkward on my tongue. My name was French, given to me by my mother, but I did not speak the language much. Some of the brothers in the monastery had spoken it, but not as much as they had Breton and Latin: tongues which I knew far more readily.

'Where are you from?'

'Dinant,' I said. I looked around the rest of the men. All of them had scabbards at their sides, and most were wearing leather jerkins, though a few had mail like their lord. They were all different sizes: some short and squat, arms folded in front of their chests; others slim and long-limbed, with piercing stares that I did my best to avoid.

'You have a family, a father or mother?' I heard the lord say.

I turned back to face him, shaking my head. My mother had died giving birth to the girl who would have been my sister. Not much later my father had followed her from this world after a feud with another man. He had not been anyone of great standing, just a minor lord with some lands near to Dinant. Neither was my uncle, his older brother, who took me in after his death. He had his own sons to provide for, and I was nothing but another mouth to feed. And so, as soon as they would take me, he gave me up to the monastery, where I had lived until just a few days before.

The lord raised his thick eyebrows but did not enquire further, regarding me without emotion. 'You fight well,' he said, and gestured towards the boy. 'Eudo has been training with me for a year and more, and still you managed to best him.'

I glanced at the one he had called Eudo, who was standing hunched over, feeling his nose, cursing and then cursing some more. He drew a grimy sleeve across his face and it came away scarlet. He did not meet my eyes.

'How old are you?' the lord asked.

'This is my fourteenth summer,' I replied, trying to work out why he was so interested in whether I

61

had a family, or how well I could fight, or how many I was in years.

'Enough of these questions,' one of the other men said. He was perhaps the shortest of them, and had a large chin and eyes that seemed set too close together. 'He was in my tent. He's a thief and he should be punished.'

'Were you stealing, Tancred?' the lord asked.

'I was hungry,' I said, turning my head down towards the ground. 'I was looking only for food, and something to drink.' Then I remembered the coins I had taken, and slowly removed them from my pocket, holding them out in an open palm. 'And these,' I added.

One of the others laughed. 'He has nerve, I'll grant him that.'

'You son of a whore,' the short one said. His face had gone a bright red. He advanced out of the ring they had formed around me, grabbing me by the wrist and snatching the silver from my hand.

'Temper, Folcard,' the lord warned him.

'I should slit your throat right now, you little bastard,' Folcard said. I stepped back quickly as his free hand went to his sword-belt; his other held fast to my wrist.

'No one will be slitting any throats,' the lord called out to him. 'Least of all the boy's.'

Folcard snarled at me, baring two uneven rows of yellowed teeth, then drew back, watching me closely. 'Then what are we going to do with him?' he demanded.

The lord stroked his beard as if in consideration, then approached slowly, his mail chinking with each step. 'Have you ever used a knife before?' he asked me. 'For fighting with, I mean, not for

62

eating,' he added sternly, when he saw what I was about to answer.

'No, lord,' I said.

He unbuckled a sheath from his belt. It was about the same length as my forearm, or a little longer. He held it out to me. 'Take this,' he said.

There was a murmur from the rest of his men, of discontent perhaps, or simply surprise. I was not paying them any attention, however, as I took the sheath in both hands, feeling its weight, turning it over. It was wrapped around with thin copper bands, off which the sun glinted.

I looked questioningly up at the lord. Did he mean to give it to me, or was this part of some test?

He nodded and gestured towards the hilt. Tentatively I curled my fingers around it and pulled. It slid out smoothly. Even to me, who knew nothing of weapons, it seemed a beautiful thing. Its edge was so thin I could barely make it out, the steel polished so clear I could see my own face in its reflection.

'It is yours, Tancred, if you wish to join me,' the lord said. He extended his hand. 'My name is Robert de Commines.'


# CHAPTER SIX

That summer's evening by the river was the first time I had ever heard that name. And it was there, the next day, in the year one thousand and fifty-seven, that for the first time I left Brittany behind. For as I was later to understand, Lord Robert had recently sworn his allegiance to the young Guillaume, Duke of Normandy, with whom lay our fate.

Of course I had no idea then that I would still be serving the same lord another dozen years later, or that our path would bring us here to England. At the time I could think only that I had been offered a chance to flee the life I had known: a chance to make myself anew. I knew almost nothing of those men or what they did, but I saw that they were if not rich then certainly comfortable. And apart from all else, I had nowhere else to go.

But there was another reason too, for that fight with Eudo had stirred within me something unexpected: a thrill that I did not understand but suddenly craved. I saw those men making their living by the sword, and the longer I travelled with them in Lord Robert's company, the more I realised that I wanted to be one of them. It was foolish thinking for one who had hardly ever seen a blade before that day, let alone wielded one, but like all youths I was easily led. My head had become filled with visions of glory and plunder: that was the life that I saw ahead of me.

I glanced at my knife, resting upon my shield beside me: the same one that I had received from Lord Robert by the river Cosnonis all those years ago. I had needed a new sheath made for it some months previously, for the blade was thinner now than it had been then, and no longer fit as snugly as it should, so often had I sharpened it in the years since. Yet that same steel had stayed with me through all these years.

A thin drizzle was falling, more like mist than rain as it swept in from the north. Beside me Eudo stirred, mumbling words I could not make out. For a time after that first meeting the two of us had been bitter rivals, and not surprisingly, for it was one thing to be beaten in a fight, but to be beaten by a boy without any training at all was far worse. But as the months passed, the bitterness receded and we gradually became fast friends.

As that year's leaves had turned from green to gold, we returned to our lord's home of Commines in Flanders. There I met Wace, who was one of the longest-serving boys in Robert's household. Then, just as now, he was headstrong and short of temper, impatient with those he considered less able than himself and full of confidence, though he was little more than a year older than me. At first he, like Eudo, was wary of me, but as I grew in strength and skill at arms, so his respect for me increased. From that time on the three of us formed a close band, swearing our swords to each other's protection, our lives to each other's service. Our days were spent learning the art of horsemanship, practising with sword and spear and shield: how to ride and how to fight. We were knights in training, and there was nothing that could harm us.

That first autumn in Lord Robert's company was the one that came to mind most clearly. The heady smell of pine burning in the hearth in the castle hall; the taste of wine upon my tongue; the sight of the orchards rich in gold and brown beneath the dwindling sun: if I closed my eyes I could imagine myself there again. But when I tried to remember all the other boys who had been there, not one of their faces came to mind, though all must have been comrades of mine at one time. Even their names I recalled only vaguely, like fragments of a dream. And it was soberly that I realised that of all of them, the only ones who were now still alive were Eudo and Wace and myself.

The sun broke through and I sat, eyes half-shut, feeling its touch upon my face. Hardly had it emerged, though, than it disappeared again behind the clouds, now the colour of slate. Soon after the rain began to fall. I closed my eyes, feeling water run down my cheeks as I thought of Lord Robert, and for the first time since Eudo had brought us the news, I wept.

\* \* \*

I roused Eudo after noon and he took the next watch while I settled down to rest. It was evening when I woke again, and the light was fading fast.

I felt a chill all through my body, and found myself shivering. My head was clouded, and for a moment I did not know where I was, or how I had come to be there, until I remembered. I tried to sit up, feeling dizzy, but only made it halfway before falling back down to the ground. Stones dug sharply into my back. Every one of my limbs was aching, but worse than that by far was the pain, the pain lancing through my leg—

'Tancred,' Eudo said. He crouched down beside me and put a hand to my brow, concern showing in his eyes. 'He's burning hot.'

'We need to get him to a physician,' I heard Wace say, though I could not see him from where I lay. 'We need to get to Eoferwic.'

Eudo held a flask out to me. 'Drink this,' he said.

He waited until I had it in both hands and then

helped me to sit up as I raised it to my lips. I sipped at it slowly; my throat was dry as parchment and I could sense each drop trickling down.

'Thank you,' I managed to croak as I passed the flask back.

'Can you stand?' Wace asked.

'I think so,' I said, though I was not at all certain.

Wace nodded to Eudo and they put their arms under my shoulders, pulling me to my feet. The two of them helped me towards Rollo, and I clambered up on to his back as they guided my feet into the stirrups. I bit back the agony. Somehow being in the saddle made me feel more secure.

We set off down the hill towards the plains below. Night fell, the stars again hidden by the clouds. All was quiet. My eyelids kept drooping, but every time they did I was quickly jolted awake again by Rollo moving beneath me.

Hills rose up and fell away. Soon we came to what I presumed was the old Roman road: a wide earthen track stretching from north to south. The way to Eoferwic, I thought, at the same time wondering how far we still had to go. I was shivering all the time now; sweat welled beneath my underarms, trickling down my side, and I felt my shirt clinging to my skin.

The hours passed. I closed my eyes, listening to the steady fall of Rollo's hooves upon the earth, trying to imagine myself someplace else, before this had all happened. I saw Oswynn, her long hair black as pitch, tumbling loose as it always was when she was with me. If I tried, I could imagine that I was touching my fingers to her cheek, feeling the softness of her skin, so smooth and pale. I wanted to speak to her, even though I knew my words would make no sense. I wanted to say the things that I never could, and now never would. I wanted to say sorry for everything. For letting her die.

The skies cleared and the stars came out. We paused at the top of a rise, and I saw the road stretch out before us, unnervingly straight all the way towards the distant horizon. So many miles yet to travel, I thought. With every passing hour the pain was growing worse, burning as never before.

I breathed deeply, feeling light-headed all of a sudden. In the distance the hills were wavering under the dim light of the moon. I leant over Rollo's flank, gasping for air. The trees, the ground itself swirled before my eyes.

I opened my mouth to say something, though what it was I never remembered. For at that moment my mind clouded, and just as it did so, the world keeled over.

*        *        *

I was lying on the ground when I came to, staring up at the stars with both Wace and Eudo crouching over me. Their faces were in shadow, the moon behind them.

I blinked, feeling the mist clear slowly from my head.

'How—?' I asked. My mind was turning, twisting, full of thoughts that did not join together, that did not make sense. Thoughts of Oswynn and Dunholm, of Lord Robert and Eoferwic. Of course, we had been riding to Eoferwic—

I tried to rise, and straightaway felt dizzy again.

'You fell,' Wace said, and placed a hand on my

68

shoulder to stop me getting up. 'Lie back for a moment.'

I heard a whicker. Eudo turned his head in its direction and then stood and walked away. He returned swiftly, reins in hand, and standing beside him I saw the dark form of Rollo, black coat faintly shimmering in the light of the moon.

'Are you fit to ride?' Eudo asked.

'He's too weak,' Wace said grimly.

'We're two days from Eoferwic, out in the open country without food or shelter, and with the enemy behind us. We can't stay here.'

Wace said nothing. He glanced at me briefly and then turned his head down towards the ground, his eyes closed as if deep in thought.

'What do you suggest we do?' Eudo asked.

'I don't know,' Wace said, and there was frustration, even anger, in his voice. His hand clenched to form a fist. 'If I did, don't you think I would say?'

'We have to get to Eoferwic.'

'I know that.' Wace stood and began to pace about, his hands clasped upon his brow.

I heard the two of them speaking to one another, though I could not make out what they were saying. At length I found the energy to sit up, but without help I could not get to my feet. And as the feeling returned to my body, so did the pain.

Eventually they came back, Wace making for his horse and mounting up without delay. 'I'll see what I can find,' he said to Eudo as he worked his feet through the stirrups and gripped the reins. 'Rest here, but don't light a fire. Give him water; keep him warm. I'll return soon.'

Then he dug his heels in and galloped away down

the hill. The sound of hooves was muffled against the mud, until it faded and once more there was silence.

'Get some sleep,' Eudo told me when Wace had gone. 'I'll keep watch.'

'Where's he going?' I managed to say. It was a struggle even to get the words out: they seemed to grind against my throat.

'It doesn't matter,' Eudo said. 'He'll be back, and we'll be in Eoferwic before long.'

I wanted to press him further, but I had so little strength. I lay back down, giving in to my tiredness. But I did not sleep, not truly. Instead I found myself slipping in and out of wakefulness: one moment staring up at the stars in the sky; the next back in Dinant, where I had spent so much of my youth, or in Commines that autumn long ago. Except that both places were different to how I remembered them, now nothing but grey wildernesses, empty of all life, the halls and houses ancient and crumbled, and though I tried many times to call out, no one ever answered.

But then at last I heard voices again. I opened my eyes. It was still dark, the night still cold. I turned my head and saw Wace, or perhaps I only imagined him. He stood beside his horse, with what appeared to be a wooden cart attached to its harness. And then there were arms beneath my shoulders and my legs, and I felt myself raised up, the ground disappearing from beneath me. I was being taken someplace I did not know, and I tried to struggle, but my limbs were weak and their hold strong, and I could do nothing.

Then there was something hard and flat beneath my back, and I was laid down once more. I tried to ask them what was happening, but could not find the words. I heard the same voices, and horses whinnying. I remembered Rollo, but then my head grew heavy and I gave in to sleep.

*      *      *

I felt myself jolted from side to side, drifting through broken dreams. Before long black skies changed to grey, and then from grey to white. About me on wooden planks were strewn loose stalks of straw, and I tried to cling to them, though they kept slipping from my fingers. The wind wrapped its icy tendrils about me, shaking me as if it had my entire body in its grip. I felt so cold, and yet at the same time my leg was burning: burning like nothing I had ever known.

The voices still murmured to one another, though I could not make out what they were saying. Later a shadow came across me and I saw a face leaning over, but his features seemed blurred, and I did not recognise him, though for some reason I felt that I should have. He pressed a hand to my forehead and spoke some more, but whatever it was that he said, I couldn't understand.

Then he was gone and the jolting began again. I closed my eyes and tried to rest, to escape the cold, to escape the pain. I no longer knew what time it was; always when I woke it was to unchanged skies. Then from above I noticed white flakes falling, dancing silently down to settle on my cloak. A few landed upon my face, and I felt the warmth drain from my cheeks as they melted.

'Snow,' someone said. Eudo, I thought, though he seemed somehow far away, and I struggled to hear him.

'We have to carry on. If we keep moving we might reach Eoferwic by dawn tomorrow. It's the only way we can help him.'

* * *

Forms danced about me in the darkness, shifting and changing like coils of smoke. Figures came and went, and I thought I knew who some of them were, but I could not be sure. For a long time I didn't know where I was, but when the shadows cleared, I found myself riding through the streets, sword and shield in hand.

Dunholm was in flames. A roof collapsed, sending up sparks; of another house only blackened timbers remained. Our men were fleeing, running and riding past me in their scores. I fought against the flow, pressing on alone, up the hill towards the fastness and the mead-hall. That was where Lord Robert was, and I knew I had to get to him before it was too late. Nothing else mattered.

Rollo's hooves pounded the dirt below. My ears were filled with the clanging of the church bell, the screams of the dying, the roars of the enemy. One Englishman after another came to challenge me, charging at me with spears and axes, and one after another they fell to my blade as I carved my path through them, riding them down. Blood sprayed across my sword-arm, but I did not feel it.

Before me stood the palisade that ringed the fastness, its tall timbers rising up to the sky. I spurred Rollo on, and then I was riding through the gates, with spears and arrows raining down to right and left. Ahead I saw the mead-hall, and in front of it, Lord Robert. He was on foot and on his own, and for every one of the enemy he felled, two more came to face him as he was pushed back towards the hall.

I called out to him, but he did not hear me. My blade swung as I pushed through the enemy's midst, but each time I looked towards Robert, he seemed ever further away, until eventually I could see him no longer. The mead-hall was ablaze and suddenly I was surrounded, fending off attacks from all sides. Beside me Fulcher was thrown from his saddle, Gérard dragged down and set upon, and I wondered where they had been, why they had not been with me when I had needed them.

And then without warning the pain rushed up on me, and I was on the ground, clutching at my leg, staring at the blood that was gushing forth. One of the enemy stood over me, grinning. He raised his spear high, ready to thrust down, to make the finishing blow. I stared back up at him despairingly as I tried to move, and found that I could not.

He gave a laugh of disdain, booming and hollow, before finally the steel point stabbed down and darkness engulfed me.


# CHAPTER SEVEN

The sun was in my eyes when next I woke, so bright that for the briefest moment I wondered if I had died and if this were heaven. But as I blinked the moisture from my eyes, raising a hand to shield them from the light, slowly the world came into view.

I found myself lying upon a narrow bed in a chamber barely larger than a horse's stall. There was a single glass slit for a window, and the light was shining straight in, glaring off the whitewashed plaster. I must have slept a long time, for the sun was high, but even so I still felt tired. A fire crackled in the small hearth. Two stools stood beside the bed, and on top of one was a wooden cup. The rest of the room was empty; there was no sign of my mail or shield, or even of my cloak or shoes.

I did not recognise this place. The last I remembered, it had been night and we were riding along the old road, making for Eoferwic. I had collapsed, fallen from the saddle; Wace had gone away and then returned. But what had happened after that I did not know. I tried to think back, but it was like chasing shadows in the night: no sooner did an image come to mind than it slipped away again, melting back into darkness.

Only the battle came back to me clearly: the one thing I would rather have forgotten. Even as I lay there I could almost feel the thunder of hooves beneath me; I could see myself leading the charge as we drove into the English line. And I remembered the moment I had been struck, the flash of heat down my lower leg as the flesh was torn open.

My leg. Apart from a dull ache I could hardly feel it now. But my head was thumping, my limbs numb with tiredness, my mouth dry. I coughed. A strange taste lingered upon my tongue—like leather, I thought, although how I could tell that I was not sure, since to my knowledge I had never

74

eaten any.

I struggled against the sheets that were wrapped around me, trying to shake off the heavy woollen blanket spread across them. My bare skin brushed against the cloth; my clothes had been taken from me along with everything else. I felt for my cross, thinking they might have taken that as well, but thankfully it was still there.

I reached out for the cup, managing to get a fingertip to it, not enough to grasp it fully, and it fell with a clatter to the floor, spilling its contents across the stone flags. I cursed under my breath, and slid back under the sheets.

Sleep came once more, and it must have been at least another hour before I surfaced. The room was still bright, but the sun had moved, no longer shining in my face, and I could see that the door lay open.

A man was standing there, watching me. He was stoutly built, and clearly used to comfortable living. His hair, brown but greying, straggled across his shoulders, but he was otherwise clean-shaven. He wore the loose-fitting robes of a priest over brown trews; on a leather thong around his neck hung a green stone, polished and sparkling in the sun. His face was weathered, and there were more than a few wrinkles around his eyes; he was in his middle years at least, even if he couldn't yet be described as old.

'Ah, I see you are awake,' he said with a smile. He glanced down, saw the cup lying on the floor. 'I will fetch some wine for you.'

I said nothing, and he disappeared from sight once more. From the accent in his voice I could tell that he was English. And yet he had spoken to me in French. My mind whirled. Had I fallen into the hands of the enemy? But if so, why would they have let me live, still less try to talk with me?

The Englishman soon returned, bearing a flagon down the side of which rolled a single red droplet. 'It is a great relief to see you awake and well,' he said before I had a chance to speak. 'In truth we didn't know whether you would survive. The Lord be praised that you have.'

'The Lord be praised indeed,' I said. It came out as a rasp, and I coughed, wincing at the rawness of my throat.

He set the flagon down upon one of the stools, and sat down on the other as he picked up the cup I had knocked over. He poured wine into it and passed it to me with pudgy fingers.

'Here,' he said. 'Drink.'

I took the cup in one hand, taking care not to spill any, and lifted it to my lips, letting the sweet taste of the liquid roll over my tongue. I swallowed; it slid coolly down.

The priest was watching me carefully, and I suddenly wondered if the wine had in fact been poisoned. But surely if they had planned to kill me, they would have done so before now.

'Where am I?' I asked. My throat still hurt, though now less than before. 'Who are you?'

'Of course,' he said. 'Forgive my rudeness. My name is Ælfwold.' He extended a hand towards me.

I glanced at it, but did not take it. 'You're English.'

If he took any offence at the accusation, he did not show it. 'I am, yes,' he said. 'Although it may interest you to know that my lord the vicomte is

76

not.'

'The vicomte?' He'd used the French word, I noticed, rather than the English, which would have been *scirgerefa*, or shire-reeve: the man charged by the king with the government of a province and everything that entailed, from the collection of dues to the maintenance of law and even the raising of armies. 'You mean Guillaume Malet?'

The priest smiled. 'Guillaume surnamed Malet, seigneur of Graville-Sainte-Honorine across the sea and vicomte of the shire of Eoferwic. I am honoured to serve him as chaplain.' He gestured around at the chamber. 'This is his house.'

I took a deep breath as a wave of relief broke over me. We had made it; somehow we had made it. 'This is Eoferwic, then?'

'It is,' he replied evenly, without so much as a flicker of impatience. 'Considering everything that has happened, you have been tremendously fortunate. God's favour shines upon you, Tancred a Dinant.'

I turned my gaze away, towards the floor. I did not feel fortunate.

'We have all of course heard the story of what happened at Dunholm,' the chaplain went on. 'You should know that so far those returned from the expedition number fewer than three hundred, many of them knights like yourself.'

Fewer than three hundred, out of the army of two thousand that had marched from Lundene only a few weeks before. How was it possible to have lost so many, and all in one night? 'I don't believe it,' I said.

'Nonetheless, it is true,' the chaplain said, his countenance grim. 'By all accounts it was a massacre. You and your companions did well to escape with your lives.'

'My companions?' I asked. 'You mean Eudo and Wace are here?'

'I didn't learn their names, but if they are the same two who brought you in, then yes, I believe they are staying in one of the alehouses in the city. They were both here for a short while yesterday.'

Yesterday, I thought, but my mind was blank. 'How long have I been here?'

'Since it is now the third day of February . . .' He paused as if in thought, fingering the green stone around his neck. '. . . I believe three days and nights in all. Most of that time you have spent either unconscious or sleeping, and burning with ague besides, so hot that at times we feared for your life. On the few occasions that you did appear to wake, you were far from lucid.' His eyes were solemn as he looked at me. 'To have suffered such an injury, endured a journey of more than fifty miles, and then still live at the end of it all—well, that is something of a miracle. You are a resilient man, Tancred. You must thank your companions when next you see them, for thcy have done you a great service. You are blessed to have friends as loyal as they.'

'I will thank them,' I said. Indeed it sounded as though I owed them my life; I hadn't realised until then how badly I must have been afflicted. Three days I had been here, and yet I remembered nothing of it.

'Will you send word?' I asked. 'I would like to see them.'

Ælfwold nodded. 'I will do my best to find out where they are staying, and despatch a messenger as soon as I can manage. Of course my lord would very much like to meet you too. He has heard a great deal about you, and I know he is interested in obtaining your service.'

I swallowed and looked away. I could not think of taking a new lord yet; Robert's death still weighed heavy upon my heart. Under him I had led a full conroi of knights: men who knew and trusted me, who would follow my every instruction without fail. He had given me mail and sword and shield, had helped to make me who I was. But now that life was gone, stolen from me, and I did not know what to do.

For without a lord a man was nothing. There were some who tried to make their way alone, swearing oaths to none but themselves, but they were few and held in ill regard besides. Often they travelled in bands, selling their swords to anyone willing to pay good silver, and often they did well for themselves. They were among the lowest class of men, for most had no honour, no scruple, no loyalty except to their purses. I had no desire to become one of them, but I had been with Robert for so long that I was not sure whether I could bring myself to serve another lord, or at least not so soon.

And at the same time I was confused, for if Guillaume Malet had heard so much about me, he must surely know that I had led my men to their deaths at Dunholm; that I had failed to protect Robert at the one time when it truly mattered. What interest could he have in me?

'I am sorry,' the chaplain said, obviously sensing my discomfort. 'I understand it is yet early to be speaking of such things. I know that you've suffered a great deal of late. I ought not to interrupt your rest any further.' He raised himself from the stool.

'What of the wound itself?' I asked him before he could leave. I felt my calf throbbing; it seemed tight, as though there was something resting upon the skin, tied to it, perhaps. Something moist and heavy, weighing my leg down so much that I found it hard to move it.

'We used the irons on it, of course, and after that applied a poultice of herbs. Again you were fortunate, for the cut, though long, was not deep.'

'How long before it's healed?'

'It's hard to know for certain,' he said. 'But you have shown yourself to be strong so far. Given rest, and provided the wound is kept clean, I should think it will not be long. I imagine you could be walking on it within a week or two. Keep praying and God will see to it; that is the best advice I can offer.'

'Thank you, father,' I said.

'I'll see that food and drink is brought to you. It is wise to build up your strength, after all.' The priest made to leave, his long vestments trailing across the floor. He reached the door and paused. 'There are servants about; if there is anything else you might require, you need only call. I'll inform my lord that you are awake. I hope that he will see you later.'

I nodded and he smiled again, just briefly, before he left, closing the door behind him.

As promised, a jug of beer was soon brought and placed beside my bed, followed shortly by some bread and cheese, apples and berries. One servant-boy helped me to sit up, placing a straw-filled pillow behind my back, while another brought some wood for the fire, which was beginning to dwindle. I ate as much as I could, but in truth I was not all that hungry, and when the same two returned later to bear away the dishes I had used, there was still most of it left.

I wondered about the chaplain, Ælfwold, and why he would choose to serve a French lord such as Malet. I thought of those English lords who had submitted to King Guillaume in the months after our victory at Hæstinges, many of whom remained in possession of their lands even now. Their oaths, though, had not been willingly given, but rather forced upon them, and more than two years later there remained much mistrust on both sides.

This priest, on the other hand, had said he was proud to serve the vicomte, and when he had spoken about what had taken place at Dunholm, it seemed to me that it was with genuine regret. Since we had first arrived on these shores, no Englishman I had met had ever regarded us with anything less than enmity. Why he should be any different, I could not understand.

I lay back for a while, listening to the sounds that I could hear beyond the window: the shouts of men practising at arms; the whinnying of horses; further off, the steady hammering of iron upon iron that was surely a blacksmith at work. Though I still felt weak, I was no longer gripped with tiredness as I had been before. As my head cleared, I sat up and spent some time in prayer, giving my thanks to God for having saved me, asking that He save the souls of those I had lost. It was a long while since I had last prayed properly, and I hoped that He would hear me.

81

It was growing late in the afternoon when I heard a knock upon the door. Even before I could answer, a man entered.

It wasn't the priest, for this man was lean and tall—as tall as myself, perhaps, although without being able to stand opposite him it was difficult to tell. His hair, cut short in the French fashion, was a dark grey in colour, his face angular, with thick eyebrows and a scar—albeit one long-healed— down his right cheek. He was dressed in a scarlet tunic, embroidered with golden thread around the neck and cuffs. Silver rings adorned two of the fingers on his left hand. He was evidently a man of some wealth, and I wondered if this were in fact the vicomte himself.

'Tancred a Dinant,' he said. His voice was deep but not harsh; nevertheless its tone was that of one used to authority.

'My lord,' I answered, and lowered my head. It was the closest to a bow that I could manage while seated.

'My name is Guillaume Malet. I am sure you will have heard of me.'

I couldn't tell if that last remark was intended to be ironic or not, but there was no sign of humour in his face.

'I'm honoured to meet you,' I said. In my time with Lord Robert I had grown well used to dealing with men of standing. As one of the men closest to the king, he was often required at court, and many were the times that either I or Wace had accompanied him with our conrois to Westmynstre.

'Similarly,' Malet said. 'Your reputation as a man of the sword is well known to me.'

He sat down on one of the stools at my bedside and held out a hand. I clasped it in my own. His grip was firm, and I noticed there were calluses on his palm, which struck me as unusual for a man of his status.

'I knew Robert de Commines,' he said as he released his hold. 'I have been praying a great deal for his soul since I heard the news. His loss will be felt most keenly by all of us. He was a good man— something that seems to be increasingly rare these days.'

I felt moisture forming in the corners of my eyes, but fought it back. 'Yes, lord.' I did not know what else to say.

'As I'm sure my chaplain Ælfwold has said, we have heard all about what happened at Dunholm. To lose so many men in one night is without precedent.'

'The enemy came upon us by surprise, in such numbers that we had no hope of defending the town.' Though if we had retreated to the fastness and rallied our forces as I had argued, perhaps we could have prevailed.

'Nevertheless, there are those who would say that the earl should have been better prepared. That he was over-confident. He gave permission for his army to go raiding the town; he let them get drunk even though he suspected the enemy were still about.'

I hesitated, surprised at how much Malet knew about events. But then he would already have heard from all those who had returned—from Eudo and Wace and other knights besides, from all the noblemen who had served under Lord Robert.

'Everything he did, he did with the counsel and

support of the other lords,' I said. I knew because I had been there with him in the mead-hall as the discussions had taken place. It was shortly after that meeting that I had been sent out with Eudo and the others to scout the hills.

'Perhaps,' Malet said, 'although with Robert dead it has become highly convenient for them to place all the blame on him.'

I remained silent, as his words worked their way through my mind. There were many among those other lords whom I had disliked, but none I had thought capable of deceit of this kind. It amounted to nothing less than a betrayal of Robert.

'And then,' Malet continued, 'there are others who would question how it came to be that Earl Robert's two most trusted men managed to survive, when he himself did not.' He raised an eyebrow.

He was suggesting that Wace and I had deliberately abandoned our lord to save ourselves. I felt a rush of anger such as I had not felt since the battle, but held it back. I couldn't afford to lose my temper before a man of such influence as the vicomte, especially given the generosity he had shown me by sheltering me in his own house.

'Do you question it, lord?' I asked instead, holding his gaze.

The corners of his mouth turned up in a faint smile. 'Rest assured I do not,' he said. Then his expression became serious once more, his lips firmly set. 'Robert trusted few men, but those he did, he always held in high regard. He knew how to win their respect and loyalty, and I have no doubt that you did all you could for him. Nevertheless, there are many who may think otherwise, and who

84

will consider twice before taking you into their employ.'

'My lord,' I said. 'It's less than a week since his death—'

'Earl Robert spoke highly of you,' he cut me off, as if he had not heard me speak. 'Indeed I have heard much of your prowess, Tancred. I know that you saved his life, and more than once. You gave him your horse at Hæstinges after his was killed beneath him. You were the one who pulled him from the mêlée when he became surrounded.'

Again I was surprised at the extent of Malet's knowledge. Everything he had said was true: I could see it all in my mind, as clearly as if it had happened only the day before. But none of it changed the fact that, in the end, I had failed in my duty.

'Why do you mention this, lord?' I asked, though I sensed that I knew the answer.

'I have need of good swords, now more than ever,' the vicomte replied. 'The enemy have tasted Norman blood; they will soon be wanting more. Dunholm will not be the end of it.'

'You believe there is more trouble to come in Northumbria?'

Malet studied me for a moment, and then he rose from his stool and made his way to the window. He peered outside; pale sunlight shone upon his face. 'The Northumbrians are a seditious people,' he said, 'proud and disdainful of outsiders. That has ever been the case, and it will not change now. You have seen their savagery with your own eyes.'

'The enemy have Dunholm,' I said. 'How can you be so sure they won't stop at that?'

He turned back to me, his face in shadow once more. 'Of course I cannot,' Malet said. 'But remember that until now they have known only defeat at our hands. The murder of the earl will have given them confidence such as they have never had. I believe it will not be long before they start to march south.' He sighed. 'And you should know that Northumbria is only a part of it.'

'What do you mean, lord?'

'Hardly a week goes by without disturbances somewhere in the kingdom. We are constantly hearing tell of Normans being murdered by bands of Englishmen in the shires. On the Welsh borderlands the enemy are becoming bolder, their raids at the same time more penetrative and more destructive. King Guillaume's forces have never been more thinly spread. And there is worse yet to come.'

'Lord?' I asked, frowning.

His eyes were fixed upon me. 'Invasion.'

'Invasion?' It seemed scarcely possible. We ourselves had held England but a couple of years.

'Indeed,' he said. 'It has been known for some time that the Danish king, Sweyn Ulfsson, has laid claim to the English crown, though he has thus far possessed neither the means nor the opportunity to pursue it. However, for some months we have suspected that he has been making plans for the coming summer. This we now know. Already he has begun to gather his ships, and it is believed that by midsummer he will have a fleet to rival our own of two years ago.'

Suddenly I understood Malet's anxiety. Even if we succeeded in driving off the rebels, there remained still a second enemy, and the Danes were fighters of some renown, feared as much for their barbarity as for their skill at arms. Indeed I remembered it being said that they had conquered this island once before, though it was many years ago now.

'Why are you telling me this?' I asked.

'It is no more than what will soon be commonly known,' he replied. 'But now you see why Robert's death could not have come at a worse time. You understand why I need the services of men such as yourself. For, sooner or later, the enemy will come, and we must be ready to fight them when they do—'

He was cut off by a sharp knock at the door.

'One moment,' Malet told me, as he went to open it.

A boy in a brown tunic stood outside. There was charcoal on his face, his tunic and light hair were unkempt, and I took him for a servant. 'My lord,' he said. 'The castellan Lord Richard is here. He wishes to speak with you as soon as possible.'

'What does he want?' Malet asked, and there was a hint of weariness in his tone.

'He didn't say, lord. He is waiting for you in your chambers.'

Malet let out a sigh. 'Very well,' he said. 'Tell him I will be with him shortly.'

The boy gave a cursory bow and hurried away.

'Forgive me, Tancred,' Malet said. 'The castellan is a tiresome man, but if I ignore him, he will only grow more persistent. I trust that you are comfortable here, that you are being brought everything you require.'

'I am, lord.'

'Very well.' He smiled. 'I do not seek an answer

from you now, but I hope that you will consider what I have said over the coming days. No doubt we shall speak again before long.'

He left, and I was alone again. I thought over everything that he had said, about Lord Robert, and about the rebellion that he believed was to come. If it did, then I wanted to be able to fight, even if for nothing else than the opportunity to avenge Robert's death. Although if Malet spoke truthfully, then there were few lords who would be willing to accept my service.

Few lords except, naturally, for him.

## CHAPTER EIGHT

Eudo and Wace came to see me the next morning, and never had I been more glad to see them. We did not talk of the battle or of Lord Robert, for there was little more to say, though I could see from the looks in their eyes that it was in their minds as much as it was in mine.

I learnt from them that Rollo had not survived the journey. They had stopped briefly at dusk to let the horses rest, but when they made to leave, he had not got up.

'The battle must have all but exhausted him,' Eudo said. 'When we saw that he wasn't going to live, we decided it was better to end his suffering ourselves. I'm sorry.'

Perhaps my heart was already so filled with grief that there was no room for any more, but for some reason I felt no sadness, only regret. I had been given Rollo in the weeks after the battle at

Hæstinges, at the same time that I was entrusted with a conroi of my own to command. He had been with me almost as long as we had been in England, seen me through two years and more of campaigning. In all my years I had known no better mount than him; strong yet at the same time quick, steady and obedient. And now he too was gone.

I changed the subject. 'The vicomte came to see me yesterday. His chaplain too, a man named Ælfwold.'

'The Englishman,' Eudo said with a look of distaste.

'You've met him, then?' I asked.

'He was the one who received us when we brought you in,' Wace replied. 'Malet has more than a few Englishmen in his household. He's half-English himself, you know.'

'Half-English?' I said, disbelieving. When I had met him there'd been nothing in his appearance or his speech to suggest that he was anything but Norman.

'It's said that his mother was of noble Mercian stock, though no one seems to know for certain,' Wace said. 'I gather he doesn't speak of it much.'

I was not surprised; it was not something that many would readily admit to.

'His loyalty to the king is not in question, you understand,' Wace went on. 'He fought alongside him at Hæstinges, and fought well at that. But his parentage means that he also has the trust of many of the English thegns.'

'Which is no doubt part of the reason he was made vicomte here,' I said. Whereas the south of the kingdom was now firmly under the control of Norman lords, much of the north was still in the hands of the same men who had held it under the usurper three years ago. As a result, whoever held Eoferwic needed to be able to treat with them. 'How do you know so much, in any case?' I asked.

'Malet was at the king's Easter council last year, when I was there with Lord Robert,' Wace said. 'All this I learnt from speaking with some of his men.'

However he had obtained it, it was useful knowledge to have, and I was grateful, just as I was for the news that they brought from outside. It seemed that there were rumours of risings in the very south of the kingdom, stories too of certain lords who had fled back to Normandy. Among them were Hugues de Grandmesnil, who had been the vicomte in Wincestre, and his brother by marriage, Hunfrid de Tilleul, the castellan at Hæstinges: some of the most prominent men in that part of England.

'I didn't realise there was so much unrest in the south,' I said. It was only a matter of weeks since we had left Lundene with Lord Robert, and there had been little trouble then. I wondered if these risings were what Malet meant when he had spoken the previous afternoon of bands of Englishmen, of Normans being killed.

'Even here in Eoferwic there is disquiet,' Wace said. 'You can see it in the way the townsmen stare at you when you ride past. They resent us, and they're no longer afraid to show it.'

'Only yesterday evening a fight broke out down by the wharves,' Eudo put in. 'Some of the castellan's knights were set upon by a group of Englishmen; I saw it happen from the bridge. It was a complete slaughter. They rode them down, killed half a dozen before the rest ran away.'

For knights to be attacked so openly meant that things were even worse than I had realised. No doubt the townsmen had learnt that a thousand Frenchmen and more had been killed at Dunholm, and now thought that they had less to fear from us. But that could not account for those risings in the south, for it was still only a week since the battle— too soon for them to have heard, and for us to have heard back. News often travelled quickly, but not that quickly.

'What will you do now?' I asked them. 'Now that Lord Robert's dead, I mean.'

They glanced at each other, and I sensed that they had not given it much consideration. Of course had Robert had a son through lawful union, I would not have needed ask the question, for then we would simply have returned to Commines and sworn our swords to him. But he had fathered only bastards, and though that in itself did not mean they couldn't inherit, none of them were of an age to take control of his manors, which would now revert to King Guillaume.

'Probably we'll try to find a new lord here,' Wace said. 'Otherwise we'll return to Lundene, maybe from there even go back to Normandy.'

'At any rate,' Eudo said, 'we won't do anything until your leg is healed and you're well once more.'

I wondered whether I should mention the offer the vicomte had made of taking me into his service, but decided against it. Though he had been generous with his praise, I was not sure that I wanted to remain in Northumbria, given what had happened in recent days. And I did not know if his offer would extend to my comrades as well— certainly he had not mentioned them when he had spoken to me. I would be reluctant to part with them, whom I had known for so long.

'You know that I'm in your debt,' I said. 'If it hadn't been for you . . .'

I did not finish the thought, for in truth I didn't like to think what might have happened. Almost certainly I would not be alive to speak to them now.

'We only did what we had to do,' Eudo said. 'We could hardly have left you there.'

'Even so,' I said, 'I owe you my thanks.'

Wace put a hand on my shoulder. 'We're at the alehouse at the top of the street the townsmen call the Kopparigat. Come and find us once your leg is healed.'

'Once the priest lets you out,' Eudo added, with a grin.

They left after that, though I was not alone for long, as soon Ælfwold came to see me, this time with a fresh poultice to place over my calf. He was pleased, for the irons had worked even better than he had hoped: the cut had closed up completely and there was no sign of any pus. I would forever bear the scar, he told me, but that could not be helped. It would only add to those I already had from battles past: upon my arm, down my side, across my shoulder-blade, although admittedly none of those were as severe as this one.

Later that same day I was visited by a monk. The hair around his tonsure was short and grey, his habit dirtied with mud, and he smelt of cattle dung. He brought with him a glass jar, which he handed to me without a word. I asked him what it was for, but he stared blankly back at me; clearly he did not speak French. But if nothing else he must have understood my puzzlement, for he held one hand down in front of his crotch, extending his forefinger, while with the other he pointed to the jar I was holding.

I tried to sit up, realising what he meant for me to do. My head was still heavy and my limbs weak from the fever, but the monk made no attempt to help me, instead merely gazing out of the window. At last I managed to perch on the edge of the bed, and with my back to the monk, I filled the jar.

He took it once I'd finished, lifting the golden liquid to the light and swirling it about, muttering some words that I did not understand as he examined it. He sniffed at the jar in disdain, and then put the rim to his mouth. I watched in disgust as he sipped at it, and he must have seen my expression for he gave me a quizzical look before walking out, nodding thoughtfully, still muttering to himself.

When the chaplain came to see me that evening, I asked him what the monk had been looking for.

'If the urine is dark and cloudy,' Ælfwold explained, 'it shows that there is more healing work to be done. But if it appears pale and clear, does not smell stale, and most importantly is sweet upon the tongue, it is a positive sign of good health. Is this not common wisdom where you are from?'

Perhaps it was, though I did not know it. It was not something the infirmarian had ever taught me at the monastery, and, to tell the truth, I was glad for it. But Ælfwold wouldn't allow me to venture out until the monk was satisfied that my waters were sufficiently clear, and so for the next few days I was kept confined to my chamber.

Whenever he could, the chaplain would sit with me and tell me the news from outside, little though there was. He made no mention of any further disturbances in the city, nor anything of the Northumbrians marching south, and I began to wonder if perhaps Malet's concerns were misplaced. At other times the priest would bring with him a squared board on which to play chess, and also a game like it called *tæfl*, which I knew the English were fond of, and which he took great pleasure in teaching me. But most of the time I had nothing to do but sit, lost in my own thoughts as I faced the same four walls from morning until night.

As the days passed, however, gradually I recovered my strength, finding my appetite once more. My head began to feel clearer, less heavy, and I found that I was spending less time asleep. By the fifth day since I first woke in that narrow bed my leg had healed enough that I was able to stand, if somewhat unsteadily, and even—with the chaplain's help—walk about the room. It still gave me trouble, but the priest assured me that the earlier I started to put my weight on it, the faster it would get better. And he was right, for it was but another two days before my piss was finally clear and he judged me well enough to venture out. I couldn't walk far without stopping to give my leg respite, but simply going beyond the door was a relief; so far I had seen nothing of the world beyond my chamber, not even the rest of Malet's house.

'This was once the residence of the Earls of Northumbria,' the chaplain told me as he led me into the great hall, 'built in the days when Eoferwic fell under their dominion. No finer palace stands in all of England, save perhaps for that at Westmynstre.'

Indeed it was a place worthy of a vicomte. The hall was easily forty paces in length and perhaps more, with a gallery running around the edge, from which were hung round shields painted in many colours: vermilion and yellow, green and azure. The sun shone in through four high windows, casting wide triangles upon the floor. In the centre stood a table long enough to seat thirty lords, with room for some of their retainers as well, while at the far end was a great stone hearth, over which was set a black cauldron, though it was still too early for the fire to be lit.

I paced about, taking in the sight. Even Lord Robert had not had a hall such as this. The chaplain was right to compare it with Westmynstre, for it could have belonged to the king himself. And perhaps at times kings had sat here, surrounded by their court.

My gaze fell upon an embroidery hanging on the wall, depicting scenes from a battle, though which battle it was meant to be, I could not tell. There were groups of horsemen charging with lances couched under their arms, while facing them was a line of foot-soldiers, their shields raised and spears set. But they were not what most drew my attention, for just beyond them I saw a lone figure standing atop a mound. His sword was raised in front of him, pointing towards the sky; to either side, strewn across the hillock, were the corpses of a dozen mailed men. I had never seen needlework so fine, nor images so detailed as these.

And then above the knight's head I noticed,

stitched in rounded, uneven letters, a legend in Latin: 'HIC MILES INVICTUS SUPERBE STAT'. It was a long time since I had last been at my studies: since I had last felt Brother Raimond's hand striking my cheek for forgetting my declensions or mistranslating a passage. But the aged librarian was not watching over me now, and in any case it was not a difficult sentence.

'"Here stands proudly the undefeated knight",' I murmured. I traced my fingers across the raised forms of the letters, wondering how long it would have taken to stitch even that one sentence; how many months had been spent in all upon this embroidery; how many nuns must have laboured together with needle and thread. Malet was wealthy indeed if he could afford such a piece.

'You know your letters,' said Ælfwold, with some surprise. Few men of the sword were able to read or write. Neither Eudo nor Wace could; in fact of all the knights in Lord Robert's household it was possible that I was the only literate one.

'As a child I spent some years in a monastery,' I replied. 'That was before I left and joined Lord Robert.'

'How old were you when you left?'

I hesitated. I had told few people anything about my time in the monastery at Dinant; the only ones who knew were those who were closest to me. They had not been the happiest of years, all told, and I did not much like to think of them. Yet even so, they had probably been happier times than these were now.

'The summer when I fled was my fourteenth,' I said quietly.

'You fled?'

I turned away, back towards the image of the knight. Already I had said more than I had meant to.

'Forgive me,' Ælfwold said. 'I do not mean to pry. It is none of my concern, I am sure. Though I do not blame you, for I have never much liked monasteries, still less monks themselves. I have always considered it better to spread God's message in the world, rather than to while away one's days in cloistered contemplation. One can so easily become lost in one's own mind, and so fail to see the glory around us. It's why I chose to become a priest rather than take the vows, all those years ago—'

'Father Ælfwold!'

The voice carried sharp and clear across the hall. I looked up to see a young woman stepping lightly towards us. She wore a winter cloak trimmed with fur over a blue woollen dress. Her head was covered by a wimple, but a few strands of hair trailed loose from beneath it, like threads of spun gold.

'Father Ælfwold,' she said, in an even, mannered voice. 'It's good to see you.'

The chaplain smiled. 'And you, my lady. You are going out, or have already been?'

'I've just returned from the market.' She looked at me then, as if I had only just appeared and she was noticing me for the first time. 'Who is this?'

She had delicate features, coupled with pale cheeks and large eyes that glistened in the light, and I guessed that she was not much older than twenty summers, and probably even younger than that. In truth I often found it difficult to judge: when I had first seen Oswynn, I had thought her

97

older than she was; there had been a wildness about her that made her seem beyond her years. It was only much later that I learnt she had but sixteen summers behind her, although it made little difference to me, for I had already found out she was experienced.

'My name is Tancred a Dinant, my lady,' I said. 'Once knight of Earl Robert de Commines.'

'He is presently under my care,' Ælfwold explained. 'He was at the battle at Dunholm, where he took an injury to his leg. Your father is giving him shelter until he recovers.'

'I see,' she said, though I was not entirely sure that she did, for she seemed to be taking little interest in what he was saying. Instead she was looking me up and down in the same disinterested manner as one might appraise a horse, until at last her eyes, tawny-brown, met mine, and then I thought I saw a flicker of a smile cross her face.

She was, it had to be said, attractive. Not in the obvious ways, perhaps, for she had less meat on her than I usually considered desirable in a woman, but attractive nonetheless: slender, with a narrow waist and full hips.

Her gaze lingered upon me a moment longer before she turned back to the priest. 'Is my father about?' she asked.

And then I understood: this was Malet's daughter. I ought to have realised it sooner, firstly from the rich manner in which she was dressed, and also from the way the chaplain had addressed her.

'I'm afraid he isn't,' Ælfwold said. 'He has gone to meet with the archbishop at the minster. So far as I know he means to be back by noon.'

'Very well,' she said, withdrawing a couple of steps. 'I'll seek him out when he returns.' She glanced once more at each of us, then without another word she hustled away, lifting her skirts so that they did not drag through the dirty rushes, though not so much that she risked baring any skin.

'She's the vicomte's daughter?' I asked as I watched her depart.

'Beatrice Malet,' the chaplain said in an admonishing tone. 'And you would be wise not to ask any further of her.' He frowned, and I saw there was a warning aspect to his gaze.

I felt the heat rise up my cheeks, and began to protest: 'Father—'

'I've seen that look before,' he said, and he kept his voice low. 'You wouldn't be the first to take an interest in her.'

I stared back at him, offended that he should even suggest such a thing. That Beatrice was pleasing to the eye could not be denied, but that was true of so many women. And in any case, compared to Oswynn she was altogether plain. Oswynn, with her hair loose and unkempt, black as the night itself. Oswynn, who had travelled with me everywhere, who had been afraid of nothing and no one. Often in the last few days I had found myself thinking of our time together, short though it had been. Hardly six months had passed since we had met for the first time under the summer sun, and now, in the silence and the stillness of winter, she lay dead.

'Come,' the priest said with a sigh as he made for the door at the end of the hall. 'It is already forgotten. There's still much I have to show you.'

He led me outside to the courtyard, where the sun was high and bright, though there were dark clouds gathering in the north, and I guessed there was rain to come. Chill air rushed over me and I breathed deeply of it, drinking it in as if it were ale, until I could feel it reaching my head. I had not been out of doors in so long that I had almost forgotten what it was like. Indeed it was as if everything had become new to me again, and at the same time somehow more real: the smell of smoke wafting upon the breeze; the songs of thrushes perched atop the thatch. Things that before I would scarcely have noticed, but of which I was suddenly now aware.

A banner fluttered from the gable of the hall, divided into alternate stripes of black and yellow, with gold threads woven into the latter so that it caught the light. Malet's colours, I presumed.

The hall and yard were ringed by earth ramparts and a high palisade, and beyond them lay the city of Eoferwic: rows upon rows of thatched rooftops, with only the minster church and the mound and timber tower of the castle rising above them. To the south, sparkling beneath the late-morning sun, ran the river. A few ships were out, their sails filled as they skimmed high over the waters. Most of them looked like simple fishermen's boats, but one stood out. Larger than the rest, she had a narrow beam and high sides which came to a sharp point at the prow. She was a longship, built for speed, for war. To whom she belonged, though, I could not tell, for her mast and sail had been taken down. A slow, regular drumbeat carried across the waters, signalling every stroke, keeping the oarsmen in time.

'Follow me,' Ælfwold said. 'You must see the chapel.'

I glanced towards him as he began making his way towards the stone building across the yard. In truth, though, I was not paying him much attention, for it seemed that there was some commotion near the gates. One group of men had lifted the bar that held them in place, while others were rushing now to open them.

The blast of a war-horn rang out, and then the gates swung open and a conroi of horsemen rode hard into the courtyard, two abreast, hooves thundering, each rider mailed and helmeted. Their lord or captain rode in front, carrying a pennon on his lance, though I did not recognise the design, which comprised four segments in blue and green.

'Whose men are they?' I asked Ælfwold, who had turned back and now stood beside me, his brow furrowed as he looked on in concern.

'They're the castellan's,' he said. 'But they're back early. He was supposed to be leading them on a scouting expedition north of the city this morning.' He began to walk faster, and I followed behind as quickly as I could, wincing at each and every step.

Already a full score of knights had passed through the gates, and still more were following. Around them a crowd was beginning to form, of servants, kitchen-girls and stable-hands.

'Where is Malet?' the one with the pennon roared at them as he untied his chin-strap, letting his helmet fall to the ground. 'Find me the vicomte now!'

'What's happened?' the chaplain asked. 'Is Lord Richard with you?'

101

The knight turned to look down at Ælfwold, and all of a sudden his expression instantly turned to anger. 'It was your kind who did this, Englishman!'

He levelled his lance at the priest's throat, just above the green stone that hung around his neck. Ælfwold stepped back slowly, his face going pale. The knight followed him, keeping the point of his weapon steady at the priest's neck. 'Tell me why I should spare your life,' he said, half choking, as his cheeks streamed with tears. 'Tell me!'

'Because he is a priest,' I called out as I drew my knife and rushed to Ælfwold's side. 'You kill him and your soul will be damned for ever.'

'He's one of them!' The knight spoke through gritted teeth, the lance quivering in his hand, and I thought that he was about to strike, but then the tears overcame him. His fingers loosened and the lance fell to the ground, into a puddle. The blue-and-green cloth lay crumpled and wet.

A shout came from close by the gates, quickly followed by a cry from one of the kitchen-girls. I looked up, and then I saw the last two men to have arrived. They were bearing a body between them. It took me but a moment to realise whose it was.

Beside me the chaplain made the sign of the cross. He was still white in colour: not yet recovered, it seemed, from his fright. He closed his eyes, uttering a prayer in Latin.

First it had been Robert, murdered at Dunholm. Now too the castellan of Eoferwic, Lord Richard, lay dead.

# CHAPTER NINE

The news of the castellan's death cast a shadow over Malet's house in the days that followed. I could see it in the anxious looks of the servants I met; I could hear it in the hushed tones they used in the corridors. Indeed I could almost feel a chill in the air when I walked between the hall and my chamber, as if there were a draught blowing in from somewhere, though that could well have been my imagination. Even Ælfwold, when he came to see me, seemed more subdued than he had been before.

For the first few hours after the castellan's men had returned there had been much confusion. A messenger was sent to the minster church to bear the news to Malet, who returned in due haste. That same afternoon he summoned all the Norman lords who were in Eoferwic to his hall, where they remained in private council for some hours. All I knew of it was what the chaplain later told me: that Malet was to assume the responsibilities of the castellan, taking all of Lord Richard's remaining men under his command.

The enemy were advancing; of that there could be little doubt. Some of their raiding parties had crossed the Use upstream of the city, and by night the horizon shone bright with the fires of the villages they had torched. But though they were growing bolder, still they did not march on Eoferwic itself.

Perhaps they were hoping to draw us out, or perhaps they were waiting for something, although what that might be, no one knew. For their full host to gather, some said, in which case it made sense to try to attack them now. But Malet had forbidden any more expeditions, probably rightly, since we could not afford to lose any more men. We had no more than six or seven hundred in Eoferwic, and while word had been sent to the king in Lundene, there was no knowing how long it would take for reinforcements to reach us. And according to the reports that came back from our scouts, the enemy numbered between three and four thousand, which if true made theirs a larger host than any we had faced since Hæstinges itself.

And so we waited for the English to come to us. All the while my leg was growing stronger, and I was spending less time indoors, and ever more in the yard outside, trading blows with Eudo and Wace as we trained at arms. My nights were filled with dreams of battle: of riding out to face the enemy, of killing those who had murdered my lord, had murdered Oswynn. If the enemy were coming, I wanted to be ready to fight them.

The chaplain didn't approve, but by then I was well enough that I didn't need his permission. In any case, it was over a fortnight since I had so much as held a sword in my hand—a fortnight in which my limbs had lost much of their strength. I knew that I could get better again only with practice, and so each afternoon I spent hour after hour with whoever would join me: perfecting my strokes, my parries and cuts, repeating the movements until they became instinctive once more.

It was close to sunset on one of those afternoons, when I was practising with two of Malet's kitchen-

104

boys, that I caught sight of Beatrice standing by the hall—watching me, or so it seemed. I was about to call to her, but at that moment the boys rushed at me, shouting and laughing as together they swung their wooden blades. One strike bounced off my shield; the other I fended off with my own cudgel, and then I was turning away, dancing out of reach so that their thrusts found only air.

What they might have lacked in skill, however, they made up for in enthusiasm. Again they came at me, and this time I stepped back, trying to give my sword-arm room, when the back of my legs struck against something hard. Thrown off balance, I staggered backwards, and I was still struggling to stay on my feet as the next onslaught came. I blocked the first blow, and the second, but the third struck me on the shoulder, sending me sprawling, and suddenly I found myself on my back facing the sky.

Dazed, not quite believing what had happened, I looked up and saw the two boys standing over me. The taller of the two, fair-haired and freckled, grinned and pointed his sword at my neck. 'Do you yield?'

'I yield,' I said, laughing as I pushed his blade away and got to my feet. Not five yards from where I stood was a wooden feeding-trough: that was what I must have stumbled into. Though it could have been worse, I thought. I could have fallen in it.

I glanced towards the hall, where Beatrice still stood, and there was a smile upon her face. I tousled each boy's hair in turn while I regained my breath, then wiped the sweat from my brow. 'Keep practising and you'll both make good knights one day,' I told them.

They seemed pleased by that, and in truth they had fought well. So much in battle was a matter of luck, whether good or ill, but the best warriors were those who made the most of their luck, who took advantage of their enemies' mistakes, and that was what these two had done. I left them to carry on by themselves as I made my way across the yard towards Beatrice.

'Defeated by a couple of boys,' she said as I approached. 'You disappoint me.'

'They show great promise,' I replied. 'Your father is fortunate to have such able young fighters in his household.'

I watched them as they finished marking out a duelling circle, and picked up their practice swords and wicker shields. They rushed together, exchanging blows before just as quickly backing away again, circling about, each searching for the all-important opening.

'There are many who can wield a sword,' Beatrice said. 'Though from what I've heard, there are few who can match your prowess.'

'If you believe that, then you couldn't have seen me fall over that horse-trough.' I spoke only half in jest. For all the hours I had spent in the practice yard of late, my sword-arm still felt slow, my body heavy. Nor was I nearly as steady on my feet as I would have liked, even without mail shirt and chausses to weigh me down.

She smiled gently as she tucked a wisp of hair beneath her hood. 'I've heard much about you,' she said. 'My father told me how you fought in the great battle at Hæstinges, how by your valour and your quick thinking you saved your lord's life.'

At Hæstinges, but not at Dunholm. 'That was more than two years ago,' I said. 'A lot of things have changed since then.'

She paused a moment, then said, 'You know that what happened to Earl Robert was not your fault.'

I frowned. How much exactly had her father told her? 'I don't want to talk about it,' I said, turning to walk away, though I didn't know where.

Within a matter of heartbeats she had fallen into step beside me, hitching up the hem of her dress to stop it trailing in the dirt. 'You can't blame yourself for his death.'

'Then whom should I blame?' I asked as I rounded on her. Though slight of frame, she was fairly tall for a woman, only a head shorter than I, and we stood almost eye to eye as she held my stare. Certainly she was determined; in that respect she seemed much like her father.

'It wasn't just your lord whom you lost at Dunholm, was it?' she asked after a while. 'There was someone else. Someone dear to you.'

A picture of Oswynn rose to my mind, her hair falling to her round breasts, and I saw myself holding her, just as I had held her before I left her that night. The night that she had died. But how could Beatrice know, and why did she torment me with such questions?

'I shouldn't have mentioned it,' she said quietly as she looked down.

'No,' I said, glaring at her. 'You shouldn't.' I had no wish to talk about Dunholm, or about Lord Robert, or Oswynn, especially not to someone like her, who knew nothing about them.

'I'm sorry. For what happened, I mean.'

'I don't need your pity.' I made for the well that

stood beside the forge, hoping that she would grow tired of hounding me. My throat was parched from the fight and I needed something to cool it. I found the bucket still half full, and I rolled up my sleeves and splashed some of the brown water into my face, gasping at how cold it was, sweet yet at the same time earthy. It trickled over my chin and neck, down the front of my tunic, like icy fingers playing across my chest.

'My father thinks highly of you,' Beatrice said from behind me.

I let out a sigh and turned, raising a hand to shield against the sun which was in my eyes. 'Why do you persist in following me, my lady?'

Her face was in shadow and I could not read her expression. 'Because you intrigue me, Tancred a Dinant.'

My face was still dripping and I wiped my sleeve across it. I felt stubble upon my chin and realised I had not shaved in the last few days. Unshaven, sweating, my hair unkempt, my arms covered with scars and bruises; I wondered what I must look like to someone like her, the daughter of one of the most powerful men in England. What could possibly intrigue her about me?

Without another word I strode past her, towards the hall's great doors and the warmth of the hearth-fire. And this time she did not follow me.

\*　　　\*　　　\*

In all that time I saw almost nothing of Malet, nor heard any word from him. Since being made castellan he had moved with his servants into what had been Lord Richard's chambers in the castle tower. Those times that I did see him, it was often from a distance across the training yard, and he was always engaged in some business with one lord or another. Most I did not know; perhaps they were lesser tenants of the king, or even men who owed their positions to Malet's patronage directly.

There was one, however, whom I did recognise, for I had met him before: Gilbert de Gand, whose long face seemed to me twisted into a perpetual sneer. He was Flemish by birth, just as Lord Robert had been, but though the two were about the same age he had never risen as high in the king's estimation. Indeed I couldn't remember a time when the two had not been rivals. We had first met when I was around seventeen years old and riding for the first time in Lord Robert's conroi. He had taken little notice of me then, though as I had grown in standing over the years, he came to recognise me as one of Robert's closest knights, and to regard me with the same hostility that he otherwise reserved for the man himself.

This time, however, he did not see me, for which I was glad. I didn't expect him to have anything pleasant to say about Robert, even now after his death, nor did I trust myself to hold my own tongue.

It was a full four days before I received word that Malet wanted to see me. He was at the castle as usual, and so the vicomte's steward supplied me with a horse, a plodding mare with a grey coat and white patches around her hocks. Not the finest mount I had ever ridden, certainly, although more than adequate, and if slow she was at least docile.

The bailey was busy that morning. In the practice yard stood a row of wooden poles, each one the

height of a man and each with a rotten cabbage set
atop it, which men on horseback were taking turns
to ride at, slicing with their swords, tearing the
leaves to shreds. By the southern gate I saw that a
quintain had been set up, with a wooden target to
tilt at. It was an exercise that depended as much
upon speed as on accuracy: strike the target too
slowly and the sandbag on the other arm would
whip around before the rider had passed the post,
hitting him in the back and knocking him straight
from the saddle. Many were the times that I had
made that mistake when I was younger.

Smoke drifted down from one of the many
workshops that ringed the yard, obscuring the sun.
The smell mingled with that of ox-dung and piss
from the tanner's place close by. I was just leaving
the mare at the stables when I spotted Ælfwold
outside the castle's chapel: a squat building
huddling in the shadow of the palisade, with only a
cross fixed atop the gable to mark it out from the
rest. He was standing near to the door, berating
one of the servant-boys, though I could not tell
what it was that he had done wrong.

He looked up as I came near, at the same time
waving the boy away. 'Tancred,' he said, and he
smiled once more. 'Forgive me. It's good to see
you.'

'What was that about?' I asked, as the boy
scurried away.

'It's not important,' he said, the redness in his
face already subsiding. 'You've heard that Lord
Guillaume is expecting you?'

'I've heard. Where can I find him?'

'He's been doing business in the tower this
morning. I'll take you to him.'

He led me across the yard, past the tents of the men who garrisoned the castle, past their smoking fires and the cooking-pots hung over them. In one a stew was bubbling that smelt strongly of fish, and old fish at that. I wrinkled my nose as we hurried past. There was a gate between the bailey and the mound, but the men there clearly recognised the Englishman, for they did not stop us.

From there a bridge took us across the ditch, and then only the mound stood before us, with a series of steps leading up to its summit, which was ringed with high wooden stakes. The tower itself stood in the middle, rising taller than anything else around, casting its shadow over the city.

'How is your leg faring?' the chaplain asked, glancing over his shoulder as we began the climb.

'Better every day,' I said. I was still carrying a slight limp, despite the many hours I had spent in training. But in all it had much improved since I had first climbed from my bed a week before. 'There's a little pain still, but not much.'

Ælfwold nodded. 'Let me know if you are in need of anything that might ease it. My own knowledge of herbs is limited, but some of the brothers at the monastery may be able to help.'

'Thank you, father,' I said, though I was not sure that I wanted the attention of any more monks. And in every other respect I was feeling well.

We had reached the top of the mound, and I could look down on the bailey below and on the men training, their blades flashing, their shouts and their laughter carrying on the wind. The castle, I saw, was bounded by water on all but its northern approach, standing as it did at the meeting-point of two rivers: the Use, which led to the Humbre and the sea; and another, the name of which I did not know.

The retainers standing guard at the door let us pass, and then we entered into a large chamber, lit only by thin slits of windows on the south wall.

'I'll see if he's ready to see you,' the chaplain said. 'Wait here.'

I gazed about at the chamber. There were no hangings on the wall, nor embellishment of any kind, only a long table and two iron braziers, at that time empty and unlit. But then this was not a palace but a stronghold.

The priest returned in short order to show me through to Malet's chambers, where he left me. The doors lay open. Inside the vicomte stood poring over a large parchment sheet spread out across a table.

'Enter,' he said without turning his gaze towards me.

I did so, closing the doors behind me. Motes of dust floated and danced in the light from the window: a slit of horn scraped thinly so as to let in the sun yet keep out the wind. On the table, beside the parchment, stood a candle, while in the hearth the remains of a fire smouldered away. A great curtain hung across the width of the room, presumably to divide the sleeping area from that intended for studying. Even accounting for what lay on the other side, it was not a large space, although these were probably not the main chambers; more likely they had been rooms intended for guests of Lord Richard, when he was alive.

'My lord,' I said. 'I heard that you wished to speak with me.'

112

He looked up. 'Tancred a Dinant,' he said, with a smile so faint it was almost imperceptible. 'Indeed I did. Come, look at this.'

He beckoned me across and stood to one side as he gestured towards the parchment. The ends were furled behind holding-stones, and he moved them back. The sheet was filled with sketches in black ink, of arches and buttresses, pillars, vaults and towers, annotated in a careful hand with measurements of each and every part.

'Plans for the refoundation of St Peter's cathedral here in the city,' Malet explained, as he traced his finger along the lines. 'Our king is most anxious that the kingdom's churches should reflect the glory of God, and is worried that the present minster is lacking. I had these drawn up last autumn.'

'It is impressive,' I said, for it was, even to one like myself who knew little of such things. From the measurements I could see that it would be a work of staggering ambition and size: more than one hundred paces in length, and as much as thirty-five from its base to the top of its tower. It would be like nothing I had ever seen. I could scarcely begin to imagine how many artisans, how many labourers, would be needed to build such a thing—nor the thousands of pounds in silver that it would surely cost.

'It is my hope that it will rival even the great church at Westmynstre,' Malet said. 'Consider the honour that such an edifice would confer upon this city—not to mention upon the man responsible for overseeing the work.' He sighed deeply, removing the holding-stones and rolling the parchment into a neat scroll, which he tied with a leather thong.

'I'd hoped that construction might begin before the spring, but as long as the rebels are marching, it will have to be postponed.'

He placed the scroll down on the desk. 'But that's not why I have called you here.'

'No, lord,' I said, relieved that he was coming to the business at hand. He had called me here because he sought an answer from me, though even now I was not sure what I was going to say.

He gestured towards a stool. I sat down as he pulled across another from beside the hearth.

'You will recall our meeting some days ago,' he said, seating himself also. 'No doubt you'll also recall the proposition that I held out to you then.'

'I do,' I replied.

He studied me from beneath his heavy eyebrows. 'As I am sure you're aware, events are moving rapidly, and for that reason it is now a different thing that I wish to ask of you, Tancred. I have a task for you.'

'What is it, lord?' I asked.

'It is a task with two parts,' Malet said, 'the first of which is this. There is a chance—a small one, to be certain, but a chance nonetheless—that if the rebels march on Eoferwic then both the city and this castle might fall. To prepare for such an eventuality, I would have you escort my wife, Elise, and my daughter, Beatrice, to the safety of my townhouse in Lundene.'

Beatrice. I thought back to the other day, when she had approached me out in the training yard, remembering the way she had kept following me, her ceaseless questions. I didn't know what to make of her: for all that made her attractive, she still seemed to me rather cold. I wondered whether

her mother, Malet's wife, was anything like her.

'And the second part?' I asked. It was a fair distance from Eoferwic to Lundene, but thus far it did not sound like a difficult undertaking.

'The second part is to help deliver a message for me.'

'A message?' I asked, taken aback. I had served Lord Robert for almost twelve years; under his command I had fought more battles than I had ever cared to count. I was a man of the sword, not a mere errand-boy.

Malet looked back at me, his face stern. 'A message,' he repeated.

I remembered whom I was speaking to, and tried to hold my temper. 'Surely, lord,' I said, choosing my words carefully, 'you must have other men who are better suited to such a task.'

'This is no small matter,' the vicomte said. 'I will be placing it in the charge of my chaplain, Ælfwold, with whom I believe you are already well acquainted. There is no one I trust more than him. But these are unsettled times, and the roads in winter can often prove dangerous. I cannot leave anything to chance with this, which is why I want you to accompany him and ensure that it is delivered safely to the abbey at Wiltune.'

Wiltune was in the very south of the kingdom: a long way indeed from Eoferwic, perhaps as much as two hundred miles, and easily more if we were to stop in Lundene first.

'I will send with you five of my household knights,' he went on. 'They are to go with you the whole way and will follow your orders.' He paused, and when he spoke again it was with a softer tone to his voice. 'I've heard much about your judgement and your ability, but I know also that you are a man with great experience. For these and other reasons I believe that you are the best person to entrust this task to. I know how faithfully you served Robert de Commines in his time, and I trust that you would do the same for me.'

He was certainly being generous with his praise, considering that he had not met me until just a few days before. And yet somehow I could not help but feel that there was more to his offer than this. For why would he tell me so much, knowing that I might not accept?

I felt the weight of his gaze upon me, but I held it with my own. 'And what if I decline, lord?'

'Naturally you have that choice. However, I believe you are an honourable man who pays his debts. Remember that while you have been recovering I have provided you with both shelter and victuals.'

I said nothing, as I realised what he meant. I owed him for the favours he had done me. And I saw that this was no ordinary debt, either: some might have said that I even owed him my life, since had it not been for the healing I had received under his roof, there was every chance that I might now be dead. The thought chilled me, and I did not linger on it. But I knew he was right. I could not ignore this debt.

'I ask only for this one thing,' Malet said. 'Do this for me and you may consider yourself free of any further obligation. Should you decline, on the other hand, I will merely seek repayment by some other means.'

I considered. I had little money left to me, save for what I might gain from selling my mail and the silver cross I carried, neither of which I wanted to part with. My coin-pouch I would never see again, for I had placed it in Oswynn's hands when I had left her in Dunholm. But I sensed that it was not silver that Malet was concerned with, even if I had enough to pay him. More likely what he meant was that he would demand a longer term of service from me—a year, perhaps, or more—and that I was not ready to give. It seemed, then, that I had no other choice.

'What of my comrades, Wace and Eudo?' I said. 'I owe them a debt too.'

'They were the two who brought you here?' But Malet was voicing his thoughts rather than asking me the question, and he didn't wait for an answer. 'Their loyalty to you is clear. And I believe I have met Wace de Douvres before, at the king's council last Easter. He seemed a thoroughly capable man, and Robert spoke well of him, too.'

He sat for a moment, as if considering, then he looked at me. 'If they are willing to accompany you, then I would gladly have them serve me. I will make sure that they are rewarded well for their troubles. But I must have their answers, and yours, by dusk. I intend for you to leave tomorrow, by noon at the latest.'

I nodded. So I had but a few hours to make my choice; a few hours to speak with the others and then return. I rose from my stool and made towards the door.

'Tancred,' Malet said as I placed my hand upon the handle.

I turned. 'Yes, lord?'

He left his seat and stood facing me, his eyes on a level with my own, his expression solemn. 'I trust that you'll come to the right decision.'

## CHAPTER TEN

The alehouse where Wace and Eudo were staying was little more than an arrow's flight from the castle gates, at the top of the street known as the Kopparigat. It meant the street of the cup-makers, or so the chaplain had told me when I had asked him the way there. Their wares were not much in demand that morning, though, since the alehouse was almost empty.

In the far corner sat two young Englishmen. They spoke in half-voices, every so often glancing towards us, as if we might be listening. At the table next to ours an old man had fallen asleep, his white hair straggling across his face where his head rested beside his cup. The place was damp and windowless; the smell of vomit, sour and sharp, hung in the air.

I told both Eudo and Wace everything Malet had said to me, about the task that he had in mind, and his promise of payment if they chose to join me.

'Did he say how much he was offering?' Eudo asked.

'It'll be more than we could make staying here, however much it is,' Wace answered sourly as he scratched at his scar, at his disfigured eye. 'Speak to any lord in Eoferwic and you'll see how little Lord Robert's name is worth. They spit at the mere mention of him; they accuse us of being deserters, oath-breakers.'

Malet had been right, then. I remembered seeing

Gilbert de Gand among those speaking with him just the other day. I wondered how much he was responsible for blackening Robert's name, even though he himself had not been at Dunholm.

'I thought they'd be desperate to take on every man they could,' I said. 'Especially with the enemy marching.'

'Obviously they feel secure enough already,' Eudo muttered.

On the other side of the common room, a serving-girl refilled the cups of the two young Englishmen, whose expressions lightened straightaway. She was short but well endowed, with full breasts and good hips. Her hair was covered and it was difficult to make out her face in the dim light, but it seemed that she could have been little younger than Oswynn.

Eudo called to her in English. Though both Wace and I knew a few words, he was the only one of us able to speak the tongue properly. His mother, like mine, had died when he was young, and his father had married an Englishwoman to whom it seemed Eudo had quickly taken a dislike. But his father had been eager for Eudo to get along with his new wife, and so he was made to sit through her chaplain's lessons, and to speak English whenever she or her servants were present, much though he had hated it.

The serving-girl turned and slowly came over to us, clutching the ale-jug tightly to her chest. Why she was afraid I didn't know. We had come armed, of course—I with my knife, the others with their swords—though it seemed to me that there were few men in Eoferwic, Norman or English, who didn't carry a blade of some kind. None of us was

119

wearing mail or helmet, and, besides, we threatened no one, sitting by ourselves.

Nevertheless, her hands trembled as she poured the ale, and she did not lift her head, but instead kept her eyes firmly fixed on the jug. Her face was round, her cheeks flushed red. She reminded me of some of the girls I had known as a youth in Commines, though I could remember none of them in any great detail.

She finished refilling our cups and Eudo held a silver penny out to her. She took it with a brief curtsy before hustling away.

'I wonder,' said Wace, after she had gone. 'Malet must be anxious if he wants to send his wife and daughter south.'

'And yet he can afford to spare six knights to do so,' Eudo pointed out. 'Including three from his own household.'

Both of them looked to me for affirmation, as if I should somehow know Malet's mind.

'I don't know what he's thinking,' I said, although I pictured him poring over the plans for the new cathedral. He had not seemed especially concerned that there was an enemy army less than a day's march from the city. But then I had no doubt that Malet, like many lords I had dealt with in the past, was careful about what he revealed to others. I did not imagine for an instant that he had told me everything he knew about the enemy advance. He had not even told me what the message was that he wanted sent to Wiltune, or whom it was meant for.

'When does he want us to leave?' Eudo asked.

I sipped at the full cup before me, enjoying the bitter taste of the ale. 'Tomorrow, before noon,' I said. 'But he wants answers from us by this evening.'

Eudo glanced at Wace. 'What else is there for us here in Eoferwic?'

'Little enough,' said Wace, with a shrug. 'We could stay, wait for the rebels to come, and hope that some lord accepts our service. But I won't risk my life without being paid for it, that's for sure—'

Sunlight burst in as the door was flung open. An Englishman in his middle years stood there, red-faced and panting for breath, hair hanging across his face, shouting something I could not understand. The two young men in the corner got to their feet, while the one with the white hair woke with a start, sending his cup to the floor. The tavern-keeper called to the serving-girl, who hurried towards the back of the room.

I rose, too quickly as it turned out, and winced as I felt a twinge in my calf. Beside me, Eudo raised his hands in a calming gesture as he said something to them in their own tongue.

'What is it?' I asked him.

He shook his head. 'I don't know.'

From outside came the sound of French voices shouting to one another, followed by a rush of feet, the pounding of hooves.

And then I heard it, faintly at first, as though it were yet some way off, but growing steadily louder: a single word, chanted over and over.

*Ut. Ut. Ut. Ut.*

I glanced at the others; they met my eyes, and I saw that they had heard it also. I reached to my knife-hilt at the same time as I saw Eudo touch the pommel of his sword.

'Come on,' said Wace. He was closest to the

door, and I followed him, with Eudo behind me. The Englishman who was standing there made no attempt to stop us, but when he saw that we were coming towards him, he ran back out into the street.

The Kopparigat was thronged with townsmen and their wives, most of whom were rushing down the hill, herding their children and their animals before them. A dog began to bark, and its call was taken up by another some way further down the road. In the distance, the wail of an infant pierced the air.

Whatever the reason for the disturbance, I knew it could not be good. Had the rebels arrived already; was the city under siege? But if so, why would their own kinsmen be running?

'This way,' Wace said, starting into a run towards the top of the hill, where the Kopparigat met the city's main street. I followed, my calf stabbing with pain, as if with every step there were half a dozen arrows driving into it, but I ignored it, pressing on through the rush of bodies, into the biting wind. A boy no higher than my waist ran into my good leg and fell backwards on to the street. He burst into tears and his mother gave a shout as she ran to pick him up. There were mud stains upon her skirts; the hood of her cloak had fallen from her head and her hair was in disarray. She glanced up at me, and I glimpsed the fright in her eyes before she took off again down the hill.

The chanting grew louder as we reached the top of the Kopparigat. To the right the road ran down towards the river, but it was from the left, the direction of the market and the minster, that the noise was coming. Some way ahead rode mailed men on horseback, their mounts' hooves spraying up droplets of mud on either side. Pennons flew from upright lances, pennons in red and blue and white and green, and I thought, though I could not be sure, that amongst them I glimpsed one in black and gold: Malet's colours.

There came a shout from behind, and I turned just in time to see half a dozen Englishmen with weapons drawn, advancing upon us from out of the crowd. They were young, perhaps five years younger than us, but all were sturdily built. Each of them carried a knife so long that it was almost a sword: what they in their tongue would call a *seax*.

'Wace!' I called, as I drew my knife from its sheath. 'Eudo!'

They turned and drew their swords, as the Englishmen came at us. None of them wore mail, nor any armour of any kind, but then neither did we, and they were six against our three.

'Stay close,' Wace said, holding his sword out before him.

Two of them rushed at me: one tall and lean; the other short, with arms like a blacksmith's. The short one came at me first, slashing wildly with his seax. I parried the blow: steel scraped against steel, but there was great strength in those arms, and suddenly I was being forced back. In the corner of my eye I saw the tall man rushing forwards, and I knew I had to do something before he reached me too.

I raised my knee into the short one's groin. He doubled over, shouting out in agony, and I smashed my hilt down over the back of his head. He collapsed, and then I was turning as the other ran at me, his blade flashing in the sunlight, half blinding me with its brightness. He thrust towards my chest and I tried to duck to one side, but the street was slick with mud and for a moment I lost my footing. I recovered just in time, raising my blade to meet his.

Sweat rolled off my brow, stinging my eyes, and for a moment I was blind as he thrust again. This time, though, he had gone too far through the stroke, and as he struggled to bring his seax back, I saw my chance. I lunged forward, hoping to drive my knife deep into the Englishman's belly, but only managed to strike his side. It was enough. The blade tore through his tunic, piercing the skin, and he roared in anguish. His hands flew to the wound, his seax falling from his grasp.

The rest of his friends had fled, all but the one I had knocked out, and another who lay on the ground between Eudo and Wace, writhing and yelling, clutching at his arm. I turned back to face the Englishman, raising my knife before me as I stepped towards him. His face, so full of anger only moments before, now held only fear as he stared at my blade, and then suddenly he turned and ran, down towards the river.

He disappeared into the crowd's midst, and I glanced at Wace and Eudo, who had already put away their swords. Neither looked as though he had been hurt.

Eudo gestured at the short one I had struck over the head, who lay on his side, unmoving. 'Is he dead?'

I kicked him in the side. He did not move, but then I saw his chest rising and falling. 'He'll wake before long,' I said.

We started off up the street. The knights I had

seen earlier had disappeared, but as we approached the marketplace and turned to the right, up towards the minster, their pennons came into sight again, quivering in the breeze. There were at least fifty of them, perhaps as many as seventy, with more riding to join them even as we approached. And facing them on the other side of the marketplace, with the minster church behind them, was a horde of Englishmen, so many that I could not count them, all shouting out with one voice.

There were men young and old, some with spears and seaxes, while others had only spades or pitchforks, and I saw more than one axe-blade, of the kind that could fell a horse with a single blow. A few were carrying round shields, and they were crashing their weapons against them in an unearthly din, like the battle-thunder I had heard at Hæstinges and at Dunholm, but somehow even wilder. For they were not beating all at once or even at the same speed, but, it seemed, simply trying to make as great a sound as possible.

'*Ut!*' they roared. '*Ut!*'

At first I thought this was the rebels' army, come to take the city, but these did not look like men trained to war. There was not one mail hauberk between them, and only a few helmets. If they had a leader, I could not see him. These were not warriors, I realised, but the townsmen of Eoferwic, come together to stand against us.

Already some of the horses on our side were shaking their heads, fidgeting where they stood, but their riders kept them steady. I looked amidst the pennons for the black and gold I had spotted before, but I must have been mistaken, for I could not see Malet there. Instead, at the head of the conroi, flying from the end of one of the lances, I saw the red fox upon a yellow field that was the emblem of Gilbert de Gand. Even at such a distance and with his helmet on, I knew from his long chin and gaunt appearance that it was him. He rode up and down in front of the men, shouting at them to keep their lines: a deep-throated roar that belied his slight frame.

We made our way through the lines of horsemen, the press of bodies, towards the front, and then Gilbert saw us. At first he must have wondered who we were, for he came riding to challenge us, but then, as he approached, a look of recognition came across his face, followed by one of anger. He slowed before us and his mount whickered, plumes of mist erupting from its nostrils.

'You,' Gilbert said, his small eyes narrowing as he looked down at me. 'You're Earl Robert's man. The Breton, Tancred a Dinant.'

'Lord Gilbert,' I replied, just as flatly.

He glanced at the others, standing beside me. 'Wace de Douvres and Eudo de Ryes.' He spoke their names slowly, and it was not hard to make out the contempt in his voice. 'Have you come just to run from this fight, as you did at Dunholm?'

'We want to help, lord,' said Wace, with far greater respect than I might have expected from him. Usually he was never one to hide his contempt of those he didn't like; his bluntness had often got him into trouble over the years. But this was no time for petty quarrels.

'I don't need help from you,' Gilbert answered, his cheeks flushing red. He spat upon the ground. 'I don't need help from any of Robert's men. Take

126

your swords elsewhere.'

A great cry rose up from the English, and Gilbert's head whipped around. 'Stand firm,' he called to the men in front of us. 'Don't let them through!' He glared at us again but did not say anything more before galloping back to the rest of his knights.

Through the ranks of horsemen I could see little of the enemy, but I didn't have to, to know that they were coming. In front of us some of the knights, over-eager for battle, raised their lances aloft and spurred their horses forward.

'Hold the line!' I heard Gilbert shout. But it was already too late, as all about him his knights broke ranks, and what just moments before had been an ordered battle-line descended into confusion. The screams of the dying filled the morning as English and Normans ran amongst each other.

Some of the townsmen had broken through, their weapons raised high. One came my way, his seax drawn as he screamed some battle-cry. I lifted my knife and parried his thrust, forcing the blade down as I clenched my free hand into a fist and smashed it into his jaw. His head wrenched back, his lower lip streaming with crimson, and as he struggled to regain his balance I followed through, stabbing my knife into his chest. He went down, the blood from his wound pooling and mixing with the dirt at my feet.

A spear belonging to one of the corpses lay in the mud. I snatched it up, passing my knife into my left hand as another Englishman came forward. He was as wide as he was tall, or so it seemed, but despite his size he was fast, deftly stepping to one side as I drove the spear towards his belly, before ramming his shield into my chest.

I stumbled backwards, but the weight was on my injured leg and suddenly I found myself falling. My back slammed into the hard earth and the taste of blood was in my mouth as the Englishman towered above me, raising his axe, and I knew I had to get away, but my limbs would not move. He lifted the blade above his head and I froze—

There was a flash of steel from behind him. Suddenly his eyes glazed over and the axe tumbled from his grasp as he collapsed forward. I came to my senses, rolling to the side as his large frame crashed on to the ground beside me. A bright gash decorated the back of his head where his skull had been shattered. I looked up, saw the sinewy frame of Eudo, who was grinning with the joy of battle. I did my best to smile back as I scrambled to my feet, spitting the dirt from my mouth. I knew how close that blade had come.

'Hold the line!' Gilbert yelled again, and this time his knights heard him, wheeling away from the slaughter to rally beneath the fox banner. We had lost perhaps a dozen men, I judged, though the enemy had lost far more. Those who faced us now had to make their way over the bodies of their fallen kinsmen first, but their anger appeared undiminished, for still they came. I gripped the hilt of my knife tightly.

From the direction of the minster I glimpsed a glint of golden thread in the noonday sun, and suddenly above the cries of all those fighting and dying came a single long note, deep but piercing, like the cry of some monstrous animal. The sound of a war-horn. A conroi came into sight, two dozen knights or perhaps even more: through the midst of so many men it was difficult to see.

'For Normandy!' they cried.

At their head, beneath the black and the gold that were his colours, rode the vicomte himself, his red helmet-tail flying behind him. He lowered his lance, couching it under his arm, as his horse started into a gallop and the horn blew again. Some of the enemy, realising the danger at their rear, began to turn to face them, but they were few. The rest saw their attackers coming from both sides and straightaway took to flight, making for the small alleys that branched off from the marketplace.

'Kill them!' Gilbert shouted to his knights as he raised his sword aloft. But the townspeople were already running and our men had little enthusiasm for the chase. Had this been the rebel army, I was sure they would not have hesitated, but it was not, and that made all the difference, since these were but peasants, and there was little glory to be had in killing them.

Corpses were strewn across the street, their shields and their weapons beside them. I was reminded of that night at Dunholm, except that this time most of the fallen were their men, not ours. Eudo wiped his blade across the tunic of a dead Englishman, smearing more blood over his back to accompany the wound that ran across his shoulders. I let the spear I had taken drop to the ground and returned my knife to its sheath.

After the rush and the noise of the battle, all was suddenly quiet, save for the bells of the minster church in the distance, their soft chimes carrying clearly to us as they rang for midday.

'That was some fighting,' Wace said with a grin as

he placed a hand on my shoulder. 'Especially for a man who's hardly picked up a blade in two weeks.'

I smiled back, though only weakly. The fight had drained more of my strength than I would have liked, and I could not shake from my mind how easily the fear had overcome me, nor how nearly I had succumbed to it.

On the other side of the marketplace, Malet passed his lance with its black-and-gold pennon to one of his knights. It was the first time that I had seen him equipped for battle, in mail and helmet and with a sword at his belt, though I had heard many tales of his prowess on the field at Hæstinges: how he had rallied the duke's men when they had all thought him dead; how he had led the counter-charge into the English lines and with his own hand slain one of the usurper's brothers.

Gilbert shouted at his men to get out of his way as he threaded his way through their lines. He glared at the three of us as he passed, but this time he had no words for us. He rode to greet Malet and, still mounted, the two clasped hands and exchanged a few words, although I could not make out what they were saying. Then Gilbert raised his lance with its red fox pennon, signalled to the rest of his men and rode off, up the street that led to the minster, leaving Malet with his conroi.

'Should we follow him?' Eudo asked.

I did not answer, for even as the spearmen were beginning to march I saw Malet riding towards us, keeping his mount to a walk as he made his way over the corpses of those who had fallen. On each flank rode one of his knights: to his left, a stocky man with a bulbous nose that was only part hidden by his nasal-guard, while the one on his right appeared not much more than a boy. If he was a knight proper, as opposed to one still in training, then probably he had only recently sworn his oath.

The vicomte untied his helmet's chin-strap and passed it to the younger of the two knights. He glanced at the English corpses that lay around us, then at each of us in turn, a grave look upon his face.

'Eoferwic is growing restless,' he said. 'The townspeople are becoming bolder.'

Behind him I heard cries of distress, and saw a woman running towards one of the bodies, throwing back her hood and clutching at her hair as she fell to her knees beside it. The wind buffeted at her dress as she leant forward, resting her head upon the chest of the dead man. Tears poured down her face.

I turned my eyes away from her, back to Malet. 'Yes, lord,' I replied. What had brought him to meet us, I wondered; did he mean to have our answers now?

'You have fought well,' he said, not just to me but to all three of us, it seemed, as he looked down at the corpses which lay around us. He turned to Eudo and Wace. 'Tancred has told you of the task I have in mind?'

'Yes, lord,' Wace said.

'Naturally I'll see that you are well paid, if you choose to do this for me. Of that you can be certain.' He turned back to me. 'I would see you again later this afternoon, Tancred. Come to the chapel in the castle bailey when the monastery bells ring for vespers. I will meet you there.'

He did not give me a chance to reply as he

tugged on the reins and pressed his heels into his horse's flank; it harrumphed and started forward. He called to the rest of his conroi and together they rode away, in the direction of the castle.

I turned back to the others. 'Will you join me?'

Wace shrugged and glanced at Eudo. 'You said it yourself,' he said. 'What else is there for us here?'

Eudo nodded in agreement. 'We'll come with you,' he said. 'And maybe after we've done everything for Malet, then we can go back to Normandy, or Italy, and take service there.'

'Maybe,' I said, smiling at the thought. It was nearly three years since we had last set foot in Normandy, and five since we were in Italy, though I was sure there would be many there who would yet remember the name of Robert de Commines, and who would happily receive us into their households.

But all that lay far in the future, for first we had to do this for Malet. And before everything else there was one task more difficult still: one that filled me with unease. I would have to give my oath to him.


## CHAPTER ELEVEN

The bells had just finished pealing, and the low edge of the sun was almost touching the rooftops to the west by the time I rode into the bailey. The heavens blazed with golden light, but there were dark clouds overhead and I felt a few drops of rain as I arrived at the chapel.

Men sat around their fires, sharing flasks of ale

132

or wine, or else honing their blades. A few I thought I recognised from the fight in the marketplace, although I could not be sure. From beyond the walls came the calls of geese, moments before I saw them lifting above the palisade, their wings beating hard as they swooped around the bailey's southern gate then headed towards the sun.

The stable-hands were nowhere to be found, and so I tethered the mare to a wooden post just outside the chapel, where there was a trough for her to drink from and a small patch of grass to graze upon. I gave her a pat on the neck, and went inside.

Malet was already there, no longer wearing his mail, but instead a simple brown tunic and braies. He was kneeling in front of the altar, upon which stood a single candle. Its flickering light played across a silver cross, in the centre of which was a gemstone the colour of blood. There was little other decoration: no scenes from the Passion painted upon the walls, nor any tapestries depicting Christ with his apostles, such as I might have expected; even the altar-cloth was a plain white in colour.

I pulled the door closed and made my way across the stone floor, my footsteps loud in the empty darkness. Malet rose as I approached the altar. His scabbard swung from the sword-belt at his waist, which I was sure Ælfwold would have disapproved of, but then the priest was not here.

'Tancred,' the vicomte said. His face lay in the shadow of the candlelight, making his long nose and angular chin seem even more prominent. 'It is good to see you again.'

'And you, my lord.'

'Events are moving quickly. Today was not the first time that the townsmen have risen against us.'

I recalled what Eudo had said only a few days before: about the fight that had broken out down by the wharves. 'No, lord.'

'They realise that our forces are weakened after the castellan's death. They await the arrival of their kinsmen.'

'Yet the rebels still haven't marched on the city,' I said. Exactly why, no one I had spoken to had been able to understand—not even Ælfwold, who of all men was closest to the vicomte and so, I thought, best placed to hear such information.

'They will, though,' Malet said, and his gaze fell upon the cross that stood on the altar. 'They will, and when they do, I do not know how Eoferwic can be defended.'

His frankness took me aback. Even though I had known him but a short while, I had not thought the vicomte the kind of man who would admit such a thing so readily, even in confidence.

'There is the castle,' I said. 'Even if the city falls, we would still hold that, surely?'

'Against a large enough army, even that may be difficult,' Malet said, and still he did not meet my eyes. 'I will be honest with you, Tancred. In all the time that has passed since the invasion, never have we faced a worse state of affairs than this.'

It was not warm in the chapel, but it felt suddenly much colder. For if Malet himself doubted whether he could hold Eoferwic, then what hope was there? From outside came the faint shouts of men, the whinnying of horses, the trundling of carts across the bailey.

134

'We will prevail, lord,' I said, although even as I said it I found that I was far from certain.

'Perhaps,' he said. 'But it is important that you understand the circumstances under which I have asked you to undertake this task for me.'

'You assume that I'll accept.' At last we were coming to the matter that he had called me here for.

He smiled, and I sensed that he was enjoying this exchange. He clasped his hands before him. His silver rings glinted in the light of the candle, and his countenance became serious once again. 'I believe that you will do what you perceive to be right,' he said. 'Should you decline, I will simply seek repayment some other way.'

I took a deep breath, felt my heart pounding in my chest. This was my last chance to consider before I had to make my decision. But already I knew what I was going to say.

'I will do this for you, lord.'

Malet nodded. He had known that I would not refuse. 'And your comrades?' he asked. 'Are they willing to accompany you?'

'They will join me.'

'Good,' he said. 'You know, then, what I must ask of you.'

I did. I knelt down on the stone paving before the altar. A twinge ran through my leg where it had been wounded, but I tried not to show it. Malet stood before me. He lifted the silver cross with its blood-red stone. As he did so, the flame of the candle wavered, and I thought it might go out, but then it straightened. Was it an omen, I wondered, and if so, what did it mean?

'In taking this oath,' Malet said, 'you swear that

135

you are and will be subject to no lord but me. You bind yourself to my service, to the protection of myself and my kin, to do as I bid you. I, for my part, will invest you with everything you need to fulfil this task, and upon your return I promise to absolve you of all further obligation to me.' He held out the cross, and his eyes bored into me. 'Do you swear to become my man?'

I clasped my sweating palms around his own fingers, around the cross. My heart pounded in my chest. Why was I so nervous?

'I swear by solemn oath,' I said, meeting his gaze, 'in the sight of Jesus Christ the Lord, my God, to serve you until my duty is done.' I knew the words that were required. Long ago I had spoken almost the same thing before Robert, except that I had vowed to serve him unto death. I had not thought then that I would ever have to give another man my oath. Nor had I known how hard it would be to do so.

I let go. My throat felt dry and I swallowed to moisten it. But it was done.

Malet replaced the cross on the altar before unbuckling his sword-belt. 'I give you this blade,' he said as he held the scabbard out to me in open palms. The leather was unadorned save for the steel chape at its point; the hilt was wrapped around with cord to aid one's grip, the pommel a simple round disc.

I rose and took it from him, slowly, so as not to drop it. It felt heavy in my hands, but then it was the first time since the battle that I had held a sword, even one sheathed such as this. I fastened it upon my waist, adjusting the buckle until it fitted.

'I will make sure you are provided with new

mail, a shield and a helmet,' the vicomte said. 'Otherwise I intend for you to travel light. Come to the wharves at noon tomorrow. I will be there to bid you all safe journey.'

'We'll be travelling by ship?' I asked, surprised. The usual route to Lundene was by land, not sea.

'The roads around Eoferwic are growing ever more dangerous, and I do not wish to take any chances,' Malet said. 'My own ship, *Wyvern*, is to take you downriver until you meet the Humbre, where you'll make landfall at one of my manors: a place called Alchebarge. There you can obtain horses before making south on the old road for a town called Lincolia, and thence on to Lundene. Ælfwold's knowledge of the country is good; you may trust in him if ever you are unsure of the way.'

'I understand,' I said.

'There is one more thing.' He produced a leather pouch from within the folds of his cloak and handed it to me.

I took it, feeling its weight, the clink of metal inside. I undid the drawstring and upended the contents into my palm. A stream of silver coins spilt out, cold upon my skin, glinting in the candlelight.

'There ought to be enough there to pay for provisions, inns for the night, and whatever else you might need on the way,' Malet said. 'If, however, by the time you arrive in Lundene you should find yourself needing more, you have only to ask my steward, Wigod, and he will provide you with whatever else you require to get to Wiltune and back.'

Wigod. Yet another English name. I wondered how many more Englishmen the vicomte had in his service.

'I trust that you will not fail me,' the vicomte said, his blue eyes fixed upon me.

'No, lord,' I said. He had given me this responsibility, and my debt to him would not be paid until I had seen it through. 'I will not fail you.'

He looked as if he were about to say something else, but at that moment the doors were flung open. I raised a hand to shield my eyes as bright light filled the chapel. The man who entered was dressed in mail, his helmet tucked under his arm. With his face in shadow and the sun behind him it took me a moment to recognise him, but as he hurried across the tiles towards us, I saw his long chin, his high brow. It was Gilbert de Gand.

'Lord Guillaume,' he said. Either he had not seen me or he did not care, but for once his arrogant air was gone, replaced by a troubled look.

'What is it?' Malet demanded.

'There is a man outside wishing to see you. An envoy from the enemy. He arrived at the city gates not half an hour ago.'

'An envoy? What does he want?'

'It seems the rebels' leader wishes to see you,' Gilbert said. 'To discuss terms.'

Malet fell silent. I thought of the doubts he had expressed to me only moments before, and wondered what was going through his mind. As difficult as our position was, he would not willingly surrender Eoferwic, surely? Gilbert was watching him carefully, waiting for a reply. I wondered if Malet had confided as much in him as he had in me.

'Let me speak to this man,' the vicomte said at last. He strode towards the chapel doors. 'Where is he now?'

He did not have to look far. The envoy sat astride a brown warhorse in the middle of the practice yard, where a crowd of knights and servants had gathered to watch. He was built like a bear and dressed like a warrior, with a helmet and a leather jerkin as well as a scabbard on his belt. If he was at all nervous at being surrounded by so many Frenchmen, he did not show it. In fact he seemed to be enjoying the attention, grinning widely and taking every insult thrown at him as if it were a mark of honour.

He bowed his head when he saw the vicomte. 'Guillaume Malet, seigneur of Graville across the sea,' he said, stumbling a little over the French words. 'My lord sends you his greetings—'

'Spare me the pleasantries,' Malet cut him off. 'Who is your lord?'

'Eadgar,' the envoy replied, loudly so that everyone in the bailey could hear, 'son of Eadward, son of Eadmund, son of Æthelred, of the line of Cerdic.'

'You mean Eadgar Ætheling?' Malet asked.

The envoy nodded. 'He would speak with you this very evening, if you are willing.'

The last surviving heir of the old English line, Eadgar was the only other figure around whom the enemy might have rallied after Hæstinges, his title *ætheling* meaning one who was of royal blood, or so at least Eudo had once told me. Until now, though, Eadgar had shown no hunger for rebellion; instead he chose to submit to King Guillaume soon after the battle and remained a prominent figure at court. It was only when whispers of plots against him were voiced last

139

summer that he fled north into Scotland, but even then none had thought him capable of raising an army.

'I would advise against this, lord,' Gilbert said, his voice low. 'We know how treacherous the Northumbrians are. These are the same savages who murdered Richard but four days ago.'

'Even so,' Malet said, 'I would prefer to look upon the face of my enemy.' But though he spoke confidently, his face was grim. He looked about, saw one of his servants and called for his sword and mail, and then to the Englishman said: 'Tell your lord I will meet with him.'

'This is unwise, Guillaume,' Gilbert said, more loudly this time. 'What if they plan another ambush?'

'Then you will accompany me with fifty of your own knights to make sure that doesn't happen.'

For a moment Gilbert looked as though he was about to protest, but he must have thought better of it, for he merely scowled and stalked off to his horse.

'Come, Tancred,' said the vicomte. 'That is, if you wish to see the man who was responsible for Earl Robert's death.'

'Yes, lord,' I replied, though the words came out more stiffly than I would have liked. I could feel my sword-arm tensing, but I tried to calm myself, difficult though that was, for Malet was watching me. As if testing me, I thought.

'Very well, then,' he said. 'Let us hear what Eadgar has to say.'

*       *       *

140

The sun was already upon the horizon by the time we rode out from the city's north-eastern gate. Almost every one of the Norman lords who resided in Eoferwic was there, each with a contingent of knights under his own banner, and at their head rode Malet.

The country around Eoferwic lay open in every direction: wide marshes rising to gentle slopes where sheep grazed. A few trees gave some cover, but they were sparse enough that an ambush was unlikely. Not that the enemy seemed to have any such intention, for no sooner had we left the city than I spied spearpoints and helmets glinting not half a mile away. Eadgar was already waiting for us.

'There they are,' murmured Ælfwold, who was riding beside me. The vicomte had brought him for counsel, although in truth I could not see what use the priest would be. This was surely a matter for men of the sword, not of the cloth.

In the low light it was hard to make out the enemy's exact numbers, but I reckoned they had brought at least as many men as we had: some on horseback, others on foot, and all of them gathered under a purple-and-yellow banner—the colours, I supposed, of the ætheling himself.

Indeed I saw him now. He was a head taller than most of his men and wore a sturdy helmet, with plates at the side to protect his cheeks and a long nasal-guard rimmed with gleaming gold. Surrounding him were men in mail and helmets, armed with spears and swords and long-handled axes, with his colours upon their shields. What the English would call *huscarlas*, I thought: his closest and most loyal retainers, his ablest fighters. Men

141

who valued their lord's life above even their own, who would fight to the last in his defence. How many of them had been there at Dunholm, I wondered; how many of my comrades had died on their blades?

We drew to a halt as Eadgar strode forward from his lines, flanked by four of his huscarls. Malet nodded to Ælfwold and myself, to Gilbert who was riding a short way behind and one of his knights, and we dismounted. The ætheling had taken off his gilded helmet and for the first time I saw his face. His eyes were dark and his lips thin, while his hair, the colour of straw, fell raggedly to his broad shoulders. He was said to be only seventeen in years, which made him hardly more than a boy, but he did not look it, for he was sturdily built, with arms like a smith's, and there was a confidence in his manner that belied his age.

This, then, was the man who was responsible for what had happened at Dunholm. For the deaths of Lord Robert and Oswynn and all my comrades. My heart was pounding and beneath my helmet I felt sweat forming on my brow. How easy would it be, I wondered, to pull my blade from its scabbard, to take Eadgar by surprise and cut him down where he stood?

Yet even as the thought came to me, I knew I could never manage it without his huscarls reaching me first. Fighting peasants was one thing, but these were experienced warriors, and four men to my one. And vengeance was worth nothing if it cost me my life. I breathed deeply as I fixed my gaze upon the ætheling.

'Guillaume Malet,' he said as he approached. 'We meet once again.' His voice was gruff, though he spoke French well enough—not that that was any surprise, given the time he had spent at the king's court.

'I didn't think it would be so soon,' Malet answered. 'I'd hoped that when you skulked away last year it would be the last we saw of your wretched hide.'

But Eadgar seemed not to hear as he nodded towards the contingent of knights Malet had brought with him. 'A formidable host indeed,' he said, with more than a hint of sarcasm in his tone. Then his dark eyes settled upon Ælfwold and he frowned. 'What's an Englishman doing keeping company with these sons of whores? You should be with us.'

The priest blinked as if startled. 'He—he is my lord,' he managed to say, shrinking back under the stare of the ætheling, who was at least a head and a half taller than him.

'Your lord? He is a Frenchman.'

'I have served him faithfully for many years—'

Eadgar spat upon the ground. 'No longer will I bend my knee before any foreigner. This is our kingdom, and I won't rest until we have taken it back. Until we have driven every last Frenchman from these shores.'

'England belongs to King Guillaume,' Malet spoke up. 'You know full well that the crown is his by right, bequeathed to him by his predecessor, your uncle King Eadward, and won with the blessing of the Pope. You swore to serve him loyally—'

'And what would you know of loyalty?' Eadgar interrupted him. 'As I remember you used to be a close friend of Harold Godwineson. What

143

happened to that friendship?'

I glanced at Malet, wondering if I had heard properly. What did Eadgar mean by calling him a friend of the usurper? The vicomte's cheeks reddened, though whether from anger or embarrassment I could not tell.

Eadgar was smirking now, clearly enjoying his opponent's unease. 'Is it true that the scourge of the north, the great Guillaume Malet, has a soft heart? That he feels remorse for Harold's death?'

'Hold your tongue, ætheling, or else I will cut it out,' said Gilbert. He rested his hand upon the pommel of his sword.

Eadgar ignored him as he advanced towards Malet. 'Tell me,' he said, 'did you feel the same sadness at the deaths of your own kinsmen? Did you shed a tear when you heard about Dunholm, when you heard how Robert de Commines burnt?'

At the mention of Robert I felt my blood rising, pounding in my ears, until all of a sudden the battle-rage was upon me and I could hold myself back no longer.

'You murdered him,' I said, striding forward. 'You murdered him, just as you murdered Oswynn and all the others.'

'Tancred,' Malet said warningly, but the blood was running hot in my veins and I was not listening.

The smile faded from the ætheling's face as he turned. 'And who are you?'

'My name is Tancred a Dinant,' I said, drawing myself up to my full height as I came eye to eye with him, 'once knight of Robert de Commines, the rightful Earl of Northumbria.'

Out of the corner of my eye I saw his huscarls'

hands reach towards their sword-hilts, but I was not about to back down. Eadgar held up a hand to stop them as he stepped towards me. He was within arm's reach now, close enough that I could see his yellow teeth, his wide nostrils; close enough that his stench, foul like fresh horse-shit, filled my nose.

'Robert was a coward,' Eadgar said. 'He didn't deserve to live.'

'I ought to slit your throat right now for what you did.' I jabbed a finger towards his breast.

He wrenched it away. 'Touch me again,' he growled, and I felt the heat of his breath upon my face, 'and it will be your throat that's slit, not mine.'

It was the wrong thing for him to say, for in my anger I took his words as a challenge. Before I could think better of it I raised my hands and, with all the strength I could muster, shoved him back. He staggered under the weight of his mail, struggling to keep his footing, until he came crashing down, landing on his backside in the mud.

'You bastard,' Eadgar said as he got to his feet, and I saw the hatred in his dark eyes. Straightaway he drew his blade, and I drew mine. His four huscarls, shields raised and spears outstretched, rushed to protect him.

I let out a laugh. 'Are you so afraid of one man that you hide behind four of your own?' I asked, shouting so that the rest of his retinue could hear me. 'You're the coward, not Lord Robert!'

'Enough,' I heard the vicomte shout. 'Tancred, put your sword away.'

But the rest of our men were behind me now: jeering, throwing insults at the ætheling, and I paid

145

Malet no attention. 'I will come for you,' I went on, 'and when I do, I'll tear out your throat and sever your head, slice open your stomach and leave your corpse for the crows to feed on. I will come for you, Eadgar, and I will kill you!'

'Tancred,' Malet said again, more sharply this time. 'We're here to talk, not to fight.'

I was breathing hard, I realised, and beneath my mail my arms were running with sweat. I watched the ætheling, but he clearly had no more words for me, since he remained tight-lipped. Slowly his men lowered their spears, and he sheathed his sword, and only then did my anger begin to subside. I spat on the ground before at last I turned and slid my own blade back into its scabbard.

'That was foolish,' Ælfwold said, as I made my way back. 'You could have been killed.'

'Just be glad that I wasn't, then,' I snapped. The battle-anger still lingered and I was in no mood to argue with him.

'You should keep your dog on a tighter leash, Guillaume,' the ætheling called. 'Otherwise sooner or later he will try to bite you too.'

'I will deal with my men how I choose,' the vicomte replied. 'Now, tell me what it is you've come to say.'

Eadgar glared at me a while longer, but I was not to be moved. 'As you wish,' he said to Malet. 'I know that neither of us wants a battle, and so I bring you this offer: surrender the city to me this evening and I will allow you and all your host safe passage as far as the Humbre.'

Of course Eadgar knew that assaulting a city was no easy undertaking, and that even if he succeeded, he would probably lose many hundreds of men in doing so. And so he presented Malet with a choice: either to stay and fight and risk his life; or else retreat in dishonour, leaving Eoferwic to the rebels, and thus invite the king's wrath. I didn't know which was worse.

'And if I refuse your terms?' Malet said.

'Then we will take the town by force,' the ætheling replied, 'and I shall look forward to killing you personally and taking my pleasure from your womenfolk.'

'My lord—' Gilbert began, but the vicomte raised a hand to silence him.

'You think you will take Eoferwic with this rabble?' he asked the ætheling, gesturing towards the purple-and-yellow banner and the men gathered beneath it.

'I have near four thousand men encamped to the north of here, each one of them hungry for battle,' Eadgar said.

Malet frowned. 'And yet I see barely one hundred here.'

'Mock me if you wish, but I've seen your scouts watching us. You know I speak the truth.'

The vicomte held his gaze. The wind was up, whistling across the marshes and the plains, while around us banner-cloth flapped. Otherwise there was silence.

'Do I have an answer, then?' Eadgar asked.

Malet looked up towards the sky, taking a deep breath. He closed his eyes—searching for guidance from God, perhaps—until, after a final glance at the ætheling, he turned his back and made for his horse.

'You are a fool, Guillaume,' Eadgar called as the rest of us followed and mounted up. 'I will show you no mercy! Do you hear me? No mercy!'

But the vicomte did not reply as we rode away, back towards the city gates. Instead he was staring out into the distance, towards the west, as the last glimmer of sun descended below the horizon. And I felt a chill come over me. For in his eyes was a look I recognised: the same one that I had seen in Lord Robert's that night at Dunholm.

A look of despair, as if he already knew his fate.

## CHAPTER TWELVE

That night I dreamt of Oswynn.

She was with me still, as beautiful as ever, her black hair whipping behind her in the wind, laughing wildly. All about us the land glowed beneath the summer sun as we rode across pastureland, through fields grown thick with wheat. Behind us lay the town of Waerwic, which was where I had first met her, though we would not be returning there. How long we had been riding neither of us knew, when we came upon a forest glade, far from anyone who might disturb us. We left our horses, and there under the shade of the trees we lay down in each other's embrace, and I was caressing her cheeks, her neck, her pale breasts before—

I woke sharply to the sound of my name, finding myself in my room once more. Malet's house, I remembered. It was still dark; a faint half-light shone in through the window. A stout figure stood over me, clad in dark robes and a thick cloak. A green pebble hung around his neck and he carried

148

in his hand a small lantern. The flickering flame lit up his face.

'Ælfwold?' I asked.

'Dress quickly,' the chaplain said.

I sat up, trying to hold on to the forest, to Oswynn, the smell of her skin, the heat of that summer's day, even as they slipped away from me. A cold draught blew in through the open door. I had kept my shirt on during the night, but it was only thin and the air was like ice upon my skin.

'It's early,' I said, which was obvious, but my mind was still clouded with sleep and those were the first words that came upon my tongue.

'So it is, my friend,' the priest answered. 'We must be up.'

Outside I could hear men shouting, horses whinnying. For an instant the chamber was bathed in an orange glow as a torch flashed past the window, then darkness took hold once again.

'What's happening?' I asked.

'They're coming,' Ælfwold said. 'We must make for the wharves without delay.'

'The English are marching?'

The chaplain frowned. 'The rebels,' he corrected me. 'Their army has been seen approaching from the north.' He set the lantern down upon the floor. 'I shall be waiting in the hall.'

He hurried out. I threw off the blanket which lay over me and got to my feet, tugging my tunic on over my shirt, pulling on and lacing up my braies, donning my mail and fastening my cloak about me. My knife lay beside the bed, and I buckled it upon my belt—on my right side this time, for the sword the vicomte had given me was now on my left. Again I could hear shouting, and the fall of hooves in the yard. I glanced about the room to make sure there was nothing else, but there was not. Soberly I realised then that I was carrying with me everything I owned.

Ælfwold was waiting for me in the hall, just as he said he would be. He was dressed not in his usual priestly robes but in what looked more like travelling clothes: a green tunic and brown trews, with a loose reddish-brown cloak in the English style, clasped at the right shoulder with an intricate silver brooch.

'You are ready?' the priest asked. 'Whatever you need you must bring now, for we cannot return later.'

'I'm ready,' I said. I checked beneath my cloak for the coin-pouch that the vicomte had entrusted to me; it was still there. 'Has word been sent to Eudo and Wace?'

'A messenger has been sent,' he answered as we made our way to the great doors, which lay open. 'They'll be meeting us at the ship.'

Outside the courtyard lay shrouded in mist, lit only by torchlight and, far to the east, the faint grey light that marked the approach of dawn. Frost crunched beneath my feet; the ground was hard and the puddles had turned to ice. The chaplain led me towards a group of knights—three in all—who were standing beside their horses, rubbing their hands to warm them. All looked up as we approached. Two of them I did not recognise but one I did, for he was one of those who had been with Malet the day before: short but firmly set, with a nose that seemed too large for his face.

'These are the men who will be accompanying us,' Ælfwold told me, then to the others said, 'This

150

is Tancred, whom Lord Guillaume has assigned to lead you.'

I held out my hand and clasped each of theirs in turn, struck by how young they all seemed. I was never very good at judging ages, but I guessed that they were easily three or four years younger than myself.

'I thought there were to be six of us,' said the one with the large nose. His voice was deep, with a slight rasp that put me in mind of a dog's bark.

'The other two will be meeting us at the ship,' Ælfwold said as half a dozen mounted men galloped past us, lances in hand, towards the gates. 'Now we await only the ladies Elise and Beatrice.'

We did not need to wait long, however, for at that moment I saw them riding towards us from the stables: Beatrice, her slender frame wrapped in a thick black cloak trimmed with fur; and beside her a woman who could only be her mother, Malet's wife. Rounder than her daughter, she rode with a straight back, and her face was stern, with a piercing gaze not unlike her husband's.

'My ladies,' the chaplain said as they checked their horses before us.

'Father Ælfwold,' Elise said, before she turned to me. 'You are the one my husband has chosen to escort us to Lundene?' she asked. Her voice was even—much like her daughter's, in fact—and I saw that despite her stern countenance she was not unattractive for her age.

'I am, my lady,' I replied, and bowed. 'My name is Tancred.'

'Forgive me,' the chaplain said, interrupting, 'but we must make haste. There will be time enough for introductions once we've sailed.'

151

A stable-hand had arrived as we were speaking, leading two horses, one of which must have belonged to the chaplain, for he now took its reins, while the other was the mare I had borrowed the day before.

'Very well,' said the lady Elise. 'We shall speak further later, I am sure.'

I took the mare's reins from the stable-hand. She was already saddled and so I mounted up and rode to the head of the party. I met Beatrice's eyes briefly as I passed—wide and full of fear—before she turned away again.

I pointed to the large-nosed man. 'You,' I said. 'What's your name?'

He regarded me with a defiant look. 'Radulf,' he said, as he settled himself in the saddle.

'I saw you with the vicomte yesterday, up at the marketplace by the minster church.'

'That's right,' he said, narrowing his eyes. 'What of it?'

I would be lying if I said that his hostility did not irk me, though at the same time I was not surprised by it. Probably he was used to leading, and so resented my being placed in charge.

'Take the rearguard,' I said, ignoring his question, and likewise ignoring the angry look that he returned. My eyes fell upon one of his companions: a thickset man who it seemed had not shaved in some time. 'And you,' I said. 'What do they call you?'

'Godefroi,' he said. 'Godefroi fitz Alain.'

'Go with him.'

They turned—the one named Radulf somewhat grudgingly—and rode to the back of the column, leaving just one. From his face I judged him to be the youngest of the three, even though he was taller than the rest—taller even than myself, I thought, though I was near six feet in height. He bore a solemn expression, but I sensed an eagerness behind those eyes.

I raised my eyebrows at him, and he understood the question even before it left my tongue. 'Philippe d'Orbec,' he replied.

'You stay with me,' I said.

A thin rain was beginning to fall, spitting down out of a still-dark sky. I glanced back over my shoulder to make sure that the rest were gathered as they should be. The chaplain was immediately behind me, just in front of the two ladies.

'We need to go now,' he said. 'The ship will be waiting for us.'

Far in the distance I was able to make out the faint beat that was the battle-thunder. I could not yet see them over the palisade, but I hardly needed to, to know that the rebels were on their way.

I kicked my spurs into my mount's flank, forgetting that it was not Rollo I was riding. The mare reared up, and I tugged hard on the reins to keep her under control as she came down, thrashing her head from side to side. I rubbed her neck in reassurance, then waved for the rest to follow as we rode out through the great oak gates into the city.

We were not the only ones on the streets that morning. It was not yet light, but already there were men everywhere, running with torches and lanterns. Some were Frenchmen like us, but still more of them were English, and they had clearly heard the news of their countrymen's approach too, for they had come out with all manner of

153

blades: seaxes and meat-cleavers, spears and axes. The air was filled with their cries.

We followed the street as it curved down towards the river, but as the crowds grew thicker, my mount's steps became shorter and I knew she was growing uneasy. I stroked her side to calm her. She was no warhorse, no destrier; she was not battle-trained, nor used to such crowds. Nor, I was sure, were the horses belonging to the priest and the two ladies.

I waved to the chaplain, who drew up alongside me. 'Is there another way to the wharves?' I asked.

'Up and past the minster, then down the Kopparigat,' he replied.

That would take us further away from the river. If anything, there was even more chance of being cut off if we went that way. But I guessed from his expression that the priest already knew this.

'There is no other way around,' he said.

I cursed under my breath. I could not afford to put the ladies at risk, which they would be if we tried to press on through these crowds, but I also knew that there was no guarantee the streets would be any clearer if we tried to go around.

'We go on,' I said to the chaplain. Whether that was a foolish idea or not we would soon see. In any case he did not argue with me, as I half expected he might, but simply nodded.

I took a deep breath and spurred the mare into a trot. She seemed reluctant at first, but I kept a firm hold on the reins with my one free hand, and she obeyed. Rollo would have been far easier to handle, I thought, with not a little regret; I had not even needed reins to control him, though it had taken months of training to master that. I had not been able to spend time with this one, learning her quirks or her strengths, and I didn't know how she would respond.

I drew my sword from its scabbard. It slid out cleanly, the edge sharp, the lantern-light glinting off its polished surface. It was a heavier blade than I was used to, balanced more towards the point than I would have liked. For now, though, it would do. It would have to.

Men scattered from our path, but the greater part of the crowd lay ahead. These were the same streets where we had fought the day before, but the townsmen's defeat had clearly not dampened their ardour, for they were out in even greater numbers than before, clamouring to the heavens: *Ut! Ut! Ut!*

'Stay together,' I shouted to the rest of the group over the noise.

Ælfwold held a small wooden cross, even as he clung to the reins. Probably the priest had never seen such a rabble before. Behind him, the two ladies looked pale as they struggled to keep their horses under control. It was a mistake to have brought them this way.

A man rushed at me with a spear held before him; I turned just in time to see him coming and bring my sword around, deflecting his blow before cutting down across his arm. He dropped the weapon and staggered back into the crowd as blood streamed from the wound, staining his tunic.

'Back!' I roared at them all, hoping that they would understand my meaning if not my words, that they would take the drawing of blood as a warning. Instead they pressed even closer, just out of sword-reach, not understanding that I had only

155

to come forward a little and I could slaughter them all where they stood.

'Back!' I shouted again, waving my sword to ward them off.

Behind me a shriek went up from one of the ladies as some of the townsmen surged forwards, grabbing at her arms and at her skirt, trying to pull her from the saddle. Her horse shied away, tossing its head from side to side, and as her hood fell from her face I saw that it was Beatrice. I pulled hard on the reins and turned, spurring the mare on as I raised my sword high, before bringing it down upon the shoulder of one, slicing into the bone, even as Radulf charged forward and plunged his lance into the chest of another. A third Englishman had taken hold of Beatrice's leg and was tugging hard, but she clung to her mount's neck, and he saw me only too late as I battered my blade across the back of his head, sending him to the ground.

'Are you all right?' I asked Beatrice. Her hair had come loose from beneath her hood, falling across her face, and a fright had taken hold of her, for she did not answer, instead merely staring at me with wide, vacant eyes. I did not know which had given her the greater shock: the men who had tried to take her, or the manner in which I had dispatched them.

The cries around us swelled. I didn't want to have to kill peasants, but we didn't have much choice. I had sworn to the vicomte that I would protect his womenfolk, and I would die before I broke that oath. I would not fail him as I had failed Lord Robert.

I placed a hand on Beatrice's arm, and nodded to

Radulf. Blood was spattered across his helmet, beneath which his face was grim and his lips tight. Waving my sword at the crowd, I rode back to the head of the column. Not a hundred paces away I could see the river, though between it and us lay a host of townsmen.

'We need to turn back,' said Philippe beside me. 'We won't get through this way.'

I glanced back up the road we had come, at the countless dozens of men at our rear. 'We've come too far,' I said. 'We have to go on.'

I looked towards the castle, a shadow against the grey skies to the east, where it rose above the houses. That was where Malet would be coming from, if he was still going to meet us at the ship. If, indeed, he could get through. But then I spotted, riding hard from that direction, a conroi of horsemen, at least two score and probably more, with a banner flying high above them. A banner which even in the dim twilight I could make out: a red fox upon a yellow field. The symbol of Gilbert de Gand.

For the first time in my life I had reason to feel relief at the sight of him. He and his men charged into the enemy's flank, tearing into the crowd with lances and swords alike. Shouts went up from the gathered townsmen, only this time they were shouts of panic rather than anger.

'For Normandy,' I heard someone call; it could have been Gilbert himself, although I was not sure. 'For St Ouen and King Guillaume!'

The enemy were fleeing now—those, at least, who were not being cut down by the swords of Gilbert's men or trampled under the hooves of their horses. Men ran past us on either side, no

157

longer caring about us, thinking only of escaping with their lives.

'On,' I shouted to Ælfwold and all the others behind me. I rode through their midst, knee to knee alongside Philippe, sword still in hand to fend off any who came too near, until suddenly we came upon Gilbert and his knights, who were pressing from the other side, and found ourselves in space once more.

'You again,' Gilbert said, drawing to a halt as he caught sight of me. 'I seem to find you everywhere.' He removed his helmet and wiped his brow with his sleeve. In the half-light of dawn he looked more gaunt than ever. A faint stubble covered his chin, and his mouth as always was drawn in distaste. 'The enemy are marching,' he said between breaths. 'They'll be at the walls before long.'

'I know, lord,' I answered as I sheathed my sword. 'I'm escorting the ladies Elise and Beatrice to the wharves, on the orders of the vicomte.'

He glanced up and saw them. Beatrice still looked white—even more so now as the skies grew brighter—though she had recovered enough to draw her hood back over her hair. Elise rode close by her side, one arm around her shoulders. The two were flanked by Radulf and Godefroi.

'Malet clearly trusts you, though God alone knows why,' Gilbert said, half muttering, as if he were speaking only to himself. He surveyed our party, and then turned back to me. 'See them safely there. You will find that the road down to the river is clear.'

'Thank you, lord,' I said.

He nodded in acknowledgement, then called out

158

to the rest of his men: 'With me! Conroi with me!'

He raised his lance with its pennon aloft and set off at a gallop in pursuit of those who had fled, his knights following close behind him. Their shields of yellow and red flashed past and their mounts' hooves drummed upon the earth, kicking up clods of earth as they went. For a moment I almost contemplated riding with them, even if that meant fighting under Gilbert's banner. If the enemy were about to attack then I wanted to be there, avenging Robert and Oswynn and all the rest of my comrades. But I knew that was not my task, and it was with heavy heart that I watched them ride away.

'Follow me,' I said to the others. Carrying on the breeze came the townsmen's chanting again; it might not be long before they returned. And there was the battle-thunder, unmistakable now as it rang out from the north: an almost unearthly din. The rebels were marching, the enemy were coming, and we could ill afford to delay.

Workshops and storehouses and wattle-work fences passed by, close on either side: in some places we could barely ride two abreast. Before us now I saw the river, grey and slow-moving beneath the mist, which lay so thick that I could see nothing of the houses on the far shore. Rain continued to spit upon us, and it seemed to me that the clouds were becoming heavier, in spite of the lightening sky to the east. The bodies of Englishmen lay in the mud, on their backs or crumpled on their sides, eyes open as they had been at the moment of their death, and I tried to ride around them.

And then all of a sudden the houses came to an end, and we had the river beside us as we came out on to the quayside. There were ships of all sizes, from simple fishing craft to wide-beamed traders, but then at the far end I spotted the longship I had seen a few days before. She was even more magnificent close at hand: a huge vessel, at least forty paces in length, I reckoned, with a black-and-yellow sail furled upon her yard. This, then, had to be *Wyvern*. It seemed a fitting name, for like the serpent she was long and sleek, and no doubt fast as well when out on the open water.

On the quayside next to her stood the vicomte himself. He was dressed again in his mail, with half a dozen knights, the rest of whom were all still mounted. He said nothing as I approached; his face was solemn, his lips tight, his eyes on his wife and daughter. I swung down from the saddle and went to help the ladies as they too dismounted, signalling for Philippe to go to Élise even as I held out my hand to Beatrice. She took it after a moment's hesitation, her fingers delicate yet firm in my own, and I saw her confidence returning along with the colour to her cheeks as she brought her leg across and gracefully slid down to the ground.

Elise rushed to her husband and threw her arms around him. 'Guillaume,' she said, and a tear rolled down her cheek.

'Elise,' the vicomte said as he held her to his chest, and then he opened his arms to receive Beatrice as well. Lord, wife and daughter embraced together.

A shout came from the ship, where a dark-haired man with a full beard was standing. The shipmaster, I guessed. He was directing men as they lifted sacks from the quayside, passing them across the gunwale to others who stowed them beneath the deck-planks.

'Aubert,' Malet called, and the man turned. 'How soon can you sail?'

'Shortly, my lord,' he said, stepping up on the side and jumping down on to the wharf. 'We're almost finished loading supplies. Is everyone here?'

'Not yet,' the vicomte said. 'We're waiting for two more to arrive.'

He was right; I had not yet seen Eudo or Wace. I only hoped that they had not been waylaid, for I understood what Malet was thinking. We might have to leave without them if they did not come soon.

Two of the deck-hands came to fetch the bags from the ladies' mounts, and from those of Radulf, Godefroi and Philippe. I helped them to unfasten the buckles that held them to the saddles, and to carry them, one in each hand, on to the ship. They were not heavy, probably containing little more than a spare set of clothes; they too must have been told to travel light. I climbed up on to the deck. It was some while since I had been aboard a ship; in fact the last time I had done so was during the crossing from Normandy, that autumn of the invasion.

'Tancred,' Malet called. His womenfolk stood beside him, speaking with Ælfwold, who kept glancing up the road that led to the bridge, an anxious look on his face. Not far off, a war-horn blew; I could hear the clash of steel upon the wind, and I felt myself tense. I left the bags for one of the oarsmen to collect and jumped back down to the quay.

'My lord,' I blurted out, 'this is not my place. I need to be here in Eoferwic, killing the men who murdered my comrades, who murdered Lord Robert—'

'Tancred, listen to me,' Malet said. 'You will have your vengeance in time. But you must understand that my wife and daughter are more important to me than anything else in this world. I am entrusting their safety to your hands. Would you abandon them if they were your own kin?'

'No, lord—'

'All I ask is that you take care of them, and extend to them the same respect as you would your own womenfolk. Do you understand?'

'I understand,' I said, bowing my head. I knew that he was right: this was the service he had asked of me, and I could not go back on the oath that I had sworn to him. Revenge would have to wait.

'As for the other matter, it is imperative that Ælfwold reaches Wiltune safely. Remain watchful, and have your hand ready at your sword-hilt at all times, for you never know when you might have to use it.'

'Of course, lord.' I would hardly be fulfilling my duty otherwise.

'These are uncertain times,' Malet said. 'I am relying on you, Tancred. Do not fail me.'

'No, lord,' I said. 'I will not fail you.'

I caught a flicker of movement out of the corner of my eye and turned to see Eudo and Wace at the far end of the wharves. They rode at a canter towards us, and across the black hawks painted on their shields there were streaks of blood.

'Are these the last two?' the man Malet had called Aubert shouted from amidships. Already the oarsmen were taking their places on top of the wooden ship-chests that they used for benches.

'They are,' the vicomte said.

The shipmaster fetched a long gangplank from beside the mast, which he laid across the gap between wharf and ship. 'My ladies,' he said. 'If you would come aboard—'

He was cut off as another horn sounded from the city: one short blast quickly followed by a longer one.

'Lord,' said one of Malet's knights. He reined in his mount as, restlessly, it pawed at the ground; behind him his comrades were glancing about nervously. 'We cannot delay any longer.'

'No,' said Malet. 'No, we cannot.' He made his way quickly to his horse, a bay with black mane and tail standing by the storehouses that fronted the quay.

'Be safe,' Elise called to him as he mounted up. 'Please be safe.' Once more she rushed to his side; this time he held out a hand to her and she took it. She seemed to have regained her composure, or else she was simply holding back the tears.

'I will,' Malet said as he gazed down upon his wife and Beatrice. 'God be with you both.' He withdrew his hand to grip the reins, and gave his horse a kick. It whickered as it started into a trot. 'Farewell.'

He waved to the half-dozen of his men who were waiting, then dug his spurs into the beast's flanks and cantered away, past Eudo and Wace who were riding in the other direction. Not once did he look back.

'The enemy are gathering,' Aubert said. 'We must go now if we're to get away at all.'

163

The shipmaster was right. Again I could hear men chanting, filling the morning with their battle-cries, and if anything it seemed that they were closer now.

Wace and Eudo drew to a halt and quickly dismounted. Both looked drowsy still, their eyelids heavy; neither had shaven, and light stubble covered their chins. Like myself they had probably been sleeping when word had arrived. It was still not fully light, the river a grey smear broken by faint ripples where the rain fell, more heavily now.

'We've been waiting for you,' the priest said to them, a little sharply, I thought, given that we ourselves had arrived only a short while before.

'We came upon some of the townsmen by the bridge,' Eudo said as he unfastened his saddlebag. 'The whole city is rising. You wouldn't believe it.'

'We saw,' I said. 'We had to fight our way through them from the vicomte's house.'

Four boys whom until then I had taken for deck-hands were seeing to the horses that we had brought, and I recognised them for some of the stable-boys I had met at the castle.

'Wait,' said Wace, when he saw one taking the reins of his horse. 'What are you doing?'

'The vicomte has asked us to take them to the castle,' the boy answered. In fact he looked to be almost a man grown, probably around sixteen or seventeen in years, although his voice had not yet deepened.

'It is all right,' Ælfwold said. 'They're Lord Richard's men.'

For a moment Wace looked doubtful. I understood: I would never have entrusted Rollo to someone I did not know. But he must have known

164

that there was not a lot of choice; we couldn't take them with us.

'Go on,' he told the boy. 'Take care with him, though. He's not used to others riding him; he'll try to bite you if he has the chance.'

The boy nodded, a little uncertainly, and climbed up into the saddle that Wace had left. The animal snorted and fidgeted, but the boy pulled firmly on the reins and kept him in check.

Eudo waited until he was firmly seated, then passed his own reins up to him. 'See to it that he's well kept,' he said sternly. 'Otherwise you'll have my sword to answer to.'

A shout from the shipmaster caught our attention and we followed the priest and the two ladies across the gangplank. Aubert waved towards two of his deck-hands—one at either end of the ship—who unhitched the ropes from the mooring posts before rushing to their seats as the rowers pushed off against the wharf's planked buttresses. On the other side, thirty oar-handles were fed through thirty rowlocks, until thirty blades broke the water, casting waves out into the river. They paddled backwards so that the prow pointed out into the midstream, and as the shipmaster began to beat his drum, larboard and steerboard fell into stroke, carving their blades through the Use's murky waters.

The four stable-boys were already almost out of sight as they led the horses in the direction of the castle. But behind us, upon the bridge by the other end of the quay, the mist was beginning to clear and through it I saw the shadows of men as they ran, like ghosts in the gloom, bearing a forest of spears and axes.

'Look at that,' I murmured to the other knights.

There were dozens of them, perhaps even hundreds, roaring as they came, the light of their torches glinting upon the calm waters below. I felt my sword-hand itch again, and I wanted to ask Aubert to turn back, though I knew that I could not. Over the roofs of the houses between the castle and the minster I saw black smoke rising, and a glimmer of flames, and I heard, or thought I heard, men's voices carrying on the wind: 'For Normandy! For King Guillaume!'

Ælfwold bowed his head. His lips moved as if in prayer and I wondered what he was feeling. He was Malet's man, and so far as I knew had been for some time, but even if he had no especial liking for the rebels or for Eadgar, they were still his kinsmen. Was he praying for them or for his lord?

'Row, you sons of whores,' Aubert shouted, beating harder on the skin of the drum. 'Row, if you want to get paid!'

The oarsmen found their rhythm and the ship surged forward, cutting through the waters with all the sharpness and speed of a sword. Stroke followed stroke, and with each one the wharves, the storehouses, the whole city receded further into the mist. Somewhere in those streets, I thought, rode Malet with his conroi. In his hands rested the defence of Eoferwic.

We passed by the castle, its palisade and tower rising in shadow high above us, and we stood there, not speaking to one another but simply watching while it grew smaller and smaller, until the river turned away to the south and even that great edifice disappeared from sight. Slowly the shouts and the battle-thunder faded into nothing. Before

166

long there was only the sound of the drum and the oars upon the water, and then at last we were alone.

## CHAPTER THIRTEEN

The banks slid past in the evening mist. Low willow branches swung lazily in the breeze, bare save for a few yellow catkins: little pinpricks of colour amidst the gloom. The first signs of spring, perhaps.

The river was quiet, stately in its progress as it wound its way through the flat country. A fleet of ducks swam off our larboard side, watching closely with beady eyes as we overtook them. All that could be heard was the soft splash of oars against the water's surface. How different it was from the crowded streets of the city; it was hard to believe it was just that morning that we had left. But night was nearly upon us again, and the darkening cloud hung low, threatening rain at any moment.

Beside me, Aubert pulled on the tiller as the river curved towards the west and the last light, and the *Wyvern*'s high prow carved a great arc through the calm water. On the right-hand bank a village came into sight, no more than a spire or two of smoke at first, but as we grew closer I was able to pick out firelight, and then a cluster of houses around a timber-and-thatch hall, a low rectangular shadow against the grey skies. I wondered who resided there: whether it was one of the few English thegns who still held land under King Guillaume, or—more likely—a new French-speaking lord.

'Drachs,' Aubert said to me as he pushed gently on the tiller. 'South-east she runs from here, down to the Humbre.'

A chorus of laughter erupted from the other end of the ship, where Eudo and Wace were playing at dice with the other three from Malet's household. They seemed like good men, from the little I had spoken to them, and I did not doubt their sword-arms, though whether they had the temperament for battle, I couldn't yet be sure.

I'd joined them earlier, but soon found myself distracted, my mind wandering and confused. So much had happened so quickly and I needed the time to think. We had departed Eoferwic in such a rush and I still did not understand how I had come to be here, why Malet had chosen me for this task.

Up ahead, the river's course bent sharply left: so sharply in fact that it appeared to come back almost on itself. Aubert shouted to his rowers, and those on the left-hand side shipped oars, taking a few moments to rest their arms, while those to steerboard quickened their pace. The ship surged forward, taking the bend in a wide curve, and as the river straightened out, the pace slowed and the larboard oarsmen once more resumed their stroke.

A gust rustled the reeds in the shallows and I caught a glimpse of shadows moving about on the right-hand bank. I watched, trying to make out more detail, but whatever it was, it remained hidden by the mist. A deer or some other animal, I thought.

Aubert steered us away, back towards the middle of the river where the flow was fastest. I looked to the sky, where the moon was up, its milky light shining diffusely through the low, bulbous clouds. There had been wind, but it had lessened as the day wore on and the black-and-gold sail was now furled, the mast taken down. But the Use was high after the recent rains and the current was strong, and so we had made good progress.

'You're from Dinant, then?' the shipmaster asked, and I was taken by surprise, not because of the suddenness of the question, but because he'd said it in the Breton tongue. I had grown so used to speaking French in recent times that the words sounded almost foreign to my ears.

'That's right,' I replied. Malet must have given him my name. 'You're from Brittany as well?'

Of course, just because he spoke the language did not mean he was a native—and I had not noticed any trace of an accent before now. The words felt unfamiliar as they left my tongue. Like the ocean on the turning tide: never really gone, only diminished, waiting for the moment when it would flood back once again.

'From Aleth,' he said. 'Not far from you.'

I had never been there but I knew of it: a port some miles downstream from Dinant, where the river flowed out into the Narrow Sea.

'It's been a long time since I was there,' he continued. 'There or in Dinant, for that matter. Not since the time of the siege, anyway.'

At the mention of the siege I felt my chest tighten. The tale was five years old, and had been related to me long before. I'd heard how Conan, the Breton count, had refused to swear fealty to Normandy; how Duke Guillaume had invaded that summer and forced him back to the castle at Dinant; how the castle had been besieged and

169

destruction wrought everywhere, until at last he submitted. But never before had I spoken to anyone who had seen it with his own eyes.

'You were there?'

'I was serving as steersman in Conan's household. It was after the siege that I left his employ and Malet took me on.'

'What was it like?'

'Houses raided, half the town razed to the ground,' Aubert said, his eyes vacant, staring off into the mist. 'Women raped, men and children murdered in the streets. The stench of death everywhere: in the castle, in the streets. It was like nothing you have ever seen.'

'I was at Hæstinges,' I said, suddenly provoked. 'I have seen thousands of men lose their lives in a single day, run through with sword and spear, trampled under the weight of the charge. You think I don't know slaughter?'

I remembered my ears filling with the screams of my comrades. I remembered seeing the whole hillside awash with blood, and whether it was the enemy's or whether it was ours, after a whole day of fighting it no longer mattered.

The shipmaster turned away. 'You live by the sword,' he said. 'That's different.'

A sense of guilt came over me, for I hadn't meant to be harsh. It was more than any man should have to witness—any man, at least, whose living was not made as mine was.

'He should have surrendered sooner,' I said. Even in those days Guillaume of Normandy had a reputation as a fierce warlord, loyal to his allies but merciless against those he considered his enemies. Conan had been foolish to think that he could challenge him.

Aubert shook his head. 'By then the war had sent him mad,' he said. 'Some days he did not even come out of his chambers. He refused to speak with anyone, and he hardly ate, though he certainly drank.' The shipmaster spat over the side into the river. 'When he finally came to his senses, it was too late for the town.'

I shook my head. Even when I'd first heard the news, it was not the Normans I had been angry at—that, after all, was how wars were fought—but our own count, for inviting it upon Dinant, for betraying his people.

'Still, the tides come and the tides go,' said Aubert. 'Five years is a long time. And we all fight for the same side now, don't we?'

'We do,' I said quietly. Conan was dead—had been for some time—and any animosity there once might have been between Breton and Norman was long buried.

A drop of rain struck my cheek, heavy and cold. The last light of day was fading and already it felt colder as the river-mist closed in around us. The drops grew more frequent and I drew up the hood of my cloak to keep them out. Dark spots began to appear on the deck.

'When do we put in for the night?' I asked.

'We'll sail until dawn if we can. With luck we'll have reached the Humbre by then, as long as there's some moonlight and we can see our way. The river's wide and deep enough here—not so many mudbanks to watch out for. Besides, I've travelled this river many times this past year. I know her curves like I do my wife's.' He flashed me a grin, and I saw that he was missing several of his

171

top teeth. I tried to smile back, though in truth I did not feel at all cheered.

'Row!' Aubert barked at his oarsmen, for they had relaxed their pace while we had been talking. He picked up his drum once more and began to beat the time he wanted. 'Stop slacking, you bastard Devil-sons! Row!'

I looked up as Ælfwold approached and sat down on a bundle of fleeces next to me.

'How are the ladies faring?' I asked him, glancing up towards the bows where Elise and her daughter stood watching the waters slide past.

'As well as might be expected,' the chaplain said, his tone somewhat subdued. 'Our prayers are naturally all for the safe keeping of the vicomte.'

He withdrew a small loaf from inside his cloak and broke it in two, pieces of crust flaking off to settle on the wooden timbers, then he offered me one half. I took it with thanks and bit into it, feeling its coarse texture between my teeth. A piece of grit scraped the inside of my cheek and I used my tongue to work it towards the front of my mouth, before picking it out and flicking it overboard.

'How long have you served him?' I asked.

'Many years,' Ælfwold said, his brow wrinkling. 'Thirteen, perhaps fourteen, or even more—I've long since lost count. Since he first came over from Normandy, at least.'

'You mean he was in England before the invasion?' Of course I remembered Wace telling me about Malet's English mother, but I also knew he had fought at Hæstinges and so had assumed that he'd come over at the same time as the rest of us.

Ælfwold swallowed his mouthful, nodding.

One question had been on my mind all day; there would not be a better time to ask it than now. I lowered my voice. 'What did Eadgar mean when he said that Malet used to be a friend of Harold Godwineson?'

The chaplain went pale as he cast his gaze down towards the deck.

'It's true, then?' I asked, frowning. 'He knew the usurper?'

Malet had been careful to keep that fact hidden. But then there were few men these days, English or French, who would readily admit to being close to the man who had stolen the crown. That the king held him in such regard in spite of it certainly marked him out.

'Knew him, yes,' Ælfwold said, speaking more solemnly now. 'Even when I entered his employ I believe they were already well acquainted. Often they hunted together; as I remember, one summer he even accompanied Harold on pilgrimage to Rome—'

He broke off as a troubled expression came across his face. 'You should know, though, that all that came to an end three years ago. For years he used to travel back and forth between Graville and his English estates. But when King Eadward died and Harold assumed the crown, he returned to Normandy to join the invasion.'

That two men who had been such great friends should so quickly have become enemies was strange. 'What made Malet turn against Harold?' I asked.

'I confess there have been many occasions when I have been unable to understand my lord's mind,' the chaplain said. 'This, I am afraid, was one of those. For certain he was opposed to Harold's seizure of the crown, which he saw as both illegitimate and perfidious. All this happened, you understand, after Harold had sworn his oath to be Duke Guillaume's vassal. But already before then their friendship was wearing thin. I remember them meeting many times in those years, and each time I recall a deepening frustration, perhaps even resentment, in my lord's manner. To this day I have never found out what happened to cause such ill will.'

'Did you go with him when he returned?'

'To Normandy?' Ælfwold asked, as if it were an absurd question, and I was taken aback by his tone. 'No, I stayed on, helping to manage his estates this side of the sea.'

'They weren't confiscated by the usurper, then?'

'No,' the chaplain said. 'Even then I think Harold still hoped the two of them could be reconciled, but for my lord it was too late.' A note of regret seemed to enter his voice. 'The damage had been wrought, and it could not be repaired.'

I fell silent. Harold had been an oath-breaker, a perjurer, an enemy of God; he'd had no right to the kingdom of England. But even so I couldn't help but think: how hard must it have been to go back on so many years of friendship, as Malet had done?

'He is a good lord,' Ælfwold said, glancing back across the ship's stern, and I imagined he was looking back towards Eoferwic, though it was of course many miles behind us now.

A loud groan came from the wooden platform at the bow of the ship; Eudo's head was buried in his

174

hands as the rest burst out laughing.

Wace cupped his hands around the pile of pebbles that lay in the middle of their circle and drew them towards his own. 'Just be glad we're not playing for silver,' he said as he gave Eudo a sympathetic pat on the shoulder.

The ladies turned their heads momentarily, before gazing back at the river. I had spoken little to them all day, save to ensure that they were comfortable, and had sufficient cloaks and blankets to keep themselves warm. At times I had brought them food and wine, though they had not seemed hungry.

I turned back to Ælfwold. 'The rebels won't take Eoferwic,' I said. I tried to sound confident, though in truth I was not entirely convinced, for it was not just their army outside the walls that I was thinking of, but also the townsmen within. I didn't doubt Malet's ability, but I was not sure whether seven hundred men would be enough to hold the city.

'The rebels are only the beginning of it,' Ælfwold replied. 'Even if they can be held off, come the summer we will have the Danes to fight, and what will happen then, none but God can know.'

'If the Danes come at all,' I pointed out.

'They will come,' he said. He met my gaze and I realised then how old he looked, and how tired were his eyes, not just with fatigue from the day's events, it appeared to me, but from something more deeply set.

'Pray with me, Tancred,' he said. He knelt down on the deck, placing his hands together and closing his eyes.

I did the same, and as he began to intone the first

175

words of the Paternoster, I joined in, reciting words practised over many years, ingrained, as it were, into my very soul: '*Pater noster, qui es in caelis, sanctificetur nomen tuum . . .*'

As the phrases rolled off my tongue, my mind wandered, and I began to think about the journey ahead, about seeing the two women safely to Lundene, and our task beyond that. What was the message that the chaplain was carrying, I wondered, and why Wiltune?

'*Et ne nos inducas in tentationem, sed libera nos a malo. Amen,*' I finished, and I opened my eyes.

Ælfwold was yawning. 'Forgive me,' he said. 'It has been a long day and I am in need of rest.'

'Of course,' I said. The time for such questions would come, I decided. There was no pressing need to air them now, and we had many days' travel ahead of us.

'I should speak with the ladies Elise and Beatrice before I sleep,' the chaplain said. 'I bid you a good night.'

'Good night, father.'

I watched him return, past Wace and Eudo and the others, to join the women at the bow. Leaving a husband and father behind to the mercy of unknown forces could not be an easy thing to do, and I had no desire to intrude upon them. We had tried to afford them space whenever we could, though there was precious little of that aboard a ship such as this. Better that Ælfwold was the one to speak with them; he knew them as I did not.

For a while I sat in silence, once again gazing out over the murky waters. To our steerboard side passed a mound, no more than thirty or forty paces in length, clustered with stubby, leafless trees.

176

Another loomed up ahead, black and featureless against the moonlit waters, but Aubert's face showed no sign of concern as he leant on the tiller, steering us around it. The river was steadily widening—had been ever since we passed Drachs—and was now easily three or four hundred paces in span, and perhaps much more. In the gloom it was hard to tell; where earlier I had been able to see shadows of the woods through the mist, now there were none as the surrounding land gave way to marshes.

I rose from the square oak chest I was sitting on and made my way along the length of the ship, between the two banks of oarsmen and around the mast, to the bow platform where the rest of the knights were still throwing dice.

Eudo looked up as I approached, and moved aside to make a space for me in the circle. 'What's the news?'

'With any luck we'll reach the Humbre by dawn tomorrow,' I replied.

Radulf scratched the side of his large nose. 'What about Alchebarge? When do we make port there?'

'You'll have to ask the shipmaster,' I said as I poured some ale from a leather flask into an empty cup.

The sturdily built one—Godefroi, I remembered—gave Radulf a sharp nudge in the side. 'We'll all be piles of bones sitting here if you don't roll those dice soon.'

'I'm warming them,' Radulf said, rubbing them vigorously in his hands.

'You've been warming them long enough—'

Radulf cast, interrupting him; the little carved

177

antler cubes clattered upon the deck, rolling and spinning before coming to rest on a five and a six. He leant forward to gather in the stakes, and then passed the dice to Philippe, who cupped his hands and threw, revealing a pair of ones.

'Are you joining us again, then?' Wace asked.

'We need someone who can challenge him,' Eudo said grimly, gesturing towards Wace's great heap of pebbles, then back to his own two. Philippe was left with only five, having lost his last throw, while his companions were faring barely better, with eight each.

'I don't wage a war I know I can't win,' I said, grinning, 'but if you're beginning another game—'

A stifled shout came from the lookout. He pointed out past the prow across towards the larboard shore. Frowning, I hurried past Ælfwold and the two ladies.

'What's the matter?' I asked, following the line of his outstretched finger. Through the mist, it was difficult to make much out.

'There,' the lookout said. He was a stout man, with a large gut and a straggling beard. 'Between those two mounds, in the distance, close to the far shore.'

Wace arrived beside me. 'What is it?' he asked.

The two islets the lookout was referring to were shrouded in bands of mist that shone ghost-like in the moonlight. Between them a dark shape, long and thin, slipped silently upstream across the white-flecked waters. I watched it for a few more heartbeats to make sure that I wasn't mistaken, but when the faint tap of a drum started to carry across on the breeze, I knew there was no doubt.

'A ship,' I murmured.

178

Except that there was not just one, for behind it appeared another, and another and another still, clustered together: a dozen of them at least, and perhaps even more.

It was a fleet.

## CHAPTER FOURTEEN

Cursing under my breath, I turned and made for the stern. Already Eudo was on his feet, but Radulf, Philippe and Godefroi hadn't noticed that anything was amiss and were still throwing dice. I kicked over their ale-cups as I passed, spilling their contents across the deck.

'Get up,' I said over their protests. 'All of you to arms.' I stepped down between the oarsmen—many of them looking spent after a day of near-constant exertion—hurrying as best I could along the narrow planking that ran down the ship's centre line. 'Aubert!'

'I see them,' he said.

Some of the men had slowed their stroke; others had stopped altogether to look over their shoulders at the band of ships, water dripping from the ends of their resting oar-blades.

'Row,' I barked at them. 'You're not paid just to sit!'

I reached the stern platform and stepped up beside Aubert, who was tugging hard on the tiller. 'Those are longships like ours,' he said. 'Built for speed. For war.'

'Could they be some of our own?'

He shook his head. 'If any fleet of ours was

179

coming up to these parts, I'd have heard tell of it for certain.'

I swore, knowing what that meant. It was only last night, after all, that an English army had arrived outside the gates of Eoferwic. That we now found an unknown ship-band sailing upriver seemed to me to be more than just chance.

'Will they have seen us?' Wace asked as he joined us.

'As surely as we've seen them,' Aubert replied. He pulled harder on the tiller, leaning back on his heels, using the whole of his weight to bring the prow over to steerboard: away from the ships to our left, out of the midstream and towards the southern shore. The tiller creaked with the strain, and I only hoped it did not break. If that happened, we would have little choice but to fight.

'Take the drum,' the shipmaster said, nodding his head towards where it lay beside his ship-chest, down near my feet.

I picked it up. It was a large instrument, heavier than it looked, and I held it in the crook of my arm, as I had seen the shipmaster himself do.

'What do we do?' I asked. 'Can we turn the ship around?'

'By the time we've done that, they'll be upon us for sure,' Aubert said.

'So we outrun them, then?'

'We can try.' He glanced towards me. His face had gone pale, and I saw the uncertainty in his eyes.

'See to the ladies,' I said to Wace. 'Get them hidden; make sure they're safe.' I couldn't have them exposed to arrows and spears and whatever else might come our way.

Wace nodded and hurried back towards the bow platform, where Elise and Beatrice stood, eyes wide in panic. But I would have to leave them to him, for just then a horn sounded from across the water, and I noticed two of the ships on the side nearest us turning, breaking away from the pack. Their oar-blades moved in unison, and their dragon-prows rose high as they skimmed over the black waters. They were not headed directly for us, but instead were moving to cut us off at the head of the next bend. Our only choice, then, was to make it there before they did, for otherwise we would be trapped with no hope of escape.

'Come on, you whoresons,' I shouted to our men as I began to beat out a steady rhythm on the drum. 'Pull!'

Beneath my feet I felt the ship surge forward, rocking from side to side as it did so. Not all the rowers were pulling in time with my beat, and the waves made by their blades were crossing over each other, interfering with the next man's stroke.

'With me,' I roared, feeling myself begin to sweat. 'Listen!' I struck the drumskin more loudly, slightly slower at first, just to get them all pulling together, but I did not want to lose too much speed, and as soon as I thought they were all in time I began to beat faster again.

I glanced at Aubert, but his gaze was fixed on the river ahead and I could see he was concentrating on our course. The river was gently curving to the right and he was trying to take us as close as he dared to the inside of that curve, to take the shortest line possible without running aground on the mudbanks which were now visible above the surface.

But the enemy were gaining speed now as they raced us towards the headland. Their vessels were smaller than ours, with roughly twenty oars to a side, but they were clearly lighter too, for they sat high above the waterline. A few hundred paces of open water still lay between us and safety.

'Row, if you want to live!' I said. 'The English will not spare you; they will not show mercy. They are wildmen, animals, the Devil's own children. They live only to kill Frenchmen like us!'

It seemed to work, for all of a sudden I sensed a fresh determination among the oarsmen, an extra burst of pace, and I responded in kind, speeding up my beat to take advantage of their renewed vigour.

'Yes,' I went on, starting to fall into a rhythm of my own, 'they will kill you, but they will kill you slowly. They will cut out your tongue so you cannot scream; they will gouge out your eyes and sever your balls; and when they have finished, they will take their pleasure from your corpses.'

The mudbanks were now less than the *Wyvern*'s own length away from our steerboard side, and I hoped Aubert was aware of what he was doing, for if he didn't judge it correctly then we could quickly find ourselves stranded and open to attack.

At the bow, Wace was lifting up planks, helping the ladies as they climbed down into the hold space below the deck. Eudo and the other knights were already donning hauberks and coifs, fastening scabbards to their belts. If it came to a fight, however, I knew we must surely lose; six knights could not hold them off for long. Of course there were a good number of Aubert's crewmen, all of whom could probably handle a spear or a knife, but they were not trained warriors.

182

'Pull!' I shouted. 'Pull, pull, pull!'

We were nearing the head of the bend now, and I could see that it was going to be far tighter than I imagined. For as quick as we were, the enemy were quicker still, and the gap we were aiming for was steadily narrowing with every stroke, with every heartbeat. Their drumbeats rang out louder than before, and even voices could be heard, jeering at us in what sounded like the English tongue, whooping with the delight of the chase. Weapons crashed against shields, raising the battle-thunder.

'Come on, you bastards, harder!'

There was a sharp whistle of air to my left, and I looked up in time to see a flash of silver as an arrow hurtled our way, arcing down until it disappeared into the water not twenty paces off our larboard side. A second followed, landing amidst the waves left by our passage, then three all at once: black lines against the moonlit clouds, soaring over the river before bearing down upon us. Two fell short, but the third flew higher and I tensed, thinking for a moment that it was going to hit us, but a gust caught it and it flew over the heads of the oarsmen before dropping beyond the steerboard side, less than an oar's length from the hull.

The distance was closing fast now; in the half-light I could even make out the faces of those aboard the other two ships. One had taken the lead, and its prow rose tall as it speared through the water towards us. Upon its deck a score and more of warriors, all dressed in mail and helmets, raised their blades to the sky in anticipation of the slaughter that was sure to come. A second volley of arrows shot towards us, and I had to duck as one

183

shot just over my head, while another stuck fast in the gunwale not far from where I was standing. We had almost made it to the headland, almost made it past them. But still they did not give up, and as they came closer, I saw that they were no longer trying to block our escape. They were trying to ram us.

'Faster,' I yelled above the noise. The painted dragon-head of the leading ship bore down upon our flank and I braced myself for the impact. 'Faster!'

A shudder ran through the ship as the deck tilted and the steerboard side jolted up. I stumbled sideways; the drum slipped from my fingers and thudded hollowly on to the deck. I was regaining my balance when the hull crashed down again, kicking up a white spray, and I fell back the other way. For a moment I thought the ship had been struck, and panic surged through me, but then I realised that we were still moving, and that the enemy were behind us.

I couldn't help but let out a laugh as I saw the two English ships in our wake, desperately trying to turn about, to pursue us. They must have just missed us, for I could see no damage to the ship, but when I looked to steerboard I saw the mudbanks perilously close to the hull. That was what we must have struck, and in doing so we had come within a fraction of grounding.

'Take us out,' I shouted to Aubert.

The shipmaster shook his head and his lips moved, but above the rush of oars and the thumping of my heart, I couldn't make out what it was he said.

'Out, into the midstream!' I said, but then I saw

what he had in mind. Less than a mile ahead, the river curved in a great arc around to the right, and at the tip of that curve was an island, a great mound of trees and rocks, much larger than any of the islets we had seen so far, with two passages around it. The first and safest of these was to follow the main stream of the river, a long, wide route around the head of the bend. The other, shorter course, took the form of a narrow channel on the inside shore, between the island and the mudbanks—and it was towards this second passage that Aubert was steering us.

If they wanted to stay close on our tail, the enemy would have to follow us through that channel, for to go around would allow us to put open water between ourselves and them. In doing so, however, they too would run the same risk of beaching there on the flats. It was a plan that relied greatly on Aubert's judgement and ability, but I did not see that we had many other choices. Already the two enemy ships had brought their prows around, carving through the dark waters, and were in pursuit. We still had a lead of several lengths on them, but they were much the faster, and I knew that lead could soon disappear. Already it seemed they were closing in again. We were far from being safe yet.

'Row,' I shouted, recovering the drum and starting to beat once more. I stepped along the middle gangplank between the men. 'Row!'

Thrown from their rhythm by the impact, some of the oarsmen were struggling to keep their strokes in time, but I could not afford to slow the pace again. Oars creaked in their rowlocks; blades crashed awkwardly into the water, not cutting its

185

surface cleanly as they had before, casting up spray, turning the water white with foam with every heave.

'Harder!' I said, but when I looked at them I saw only tired arms, tired faces, and thought they might collapse if I tried to press the pace further.

Up ahead rose the island, which I saw now was no great mound but in truth little more than a low rise, bolstered on its upstream side by wide banks of silt. Indeed, had *Wyvern*'s mast been raised, the island would have been barely taller, but set against the flatness of the surrounding land, it stood out like a wart upon the skin of the earth. To the right of it lay the channel for which we were aiming, which at closer sight seemed even narrower than at first it had appeared, wide enough only for two vessels like ours to run abreast, with barely enough space for oars as well. I shivered at the sight.

In the bow of the ship, the rest of the knights were still putting on their mail, Wace and Philippe adjusting their coifs over their heads, Radulf and Godefroi tying their helmets' leather straps under their chins. Only Eudo was fully ready, looping the strap of his shield around his neck.

I called him over. 'Take the drum,' I said, releasing it from my arm and pushing it towards his mailed chest. He slung his shield across his back and took it without a word, his expression grim. I thought of all the times we had charged upon enemy shield-walls bristling with spears, staring fate in the face, never knowing whether that battle would be our last. But at least then we'd known we could trust in the strength of our own sword-arms to see us through.

'We have a priest with us,' I said. 'God won't let us come to harm.'

He did not look certain, nor did I feel it, but I could think of nothing else to say. I left him and crossed towards the bow platform, where Wace was fastening his helmet-strap.

'Are the ladies safe?' I asked.

'They're safe,' Wace said. I nodded, feeling that I should check on them but knowing there was no time; I had his word and that would have to be enough.

From behind came another muted rush of air as more arrows were given flight, though they dropped short of the stern by half a length. I had spotted only half a dozen archers on each ship, but that was scant relief, for it would only take a few of their shafts to strike home to start causing panic amidst our rowers.

I turned my attention to Malet's men, who were beginning to pull chausses up over their legs.

'Leave them,' I said. 'A hauberk you can remove quickly if you fall in. Chausses will only weigh you down.' I spoke from experience: I had seen men drown in circumstances none too different, held under the surface by the very weight of their mail, floundering, struggling for breath with no one to help them.

I shrugged off my cloak and fastened my sword-belt to my waist, then found my gambeson and pulled it on over my head, followed by the hauberk and finally the helmet. I fed the hilt of my sword through the slit in the hauberk, just as a cry of agony went up from one of the rowers on the larboard side. His oar-handle slipped from his grasp, through the rowlock and out into the water.

187

I rushed to the young man's side as a great cheer erupted from the boats of our pursuers. A feathered shaft had pierced his gut, and blood was spilling out on to the deck.

'It hurts,' he whimpered, eyes shut tight. 'It hurts!'

'Ælfwold,' I called, and then because some of the oarsmen around him were drawing their attention away from their stroke, 'Row, you bastards!'

'Pull,' Eudo said. 'Pull!'

I put my arms around the man's chest and hauled him over so that he lay on his back rather than his side; he had been struck on his right and I could not easily get to the wound otherwise. He let out another cry and his hands clutched at the arrow. I saw that it had pierced deep, the whole head buried into the flesh and some of the shaft too. I pushed the man's hands away and snapped off the flighted end to leave only the point in the wound, then took hold of a corner of the man's cloak. It was wrapped awkwardly around his body, but I was able to free enough that I could gather it and press it in a wad against the wound. Even as I did so, though, I knew it was in vain: the wound was too severe, the blood flowing too quickly to be staunched.

The oarsman gasped and his head wrenched forward. I heard footsteps along the deck and Ælfwold knelt down next to me.

'How badly was he struck?' he asked.

I shook my head. 'See to him,' I said, standing back up on the centre plank and letting the chaplain get closer. I waved to the rest of the knights to follow me towards the stern; if we ran aground that was where I wanted them, facing the first line of the English assault. 'A shield,' I called to them as I stepped up on to the platform. 'Bring me a shield!'

We were almost at the island, at the point where the river forked, still clinging to the steerboard shore as Aubert tugged hard on the tiller, taking us into the channel. The closest of the English ships was no more than three lengths up in front of us now; both were filled with men, roaring, battering the hafts of their spears against their round shields. The few archers they possessed were lined behind them, letting fly as quickly as they could draw the shafts from their arrow-bags, without regard for aim.

'How is he?' Aubert asked, his gaze not turning from the channel ahead.

I looked back towards the chaplain, who was kneeling there still, his head bowed and his palms together. The oarsman was no longer moving, his eyes closed, his expression fixed in anguish.

'He's dead,' I replied.

The shipmaster said nothing, gritting his teeth as he wrestled with the steerboard. His face was red, his cheeks wet with perspiration.

On either side of us the marshes were closing in, and it seemed like the water itself was receding. From the island came a clatter of wings as a flock of crows took flight, cawing as they went, spiralling up into the sky before swooping low over our heads. Ahead, the channel glistened: a thin course of white showing us the way between the darkness of the two shores.

Wace headed the knights as they stepped up on to the platform, unslinging one of the two shields from around his neck and passing it to me. I looped the strap over my right shoulder and put my arm through the leather brases, gripping the cross in my hand, just in time as Wace yelled out: 'Shields!'

A cluster of silver points flew out of the western sky. I brought my shield up to cover my face, moments before a shaft thudded into it, sending a shock down my arm and into my shoulder, but I held it firm. Behind me on the platform there was a crash of mail upon timber; Philippe lay face upwards on the deck, shield lying across his chest, and at first I thought the enemy had claimed another kill, but he was breathing and moving with no sign of injury, running a hand along the side of his helmet where there was now a dent in the plate.

'Up!' I said, for already more arrows were flashing towards us. These ones flew wide, falling harmlessly amongst the reeds, albeit no more than a couple of oar-lengths away from *Wyvern*'s side. Blinking and clearly more than a little dazed, Philippe got to his feet, stumbling a little as the prow swerved violently to larboard and we came desperately close to the shallows that marked the island's shore. A dark shoal passed by, long and low, barely visible above the surface.

'Come on, you bastards,' Eudo said. 'Harder! Harder!'

The ship shuddered again and I staggered forwards. A great grinding noise sounded up through the deck as the hull scraped along the riverbed. I thought we had run aground, and I waited for the moment when the bows would drive up on to the flats and we would become stranded, but the moment never came; instead the grinding ceased and suddenly we were free. Relief washed over me, if only briefly, since the enemy still followed, their war-cries growing ever louder to match the beating on their shields. I wiped the sweat off my brow and adjusted my helmet so that the nasal-piece sat more comfortably. It would not be long before they caught us and the slaughter began.

'Larboard, lift oars—' Eudo shouted, before he was interrupted by a series of loud cracks near the front of the ship. I looked over my shoulder, saw the first half-dozen or more oars sheared through, blades missing from their ends. We had struck something, though what it was I could not see. Another roar went up from the men massed in the enemy's bows, and they raised axes and swords to the sky. Their leading ship surged forward, less than a length behind us, so close now that I could see the emblems on their shields. A spear sailed through the air, hurled by a tall Englishman; next to me Radulf caught it on his shield and deflected it aside, into the water.

I drew my sword. 'Shield-wall,' I said to the knights. 'Keep close and don't let anything through.' I overlapped my shield with that of Philippe to my right; on my left, Godefroi did the same. I would soon see how well they could fight.

'Larboard oars, pull!' Eudo said.

A rock passed by the stern, the length of three men and the width of one, surrounded by a floating mass of broken beams, and straightaway I knew that this was what we had hit. But so close were the enemy following that as we left it in our wake, I realised that the steersman of the ship behind could not have seen it.

A cry went up from the men in their bows, but it

was too late, and they struck it full on, the prow heaving up, the rock slicing into the boat's underside, tearing timbers into savage splinters. Men fell backwards, or were pitched over the side, plunging into the water, thrashing about to keep their heads above the surface, struggling to free themselves from their mail hauberks, which were dragging them down. Their ship ground to a halt, pitched over to one side with its larboard gunwale high, a rent along the length of its hull. Some of the oarsmen leapt overboard, trying to push it free from the rock, while those nearer the stern began to back-paddle. Behind it, the second ship drew up, the channel too narrow to allow it past. Angry shouts filled the air.

'Break,' I told the others in the shield-wall. Arrows continued to spit down from the sky, but I sensed they were loosed out of frustration rather than with any aim in mind, and they sailed high, far to larboard as the *Wyvern* steered right, following the channel. Stroke by stroke we pulled away, opening the range as they laboured to free their stricken vessel.

'Row,' Eudo shouted from amidships. 'No flagging, no slacking! Pull! Pull!'

The enemy receded into the distance, their ships continuing to dwindle until at last they disappeared into the night. Gradually the pace slowed and I began to breathe more easily as their shouts faded away to nothing, until all I could hear was the gentle creak of our own oars in their rowlocks, the splash of the blades as they entered the water, the slow beat of Eudo's hand upon the drum. The men looked spent, hardly able to lift the blades any longer, their backs hunched over, their arms almost limp with exhaustion.

Wace made his way to the bows, where he lifted the deck-planks and gave his hand first to Elise, then to Beatrice, as he helped them climb out from the hold. I noticed the flighted end of an arrow jutting out from one of the timbers; it was as well they had been hidden, or that same arrow could have struck one of them.

I stepped over to the shipmaster and slapped a hand on his shoulder. 'We owe you our thanks,' I said, offering my hand.

Aubert took it wearily, his palms chafed and raw. 'I don't need thanks,' he said between breaths. 'Let's just hope we don't meet any more of the enemy tonight.'

I nodded. In front of us the channel was widening once more; the open river was almost upon us. If our luck held then by morning we would be in Alchebarge.


## CHAPTER FIFTEEN

Darkness settled around us as *Wyvern*'s prow carved its way from the shore out towards the midstream. Aubert left the tiller and strode along the length of the ship, giving the order to ship oars. Eudo ceased beating the drum and the long poles were slowly hauled aboard, dripping water on to the deck. All else was still. What breeze there had been had now died completely, and the clouds hung low, bathed in the glow of the moon and the stars. For the first time in what seemed like hours, silence filled the air as we drifted on the current.

I untied the strap under my chin and removed my helmet, setting it down on the deck by my feet. I glanced towards my fellow knights and saw the relief in their eyes. At the same time, though, I could sense a frustration in them, a frustration that had I been the same age I would surely have felt too. For there were few things worse for a young warrior hungry for battle than to be denied the chance to test one's sword-arm, to prove oneself. Death was not something one even considered, though that seemed to me due less to the arrogance of youth than to an innocence of the true nature of battle. Many were the times I had seen such men charge happily to their deaths. More than once I had come close to doing the same. The fact that I had held myself back was— above all else, above skill at arms or bravery or strength—the reason why after all these years I was still alive, when so many others I had known were not.

I gazed past the stern into the night, searching upstream for any sign of the enemy, but there was none. Indeed I could barely make out the line of the shore, lost as it was in the mist. But in truth I didn't expect them to continue the pursuit; the last light of day was gone and they could not hope to find us by night. We were out of danger, for the present at least.

Wace returned, having already divested himself of his mail, though he was still wearing his scabbard. He stood beside me, arms folded as he leant on the gunwale, soon joined by Eudo.

'Malet will need God on his side if he's to defend Eoferwic,' Wace said.

'He was on our side tonight,' I pointed out.

Eudo grinned at me. 'Because we have Ælfwold with us.'

It was a weak attempt at a jest and I did not smile. I was thinking of the twelve English ships I had counted, and my heart sank as I realised that each one might carry as many as fifty Englishmen, and even if only half of those were fighting men, it meant that Eadgar would have another three hundred spears under his banner. Together with those already besieging Eoferwic it made for a considerable host, several times larger than that which Malet had left to him. Wace was right: the vicomte would need God's help.

'He'll hold out in the castle even if the city falls,' I said.

'But for how long?' Wace asked.

'For as long as he needs to.' Otherwise the whole of Northumbria, from Dunholm to Eoferwic, would lie in the hands of the English rebels.

Wace gave me a wry look but said nothing.

'No doubt we'll hear soon enough,' I said. It did not warrant dwelling upon. Our task was to see Malet's womenfolk safely to Lundene; all we could do was carry that out.

I turned away from the river, towards the oarsmen, exhausted after the chase. Some sat bent forwards, hands on their heads, heads bowed low between their legs. Others lay collapsed across their ship-chests, on their backs or on their sides, breathing deeply of the night air. One of the younger men leant over the side, spewing forth a long stream of vomit, some of which dribbled down into his beard and on to his tunic.

A dozen or so had crowded beside the man who had been killed, those behind peering over the

195

shoulders of those in front. The shipmaster himself was there, and he murmured a few words before standing and making his way back towards the bow. It took two of the men to lift the youth's body: one taking the legs, the other the shoulders. Together they followed the shipmaster, who lifted away some of the deck-planks, revealing the hold space where Elise and Beatrice had hidden. He motioned the two men forward and gently they lowered the body into the gap. They stood there a while, not speaking, just looking down upon him, until the shipmaster lay a sheet of spare black sailcloth over him and replaced the boards.

'We'll pay our dues to him properly when we reach Alchebarge,' he said.

The others nodded and returned to the rest of their companions. Too tired even for tears, I thought, or simply numbed by the tide of emotions. Exhilarated by the victory, at having themselves evaded death, yet at the same time grief-stricken for their fallen friend. I knew such feelings well.

Aubert returned to the tiller and sat down. I went and placed a hand on his shoulder in sympathy.

'He had only been with me since last summer,' the shipmaster said, and swallowed. 'Strong lad, he was. Always eager.'

I wanted to say something, but in truth there was nothing more to add. Privately I couldn't help but think that we had been lucky to lose only one man; it could so easily have been worse.

Aubert rose, shrugging off my hand. I looked up as Lady Elise hustled her way along the length of the ship, her daughter and the chaplain close behind. The ladies' skirts were raised above their ankles, prompting stares from more than one of the rowers as they picked their way between them. The embarrassment on Beatrice's face was clear but she held her head high and tried to ignore them, almost tripping over one of the cross-beams in so doing. Elise paid them no attention; her face was a shade somewhere between distress and anger.

'My lady,' I said. 'You look troubled.'

'We must send word to my husband.' Her dress was damp; a few strands of grey hair had come loose from beneath her wimple to fall across her face. 'An English fleet sails towards Eoferwic. We must warn him.'

'There is nothing we can do,' I said. 'The river is closed to us, and no message that we might send overland will reach Eoferwic before them.'

She turned to the shipmaster. 'And what do you say?'

'He's right,' Aubert replied. 'The enemy will be rowing against the current, but if they travel through the night they'll be there by dawn. Given horses and open country, we might get word through in time, but not on foot and across these marshes.'

'We must do something,' she protested.

'There is nothing we can do,' I repeated, my ire rising. Why could this woman not understand this? 'I swore an oath to your husband—an oath that I would protect you and your daughter. That is what I intend to do.'

I looked for support from Aubert, who nodded in agreement. 'We have no choice. The best we can do is to get to Alchebarge as soon as possible.'

'And leave my husband in mortal danger?' the lady Elise said, on the verge of tears. She clasped

197

her daughter's hand tightly. 'How are we to live with such uncertainty?'

I felt myself tensing, my patience nearly ground down. We had only narrowly escaped danger ourselves; I was tired and not much given to being harassed with questions that didn't have answers.

'These are uncertain times,' I said sharply. 'Not just for you, but for all of us.'

Ælfwold, standing behind the two ladies, fixed me with a stern look. Elise remained where she was, looking at me, tears forming in the corners of her eyes, lips pursed and shaking her head. But I had said only what needed to be said.

'My lady,' the chaplain said, at last turning his eyes from me, 'Lord Guillaume is a thoroughly capable man. I am sure that with or without our help, he will succeed.' He took a deep breath. 'Now, it is growing late and the road to Lundene will be long. We should try to sleep.'

'A wise idea,' I said, unmoved. It had indeed been a long day. Had anyone tried to tell me then that it was only the night before that the rebel army had arrived outside Eoferwic's gates, only the night before that we had gone to meet the ætheling, I would not have believed them. 'We have a good few days' travel ahead of us. Best to rest now while you have the chance.'

Still Elise looked at me, her lip trembling, and she did not move until Ælfwold said softly, 'My ladies,' and she spun away, hoisting her skirts once again. Beatrice waited a moment longer, her plaintive eyes unblinking, holding my gaze, then she too turned to follow her mother towards the bow.

'That was harsh,' the chaplain said when they

were out of earshot.

'What would you have me say?' I asked. That all would be well, perhaps, that Malet would come through unharmed? But I could not know that and they would not have believed me even had I told them so.

'They aren't used to this,' Aubert put in. 'Some comfort is what they need.'

'Even if that comfort is false?' I didn't mean to hurt them, but neither could I bring myself to say anything that was less than honest.

'At the very least I would expect you to extend them your courtesy,' Ælfwold said. 'To show some politeness.'

I looked away, out across the river, shaking my head.

'Tancred,' the priest said, and there was a note of warning in his voice. 'Remember what Lord Guillaume has done for you, and consider what he would like you to do in return for his womenfolk. You don't have to enjoy their company, only offer them the respect they deserve and not antagonise them.'

'I'll try, father,' I said, though more to please him than because I truly meant it.

'That's all I ask,' said Ælfwold. 'Now, I intend to get some rest. I bid you a good night.' He went to join the two ladies again, helping them as they spread blankets upon the deck and settled down.

Aubert still watched me, a disapproving look in his eyes, but I'd heard enough words of reproach already, and I wasn't about to listen to any more.

'What?' I said.

He did not reply, but instead picked up a sack lying close to the tiller, reaching into it and tossing

199

small loaves down to each of the rowers as he walked the length of the ship. 'Eat,' he said to them. 'Eat and gather your strength, for soon we row on.'

A concerted groan went up from the men.

'That's right,' he said, raising his voice above their shouts. 'The enemy might be behind us but there's still some way to Alchebarge.'

'Aubert,' said one, older, more grizzled than the rest. 'Most of us have been rowing ever since we left Eoferwic. We can't go much further tonight.'

The shipmaster turned, stony-faced, towards him, then he cast his gaze up and down the length of the ship, surveying the rest of the men. 'The more progress we make tonight, the less we have to do tomorrow morning,' he said. 'And if there are any more English ships downriver, it's better that we pass them under the cover of darkness while their crews might be sleeping, than when it's light and they're fresh.'

He began to pace once more. 'I've seen you work harder than this before. All I ask for is thirty men rowing at a time, for a few hours at most before changing over. That way we keep going through the night.' He delved into the sack for more loaves as he neared the end of the line. 'For now, though, we eat.'

Nonetheless, it was not much longer before the oars were lowered back into the water and Aubert began to sound the time, a slower pace than before but constant nevertheless. The beat was quickly taken up by the oarsmen, whose ranks I had joined, together with Eudo, Philippe and Radulf; Wace and Godefroi had taken the opportunity to rest, along with the other half of *Wyvern*'s crew. It

200

was many years since I had rowed, and I was surprised by the strength needed to pull the blade through the water, and to lift it clear again for the next stroke, such was the weight of the oar-handle. But though at first my arms and back protested, the feeling soon subsided as I became lost to the rhythm. All thoughts of Malet and Eoferwic fled my mind; for the moment at least nothing else mattered, nothing else existed but myself, the oar in my hands and the constant, driving *beat, beat, beat.*

\* \* \*

I woke the next day just as the sun was coming up, a glimmer on the distant horizon that turned the waters into a sea of shimmering gold. The oars had all been stowed inboard and most of the men lay curled up in their blankets beside their ship-chests. But the wind was rising, gusting at us from astern, and Aubert was amidships giving orders as the mast was raised and the sail unfurled, its alternating stripes of black and yellow billowing out, pushing us on downriver.

The river had broadened, so much so that I could hardly pick out the shores to either side. Blinking, rubbing my eyes to clear the last traces of sleep, I breathed in a deep draught of frigid air. A lone gull swooped low in front of the ship, soon joined by another which flew up from the river, and the two rose to the blue sky, dancing in flight, twisting around and about each other, crying as they did so.

It was a clear dawn, but a cold one. I blew warm air into my hands as I shook off the woollen blankets that covered me. Around me the other knights were all still sleeping; of our party Ælfwold was the only other up and he was at prayer. Aubert soon returned to take the tiller and I spoke to him for a while, though he was bone-tired. He had not slept all night; his eyes looked dark and heavy and he kept yawning. I offered to take his place for a few hours while he rested, and he readily accepted. With open water around us and a following wind, managing the tiller ought not to be difficult, he said. As long as I kept her facing into the sun I could not go wrong.

And so I sat on his ship-chest, gazing out across the wide river, towards the many small islands which drifted past, and beyond, to the south and a shoreline dotted with trees, with low hills in the distance: the part of England known as Mercia.

A sudden shadow was cast over me and I looked up to see Beatrice leaning upon the side of the ship, the profile of her face sharply outlined in the low sun. Her eyes were closed and she wore a slight smile, as if she were enjoying the play of the breeze across her cheeks.

'My lady,' I said, a little surprised to see her there. I had expected one of the other knights, or perhaps Ælfwold. 'Did you sleep well?'

'Well enough,' she replied. The smile faded from her face but she did not open her eyes.

I wondered if she was angry about what I had said the night before, and almost opened my mouth to apologise. Our flight from Eoferwic, the encounter with the English fleet, the pursuit: it had all left me on edge, and I had not been thinking clearly. But I stopped myself long before the words formed on my tongue. I had meant what I said, and there was no point in denying it.

'Tell me,' she said abruptly, 'have you ever been married?'

I stared at her, taken aback by the question. She turned and met my look, but I could not read anything from her expression; her brown eyes gave no clue. The breeze tugged at her cloak but she did not try to pull it closer, cold though she must have been. Her demeanour, the way she carried herself, suggested a maturity which her youthful appearance belied, and I wondered if she were a little older than I had first thought.

'Only to my sword,' I answered, when I'd recovered my wits.

She gazed back out upon the river, nodding as if she were coming to some new understanding, but she did not speak. The silver bands she wore around her wrists shone brightly in the morning sun.

'Why do you ask?'

'Only because if you had,' she said, 'you would know what it means to have to leave a loved one behind.'

An image of Oswynn came to mind: an image of her as I had last seen her, that night at Dunholm, with her dark hair falling across her smiling face. And I recalled the moment Mauger had stood before me in the street and told me she was dead, and I felt something of the same fire that had consumed me then returning.

'I know what it means,' I said, rising from the ship-chest to face Beatrice, my cheeks burning.

She stared back at me, impassive, though I stood a whole head taller than she. 'You do not show it.'

'There's a lot I don't show,' I said, though what I truly meant by that, I didn't know. All I wanted were words that I could throw back at her.

She smiled again, though it was less a friendly smile than one of derision—almost as if she understood all this and was enjoying my discomfort.

'And what about you?' I asked, turning the attention away from me for one moment. 'Have you married?' I didn't see how she could not, if she were as old as I thought—but on the other hand I had not seen her with any man back in Eoferwic, nor did she wear a marriage-ring on her hand.

A strand of golden hair had fallen loose from under her wimple and she tucked it back behind her ear. 'Once,' she said quietly. 'It was before the invasion, four years ago. We were wed in the summer; he died before Christmas. I didn't know him long, but the end, when it came, was nonetheless hard to bear.'

Oswynn had not been with me long when she died, either: a matter of months at most.

'I'm sorry,' I said.

She nodded and for a while did not speak, as if she were considering whether or not to accept my apology.

'Just remember that you are not the centre of the world, Tancred a Dinant,' she said at last, and there was a hard edge to her voice now. 'Perhaps next time you'll think more carefully before you open your mouth.'

Before I could say anything more, she turned on her heels and went. I watched her go, surprised by her sudden change in manner. I still couldn't see what she, what Aubert and Ælfwold, wanted from me. I had no time to wonder then, though, for the wind was changing direction and one of the men

204

shouted to me to bring the ship around more to steerboard. I pulled on the tiller, leaning back on my heels as I put the weight of my body into it, until the prow pointed into the sun, the full circle of which had risen above the horizon. Above us the gulls circled still, swooping, screeching.

A few others were waking now, sharing bread with each other, pouring out cups of ale to break their fast. Before long Lady Elise also rose and she and Beatrice joined Ælfwold in prayer. Beside me on the stern platform, Wace and Eudo and the rest of the knights were still asleep, as was the shipmaster himself, gently snoring.

The sun climbed higher and the day grew brighter. Aubert woke after an hour or two more and took back the tiller, though he still looked exhausted. The oarsmen took their places on their ship-chests, soon settling back into their rhythm as the shipmaster beat a languid pulse on the drum, and *Wyvern* soared across the calm waters.

It was mid-morning by the time Alchebarge was spotted ahead of us: first as a few wisps of grey smoke rising above the horizon, then as a long ridge dotted with trees, rising over wide flats. From our steerboard side, across bare fields and past dense thickets, a second river wound its way to meet the Use, the two joining to form a single broad expanse of blue.

'The Trente,' the shipmaster said to me. 'Where the two streams meet, the Humbre begins.'

I nodded, but I was paying him little attention. Instead I was watching the ridge in the distance and the smoke blowing towards the east, and growing puzzled, for it wasn't the kind that I would have expected to see from houses during the day,

205

and especially not on such a cold day as this. For there were no thick clouds billowing up, as there should have been if their hearths had been freshly stoked, but rather a collection of thin, feeble threads weaving slowly about one another, as when a fire has nearly burnt itself out.

We drew nearer, leaving the Use behind us. I began to make out more clearly the houses there, dotted against the bright sky. Or rather I saw what remained of them: their blackened timbers and collapsed roof-beams, smouldering still. The stone tower and nave of the church were all that was left standing; all else along the ridge lay in ruins.

Aubert's hand stopped beating upon the drumskin, and the splash of oars against the water ceased. Silence fell like a shadow across the ship. I saw the chaplain cross himself and murmur a prayer in Latin, and I did the same as I stared up at the twisted wreckage of what once had been Alchebarge, but was no more.

The enemy had been here before us.


## CHAPTER SIXTEEN

We approached slowly, drifting on the current with only the occasional pull on the tiller from Aubert to keep us on the correct course. The shipmaster had ordered the sail furled and the mast lowered. We didn't know whether there were any more of the enemy still watching us from the ridge, with their ships perhaps hidden amidst the reeds and mudbanks that lay beneath, in which case it was better they did not see the black and gold, since then they would know straightaway that we were not of their own fleet.

But if the enemy were there, they did not show themselves. I kept watching for any flicker of movement or a glint that might be steel, and I saw nothing.

The ridge on which Alchebarge stood loomed steeply before us. From its top it must have been possible to see for miles around, and it seemed to me that it would make for a strategic place—if one could hold it—for it commanded the two rivers, the Use and the Trente, at the place where they joined. And it ought to be easily defensible from the water, too, owing both to its steep slopes, and to the mudflats that lay at its foot: a wide expanse of reeds and long shoals, which glistened under the light of the sun.

The tide seemed to be on its way out, for though the part of the flats nearest us was still submerged, on their landward side I could see myriad pools and channels where the river was retreating. If we were to reach Alchebarge at all we would have to make our way—whether by ship or on foot— through that maze.

'Can we make it across before we lose the tide?' I asked the shipmaster.

'It'll be difficult,' he said. 'The channels through the marsh aren't deep and it's easy to get stuck upon these banks. But if we don't try now, we'll have to wait until the waters return.'

I looked again towards the ridge and the black remains of the halls. 'Get us as close as you can.'

Aubert shouted to the oarsmen and tugged hard on the tiller; *Wyvern* carved her way between two banks of reeds, which rippled in waves as the

207

westerly breeze played across them. Ahead, a pair of moorhens flapped their wings, shrieking loudly as they skimmed across the surface of the murky water. They took off away from us, flying around in a great loop until we had passed, before settling once more. Amidst the reeds on the banks to either side more birds stretched their wings as if preparing to flee, but they did not; instead they watched us carefully with dark beads of eyes as we scythed our way around the larger islands.

One of the oarsmen stood at the prow, lowering a long pole into the murky water, testing its depth. The tide was flowing fast and the channels were growing narrower the further we went. Eventually the man gave a shout and raised his arm.

'Slow,' the shipmaster called to the rest of his crew. He looked to me. 'I can't take us much further in,' he said. 'You'll have to go the rest of the way on foot.'

I waved my thanks to the shipmaster, and then called to the rest of the knights. We put on our hauberks and helms, slinging our shields over our backs. Again we left behind our chausses; they would only slow us down over the marshes. Besides, they were more useful when mounted, when blows would naturally come from below. On foot, however, opponents tended to aim their strikes more towards one's chest and head. In such situations speed was all-important; the extra weight of mail would be a burden if we needed to fight.

'I should come with you,' Ælfwold called. 'If there are any dead in the village it's only right that they be accorded a proper burial.'

'No,' I said. 'Stay with the ladies. The enemy

could still be about. If so, it's better that you stay away from danger.' I still had to make sure he reached Wiltune to deliver Malet's message; I could not have him at risk. Besides, it was not the dead that I was concerned with, but rather the living: if there were any Normans still left alive in Alchebarge, it was important that we found them.

'You're leaving us?' Elise asked. She strode towards me, her cloak swirling behind her.

'We'll be back before long,' I said. 'We have to know if there is anyone left on your husband's manor. It'll be safer for both you and your daughter if you stay here on the ship.'

'And what if the enemy find us while you are gone?'

'If they were to come upon us in numbers,' I said, and I spoke honestly, 'it would make little difference whether or not the six of us were here to help protect you.'

She didn't look comforted by that, nor had I expected her to, but she said nothing more. And in truth I could not help but feel a little uneasy, even though we had seen no sign of the enemy since the previous night.

'My men will be here with you,' Aubert assured her.

'Can they fight?' she asked.

'Well enough, my lady. What they lack in skill they make up for in strength. There are more than fifty of them on the *Wyvern*; that ought to be sufficient.'

'And what of yourself?'

'I'll be going with Tancred.' He saw my glance but he cut me off even before I could open my mouth. 'If you're to take anyone it should be me.

209

You'll need someone who knows the village well.'

'We also need the ship prepared,' I pointed out. 'We might need to leave suddenly.'

'That's easily done without me.' He turned to one of his men, older than the rest, and I noticed that it was the same grizzled face who had challenged Aubert the night before. 'Oylard,' he said. 'I leave you in charge of *Wyvern* until we return.'

'Yes, Aubert,' he replied, with a slight bow of his head.

'Keep her out of sight from the river if you can, hidden amongst the reeds, but at the same time ready to sail in case you see us running down that hill with the enemy behind us.'

'I'll make sure of it,' Oylard said.

Of course, if more rebel ships were to come, there would be little chance of us making a quick escape, but I kept that thought to myself.

'Are you ready, then?' I asked the shipmaster. 'I don't want to spend any longer here than we have to.'

'Let me fetch my sword,' he said. 'Then I'll be ready.'

I waited while he did so, and while he donned a leather jerkin, then I jumped down from the ship's prow. Straightaway my shoes sank into the mud, and already I was beginning to wonder whether this was so wise after all. But I found firmer footing along the top of the bank, and I waved to Aubert and the other knights to follow. Once the seven of us had climbed down the shipmaster waved to Oylard, who shouted to the oarsmen to push *Wyvern* off.

'Don't take her too far,' Aubert warned him. 'We

have to be able to find our way back to you.'

Oylard waved back in acknowledgement and then we set off, trudging on through the reeds and over the mudbanks, splashing through the pools that remained where the tide had gone out. Water seeped into my shoes and with every step I felt a fresh bite of cold at my toes. Wading birds flocked down upon the flats, digging in the bare mud for worms and whatever else they might find. They scattered as we approached, lifting up into the sky as if with one mind, and I shivered at the sight, for if we had not been spotted before, we almost certainly would have been now. The hairs on my neck stood on end; I had the feeling that we were being watched. I kept glancing up at the buildings upon the ridge, and once or twice I thought I saw a shadow moving in between them, but I could not be sure. I did not want to mention it, in case the others took it wrongly for a sign that I was growing nervous.

The footing became easier the further we went on, as the land became firmer and the waters receded yet more, until at what I guessed would have been the line of the high tide we came upon a wooden landing stage. To its timbers were roped a collection of rowboats and small punts, with poles for pushing them across the flats, and fine nets for catching eels. Beyond it the hill itself rose steeply, affording little by way of cover, apart from the occasional bush. At its crest stood the remains of what was once a large building, around the same length as *Wyvern*'s hull.

'Lord Guillaume had that hall built last summer,' Aubert said, shaking his head. 'Not that he came here much; I don't believe his womenfolk ever did.

Since he was made vicomte he's rarely been away from Eoferwic.'

We continued up the hillside, hands ready at our hilts in case we should find any of the rebels waiting to ambush us when we arrived at the top. But the air had gone still and, save for the cawing of the carrion birds circling above the village, the day was quiet. Nor was there any sign of the shadows that I thought I had seen earlier, but even so we trod carefully, taking care not to let our mail make too much sound.

At last the ground began to grow less steep and we could see the whole of Alchebarge before us. It didn't look as though it had been a large village—perhaps a dozen families at most—and there was even less of it now. Where houses and workshops had once stood, all that now remained were piles of quietly smoking timbers and ash. There were bodies everywhere: men, women and children, oxen and cattle all lying together in death. The stench of burnt flesh wafted on the wind.

'They didn't leave anything,' Wace said as we walked amidst the corpses. Crows picked at them with black beaks, tearing skin from bone, flapping their wings angrily at any others of their kind who tried to come near. They watched us closely as we approached, hopping aside grudgingly before flocking back as soon as they thought we were far enough away.

Many of the bodies were hacked to pieces, missing arms and even heads. Several of them were Normans; indeed some were still in their mail, with shields lying by their sides. Most, however, seemed to be English, and from their dress I took them mostly for the villagers of Alchebarge rather than the ones who had wrought this destruction.

'They killed even their own kinsmen,' I said, scarce believing what I saw, before I recalled that they had done the same to Oswynn. I imagined her body lying unburied at Dunholm, just as these did here, and hoped that if we met again at the end of days she would forgive me.

Eudo spat upon the ground. 'They're no better than animals,' he said.

'Why would they do this?' Wace asked.

'Perhaps the villagers tried to fight them,' Aubert suggested. 'Or perhaps there was no reason.'

I wondered how long Oswynn had been able to fight. Before our march to Dunholm I had gifted her with a knife, and had spent many hours showing her how to use it: how to thrust and how to slice; the places to aim for; how to twist it in a man's belly to kill him quickly. I hoped she had remembered. I hoped she had sent many Northumbrians to their deaths that night.

We walked on in silence, up towards Malet's hall. The only parts still standing were the posts which supported the roof, and those only up to waist height. The roof-beams themselves, along with the walls, had all collapsed, and in most places there was nothing more than a thick pile of grey ash. Beneath some of the broken timbers, huddled together in the middle of the hall, lay several blackened corpses, burnt away so that only their bones and teeth were left.

'A hall-burning,' Radulf muttered.

I nodded grimly. 'They would have trapped them in here before setting the torch to the whole building.' It would have taken mere heartbeats for the flames to sweep through the thatch, and hardly

213

much longer to spread downwards and engulf the rest of the hall. The terror those inside must have felt as the blaze surrounded them, growing ever closer, ever hotter—

'Just as they killed Lord Robert,' Eudo said. He glanced first at Wace, then at me, long enough that I could see the anger building within him.

I lowered my head and shut my eyes, trying to push the image of the fire, of Lord Robert from my mind. This was not the time to be thinking of such things.

'They did the same here,' I heard Godefroi call.

I opened my eyes; the sunlight flooded back. Godefroi was beckoning us over to what I realised must have been the stables, for under a fallen roof-beam lay a horse's head. The hair and skin had burnt away to expose the yellow-white of the skull, its jaw set wide as it would have been at the moment of death. As we rounded the smouldering remains, I saw the charred corpses of two more animals.

'The enemy couldn't have been interested in plunder, or else they would have taken them,' I said.

'Or they might not have been able to carry them away easily,' Wace said. 'If they came by ship, they probably didn't have space.'

'But if they approached by river, why did no one in the village spot them coming?' Eudo asked. 'In the time it'd have taken them to cross the flats, the villagers could all have fled. Instead they held their ground and died.'

'Unless the enemy landed somewhere further downriver and marched overland,' I said. 'Any retreat into the country would have been cut off,

214

and if the tide was out at the time, the villagers would have been trapped by the marshes.'

'That would make sense, given the punts still moored by the jetty,' Wace said.

Aubert gave a cry. I turned quickly, my hand darting towards the sword-hilt at my waist, imagining hordes of Northumbrian warriors rushing upon us from the south. But there was no enemy; instead the shipmaster was kneeling beside one of the bodies, not far from the eastern end of the hall.

'His name was Henri,' he said as we approached. 'He was Lord Guillaume's steward here.'

The man's face was crusted with blood and crossed with sword cuts, but it seemed to me that it would have been a handsome face, strong-featured and youthful too. Henri could not have been much older than I when he died. There was a gaping wound at his breast, across which lay one of his hands; his fingers, like his tunic beneath, were stained a dark red. His other arm was stretched out by his side, palm facing the sky, fingers curled as if he meant to be clutching something in them. If there had been anything there, however, then the enemy had already taken it.

'Did you know him well?' I asked.

Aubert got to his feet, still gazing down upon Henri's body. 'Hardly at all,' he said. 'I met him only once, a few months ago when we put in here on our way up to Eoferwic. He was a generous man, as I knew him. He arranged a feast for the whole crew.' The shipmaster sighed. 'Have you found anything?'

'Nothing,' I replied. 'The enemy left nothing.'

'There's the church,' Philippe said. 'They didn't

215

take the torch to that.'

I glanced up towards its stone tower and nave, overlooking the village. It was built on the highest point along the ridge, its yard marked out by a narrow ditch which ran in a continuous circuit, broken only at its eastern end. If the villagers had taken refuge anywhere, it was likely to be there, for that was the only place that seemed in any way defensible. Even so, I didn't have much hope of finding anyone alive inside.

Indeed, as it turned out there was no one; the church was small and it did not take long for us to search. Surprisingly, the rebels' respect for the building had extended to its property, for there was much of worth that had not been taken: a large pewter dish displaying the Crucifixion, inlaid with silver lettering; three silver candle-holders; and a small gold cross. But of any priest, or indeed of anyone at all, there was no sign. Of course, I realised, if the same rebels we had encountered last night were responsible for what had happened here in Alchebarge, then the attack was already one day old. If anyone had survived, they would have long since fled.

We stayed a short while in the church, praying for Malet's men who had died. It was the best that we could hope to do, considering that we had not the time to give them the burials they deserved. I was aware that the day was wearing on, and so as soon as we had finished we returned through the village and down the hillside, back across the marshes to the ship.

The tide was at its lowest point and so *Wyvern* was waiting for us not far from the edge of the flats, where there was still enough water that she

216

could float. Oylard had done well, for he had found a place between two large mudbanks, both of them thick with reeds, which ensured that she could not have been seen from the river.

The sun was high by the time we returned to the ship and related news of what we had seen in the village.

'What do we do now, then?' asked Elise, a worried expression on her face. She had paled on hearing of the hall-burning. 'We have no horses, and we can't travel to Lundene on foot.'

'The Trente flows through Lincolia,' the chaplain said. 'Surely we could sail upriver and meet the old road there.'

The shipmaster stroked his chin, looking doubtful. 'The tide is still on the ebb. We'll need to wait for the next flood before we can sail upriver,' he said. 'No, you'd be quicker going by land. If we carry on down the Humbre, there's a town not more than an hour or two from here called Suthferebi, where you should be able to purchase horses.'

'You know the river better than all of us,' I said. 'I leave the decision to you.'

Aubert nodded. 'Suthferebi it will be, then.' He gave the order to the oarsmen, retaking the tiller and slowly steering *Wyvern* clear of the flats, until we were back out upon the open water. More villages passed by as we travelled downriver, many of which had suffered the same fate as Alchebarge, though there were some the rebels had left untouched. Indeed in the distance I heard cattle lowing, and could see men and women out in the fields with their oxen, ploughing the earth. But why those had been spared, and not the rest, I could not discern. I only hoped that Suthferebi had escaped the devastation.

True to the shipmaster's judgement, it was but a little after midday that the town was spotted off our steerboard side, first as a few spires of smoke, then as a cluster of hovels along the shoreline, until as we grew closer it was possible to make out a palisade, a church, a hall. I smiled at Wace and Eudo, who were watching too, and they returned the same expression. We had made it safely from Eoferwic, and Northumbria was at last behind us.


## CHAPTER SEVENTEEN

We rode south that same afternoon, as soon as we had mounts for the journey. I had half hoped there would be a stud nearby where we might find good warhorses for myself and the rest of the knights, but there was not, and so we had to settle for what we could come by in the town.

Fortunately Suthferebi turned out to be a thriving port: a favoured stopping-place both for trading ships on their way to Eoferwic, and for travellers on the way north, before they crossed the Humbre. Among the many alehouses, we learnt, was one whose owner kept a trade in horses. His name was Ligulf; a large-bellied man in his middle years, he had fair hair, blue eyes and a gruff manner, and I sensed there was more than a little Danish blood in him. Swigging from a flagon, he led us around into the yard behind the alehouse, and showed us more than a dozen of the animals that he stabled. Most of them were beyond their

218

best years, while a few were so thin that I wondered if they had been fed at all this week, but it wasn't as if we had much choice and so I chose the nine who looked strongest.

'They only need to get us as far as Lundene,' Eudo pointed out. I had brought him to translate for me while Ælfwold stayed with the ladies back at the ship. 'We can sell them there and recover their cost.'

'We'll never recover what he's asking,' I said, and I kept my voice low, though I did not know why, since the man could not understand me anyway. He wanted no less than four pounds of silver for the nine animals: a ridiculous amount, and more than Malet had given me for the whole journey.

'I might be wrong. He speaks with a strange accent and I don't understand all of his words.'

'Tell him we'll give him one-and-a-half pounds.' That was a fair price, considering the animals' condition.

Eudo talked at length with Ligulf, who made a face as if he were being insulted.

'*Threo pund,*' he said at last. His cheeks flushed red, although whether it was because he was angry or rather due to the mead I was not sure.

'Three pounds,' Eudo translated, a little unnecessarily, for though I knew little of the English tongue, I had understood that much.

'*Threo pund,*' Ligulf said again. His breath smelt stale as he strode up to me, waving his flagon in my face. Mead dripped from his beard on to his paunch.

I spat on the ground and made to walk away, but he hurried after me and in the end settled for taking just two pounds, which was still far too much for what they were worth, but it seemed the best price we were going to get. In any case Eudo was right: all they had to do was get us to Lundene.

I left him there to watch over our purchases while I rode down to the shore to gather the others and to say our farewells to the shipmaster. We were not far from where the Humbre emptied into the German Sea, and the smell of the ocean filled my nose. Several dozen figures had flocked around the ship, which I saw had been dragged high up the beach, over the wrack that covered the stones, above the tideline. There was no wharf at Suthferebi but rather a wide expanse of sand, pebbles and mud that separated land from river. Several other vessels were drawn up there, from the rowboats that probably belonged to fisherfolk, to others with high sides and broad beams, which I took to be the ferry craft that, Ælfwold told us, gave the place its name. But none of those was nearly as big as *Wyvern*, and clearly that was what had attracted the townspeople's interest: they understood that a ship of her size meant wealth. Not that we had much to sell them; she was built for war rather than for carrying goods, and besides, we had left Eoferwic in such a hurry that we carried little beyond the provisions we needed.

Water dripped off the ship's exposed hull, and as I rode closer I could see places where the keel and garboard strake had splintered when we had nearly run aground. The shipmaster was walking around the ship, inspecting each one of the planks that made up the hull. I left my horse to graze on the bank above the beach and strode down to meet him, feeling my boots sink into the gravel. The wind was blowing strongly now and the skies were turning grey. Drizzle hung in the air and I felt its cold moisture on my cheeks.

'Aubert,' I called.

He raised his head, saw me and beckoned me over.

'Is there any lasting damage?' I asked, slipping back into the Breton tongue. I knew that I might not have the chance to use it again for some time.

'Just a few scrapes and scratches,' he replied. Absently he ran his hand along one of the timbers and picked off a splinter. 'She'll still float.'

'That's good to hear.'

'Aye, although it will be better still if we can get some good news from Eoferwic in the next few days.'

'And if you don't?'

'If the signs are bad, we'll sail down to Lundene,' he said. 'We might see you there.'

'You might,' I said, though in truth I wasn't sure whether he would. Once we had been to Wiltune I didn't know where we would be going.

He glanced up the beach, in the direction of the town, and nodded towards my mount, which was grazing upon the bank. 'Are you leaving now?'

'We are,' I said. 'The day is wearing on and we need to go soon if we're to have any chance of reaching Lincolia tonight.'

He looked up towards the sun, which was obscured behind the thickening clouds to the south and west. 'You'll be doing well if you make it that far.'

I shrugged. 'We can but try. Otherwise, we'll find an alehouse to overnight in.'

'Take care on the roads,' Aubert said. 'These have always been lawless parts in my experience, and most people here have little love for Frenchmen either, so be safe.'

'And you too.' I clasped his callused palm. 'May we meet again soon.'

'May we meet again soon,' he replied, and smiled.

I saw Ælfwold speaking with a group of the townsmen not far off, and waved to catch his attention. He raised a hand in acknowledgement, made his apologies and broke off from his conversation, before calling to Wace and Radulf, Godefroi and Philippe, who were all standing with Elise.

Beatrice was not with them, but then I saw her down by the shoreline, away from the crowd. She was gazing out across the river to the north, her face falling into sharp shadow as the sun emerged briefly from behind a cloud. There was a keen wind blowing in from the sea; it tugged at her dress, and I wondered that she was not cold. I made my way across the beach towards her, the stones crunching beneath my feet.

She must have heard me, for she glanced over her shoulder, long enough to see that it was me, before turning back to face the river. 'What do you want?' she asked.

'We're leaving,' I said. 'Gather your belongings.' What she had said on the ship was still fresh in my mind and I was not inclined that morning to be deferential, even if she was the daughter of my lord.

She did not reply, though I knew she was listening. She had taken her shoes off and the waters lapped at her feet. Her long toes were pink with the cold, glistening wet where they protruded

222

from beneath the hem of her skirt, which was likewise damp.

I picked up her shoes from where they lay, beside a gnarled log that must have washed up with the last tide, and held them out to her. 'Put these on,' I said.

She snatched them from my grasp and clutched them to her chest as she sat down upon the log, glaring at me all the while, before finally doing as I'd asked. I held out a hand to help her up, but she ignored it.

'I can manage by myself,' she said, almost spitting the words as she rose and hustled past me, following the others up the beach towards the town.

For a moment I watched her walk away, wondering why she was being so difficult. Inwardly I was dreading the thought of the week to come, for it would take that long for us to reach Lundene. Whether I could keep my temper with the ladies for that long I did not know.

I went to round up my horse, who was still grazing upon the bank, though he had wandered a short way downwind. As I climbed up into the saddle, I paused to gaze back down at the ship. Aubert saw me and waved one last time; I returned the gesture before at last pressing my spurs in.

\*　　　\*　　　\*

We made good progress over the days that followed. Each morning we rose at first light, while each evening we stayed on the road until almost dark. Though the mounts we had purchased were not as strong as the warhorses with which I was familiar—they couldn't be pushed too hard or too long—we were still, I reckoned, able to make between twenty and thirty miles each day.

We overnighted in alehouses to begin with, and there were many of them, since this was the old road from Lundene to the north of the kingdom. But while the innkeepers we met were happy enough to take our coin, I was wary of bringing too much attention upon ourselves. A party of just seven men and two women, with horses and silver to spare, would not go unnoticed. Everywhere we heard stories of Frenchmen being set upon out on the roads: merchants and knights and even monks killed not for what they carried but for who they were. Though I tried not to set much store by such rumours, it was not only my own safety that I had to consider, and so after a couple of nights we took to camping in the woods.

Elise did not like the idea of sleeping in the wild, and while the rest of us set up tents and built a fire, she complained loudly of the cold, the damp, the wolves that she had heard howling up in the hills. This was not how a vicomte's wife should live, she said; her husband would not be happy when he came to hear how she had been treated. She soon fell silent when I made it clear we wouldn't be going any further, but as we set off the next day she began again, and when later that morning we stopped by a stream to refill our wineskins, I saw the irritation in the faces of the other knights. Only Wace seemed unperturbed, and Beatrice, who accepted everything with a quiet dignity that I could not help but admire. Even Ælfwold seemed to be growing weary, especially when Elise suggested that the priest was taking my side, at which point he spoke a few words in her ear. What he said I could not hear, but inwardly I gave my thanks to God, for thereafter she stayed quiet.

The next night we spent in a clearing a short way south of the town of Stanford. Ælfwold and the two ladies were already in their tents, though it had been dark but an hour or so. The rest of us were sitting around the fire, eating from our shields laid across our laps.

No one had said anything in a while, when Eudo delved into his pack and brought out a wooden pipe, about two hands' spans in length and with half a dozen holes along its length. His flute, I realised, with some surprise; it was a long time since I had heard him play.

'I thought you'd lost it months ago,' I said.

'I did,' he answered. 'Some bastard stole it from my pack around Christmas. I bought this one while we were in Eoferwic.'

He held it before him, closing his eyes as if trying to remember how to use it, then put the beaked end to his lips, breathed deeply, and began: softly at first but slowly building, lingering on every wistful note, until after a short while I began to recognise the song. It was one I remembered from our campaigns in Italy all those years ago, and as I listened and gazed into the fire I found myself there again: feeling the heat of the summer, riding across the sun-parched fields with their brown and withered crops, through olive groves and cypress thickets.

Eudo's fingers danced over the holes as the music quickened, rising gracefully to a peak, where it trembled for a while, before settling down to a final pure note and fading away to nothing.

He lifted it from his lips and opened his eyes. 'I ought to practise more,' he said, flexing his fingers and laying it down beside him. 'I haven't played in a long while.'

If he hadn't said so, though, I wouldn't have been able to tell, so confident and sweet was his playing.

'Give us another song,' Wace said.

The fire was dwindling, I noticed, and most of the stack of branches we'd collected was gone.

'I'll go and find some more wood,' I said, getting to my feet.

It had rained earlier that day and so there was little dry wood to be found anywhere, but eventually I'd gathered enough to keep the fire going, for a few hours at least. I began to make my way back, a bundle of damp sticks beneath my arm, when I thought I heard a voice amidst the trees, not far off.

I stopped. The night was still, and for a moment the only other sound I could hear was that of Eudo's flute, this time playing a quicker song: one that was lighter and more playful. But then the voice came again, low and softly spoken. A woman's voice, I realised, and as I came nearer I saw that it was Beatrice.

She was kneeling upon the ground, her head bowed and her hands clasped together in prayer. Her back was to me, the hood of her cloak drawn back to reveal her fair hair, which was bound in a tight braid at the back of her head. My footfalls sounded softly upon the sodden earth and she showed no sign of having heard me.

'My lady,' I said. 'I thought you were abed.'

She looked up with a sharp intake of breath, her expression putting me in mind of a deer that has just heard the sound of the hunting-horn.

'You startled me,' she replied crossly, her lips tight.

'It isn't safe to be wandering the woods. You should be with the others.' I glanced back towards the fire, wondering how they could have let her from their sight. I would speak with them later.

'I'm not wandering,' she said. 'And I don't need you to watch over me.'

She turned and again bowed her head, closing her eyes, hoping perhaps that if she ignored me, I would soon go away. As the faint moonlight fell upon her face, however, I saw that her cheeks were wet, and I realised she had been crying.

'What's wrong?' I asked.

She said nothing, but she did not have to, for no sooner had the question left my lips than I already knew the answer. 'You're thinking about your father, aren't you?'

She raised her hands to her face, as if hiding her tears from me. 'Leave me,' she said between sobs. 'Please.'

But Ælfwold's words from a few days ago were still fresh in my mind, and the sight of Beatrice on her knees and trembling was more than I could bear. Here was a chance to set things right.

I crouched beside her, setting down the firewood before gently resting my hand upon her shoulder. She flinched at my touch, though she did not try to get up, or to shake my hand away.

'You don't understand what it feels like,' she said, 'not knowing whether you will ever see someone again.'

Lord Robert, Oswynn, Gérard, Fulcher, Ivo, Ernost, Mauger: I would not see any of them

227

again. Not in this life, at least. But I knew that wasn't quite what she meant.

'No,' I said instead, 'I don't.'

I didn't know what more I could add, nor did she speak, but I stayed there, until my legs began to ache and I felt my wound twinge and I sat down on the wet leaves instead. The damp seeped through the thin cloth of my braies, cold against my skin, but I did not care.

'I barely knew my father,' I said quietly, after a while. 'Or my mother either. Both died when I was young.'

Almost twenty years ago, I realised. What would they think of me, were they here to see me? Would they recognise the man I had become?

'The closest to a father I ever truly had was Robert de Commines,' I went on. 'And now he is gone too, along with all my sworn brothers, and Oswynn—'

I broke off, suddenly aware of Beatrice's gaze resting upon me. I had hardly spoken of my family in years. Why was I doing so now, and to her? Why was I telling her about Robert, about Oswynn?

'Oswynn,' Beatrice said. Her tears had stopped, and in the soft light her skin was milky-pale. 'She was your woman.'

I sighed deeply, letting the bitter night air fill my chest. 'She was.'

'You cared for her.'

Not as much as I should have, I thought, though at the same time probably more than I had ever dared admit to myself. Would I ever have made her my wife, had she lived? Probably not; she was English, and of low stock besides, the daughter of a blacksmith. And yet she'd been unlike all the other

228

girls I'd known: strong-minded and fiery in temper; unafraid of anyone; able to face up to even the most battle-hardened of Lord Robert's knights. There would never be another like her.

'I did,' I said simply, leaving Beatrice to take from that what she would.

'How did she die?'

'I don't know. It was one of my men who told me. I never saw what happened.'

'Perhaps it was better that way.'

'Better?' I echoed. 'It would have been better if I had never left her in the first place. If I had been with her, I could have protected her.' And she would still be alive now, I thought.

'Or else you might have died with her,' Beatrice said.

'No,' I said, though of course she was right. If the enemy had come upon them suddenly, as Mauger had said, there was probably little I could have done. Yet what did it matter to Beatrice what had happened to Oswynn?

Discomfited all of a sudden, I got to my feet. 'We should get back. The others will be wondering where we are.'

I held out my hand to help her up; she took it in her own. Her fingers were long and delicate, her palm cold but soft. She rose, smoothing down her skirt, brushing off the leaves and twigs. There were patches of mud where she had been kneeling, but that could not be helped. She pulled her hood back over her hair, while I gathered up the wood for the fire, and together we returned in the direction of the camp. Eudo had finished playing, for the meantime at least, and the knights were laughing amongst themselves as they took draughts from a

229

wineskin that they passed around.

We arrived at the edge of the clearing, where I bade her a good night and watched her make her way back to her tent. For the first time in weeks, I realised I felt free, as if merely by talking about Robert and Oswynn a weight had been lifted from my heart.

I was going to join the others by the fire, when I glimpsed Ælfwold standing in the shadows beside his tent. How long had he been there? I made to walk away, ignoring him, but hardly had I gone five paces when he called my name. For a moment I considered pretending that I had not heard, had not seen him, but then he called a second time and I turned to see him marching towards me.

'What were you doing?' he demanded.

I stared back at him, surprised. I had known the chaplain only a few weeks, but never before had I seen him provoked to such anger. 'What do you mean?'

'You know what I mean,' he answered, and gestured towards the ladies' tent.

I realised then that he must have seen me with Beatrice. Indeed, how must it have looked, the two of us emerging together from the trees?

'She was upset,' I said, feeling the blood rising up my cheeks. Yet I had no reason to be ashamed, and if the priest thought I did, then he was mistaken. 'I was comforting her.'

'Comforting her?'

'What sort of a man do you think I am?' I asked, trying to restrain my temper. I looked him up and down, disgusted that he would so much as imply such a thing. 'You don't know what you're talking about.'

'I know exactly—'

I did not let him finish, as I pointed my finger towards his face. 'You should hold your tongue, priest, in case you say something you might regret.'

He froze, blinking at me, but heeded my warning and stayed quiet.

'I would never besmirch the lady Beatrice's honour,' I said as I drew away. 'And if you doubt my word, you can ask her in person.'

I half expected him to offer some retort, but instead he turned his back and disappeared into his tent, leaving me standing there, alone and confused. How could he think so little of me, when all I had done was try to follow his advice?

I heard the fire crackling, the other knights laughing. I shook my head, trying to clear it, and went to join them.


## CHAPTER EIGHTEEN

I kept my distance from Ælfwold the next morning, and from Beatrice as well: I didn't want to give the priest any reason to think that his suspicions might be founded. Once or twice I exchanged a glance with him, but most of the time he rode on in front, never so far that he was out of sight or hearing, but always apart from the rest of us.

It was only when we stopped to eat at noon that the Englishman approached me again. His temper had cooled, for he came with head bowed and hands clasped sombrely in front of him.

He sat down beside me. 'I've been meaning to

231

apologise for last night,' he said. 'It was wrong for me to imply that anything'—he hesitated, as if searching for the right word—'anything *untoward* might have taken place.'

I did not reply, nor even look at him as I took another bite of bread.

'I fear I may have been too hasty in my presumptions,' the chaplain went on. 'I was merely concerned, for Beatrice's sake. I have known her since she was very young, and she is dear to me. I hope you understand.'

'I thought nothing of it,' I lied. In fact I had spent a great deal of time turning it over in my mind. I hadn't thought the chaplain the kind of man to anger so easily—not, at least, until last night.

'That is good,' Ælfwold said, nodding, and once more produced that gentle smile I had grown used to seeing.

Still, I could not help but feel uneasy, and I kept a close watch over him over the next couple of days, though exactly what I was looking for I was not sure.

The rest of the journey was passed in an ill humour: little was said and the rain and wind did nothing to lift the mood. Nothing more was said of Eoferwic or Malet, and the fact that none of the towns we passed through had heard any news only unsettled me even more.

So it was that on the following Sunday, the twenty-second day in the month of February, and the sixth after we had left Suthferebi, we finally left the woods to the north of Lundene. The familiar Bisceopesgeat hill came into sight, its crest occupied by the stone church and attendant buildings of the convent of St Æthelburg, lit orange by the low sun. Since first coming across the Narrow Sea two-and-a-half years before, I had been to Lundene more often than I could recall; more than anywhere else in England, it felt like home.

Fields gave way to houses as we made our way up the other side of the valley towards the Bisceopesgeat itself, which was one of the seven gatehouses, built of stone and more than thirty feet high. The city was girded on its landward sides by great stone walls left by the Romans, the first people to have taken this island, so many centuries ago. I remembered how, the first time I had arrived, I had marvelled at the sight: it had seemed more of a fortress than a town. But a town it was, by far the largest in the kingdom: more than twice the size of Eoferwic and easily a rival to Cadum and Rudum, the great cities of Normandy.

The road was quiet; it was growing late and I imagined that most men would be at home with their wives, drinking ale or mead by the warmth of their hearths. Children played in the road, chasing each other between and around the backs of the houses, hardly noticing us. It was a pleasant change after Eoferwic, where Frenchmen were still greeted in the streets with hostility or, at the very least, suspicion. Of course the south of the kingdom was long accustomed to our presence, having made its surrender within a month of our victory at Hæstinges. In the time since, the people in Lundene had come to understand that we were here to stay, in a way that the northerners so far had not.

The gatehouse rose tall in front of us, solid and imposing as it must have appeared for hundreds of years, although I could see from the lighter coloured stone in the upper courses where it had been repaired and added to. Behind a wooden parapet on its roof, two men stood silhouetted against the yellowing sky, facing out across the fields towards the north, spears in hands, their long hair blowing in the wind where it protruded from beneath the rims of their helmets. How many sieges, how many assaults had these walls withstood? How many others had kept watch atop the same tower?

We passed in single file beneath the shadow of its archway; hooves clattered against the paving stones, echoing in its darkened confines. There were four knights guarding the gate, pacing about, blowing warm air into their hands. When they saw that most of us were Normans, however, they let us pass, and then the low sun was on my face again.

We carried on climbing the hill until we had passed the church, whereupon the road fell away once more, straight down towards the river. The whole city sprawled out before us. Houses and workshops clustered together along the main streets, sending up coils of smoke that wound about each other in the still evening air. Beyond them the murky waters of the Temes swept in great curves across the land. A number of ships were out on the river that evening: fishing boats returning from the estuary with their day's catch; trading vessels, wide-beamed and broad in sail; a solitary longship, fighting its way against the current. I remembered what Aubert had said back in Suthferebi, and for a heartbeat wondered if it might be *Wyvern*, before I saw her sail, which was blue and white rather than black and gold.

234

In the south-eastern quarter of the city stood the castle, more impressive still than the one at Eoferwic, while in the far distance, a mile and more upriver of the city, was the great abbey church of Westmynstre, its towers rising high above the stone-and-timber halls of the royal palace and the houses and farms of Aldwic, the old town.

'Where from here?' I asked the chaplain.

'Down to Wæclinga stræt,' he replied. 'Lord Guillaume's house lies the other side of the Walebroc.'

I nodded, picturing both street and brook in my mind as we carried on down the hill, towards the bridge which carried the road across the Temes to Sudwerca and thence on to the southern coast and the Narrow Sea. Squawks pierced the air as a lone chicken scurried down the road in front of us, flapping its wings; a young girl chased after it, shrieking with excitement while a woman in a grey dress called after her. A dull clanging sounded out from the open front of one of the workshops, where a blacksmith hammered away at a glowing red horseshoe, throwing up sparks, before taking it in a set of tongs and thrusting it back into the forge.

The sun had fallen below roof-level by the time we reached Malet's townhouse. It was a simple long hall, two storeys high and built of timber and thatch, distinguished by the banner of black and gold which flew from its eastern gable. After seeing his residence in Eoferwic it was in truth something of a disappointment. There were no walls or gatehouse, although there was a small fenced enclosure running around the side of the hall, with a yard and stables behind. Its oak door opened almost directly out on to the road and was guarded by a single servant.

Ælfwold rode up to him and spoke some words in English; the other man disappeared inside the hall. I dismounted, motioning for the rest of the knights to do the same, and then offered my hand to Elise to help her. She accepted but did not meet my eyes as she climbed from the saddle. Beside her, Beatrice gratefully accepted Wace's hand, leaning on his shoulder and stepping down with grace.

The oak door opened again and a tall, red-faced Englishman appeared; he smiled when he saw the chaplain standing there and the two briefly embraced, speaking in their own tongue.

Ælfwold broke off. 'The ladies Elise and Beatrice,' he said, gesturing towards them.

The Englishman knelt on the ground before them, leaning forward to kiss each of them on the back of the hand. 'My ladies,' he said. 'It's a relief to see you safe. When we heard the news from Eoferwic, we feared the worst.' Like the chaplain, he spoke French well.

'Wigod,' said Ælfwold, 'this is Tancred a Dinant, to whom Lord Guillaume has entrusted our safety. Tancred, this is Lord Guillaume's steward, Wigod son of Wiglaf.'

The steward rose, looking me up and down with indifference. He had dark hair, cut fairly short for an Englishman, with a pink patch of scalp showing where he was beginning to bald. His upper lip bore a thick moustache, though he was otherwise clean-shaven. He extended a hand and I clasped it.

'Wigod, I must know,' Elise said, interrupting, 'what news is there from Eoferwic?'

236

The Englishman stepped back, his expression solemn. 'Perhaps it is best if you come inside, into the warmth, rather than discuss such matters in the open.' He gestured towards the door. 'My ladies, Ælfwold,' he said, and then to the rest of us: 'I'll have the boy show you the stables.' He put his head around the doorframe into the hall. 'Osric!'

A boy of about fourteen or fifteen emerged. Tall and wiry, he wore a brown cap on his head and a sullen expression on his face. His tunic and trews were marked with dirt and there was hay in his hair. Wigod placed a hand on his shoulder and said something quietly in English, before following the chaplain and the ladies inside.

'Whatever news he has, I'm guessing it's not good,' Wace murmured.

'We'll see,' I said, although I'd had the same feeling. 'If it were so bad, wouldn't he have told us straightaway?'

Wace shrugged. Osric took the reins of the chaplain's mount while Philippe and Godefroi took those of the two ladies, and we followed him around the side of the hall, alongside the brook and into a wide courtyard bounded by a picket fence.

'Here we are, then,' said Eudo. 'In Lundene again.'

'Enjoy it while you can,' I replied. 'We might not be staying here long.' The fact that we had been travelling a whole week would likely count for nothing with Ælfwold; I suspected that the priest would want us on the road again before long. So far he hadn't said anything more regarding the message he carried, or the person for whom it was intended. I had asked him more than once while

237

we had been on the road; each time, however, he had refused to answer. It made me uncomfortable, for it meant that although we were soon to be on our way, I was no wiser as to exactly why.

'I might ride over to Sudwerca tonight, if I'm to see Censwith before we go,' Eudo said.

I grinned. 'You're nothing if not loyal.'

'Sudwerca?' Radulf put in. 'You know there are far better whorehouses this side of the river, don't you?'

Eudo turned to face him. 'And what would you know of whores, whelp? I'd wager you've not so much as seen a naked woman in your life.'

Radulf smiled sarcastically. 'More times than you could count.'

'He means women other than your sister,' Godefroi said.

I laughed with the others; Radulf's eyes narrowed and he sneered at Godefroi, who stared back, impassive.

We were led to the stables, where Osric showed us the stalls, then left us while we removed the packs from our saddles and untacked the animals. They had worked hard these last few days with little by way of reward. I hoped we would be able to obtain fresh horses for the next part of our journey; it seemed that Malet or members of his household owned several, including four fine-looking destriers, of which one, a black, reminded me of Rollo. Two stable-hands were at work, scrubbing down their coats and brushing out their manes.

Osric returned shortly, bearing water-pails and sacks of grain, with bundles of fresh hay under his arms, and as soon as we had finished seeing to the animals, led us back across the courtyard in the fading light, into the hall. He said nothing the whole time: not even to the stable-hands who I presumed shared the same tongue.

It was dark inside; there were no windows and the walls were hung with leather drapes to keep out draughts. The hearth-fire, recently stoked with fresh wood, was crackling, hissing with white smoke. Ælfwold and Wigod sat on stools at a low round table beside it, with a pitcher and cups and the smell of mead thick in the air around them. The ladies were not to be seen and I presumed that they had—for now at least—retired to their rooms.

Wigod looked up as we entered. 'Welcome,' he said to us, before muttering some words to Osric in their own tongue.

The boy grunted and slunk away, out of the door we had come in.

'My apologies for his manners,' the steward said.

'He doesn't say much,' I observed, sitting down on one of the stools that had been set out for us.

'He doesn't say anything, though he understands well enough. Don't worry about him; he may be dumb and none too bright either, but he works hard and that's why I keep him on.' He poured out six cups of mead from the pitcher and then took a sip from his own. 'I hear your journey was eventful.'

'Ælfwold has told you what happened out on the river, then.'

'I only wish I'd been there to witness it.'

I looked at him sternly. 'If you had, you wouldn't be saying that.' Even though in the end we had come through mostly unharmed, I hadn't forgotten

239

how close it had been. 'What word has there been?'

The steward leant closer. 'Little that will be easy to hear, I am afraid,' he said. 'About four days ago it became known that an army had gathered outside Eoferwic and was laying siege to it. Shortly thereafter we heard of a rising by the townsmen.' He sighed. 'And then yesterday came the news that the rebels had taken the city.'

'Taken the city?' I had known it was possible and yet at the same time found it hard to believe. Malet's doubts had been well founded, it seemed.

'It is so,' Wigod said. 'Close to dawn last Monday a band of townsmen managed to seize control of one of the gates. They killed the knights who were there on guard and opened the city to the rebels, who swept into the town.'

'Was there no resistance?' Wace asked.

'Lord Guillaume rode out from the castle with more than a hundred knights,' Wigod said. 'He tried to head them off, and succeeded in killing a good many of them too. But even as he did so, a fleet of more than a dozen ships had appeared from downriver.'

'The fleet we saw,' Eudo muttered.

'Most probably,' Wigod said. 'They landed and attacked Lord Guillaume's conroi in the rear. He was forced to retreat to the castle, along with Lord Gilbert and what remained of their host. It is thought that in all as many as three hundred Normans were killed.'

I cursed under my breath. The loss of three hundred men would be hard for the defenders to bear.

'There is more,' the steward said. 'Already it

240

seems Eadgar's own men are proclaiming him king—and not just of Northumbria, but of the whole of England.'

I shook my head; events were moving too fast. It was a matter of weeks, after all, since we had ridden victorious into Dunholm. How could things have changed so much since then?

'What's happening now?' I asked.

'The king is raising a relief force to march north as soon as possible. His writ has gone out to all his vassals around Lundene and along the north road. There is even talk that he may try to muster the *fyrd*, as he did last year when he marched upon Execestre.'

'The fyrd?' said Philippe.

'The English levy,' Ælfwold explained, 'raised according to shire by the thegns—the local lords—from the men who dwell on their lands.'

'A peasant rabble,' I said. In my experience most of the men who made it up could hardly even hold a spear, let alone kill with one. They were farmers, accustomed only to tilling the soil and sowing their crops.

'Would they march against their own kinsmen?' Philippe asked.

'They did at Execestre,' Eudo answered.

'The town submitted shortly after we laid it siege,' Wace pointed out. 'They didn't have to fight.'

'But they would have, had they been called to,' the steward said. 'As they will fight any who rise against their lawfully crowned king.'

'Times have changed,' Ælfwold added. 'King Eadward is dead and Harold too. The men of the south understand this; they hold no desire to see

241

Eadgar Ætheling as king in place of Guillaume.'

'You can't be sure of that,' I said. The chaplain had been close to Malet for many years, and I could well believe that for him—as perhaps for Wigod, too—the ties of lordship took precedence over any allegiance he might owe his countrymen. I myself knew how powerful such ties could be, having served Lord Robert through a dozen campaigns. But I was sure that most Englishmen wouldn't share their sentiments. For although over time they had learnt to live with us, I could not bring myself to believe that they would not rather have one of their own race as king. These were, after all, the same people who little more than two years ago had stood in their thousands against King Guillaume; who had fought under the banner of the usurper at Hæstinges.

'In their eyes Eadgar is a foreigner,' Ælfwold said. 'He was born and raised in lands far from here; only indirectly is he of the old royal stock. They have no love for him—no more, at any rate, than they do for King Guillaume.'

'The hearts of the people are fickle, though,' Eudo put in. 'If Eadgar holds Eoferwic and the king's army fails to drive him out, they may start to think differently.'

I sipped at the mead in my cup, but it tasted sickly and I swallowed it fast. 'How many men does the king have with him in Lundene?' I asked the steward.

'Around three hundred knights, and perhaps as many as five hundred foot,' he replied. 'More of course will join them as they travel north.'

'Remember it's winter,' Wace said. 'The king might call on his barons but at this time of year they're unlikely to be ready to fight. It'll take time for them all to gather.'

He looked towards me. I was reminded of our conversation back on the *Wyvern*, and wondered again how long Malet would be able to hold out in the castle. And how long could the king afford to delay, if he was going to arrive in time to relieve him?

'He'll need every man he can gather if he's to retake Eoferwic,' Eudo said. 'We're needed there more than we are here.'

My sword-arm itched as I thought of the Northumbrian host waiting for us in Eoferwic: of Eadgar Ætheling, who had murdered Oswynn, murdered our lord. But at the same time I knew that my oath would not be discharged until I had seen Ælfwold safely to Wiltune with his message, whatever it was.

'We have our duty to Malet,' I said.

'Indeed we do,' the chaplain said, as he glanced at each of the other knights in turn. 'Lest you all forget.'

'But he couldn't have known when we left that he'd soon have another thousand men at his gates,' Eudo said. 'He couldn't have known the danger.'

I looked at Wigod. 'How long will it take us to ride to Wiltune from here?'

'Wiltune?' he asked. 'Why do you want to go there?'

'It's not important why,' Ælfwold said. 'All that matters is that we get there safely.'

Wigod looked first at him, then at me, plainly puzzled. 'At a steady pace, I should think no more than three days.'

'So if we left tomorrow, we could be back here in

243

Lundene within the week,' I said.

'It is possible, yes,' said the steward. 'It will probably take that long for the king to ready his forces. And even if they had gone by the time you returned, you would still catch them on the road north.'

'In that case we leave tomorrow morning,' Ælfwold said.

I lifted my mead-cup and drained what was left; the liquid rolled off my tongue, sliding down my throat, and I tried not to grimace at the taste for fear of offending the steward.

I placed the empty vessel down upon the table. 'To Wiltune, then.'


## CHAPTER NINETEEN

It was long past dark and the house lay cold and silent. The fire in the hearth had dwindled since earlier but nonetheless remained smouldering, the undersides of the logs still glimmering a faint orange. Every so often a finger of flame would rise up and lick over them, and I would feel a flicker of comfort as the warmth played across my face. Out in the street a dog began yapping, only to be silenced by a man's shouts. Otherwise all was still.

I sat before the hearth on one of the low stools, sword in hand as I scraped a whetstone along its edge, firmly enough to sharpen it, yet not so loud that I would wake the others lying on the floor behind me. Wigod and Ælfwold had long since retired to their rooms, leaving the six of us to bed down on rushes in the hall. It was no less than I was used to, and I had hoped that so many days spent in the saddle would have more than tired me, but instead I had found myself unable to sleep— and not for the first time of late. My mind kept returning to the river and the chase, and Malet in Eoferwic, and myself here, bound by this duty I had to him and yet unable to do anything to help. And so even though we had hardly been in Lundene half a day, I was already eager to be on the road again, for the sooner we were in Wiltune to deliver whatever message it was the vicomte had sent, the sooner we might be back.

How long I'd been sitting there I didn't know; it could have been hours. I drew the whetstone up the length of the blade one last time, then I set it down upon the paved floor and turned the sword in my wrist, examining its edge. It gleamed in the firelight, keen enough to slice through flesh and even bone. Lightly I put my fingertip to its point, just to test its sharpness for myself. At first it was like touching ice, but then I felt warm liquid oozing forth and I lifted away, watching the blood run down and drip once, twice on to the floor. There was no pain.

I wiped my finger on the leg of my braies and sucked at it to clear away the rest of the blood, then held the flat of the weapon up to the fire. The dim light showed up well the pattern in the metal where the swordsmith had twisted and welded together the iron rods from which the blade was fashioned. Swirls and lines ran the length of the blade, decorating the fuller, the narrow channel which ran down the blade's centre, into which, I saw for the first time, some words had been inlaid. 'VVLFRIDVS ME FECIT', it read, in what appeared to be silver. *Wulfrid made me.* I turned the sword over, to see if the reverse bore a similar legend. Often the swordsmith would inscribe, as well as his own name, a phrase from the Bible or the readings for Mass, 'IN NOMINE DOMINI'' or something similar. And more often than not it would be misspelt, but then those who made the engravings were not men of letters. But there was no inscription here, only a single small cross roughly halfway up.

How I longed to find such words then, and the small solace that they might provide. I could have talked to Ælfwold, I supposed, but ever since that night in the woods it seemed he had grown more distant. Nor did I like the fact that he was withholding information from me, whom his lord had placed in charge of this party. Though I could not force him to tell me, it troubled me that he could not entrust me with such things. For how then could I trust him enough to speak about matters so close to my soul?

Even if I did, however, I knew he would not understand, not truly. Priests never could.

I picked the scabbard up off the rushes beside me and slid the sword back into it, glancing back over my shoulder to make sure that I hadn't woken any of the others. All were soundly asleep. Even Eudo, after hearing the news from Eoferwic, had decided he was no longer in the mood to see Censwith that night and was now snoring gently.

I removed the chain that held the little silver cross from around my neck and sat for a while, staring at the tarnished metal shining in the firelight. I'd had it so long that I no longer knew exactly when or where I had acquired it. All I remembered was the bearded face of the man I had taken it from, with his broken nose, his eyes and mouth wide open in death, and the sounds of slaughter ringing out across the field of battle. It had failed to protect that man from his fate; why I thought it might aid me I had no idea. True, it had served me well enough thus far, but for how much longer?

I had come close to death at Dunholm, and again in the days after; I had the scars to prove it. Had it not been for the help of my friends, I would now be dead and—the thought made me cold—most likely gone to hell. For though I'd tried in my own way to serve the Lord as best I could, I knew that it might yet not be enough. Not after the life I had fled so long ago. The life that perhaps I was running from still.

Ever since I'd met Lord Robert all I had wanted was to bear arms, to be a warrior, and indeed I wanted it even now. It had been my life for a decade and more, in which time I had followed the hawk banner across the breadth of Christendom, from Normandy as far south as Italy and Sicily, and for the past two years in England. I had ridden to battle in summer and in winter, under scorching sun and the cold light of the moon. I had killed more men than I had ever cared to count, each one of them an enemy of my lord, each one of them an enemy of Christ. But it was half my lifetime since I had been called to that task. Was Dunholm the sign that I was being called back?

The walls felt close around me and I found my palms damp with sweat. I needed space, and to feel the chill of the night air. I replaced the chain around my neck, rose from my stool and fastened my sword-belt to my waist. Even in Lundene, one could never be too careful in these times, especially after dark. I stepped between the sleeping forms of the other men, across the rushes to where I had made my own bed on the floor. I lifted my cloak and shrugged it on, then made for the door.

Outside it was snowing, a few light flakes which melted the instant they touched my skin. There was no wind to speak of and they fell gently through the air, spiralling, dancing about each other.

A small timber bridge spanned the black waters of the Walebroc, but it was too chill to be standing in one place, and so I did not stop there. Instead I walked on down Wæclinga stræt, towards the river Temes, letting my feet take me where they would. The ground lay hard beneath them. Where during the day mud had lain thick and soft across the road, now it was solid; where water had pooled in its many ruts and holes, now there was ice. Already the snow was beginning to settle: a white dusting across the thatch of the houses and on the branches of the trees. The street was silent, as empty of people as the skies were of stars. The moon was new, too, and I regretted not having brought a torch, but then I wouldn't be going far.

I came to the end of Wæclinga stræt and gazed down towards the bridge, its tall stone piers rising out of the water, defying the current. Across the swollen blackness of the river there was firelight still. While Lundene slept, Sudwerca plied its trade.

Turning, I began the climb up the road towards St Æthelburg's convent and the Bisceopesgeat, both buildings hidden from sight by the snow,

248

which was starting to fall more heavily, swirling about me in great clouds. I crunched my way over the frozen surface of a puddle, not realising how deep it was. I cursed as icy water gushed into my boots and the hem of my trews stuck, soaked, to my skin.

I shivered and trudged onwards, up the hill in the direction of the church dedicated to the martyr St Eadmund, who had been king in these parts in the days when England was more than one kingdom, who was brutally slain by the Danes raiding his lands. So I recalled from my studies, at least: I could picture in my mind the richly decorated leaves of parchment, and my own trembling hand as I copied out the letters by candlelight, inscribing them upon my wax tablet. And I could see all too plainly the stern face of Brother Raimond watching over me, waiting for me to err. How easily such things came back to me, even after so many years.

Of course, in King Eadmund's time, the Danes were still pagans and enemies of the English. Now they claimed to be Christians and the two peoples were sometimes hard to tell apart, so alike were their customs and their tongues, so completely had they interbred in the years since. But though they might have changed their faith, they had not yet changed their warlike ways. Indeed, if the stories from Denmark were true, we would have to contend with them yet for the right to possess England.

The stone tower of the church rose over the houses on my left, lit by a flickering orange glow. A glow like torchlight. I stopped, surprised, for torches meant people, and I had not expected to

249

find anyone else out in the city this night—especially not at this hour.

There were voices, too. I moved into the shadows, close by the houses. Two roads met here: the first going down from Bisceopesgeat to the bridge; the second running in the same direction as the river. I edged closer to the corner, where, abutting the wall of the house, was piled a great mound of manure.

There were two of them, standing under the branches of an old oak tree by the eastern end of the church, about fifty paces from me. One was a priest, if the black robes he wore were any indication. He was short of stature, with a round face and ears that stuck out from the side of his bald head. Even in the dim light I could make out the ruddy complexion of his cheeks. Beside him a grey horse stood patiently, waiting.

The other man had his back to me, but from the manner of his dress and the length of his hair I knew him instantly for an Englishman, and not just any Englishman.

Ælfwold.

I could not see his face but I was sure it was him. It was there in his stance, the broadness of his shoulders, the grey of his hair. But I had been in the hall, close to the door, all night. How could he have gone out without me noticing? Unless there was a back entrance to the house out of which he might have slipped, though I had not seen one.

Ælfwold handed the priest a leather pouch, about the same size as the one he used to carry his coin. I tried to make out what they were saying, but could not. Then I heard hooves and the clink of mail, and I shrank back, crouching low behind the mound. The stink of shit filled my nose as a knight rode up to the priest.

'*Dominus tecum in itinere*,' Ælfwold said to the priest, who was mounting up, and then he nodded to the knight.

I retreated as far as I could back into the shadows, watching them as the knight and the bald-headed man rode not ten paces in front of me, turning up towards the Bisceopesgeat. I looked back towards the church, to where Ælfwold had been standing, and saw him hurrying away from me, up the road. I rose, meaning to follow him—

Cold steel pressed against my neck.

'Say a word and I will kill you,' a voice said from behind me.

I felt warm breath on the side of my face. All I could see was the blade and the hand holding it. I tried to turn my head but straightaway the knife was drawn closer and I swallowed, feeling the sharp edge press against my skin.

'Don't turn around.' The voice was gruff and spoke with a tone of conviction, and I knew he meant what he said. 'Take off your sword.' He spoke French well, I noticed, without any accent that I could discern. 'Slowly,' he added.

I did as I was asked, undoing the iron buckle and letting the sword-belt fall to the ground beside me. Out of the corner of my eye I saw him extend a foot, using his heel to kick the scabbard back towards him.

'Now, on your knees.'

I did not move, trying to work out how I might escape. Who was this man?

The blade pressed tighter. 'On your knees,' the

voice repeated.

I had little choice, I realised, and so did as he said. The ground here was still soft, and the water standing on its surface made it slightly slippery. The knife remained at my neck; a hand clamped down on my shoulder.

'What's your name?' he asked.

'Fulcher,' I said, after a moment's hesitation. I only hoped it was not a moment too long. 'Fulcher fitz Jean.' I was not going to give him my real name, and my old friend's was the first that came into my head.

'Whom do you serve?'

My mind raced. I did not dare mention Malet's name after lying about my own. 'Ivo de Sartilly,' I said. 'The lord of Suthferebi,' I added, as if to bear it out.

'I've never heard of him,' the voice said. 'Or this place Suthferebi. He sent you here?'

I was not sure whether that meant he did not believe me. 'He did.' How far I could go with this ruse I did not know.

The man grunted. 'Then he is a fool. As are you for serving him.'

I did not know what to say, and so I said nothing.

'Who else knows?'

'Knows what?' I asked. It was a stupid response, likely to anger him more than anything else, but I needed time if I was going to think of a way out, and I had no answer that was more sensible. And what did he mean, in any case?

'Don't play games with me,' he warned, speaking directly into my ear. 'Ivo de Sartilly and who else?'

'Would you spare me if I told you?' I asked.

He laughed, and at that moment I jerked my

head back, connecting with some part of his face, as I threw my whole body backwards. The knife-blade followed, flashing across my cheek, but I did not feel it as I twisted and threw myself at the man's legs. Cursing, he fell forward, across me, and I heard the thump as he hit the ground. I scrambled forward over the ground to reach my scabbard, just as I heard him rise and draw his own sword free. I tugged my blade from its sheath; it slid out quickly and I turned to face him, still on my back, sword raised above my face.

'Bastard,' he said as he towered over me, and I saw his face for the first time. Blood streamed from his mouth and his eyes were full of hate. He wore mail, but had neither helmet or coif to protect his head, and I saw from the cut of his hair what I had suspected from hearing his voice. He was a Norman.

'Bastard, bastard, bastard,' he said, and he came at me, raining blows wildly. I parried the first, but his sword-edge came perilously close to my face, and so I rolled away from the second, and again from the third, his blade coming crashing down each time inches from where I lay. He lifted his weapon too high for the fourth and I saw an opening, driving my sword up towards his groin, but I missed, managing only a glancing blow on his chausses. He stumbled back out of sword-reach, for a heartbeat looking as though he might fall to the mud again. He did not, but it gave me time to get to my feet.

'You'll pay,' he said, wiping some of the blood from his face. 'As will your lord.'

I stared silently back at him, wielding my sword before me. His prominent chin was unshaven, and his eyes were deep-set, with an ugly scar above his left. In all he looked perhaps five years older than myself.

He lunged forward, aiming for my chest. I took his sword on my own, quickly stepping around to my right, hoping to kick or trip him from behind, but I was not quick enough, for he had already turned by the time I was ready.

He gave a sarcastic smile. 'You fight well, Fulcher fitz Jean,' he said, and he stepped forward, feinting with his sword, tempting me into an attack, but I was well used to such tactics and refused to be drawn in. We circled about, watching each other intently.

He lunged again. Perhaps he thought that his feints had put me off my guard, but I had seen it coming and was ready this time, again stepping right and this time thrusting my boot out, hooking it around his leg. He stumbled forwards and went down with a cry.

I hesitated, thinking to finish him off, but he was already rolling on to his back, his sword raised and ready to face me, and I knew that I would be hard pressed to find the killing blow. He had mail and I had none, and it was I who was the more likely to die than he, if this continued much longer. My scabbard lay at the side of the street, in the mud, and I knew I had no time to pick it up and sheathe my blade, but neither could I run well with a sword in my hand.

I ran—while my opponent was still on the ground, while I still could—dropping the blade and taking off back down towards the bridge. I didn't know where I was going, only that going straight back to Malet's townhouse would be foolish, since if the knight followed me, then he would know I was not who I said.

I heard cursing and glanced behind to see him getting to his feet, giving chase. The weight of his hauberk would slow him down, but I could not rely on that alone and so I pounded on down the hill, through the snow which filled the air, ducking left across the cobbles of the market street, and then straightaway right, into a side alley between two low-gabled houses, hoping to lose him. The river was ahead, and the wharves; the shadows of the ships rose before me.

I came out on to the riverfront, on to the packed earth and wooden planking of the quay. Above my own breathing and the beating of my heart I heard the clink of mail and heavy footsteps following.

'This way!' the man shouted. I heard hooves, and understood that there was more than one of them chasing me.

Only one other street led up from the quay, and I could have run on, but it was clear that I could not outpace a man on horseback. There were a number of long sheds along the wharf, and I briefly considered hiding in one of them, but I would have to break in and it would then be obvious where I was. Of course there were the ships too, but I spotted figures asleep on the decks; often shipmasters would leave a part of their crew sleeping on board to ensure the vessels and their goods were not stolen, and I could not afford to wake them.

The sound of hooves grew louder. I ran to the far western end of the quay, closest to the bridge, where two ships were moored closely together, then, bracing myself for the cold, I slipped down between them, off the side.

I gasped in shock as I slid into the water. It was far colder than I had thought possible and immediately I was struggling to keep my head above the surface, to free myself from the thick cloak, which was weighing me down; but I knew if I made too much noise they would spot me and all would be lost.

There was a slight gap between the quayside and the ships' hulls, and it was through this gap that I saw them now. There were two of them: the man I had been fighting and another, mounted, whose face was in shadow. Both were looking around and I was sure it would not be long before one of them would see me. I almost prayed they would, for the cold was seeping into my arms and legs; I could feel them tiring already and I knew I would not be able to stay in the water for long.

'He's gone,' said the one on horseback. His was a deeper voice.

'Bastard,' said the other.

They disappeared from view, moving on down the quay, still speaking.

'Have you seen anyone come this way?' I heard the mounted one call.

'Not tonight, my friend.' One of the ship-men, perhaps.

The man on the horse cursed, and I heard the two knights talking to each other though the words were no longer distinct. I kept as still as I could; there was a little ridge of rock where I could put my feet. All feeling in my hands and arms was gone, and I found myself gasping, as if the cold had stolen all the air from my chest. The black water lapped around my chin, some of it finding its way up and into my open mouth, and I had to swallow it so as not to choke. I closed my eyes, willing the two men to leave.

It seemed like an eternity but eventually the voices ceased and distantly I heard hooves clattering on the planking, riding away. I could not delay, or else I was sure the waters would drag me down. I swam along the side of one of the ships to where there were steps set into the wharf, looking about to make sure that the two men had left.

There was no one. Clumsily, with hands that were all but numb, I managed to haul myself out of the river, dripping, shivering. Snow whirled about me. I spat on to the ground.

'Hey! Who are you?'

I turned; it was one of the ship-men, standing at the stern of his vessel, holding a lantern. I ignored him and ran, clothes plastered against my skin, and I did not stop running until I reached the house.


CHAPTER TWENTY

I burst into the hall, sending the door crashing against the inside of the wall. The snow billowed around me as, shaking violently, I stumbled in. My breath caught in my chest. I hadn't realised how far it was back from the wharves.

I closed the door fast against the outside and lifted the thick timber plank that rested against the wall. My arms protested, drained of all their strength, as I set the bar in place across the door. A large brass key rested in the lock and I tried to turn it, but there was little feeling in my fingers and it slipped from my grasp, falling with a dull clang on to the flagstone paving. I cursed out loud but did not stoop to pick it up, instead making my way straight to the hearth. There was a stack of firewood beside it; I picked up several of the smallest pieces, casting them liberally on to the embers, and huddled down on the stool in front of them. I needed fire. I needed warmth.

'What's going on?'

I looked over my shoulder as Eudo sat up, rubbing his eyes. I wondered what I must look like, wet and trembling by the fire, but only briefly, for the cold was seeping into my bones.

'Fetch me a dry tunic,' I said, my jaw quivering. 'Braies and a cloak too.'

He saw me properly then and got quickly to his feet. 'What happened?' he asked.

'First get me some dry clothes,' I said, as I stripped off my tunic and undershirt and cast them on to the floor. A few tiny flames began to lick at the dry wood I had added; I blew on them to encourage them, trying to will them larger as I tossed more pieces on. I gathered up some of the rushes from the floor in my arms and added them to the smouldering pile. They were dry and ought, I hoped, to burn easily.

Stepping over the sleeping forms of the other knights, Eudo went to where my pack lay beside the round table, and fumbled inside. Wace sat up, dazed and blinking, while the three younger men began to stir. Light appeared, bobbing down the stairs. It was the steward, a candle in his hand.

'I heard noise,' he said, frowning. His bald pate gleamed in the firelight. 'Is everything all right?'

I rose from the stool as Eudo brought me my

spare clothes, and his own cloak. 'I was set upon,' I said. 'In the streets by St Eadmund's church.'

The steward stopped where he was, clearly confused by my appearance, as he looked me up and down. 'You were—?'

I pulled the dry tunic over my head. 'I was attacked. By another knight.' I belted up the cloak while I waited for the impact of that to settle. 'A Frenchman,' I added.

'A Frenchman?' Wace asked, through the middle of a yawn.

'You must have been mistaken,' Eudo said.

'No,' I replied. 'I saw him. I heard him speak.'

Eudo shook his head. 'Why would a fellow Frenchman attack you? Especially in the king's own city.'

'It's the truth,' I said, and turned away as I unlaced my wet braies, letting them fall to the floor. The air was cold against my bare skin, and I hastily tugged on the dry pair. Straightaway I imagined I could feel the heat returning to my legs, the blood beginning to course through them once more.

I turned to the steward even as I finished lacing the braies up. 'Where's Ælfwold?' I asked him.

'Asleep in his room, I should think,' Wigod said.

'Are you sure?'

The steward looked at me, puzzled. 'What do you mean?'

If Ælfwold was missing, then I could be almost sure that it was him I had seen with the priest. 'Wake him,' I said.

'Why, are you hurt?'

After everything that had followed, I had all but forgotten about the fight and the blow I had taken

259

to the cheek. I pressed a hand to it; my fingers came away warm and smeared with crimson, but I was too numb to feel any pain.

'Just bring him here,' I said.

While Wigod hurried away to find the chaplain, I related to the rest what had happened: how I had been unable to sleep and had gone for a walk to clear my head; how suddenly I had found a knife at my throat; how I had managed to fight off my attacker; how I was chased down to the wharves; how I'd had to jump into the river to evade them. I did not mention anything about the two men I had seen speaking by the church, or that one of them I had thought to be Ælfwold; on that matter I wanted to confront him in person.

Besides, now that I had sat down and my heart was no longer beating quite so fast, I found that doubts were beginning to form in my mind. After all, it had been dark and I was tired; the man had had his back to me and I hadn't been able to see clearly through the snow.

'What did your attacker look like?' Eudo asked.

'He was tall, with a scar above his left eye,' I said. 'His hair was cut in the Norman style; in all he looked about five years older than me.' I ran my finger across my cheek again. The flesh stung this time and I winced. 'He was a good fighter, too.'

'And what about the other—the one on horseback?'

I shook my head. 'I didn't see him well enough.'

There were footsteps on the staircase and the steward returned, this time with two servants. One of them was Osric, the other a boy I had not seen before, shorter and, it appeared, younger, with dark hair that was a tangle of curls.

'He'll be with us shortly,' Wigod said, which surprised me a little, as I had thought he would have found the chaplain missing. But on the other hand I had been gone some while; he would have been able to return to the house long before me. I felt my heart begin to pound; at least I would have the chance to challenge him in person. I wanted an explanation.

The two boys saw to the fire, and soon it was burning fiercely again, though a chill had taken hold of my body and I realised I was still shivering. Osric went and came back in with two iron pails filled with water, which he suspended on the spit over the flames.

'Bring me some food,' I said to him.

He looked back at me with a blank expression on his face, and I recalled that he did not speak French. I looked to Wigod despairingly.

'*Breng him mete and drync,*' the steward said loudly. Osric grunted and hurried away through a door at the end of the hall.

'Do you know why he attacked you?' Wace asked.

I shrugged, though it was clear to me that whatever business the two churchmen had had, they had not meant it to be witnessed by anyone else. The two knights had to be in the pay of one of them. I couldn't think of any other explanation which made sense.

'He might have been drunk,' I suggested, though I was fairly sure that he was not.

Wace frowned, his good eye narrowing, the other all but closing, so that if I hadn't known better I might have thought he were winking at me. 'Did you provoke him?' he asked.

'Provoke him?' I choked off a laugh. 'I didn't

even see him.' That at least was true enough. 'The first I knew of him was his knife at my throat—'

Ælfwold emerged from upstairs and I broke off. I rose sharply from my stool—too sharply, for a sudden dizziness overtook me. My feet felt uncertain of their grounding and I had to put a hand out against one of the hall's wooden pillars to steady myself.

The chaplain was dressed in the same tunic and trews he had worn on the road; his hair was loose and stuck up in tufts from his head. 'What's the matter?' He looked at me and stopped, and he must have noticed my cheek for a look of concern spread over his face. 'You're wounded,' he said.

'I was attacked,' I said flatly. 'Tonight, by St Eadmund's church.' I watched him carefully, in case my mention of the place yielded a response, but his face did not so much as flicker.

'Attacked?' he asked.

I did not reply, still trying to determine from his expression whether there was anything he might be concealing, but I found nothing.

'By another knight,' put in Eudo.

The chaplain's eyes opened wide. 'Is this true?'

'It's what I said, isn't it?' I asked.

'Do you know who it was? The name of his lord?'

I stared back at him, searching. Either he was able to control himself far better than most men, or truly it had not been him. 'No,' I said eventually.

'How did this happen?'

Osric came back in, carrying in one hand a wooden platter with bread and some kind of meat, and in the other an iron pot with an arched handle, which he hung over the hearth. He placed the platter down beside the stool; my stomach gave a

262

low rumble, but I ignored it for the moment.

'How it happened isn't important,' I said. A flash of pain ran through my cheek, and I put my hand to it.

'Are you still bleeding?' Ælfwold asked as he approached.

'It's nothing,' I replied, stepping away from the wooden post and sitting back down on the stool. 'No more than a scratch.' If it wasn't Ælfwold I had seen earlier, then who was it? Who had hired those men?

'It looks deep. Let me see it.' He squatted down beside me, digging out a small cloth from his pocket and raising it slowly up to my cheek.

'It's nothing!' I repeated, wrenching away from him and towards the hearth.

He drew back, and from the look of sheer confusion that crossed his face I knew that it could not have been him. Anger flared up inside me and I felt suddenly foolish. I had thought to accuse a priest, a man of God and the Church, who had helped me recover after my fever only three weeks before. The same priest who was chaplain and confessor to the man who was now my lord.

The hall fell silent but for the water bubbling on the hearth and the crackling of the logs beneath. I felt the eyes of the others upon me, and wondered what they must be thinking.

'It's nothing,' I said again, more quietly this time. I sat down again on the stool beside the fire, tore off a corner of the bread and dipped it into the broth heating in one of the iron pots. 'I just need to eat, and then to rest. We have another few days' travel ahead of us.'

I took a bite of the bread. The broth it was

soaked in tasted of heavily salted fish, and while it was not especially pleasant, neither was it distasteful. It was warm and that was all I cared about, though perhaps the heat of my anger had done something to dispel the chill, for I found that I had stopped shivering. I ladled some more into a wooden bowl which Osric had brought, and lifted it to my lips, sipping it slowly.

'We should send word straightaway to the town-reeve,' said Wigod. 'We could bring a plea before the hundred court.'

'On what grounds?' the chaplain replied. 'There was no injury, short of a mark to the cheek.'

'Disturbing the king's peace,' Wace offered. 'Isn't that reason enough?'

'It would do no good,' said Ælfwold. 'Without at least a name to attach blame to, there can be no case.'

The steward sighed. 'You're right. And the court here in Lundene isn't due to sit for another two weeks.'

'By which time we'll have gone north with the king's army,' I said, defeated. I was no closer to knowing who any of those men were, and indeed it seemed had no way of finding out.

'I'll go to the reeve in the morning,' Wigod said, obviously sensing my frustration. 'For whatever that might be worth.'

The hall began to empty not long after that, and one by one the other knights fell back asleep, until once more I was the only one left awake. I sat by the fire for a while longer, drawing out the last of the cold, for it had worked itself deep into my bones. The two servants had brought in more wood from the store outside and I added it to the

264

hearth, keeping the flames roaring until my skin had dried completely. Eventually I let the fire be and I lay on my back upon the rushes, gazing at the whorls and splinters in the timber planks that made up the ceiling. My body ached and my limbs clamoured for rest, but my mind was still awake as I fingered the cross at my neck. I saw the fight clearly in my mind: every stroke of my blade, every parry, every thrust. It was then that I remembered I had left my sword behind. I was not going to fetch it then, however; that could wait until the day.

I had thought when we arrived in Lundene that in some small way I would be returning home. Now, though, I wanted nothing more than to be away from here.

Not far off, bells began to chime, marking the beginning of the matins service at one of the monasteries nearby. It could not have been much longer until I did manage to sleep, for in my dreams they were chiming also, and I was there with the monks in their cold stone church, and I was twelve years old again.

\*        \*        \*

We'd hoped to set off for Wiltune at first light, but the snow fell heavily that night, so heavily that in the morning it came halfway to my knee: a blanket across the whole city and the countryside beyond, making it impossible to travel.

I walked on my own, crunching my way down Wæclinga stræt, retaking my steps from the night before. I had left the others at the house, including Ælfwold, who protested when he caught me slipping out unannounced. It was too cold to be out, he said; far better that I stayed inside, where the fire was warm and I could take the time to recover. But save for the scrape I had taken during the fight I was feeling fine, and in any case I was in no mind to listen to the chaplain. I needed the time to think.

What men of the church employed knights to serve as their personal guards? The one I'd thought looked like Ælfwold was English: that much had been clear from his appearance. As for the priest in the black robes, I could not be sure, although if he was from Normandy then it was more likely that he was the one who had hired them, for few Frenchmen I knew would choose to serve an English lord.

Then again, these were no doubt men who made their living through selling their swords, without thought or scruple. Many such had at one time been oath-breakers, little better than murderers, since by severing those ties—the only things that bound people together—they had defied the natural order. Such men never questioned whom they served or for what purpose, so long as they were rewarded well—and that made them dangerous.

I stopped by the little wooden bridge that crossed the brook. Ice had formed around some of the larger rocks and the ducks were huddled together by its edge. Some had their heads tucked under their wings; others dipped the tips of their beaks into the fast-flowing water, as if testing it. None dared swim.

A bitter wind gusted from the east, piercing through my cloak. I pressed on, into the wind. Across the Temes, the land was a single field of white stretching from east to west, broken only by the cluster of houses that was Sudwerca, and by the woods that lined the distant horizon. In all the years I had spent growing up around Dinant, I had never seen snow like this; only since coming over to England had I known weather so cold.

I wasn't the first to be out that day. Already the street bore the marks where feet and wheels had pressed, though they were few. Smoke rose thickly from the chimneys of every house; most of the townsmen would still be inside by their fires, for the sun was just rising. Only when I came near St Eadmund's church again did people come into sight. Two boys drove a herd of pigs up the hill, poking them with sticks to keep them from stopping to dig in the snow. Further up, a man led a team of oxen hitched to a cart, the wheels of which wobbled violently as it trundled on. And there, waiting by the corner from where I had watched the two churchmen last night, were five men on horseback. Four of them were mailed and had spears in their hands, but the other wore a deerskin cloak covering a loose tunic with long, bunched sleeves. He was speaking with a decrepit woman who was clearly in some distress, since she was waving her arms violently, though for what reason I could not discern.

I paid them no more attention, for a glint of metal had caught my eye from the bottom of a rut, where a passing cart had carved its tracks. It was roughly where I remembered, to one side of the street. I rushed over and knelt down on the packed snow, clawing it away with my bare hands to reveal the whole length of the shining blade and the legend inscribed thereon: 'VVLFRIDVS ME FECIT'.

267

I lifted it free with both hands, then with my glove wiped the dirt off its underside as I examined it closely for signs of damage. It appeared to be in good condition, despite obviously having been run over. Snowmelt ran down the steel, causing it to gleam in the new day's light.

I heard a shriek and looked up to see the woman pointing a finger at me. '*Hwæt la!*' she screamed, and she glanced up at the five men on horseback. '*Hwæt la!*'

The men rode at a trot towards me; were they friends of those I had seen last night? I stood where I was, sword in hand, uncertain whether to run or to fight. I was on foot and there was no way I could get away from them even if I had wanted to. And five was more than I could hope to fight on my own. Two I might have handled, and on a good day even three—if I were less tired, perhaps, and luck were on my side.

'You,' said one of those in mail as he slowed to a halt. A red pennon was attached to his spear and I took him for their leader. His face was pockmarked, his chin covered with a sparse stubble. 'Who are you?'

The other three knights formed a half-circle around me, spears couched and ready under their arms. The other man, the one with the deerskin cloak, kept back, alongside the woman. He was dressed like an Englishman, his cloak clasped at the shoulder with a silver brooch, though his hair was cut short in the Norman style, and I guessed that he was an interpreter of sorts.

I thought about lying again, but something about their demeanour told me that would not be a good idea. 'Tancred,' I said stiffly. 'A knight in the employ of the vicomte of Eoferwic, Lord Guillaume Malet.'

'Malet?' He gave a short laugh. 'And what is a knight of his doing so far south, in Lundene? A deserter, are you?'

I was about to reply that if I were, I was hardly likely to tell him that, but thought the better of it. 'I'm here with the vicomte's chaplain.'

He raised an eyebrow. 'For what reason?'

It seemed clear that these men were not here to finish me off, or they would surely have done so already, and I was growing tired of his questions.

'Why should I tell you?'

A crowd was beginning to gather—of those men and women who were about at such an hour, at least. There were no more than a dozen of them, all standing at a respectful distance, I noted, for no doubt they had spotted that these men held swords.

The pock-faced knight drew himself up in his saddle and gestured towards the woman standing with the interpreter behind him. 'This peasant claims that she saw you here last night. Do you deny this?'

I said nothing. It hadn't even crossed my mind that I might have been seen.

'She swears that she saw you fighting,' he went on. 'Here, on this street, with another knight. Is this true?'

'I was attacked,' I burst out, which on reflection was not the wisest thing to say, for straightaway I knew he would take that as an admission of guilt, but I had committed myself and had no choice but to press on. 'I was defending myself.'

He lifted his head slightly, so that he looked at

269

me along the length of his nose. A faint smile spread across his face. 'Do you know', he asked, 'what the penalty is for bearing arms against another in the king's own city?'

'Tell me.'

'The penalty . . .' he said slowly, as if to ensure that I did not miss a word, 'is no less than the forfeiture of your sword-hand.'

I swallowed, and wondered whether this was the time to run. I knew it would be a useless gesture, though: they were mounted and would easily catch me, and it would only reinforce my guilt in their eyes.

'Give me your sword,' Pock-face growled.

I held it by the steel and carefully, so as not to cut myself, held it up to him, hilt first.

He looked questioningly down at me as he took it. 'You carry a naked blade in the streets,' he said.

'My scabbard is there,' I said, and I pointed to the patch of snow which now covered the place where I remembered dropping it.

He looked where I was pointing, and then back at me. The contempt in his eyes was clear.

'It's the truth,' I insisted. 'Everything I have said is the truth.'

'You will come with us,' he said. He gave the signal to two of his men, who swung down from their saddles and grabbed me roughly by the shoulders. I tried to shake them off but they held firm, twisting my arms behind my back.

'Malet will hear of this,' I said through gritted teeth as they began to march me up the street. 'He will have *your* sword-hands, I swear it.'

'Wait!' a voice called.

The knights stopped. I turned my head, though

my shoulders were held. The voice had come from amongst the crowd.

The circle of onlookers parted as a man, dressed in a fine-looking cloak of black wool, rode forward. His face was angular, his nose prominent; he looked about the same age as myself or a little older. I had the feeling that I had seen him before, but I could not place when or where. He sat tall in the saddle as he came towards us. From his belt hung a scabbard, decorated along its length with scarlet gemstones, with an intricate design of golden lines weaving between and around each one.

'What's your name?' he asked me, his voice stern. Behind him rode a man of more modest dress—a servant, I presumed. He was thin, with a large boil on the side of his neck and skin so pale that I wondered if he hadn't ventured outside of doors in some while.

'Lord,' said Pock-face. 'If you will forgive us, we are taking this man to the town-reeve. He is not to be spoken to—'

'My name is Tancred a Dinant, lord,' I interrupted him.

The man fixed his eyes upon me, though not in an unfriendly manner. 'You know my father?'

'Your father?' I said, before realising how it was that I recognised his face. Indeed now that I saw it, the resemblance was clear, not just in his angular features but also in his high brow and the slope of his shoulders.

'Guillaume Malet, seigneur of Graville across the sea. You know him?'

'I am a knight in his service, lord.' As far as I could recall, the vicomte had made no mention of

271

any son. Of course that by itself meant little, for why should he have done so?

'My lord,' said the pock-faced one, a note of despair in his voice. 'If I may say, this is not the time to be making idle conversation. We are—'

'What business do you have with him?' asked the man who called himself Malet's son.

'He is accused of bearing arms in anger against a fellow Frenchman.'

'You have witnesses to this?'

'We have one, lord,' said another of the knights, a portly and rough-kempt man who looked too large for his mount. He pointed towards the aged woman; she shrank back into the crowd.

'One witness,' Malet's son said. 'But she is English, and a woman at that.'

'Others can always be found,' Pock-face replied mildly. 'This is not a matter to be dismissed lightly.'

Malet's son turned to me. 'And what do you say? Did you bear arms against a countryman?'

I hesitated, tempted this time to deny the accusation outright, so that he might be more inclined to help me. But if I did that, then the others would see that I had openly perjured myself—an offence which was potentially as bad, if not worse than a breach of the peace.

'I was attacked, lord,' I said, repeating exactly what I had said before. 'I was only defending myself.'

He nodded slowly, and I felt my heart sink; that surely had been the wrong answer to give. He looked at his manservant, who merely blinked and shrugged in return. 'Have you considered that he may be speaking the truth?' he asked at last.

'Whether he is or not,' said Pock-face, 'he was seen using weapons in the king's own city!'

'And where is the man he was seen with? He can speak for himself, I presume.'

The knight opened his mouth, but then fell silent, instead glancing about the rest of his men.

'Well? Where is he?'

'My lord, he is not—'

'So,' said Malet's son, his voice suddenly harsh, 'neither do you have true witnesses to this event, nor, as far as I can see, was harm done to anyone present here.' He turned to the men flanking me. 'Release him.'

'You cannot do this,' said Pock-face.

Malet's son glared at him. 'I will do what I wish, or else I will go to your lord, the town-reeve, and inform him of your insolence. Now release him,' he repeated with greater force. 'I'll deal with him myself.'

Pock-face said nothing as he stood still as stone, his face reddening. Eventually he waved an arm and his two men lifted their hands from me, before remounting their horses. I glared at each of them as I rubbed my forearm, easing the pain where they had twisted it.

'Give him back his sword,' Malet's son said.

Pock-face's eyes were seething as he tossed it down. It landed in the snow; I bent down to pick it up and watched as the five men began to ride off back up the street, in the direction of the markets at Ceap.

Pock-face was the last to leave. 'The reeve will know of this,' he called.

'As well he might. And when you tell him, make sure to mention the name of Robert Malet. If he pleases, he may take the matter up with me.'

Pock-face snarled and then dug his heels in, riding back to join his men. The crowd had swelled in numbers since last I saw; several dozen had now come out of their houses to watch.

'Go,' Robert said to them, waving an arm at the same time to send them away. He leant down from his mount to speak to me. 'I'll seek an explanation for all of this in due course. For now, however, we should return to my father's house.' He glanced about. 'You have brought a horse with you?'

'No, lord,' I replied.

'Then, Tancred a Dinant, we shall walk.' He swung down from his saddle, and then signalled for his manservant to do the same as he patted his mount on the neck and took up the reins.

I nodded, not knowing what more to say. For I now owed debts to two members of the Malet house, and neither, I sensed, would be easily paid.

## CHAPTER TWENTY-ONE

The sun was creeping above the marshlands to the east, shrugging off its veil of wispy cloud, tingeing the eastern skies yellow. Beneath it, Lundene was waking.

Already the streets were growing busier: there were women carrying wooden pails; men with firewood under their arms. A group of children shrieked as they ran after each other with clods of snow in their hands, almost colliding with two burly men carrying large sacks over their shoulders. Down on the river, some of the smaller craft were putting to sail, making their way out towards the estuary and the sea beyond.

My sword-belt was buckled on my waist once more, and I was glad to feel my scabbard by my side. Malet's son walked alongside me, reins in hand, his manservant trailing close behind with his own horse.

'What news do you have of my father?' he asked as soon as we had left the crowds behind us.

'You haven't heard?'

'I've heard nothing since we sailed from Normandy yesterday,' he said. 'What is it?'

I stopped by the edge of the narrow street to make way for an ox-cart which was coming up the hill. 'The news isn't good, lord,' I said as the beasts plodded past us, clouds of mist erupting from their nostrils. I told him everything that Wigod had said the evening before: how the rebels had broken into the city, killed three hundred men and forced the vicomte to retreat to the castle. 'So I've been told, at least,' I said. 'The king is even now gathering an army to march north.'

Robert looked to the sky, and then closed his eyes. His lips moved but made no sound; no doubt he was saying some prayer. 'When we left Saint-Valery yesterday morning, all we knew was that the city was still under siege,' he said at last. 'But my father lives?'

'As far as I know,' I said. 'Your sister and mother too—they're here in Lundene.'

'They're here?' Robert asked, wide-eyed suddenly. 'You know that for certain?'

'I was the one your father charged with escorting them,' I said. 'I brought them from Eoferwic, along with your father's chaplain, Ælfwold. They're all at his townhouse.'

'Ælfwold too,' he murmured. 'I haven't seen him in a long while.' He took a deep breath and turned to face me, clapping a firm hand on my back. 'That is easily the best thing I've heard in the last few days. I owe you my thanks, Tancred.'

'As I owe you mine, lord.'

'Tell me,' he said, smiling as we began to walk once more, 'how long have you been in my father's service?'

I counted back in my head. 'Eight days, lord,' I said, and for some reason felt embarrassed to say it, for it felt far longer. But it was true: it had been the fifteenth day of the month when the vicomte had called me to his chamber at the castle, and it was now still only the twenty-third.

'Eight days?' he asked, with a look of disbelief.

'Before then I was sworn to the Earl of Northumbria, Robert de Commines,' I explained, holding his gaze. My throat was dry. 'That was until Dunholm.'

He nodded gravely for a moment, his brow furrowed. 'Eight days ago I was minding affairs back at home in Graville. Even then the Northumbrian rebels seemed but a distant threat. Yet now I return here to find that my father's very life is in danger. You see, Tancred, how quickly both our lives have been changed by recent events. There is much that we have in common.'

My fingers tightened into a ball. How could he compare his troubles to my own grief? At least Malet was still alive. But I remembered how I had been just as insensitive towards Beatrice and Elise back on board the ship, and so held my tongue.

We trudged on down the street. Snow slid in

drifts off the roofs to either side, exposing the thatch beneath. Men and women approached us, trying to sell us bundles of firewood, or shrivelled carrots that were almost as pale as the snow, but I waved them all away.

'It's good to be in Lundene at last,' Malet's son said. 'It has been a long journey. The moment I heard that Eoferwic was under siege, I began making the preparations to sail. We left Graville that same afternoon. That was three full days ago; bad weather prevented us sailing any sooner.' He shook his head. 'And all that time we could only wait, praying to God to preserve my father.'

It was not as long a journey as ours from Eoferwic had been, but I did not say it. If anything he should have been thankful that he hadn't been delayed more than he was; February was not the best time of the year to make the crossing. I had often heard it said that the Narrow Sea was changeable: that what looked at sunrise like calm water could by midday turn into a maelstrom. And they were lucky, too, if they had missed the snow that had fallen here, since it would have been impossible to sail through such conditions.

We soon arrived back at the house. The same servant who had guarded the door on our arrival was there again now; he and Robert's retainer led their mounts around to the stables at the back.

Inside, the rest of the knights had risen and were seated around the hearth as they broke their fast on cheese and bread. The chaplain sat at the table, sipping quietly from a cup as he squinted at a sheet of parchment. He looked up as we entered, almost dropping the cup in surprise as he saw Malet's son. He threw out his arms as he got to his feet, and they greeted each other like old friends, speaking in both English and French, until Wigod came in and Ælfwold hurried to find the two ladies.

I sat down beside Wace and Eudo, taking off my gloves and warming my fingers by the flames.

Wace poured me some beer into a cup. 'Who is this?' he asked, nodding his head towards the newcomer.

'The vicomte's son,' I said. 'Robert Malet.'

'I didn't realise Malet even had a son,' Eudo said.

'Nor did I,' I replied, and glanced up at Robert, who was speaking with the steward.

'It's certainly good to be back in this house,' he said, gesturing animatedly at everything around him: at the hearth-fire, the wall-hangings, the ceiling. 'The last time I was here was for King Guillaume's coronation.'

'I'll admit I didn't think it had been that long,' Wigod said. 'Two years is quite some time—'

He broke off at the sound of quick footsteps on the stairs. Beatrice came rushing down, dressed in a dark green gown, her skirts raised just above her ankles. She caught sight of her brother and straightaway burst into delighted laughter, running across and flinging her arms around him. Her mother was not far behind and soon joined in the embrace.

I turned away. I was not much used to families, and the sight of them all together was more than I wanted to see. Mauger, Ernost, Ivo, Fulcher, Gérard: they had been my brothers, in life as well as in arms; the closest to a family I had ever known.

*You live by the sword*, Aubert had told me, back when we were on the ship, just after we had fled

Eoferwic. Until now I hadn't realised how truly he spoke.

Beatrice released Robert and stepped back, smoothing down her skirts. The gown she wore was cut for her figure, embroidered with yellow thread on the bodice and down each of the sleeves, and I could not help but notice the swell of her breasts beneath it.

'When did you arrive?' she asked her brother, wiping a tear from her eye.

'We put in at Stybbanhythe at high tide, not an hour before dawn. I rode straight here with my manservant. He's seeing to our horses.'

'What about the rest of your men?' Wigod asked. 'Did you bring any over from Normandy?'

'A full twenty of my household knights, their horses following in a second ship. They were all I could muster in the time I had before we left. I came as soon as I heard—'

'And your brother?' Elise asked, cutting him off. 'Where is he?'

'I left him to manage affairs at home in my absence. I thought it unwise that he should risk himself as well. One of us had to stay.'

'You have heard, then, about Eoferwic and your father?' Ælfwold said, now that he had returned.

'Only since arriving here—Tancred told me all that has happened.' He looked to the two ladies. 'I hear he has been looking after you on the journey.'

Elise met my eyes. 'He was,' she answered, tight-lipped. In truth I had half expected to hear some word of thanks, now that we were in the presence of her son. I should have known better, though, for she said no more.

The priest looked puzzled. 'Tancred told you?'

he asked Robert.

'I found him up by one of the churches on the Bisceopesgeat hill,' Malet's son replied. 'He was there with some of Ernald's men. They were about to take him away, when I heard him mention my father's name. That was when I intervened. Their leader was not best pleased.'

The chaplain gave Wigod a glance, then he looked sternly at me. 'You ran into the town-reeve's men,' he said, plainly unimpressed.

I shrugged. 'I'd gone to find my sword.'

'They had accused him of fighting in the streets,' Robert put in. 'Though they had no one able to swear on it.'

The steward sighed and shook his head. 'You should have waited until we had gone to the reeve ourselves.'

'So it's true, then?' Robert asked.

'It's true,' I said. 'I was attacked last night, on the same street on which we met today.' I sensed the stares of the two ladies upon me; of course they hadn't been here last night when I came back. 'There were two of them—one on horseback, the other on foot.' I put a finger to my cheek, feeling for the line of dried blood, showing them where I had been cut. 'It was one of them who gave me this. I was fortunate to get away with my life.'

I caught Beatrice's gaze as I looked up, and saw a hint of concern in her eyes, though it was only the briefest of flickers before she bowed her head.

'It is a serious matter,' the steward said as he rubbed the bald patch on his head. 'I was going to see the reeve myself this morning to report it. But now it seems that he already knows.'

'I'll deal with him if he comes,' said Robert,

shrugging. 'I told his men that he could pursue the matter with me.'

'You should be careful how you treat with him. To those who oppose him, he can be dangerous. He holds considerable influence with the king.'

'My father is the vicomte of the shire of Eoferwic, one of the most powerful men in the kingdom.'

'Even so,' Wigod said, 'it is better to have him as a friend than as an enemy.'

The hall fell quiet, the steward's words hanging like smoke in the air.

'Come,' Elise said with a smile, and she began to walk towards the stairs. 'We shall go to our chambers. You must tell us about the crossing, tell us what news you bring from home.'

Robert made to follow her. 'I fear there is little to say, but very well. You must also tell me of your journey.' He bent down as he passed me. 'I would speak with you later,' he said, his voice low as he spoke in my ear.

He straightened and walked away, and I wondered what he meant. I had already told him what the town-reeve's knights had wanted with me. What more was he after?

I let out a yawn; I had hardly slept last night again. Indeed I could not remember the last time I'd had a full night's rest with four walls and a roof around me, rather than under canvas, on the hard earth. It was longer than a week—that much was certain.

Eudo gave me a nudge. 'Wake up.' He picked up a loaf from on top of the hearthstones and held it out towards me. 'Here, eat.'

It occurred to me that I had not yet eaten that

morning, but I did not feel hungry. In fact the smell of the bread, fresh baked by the fire, made my stomach turn.

'I don't want it,' I said, pushing it away.

He shrugged and began to eat it himself, pausing once in a while to pick some grit out of his teeth.

'Are you going to tell us what happened, then?' Wace asked.

'For what it's worth,' I said. 'There isn't much to say.' And I explained to them the events of that morning.

'You shouldn't have gone alone,' Eudo said, frowning, after I had finished.

I heard footsteps behind me and looked up to see the chaplain standing there.

'I'm not interrupting, I hope,' he said.

I got to my feet. 'What is it, father?'

He looked about at all six of us, the light from the fire playing softly across his face. 'I wished only to say, given that the snow is unlikely to clear today, it might be best if we wait until tomorrow to leave for Wiltune.'

'This message of yours isn't urgent, then,' Eudo said, his mouth full of bread.

'It can afford to wait one more day,' Ælfwold said. 'But I want us to leave at dawn tomorrow.'

He stepped away, towards the door at the far end of the hall, gesturing for me to follow him. I frowned, not understanding what he meant, and glanced at the other knights, but they were talking amongst themselves, and so finally I followed him.

'I sense there's something troubling you,' he said, once we were far away from the others.

He was right, of course, there were many things that had been troubling me of late. But I wasn't ready to speak with him yet; after what had happened last night I still felt uneasy around him.

'I'm just tired,' I said.

He narrowed his eyes. 'If you're quite sure.'

'I'm sure,' I answered.

The Englishman didn't look convinced, but he placed a hand on my shoulder. 'Remember that the Lord is always listening, if ever you wish to speak to him.'

'I'll remember,' I said. With everything that had happened recently, I had managed to neglect my prayers.

'That's good.' He let go and stepped away. 'For now I must go and discuss matters with Robert. However, if you wish, we might talk later.'

'Perhaps.' I didn't think there was anything more I had to say to him. I felt another yawn building and did my best to stifle it.

He nodded. 'Very well.'

He turned and crossed the hall towards the stairs, and I made my way back to the hearth, where the fire was still burning strongly.

'What was that about?' Eudo asked.

'Nothing important,' I said, and yawned as I sat back down on my stool.

'Nothing to concern us, you mean.' He was glaring at me, his face half in shadow from the firelight, his eyes unfriendly.

'What?' I looked at him for a moment, confused as to what he meant, but he said no more, merely returning a bitter gaze.

Wace stood up and I turned to him, breaking off the uncomfortable stare. 'We're going to train at arms in the yard,' he said. 'Are you joining us?'

I shook my head. 'Later.' My limbs still ached

from the night before, and I did not feel awake enough to be of much use, even in a mock fight. 'I think I'll try to sleep some more.'

Wace nodded, buckling on his sword-belt, then went to the door at the back of the hall. Radulf, Philippe and Godefroi all followed. Eudo was the last to go, pausing as if he were about to say something to me, but then he seemed to think better of it, and stalked out after them.

I sat alone, wondering what I might have done to cause Eudo offence, but couldn't think of anything. Eventually I gave up, and for a while after that I tried to rest. The morning was wearing on by now, however, and the streets outside were filled with the sounds of animals and the shouts of men. At the same time I could hear the other knights in the yard behind the house, their laughter interrupted by the crash of oak against limewood.

Soon I abandoned any hope of sleep, sitting instead by the table in the hall, attending to my sword. Its edge had been blunted again during the fight, and where my sword had clashed with that of my opponent there were nicks in the blade. I tried to smooth them out as best I could with my whetstone, but he had struck hard and the steel was marked deep.

How long I sat there, sharpening the blade, entranced by the patterns in the metal, I did not know, before I heard the stairs creak and saw Robert descend.

'My lord,' I said.

'Tancred,' he replied. 'I expected to see you with your comrades outside. I could hear them from the chambers upstairs.' He gestured at the blade in my hands. 'That's a fine weapon.'

284

I placed it down on the table, the whetstone beside it. 'Your father gave it to me when I entered his service,' I said.

'I remember I had one much like it when I was younger. Nowadays, I prefer a quicker blade.' He drew his own from the gilded scabbard at his side and rehearsed a few cuts at the air. It was thinner than mine, and half a foot shorter too, with a more pronounced taper; in some ways it was more similar to the English seax in appearance. But I knew there would be no weight in such a weapon, weight one needed to batter down an enemy's shield, to slice through leather and mail. His was a thrusting blade, ideal when it came to close fighting, but of little use when mounted. I hoped it was not the only sword he owned.

He sheathed it again and sat down. 'Ælfwold tells me you'll be leaving again tomorrow.'

'For Wiltune,' I said. 'Your father has a message he wishes delivered there.'

His face bore a grim look. 'That is most like him,' he said, 'sending his men on worthless errands even as the enemy presses at his gates. Do you know who this message is meant for?'

'No, lord.'

'Wiltune,' he said, absently picking at a splinter on the table. 'I can only think it must be for Eadgyth.'

'Eadgyth?' It was not a name I had heard before.

'She is a nun at the convent there,' Robert said, 'although previously she was much more.'

This was altogether new to me. Until now I had learnt nothing beyond what Malet had told me that day back at the castle. 'What do you mean, lord?'

The splinter came free; he flicked it aside. 'It

matters not,' he said, sighing. 'What matters is that you return in time for the relief of Eoferwic.'

'Of course,' I said, unsure whether he had even heard the question, and wondering whether it would be rude to ask it a second time. The chaplain was evidently not going to tell me anything, or he would have done so already. Therefore if Robert had even a hint of what the message might concern, I needed to know from him. 'My lord—'

'My sister and mother were telling me how you looked after them on the way from Eoferwic,' he said.

I felt myself tense. At least with Beatrice I felt that I had come to an understanding, but I did not expect Elise to have had anything favourable to say about me. 'What did they say?' I asked.

He must have sensed the wariness in my tone, for he laughed. 'There is no reason to be worried,' he said. 'I am well used to their exaggerations. They might be my own blood, but they are still only women, and not much used to hardship. But they are here and they are unharmed, and that—as far as I am concerned—is all that counts. Again I thank you.'

'I have no need of thanks, lord,' I said, though not out of modesty. I was here because of the debt I owed his father; I wasn't looking for reward.

'There is one other thing I wanted to discuss with you,' Robert said. 'These men who attacked you last night—do you know why they did so?'

'No, lord,' I said. It was the truth, for I had nothing more than my suspicions.

Robert studied me carefully, much as I recalled his father doing. His eyes were hard, revealing nothing. 'You didn't recognise them?' he asked. 'They had no feud with you?'

I shook my head. 'What difference does it make?'

'It intrigues me, that's all. For a knight to set upon a countryman in the streets, and without apparent reason, is more than unusual. But perhaps it's a riddle that will have to remain unanswered.'

'Yes, lord.'

He rose from his stool. 'Take care, Tancred,' he said. 'In these times it is all too easy to make enemies. Be careful that you don't make any more than you need.'


## CHAPTER TWENTY-TWO

The skies were only just growing light and a steady rain was falling as we gathered in the yard to prepare our mounts for the road. Ælfwold's horse, a dappled grey mare, was already saddled, but there was no sign of the priest himself, and none of the others had seen him when I asked them.

'I'll go and find him,' I said, trudging back towards the hall. The snow had all but melted, and the yard was thick with mud. Water pooled in every rut, every hollow, reflecting the leaden skies above.

The hour was yet early and the house was quiet, but I found Osric by the hearth, scraping out the ash from the previous night's fire. He looked up as I entered, his hair sticking out in tufts from beneath his cap, his hands and face grey with dust.

'Ælfwold,' I said loudly. *'Preost.'* It was one of the

few English words I knew.

Osric merely blinked; obviously he hadn't seen the chaplain either. I frowned. It was Ælfwold who had been most anxious to set off early.

I left the boy by the hearth as I made for the stairs at the far end of the hall. The chaplain's door was the first on the landing at the top. I knocked upon it, but there was no answer, and when I pushed, it opened easily, without a sound.

He was not there. A wooden plate with bread half-eaten stood on the floor beside a cup of wine and small lantern; a woollen coverlet lay crumpled upon the bed. The shutters were open, letting in a chill draught, and I went to close them, my mail hauberk and chausses clinking as I did so. The room faced over the Walebroc, which ran beside the house, though its view was partly blocked by the thick branches of the oak that stood outside the window: the kind of tree that in my youth I had loved to climb, with branches that were evenly spaced, and knots on its bark that made for good handholds.

'Tancred,' a voice came from behind me.

I turned with a start. Beatrice was standing in the doorway. I hadn't even heard her approach.

'My lady,' I said. 'You're risen early.'

'As soon as I heard you all outside I knew I wouldn't be able to sleep any longer,' she replied.

'We didn't mean to wake you.'

'It doesn't matter,' she said, waving her hand dismissively. 'You're looking for Ælfwold, I assume.'

'Have you seen him?'

'He's in the kitchens, fetching provisions for the road. Robert is with him, I think. He wanted to see you on your way.'

At least he had not gone far. The days were still short and so we had to make the best use of them. The sooner we left, the better.

'Thank you,' I said, closing over the shutters and making for the door. Beatrice didn't move, but stood blocking my path.

'I have to go, my lady,' I said, and tried to edge past her, through the narrow doorway.

She placed her hand upon the sleeve of my hauberk. 'Wait,' she said, and I turned. 'I never had a chance to thank you properly for the other night. For staying with me. For not leaving, even when I asked you to.'

I shrugged. 'I could hardly have left you on your own, in the middle of the woods. I swore to your father that I would protect you, and I intend to honour that pledge.'

'All the same,' she said, reaching out, touching the back of my hand, intertwining her fingers with my own, 'you should know that I'm grateful.'

I looked into her soft, smiling eyes. From down in the hall came Wace and Eudo's voices—wondering where I was, no doubt. I heard the chaplain greet them, and Robert too.

'They're waiting for me,' I said.

She did not say anything but lifted her other hand to my cheek, gently running her fingers along the cut. The skin was still tender, and I winced inwardly as it stung, but resisted the urge to pull away. Something like a shiver ran through me; I could feel my heart thumping despite myself. I tried not to think what the priest might say if he happened upon us now.

'Be safe,' she said, and before I could reply she

leant towards me, standing up on her toes, pressing her lips to the spot where her hand had just been. It was the lightest of touches, but it lingered there, for how long I could not say, and when she drew back, I could feel the moisture that was left.

She squeezed my hand. 'Take care, Tancred.'

My throat was dry and I swallowed, wondering what had just happened. 'I will, my lady.'

My fingers slipped through hers as she let go, and then straightaway I was turning, my cheeks burning as I started down the stairs. After I had descended a few steps I paused to look back over my shoulder, but she had already gone.

*       *       *

Robert was there to see us leave, just as Beatrice had said. He had on the same black cloak he'd worn yesterday, this time with tunic and braies to match. His scabbard, with its red and gold decoration, was the only mark of colour on his person.

'We hope to return within the week,' Ælfwold told him.

Robert nodded as he looked from the chaplain to me, and then to Eudo and Wace, and the rest of his father's knights. 'I don't know how long it will be before the king intends to march, but if I'm gone when you return, ride north on Earninga stræt and look for the black and gold. I have only twenty men with me; I'll be glad of another six.'

'We will, lord,' I said, but at the same time felt my spirits sink. When I pictured it in my mind, I saw myself leading the charge, as I had at Dunholm and countless times before, but I no

290

longer commanded a conroi of my own, I remembered; the only men under my authority were the five with me now. It was in numbers that the charge found its strength: in the weight of horse and mail it could bring to bear upon the enemy. Which meant that we would have to fight under the banner of Robert Malet—and under his orders rather than my own.

'We'll be praying for your father's safety,' the chaplain said.

'As will I, Ælfwold,' Robert answered. 'I wish you a safe journey.'

We bade him farewell and rode away, up the hill and away from the river. The road widened as we came upon the markets at Ceap, where the traders were setting up their stalls. Baskets lined the side of the street, some full of fish, no doubt fresh from the river; others held crabs, and they were even fresher, for many of them were still alive, clambering over each other in sideways fashion as they tried to escape. Further along, a man lifted wicker cages packed with scrawny chickens down from his cart. Merchants, recognising us for Frenchmen, called to us in our own tongue, trying to sell us rolls of Flemish wool-cloth, or flagons of Rhenish wine.

We rode on past them, towards the city's western gates and beyond. The road followed the line of the Temes as it curved around to the south, towards Westmynstre church and the royal palace. A number of boats were moored there, from small barges to great longships. Among the latter I recognised *Mora*, King Guillaume's own ship—the very one, indeed, in which he had sailed from Normandy during the invasion. There were few vessels known to be larger; at thirty-three benches she was longer even than *Wyvern*. Today she was at rest and sat high in the water, empty of all but a few men. Had she been out on the water I knew she would have been more impressive still. I could readily imagine her great sail, decorated in the king's colours of red and yellow, billowing in the breeze.

On the higher ground beyond Westmynstre stood hundreds of tents, with banners of every hue flying high above: reds and greens, blues and whites. A wooden stockade had been erected on the slopes beneath the camp, forming an enclosure within which all the horses of the king's host were gathered. How many men were encamped there, I could not say. Wigod had said that the king had eight hundred with him, and to judge by the number of tents and banners, that seemed about right. But even if all of those were fighting men, which was doubtful, it did not look like an army that could take back Eoferwic.

I breathed deeply but said nothing, though I glanced at Wace and saw his expression, and knew that he was thinking the same.

The Temes wound away to the south and we found ourselves amidst recently ploughed fields and rolling hills covered in woodland. The country all about lay silent, save for the calls of birds in the distance, the creaking of branches in the wind, and the crunch of small stones under our horses' hooves. Every so often we met other travellers: peasants driving their animals to market in Lundene; pedlars and merchants; a group of monks with brown hoods. The further from the city we travelled, however, the less we saw of such

292

people, and the more we were alone.

My mind kept returning to my conversation with Robert and his mention of the nun, Eadgyth. She was once much more than just a nun, he had said. Did he mean that she and Malet had once been lovers? But even if that were so, why send to her now?

I was jolted from my thoughts by Eudo and Radulf laughing as they exchanged bawdy jokes. I glanced behind me, trying to catch Eudo's eye, but he merely ignored me. He had hardly spoken to me since yesterday; in fact he had spent the rest of that day away from the house, probably across the bridge in Sudwerca, although he never told us. Only as we were breaking our fast did he at last come back. He gave no reason for his absence, and when he looked at me his eyes were hard, his mouth set firm, as if in disgust.

'What's wrong with Eudo?' I asked Wace, when we stopped at noon.

'Maybe you should ask him,' he said.

I had no wish to start an argument, though. Whatever the reason for Eudo's foul mood, I knew that it would soon pass: it usually did. And so I ignored him as the seven of us sat beneath the drooping arms of an old oak and ate what food Wigod had provided us with: bread and cheese and salted bacon. Ælfwold made sure we did not linger long, however, reminding us that we still had many miles to make, and so shortly after we had finished we returned to our horses.

I was placing my flask in my saddlebag while beside me the chaplain mounted up, when I saw something drop from his cloak pocket. He did not seem to notice as he began slowly to make his way back towards the path, following the others who were laughing between themselves.

'Ælfwold,' I called, raising my hand to catch his attention.

It was a parchment scroll, about the same length as the distance from my elbow to my wrist, tightly bound with a simple leather thong. I crouched down and picked it up from where it lay on the grass. It felt crisp and new, although the parchment was not the best: the surface was not even but grainy, while the sides were rough where the sheet had been cut from the edge of the animal's skin.

The chaplain turned the mare about and rode back over towards me, a frown upon his face all of a sudden. 'Give that to me,' he said.

I held the scroll out to him; he reached down and took it carefully, watching me all the time as he replaced it inside his cloak.

'What is it?' I asked him.

'Nothing,' he said. 'Nothing important, at least.' He gave a smile, though I could not detect any humour behind it. 'Thank you, Tancred.'

He turned and started to ride away. I stood there for a moment, puzzled by the change in his manner.

'Are you coming?' Wace called from the road.

I looked up, blinking as the glare of the sun struck my eyes. There was something important about that scroll: that much was clear, at least. And I couldn't help but connect it with this mission of his, this journey to Wiltune and Eadgyth. But what reason would Malet have for sending to a nun in any case, and to an English nun at that?

'I'm coming,' I muttered, mounting up at last.

Like Earninga stræt, this was one of the ancient roads, and made for easy riding, which meant that we covered many miles that day. Nevertheless, the sun was growing low and bright in the sky ahead of us by the time we arrived at the Temes again. The river was narrower here than when we had last seen it back near Lundene, but the waters were high and the current fast, swelled by the snowmelt running down from the hills. A stone bridge traversed it; on the other side a scattering of houses nestled beside a small timber church, while amidst the reeds at the water's edge a number of small rowing boats had been drawn up on to the shore.

'Stanes,' Ælfwold said, when I asked him the name of the place. 'Over on the other side lies Wessex, the ancient heartland of the English kings.'

'Wessex,' I murmured to myself. How far we had come, I thought: from Northumbria to here, the southernmost province which made up the kingdom of England. It had belonged once to the usurper Harold, before he had seized the crown. Now it lay under the charge of Guillaume fitz Osbern, who was one of the realm's leading noblemen, alongside Malet—and Robert de Commines, I thought, before I remembered.

We had come upon many other villages that day. Some were larger, some were smaller, but all were alike in character, inhabited by gaunt and sullen peasants who spat on the ground as we passed by. I wondered whether they had heard of events in the north, and what that might mean to them. Of course it might not concern them at all; Eoferwic was two hundred miles and more from here. In any

295

case, they could spit and stare as much as they wanted. I knew they would not harm us, for we had horses and mail and swords, and they did not.

That night we spent in our tents, a short way off the road. It was a fitful sleep, though, for I dreamt again of Oswynn, except that her face was shrouded in darkness, and every time I tried to come near her, she melted away into nothing. More than once I woke to find myself breathing hard, sweat running from my forehead, and though I managed to return to sleep each time, it was always to the same dream. When morning came I felt as if I had hardly rested.

The hills lay thick with the night's frost, and for some time after we resumed our journey we travelled through a landscape glistening white as the fields of heaven. Soon, however, the rime began to melt, the clouds passed in front of the sun, and as the horses settled into their rhythm, so the day wore on. Hour after hour we passed fields and farms nestled amidst gently sloping hills, and it struck me that the country here was not so different from that in Normandy or Flanders. More than once I found myself gazing out across a certain valley or forest, only to be reminded of somewhere I had known in my youth, and for a moment I could imagine myself there once again. But of course it was never quite the same; most times we only had to go on over the next rise or merely beyond the next tree before its appearance suddenly changed and the feeling faded.

Close to midday the road climbed a steep hill, at the top of which we came upon crumbling stone walls and what looked as if it had once been a gatehouse. Its arch had long since collapsed; great blocks of lichen-covered stone, dressed and evenly shaped, littered the side of the way. As we passed within the gates I saw the remains where more buildings had once stood: neat rectangles and half-circles of stone foundations, many with trees and bushes growing in their midst. The air was almost still, the skies filled with shadows as rainclouds loomed overhead. Aside from the seven of us, there was no one.

'*Ythde swa thisne eardgeard,*' Ælfwold intoned as he looked about, '*ælda scyppend, oththæt burgwara breahtma lease, eald enta geweorc idlu stodon.*'

'Thus He, the creator of men, destroyed this city,' said Eudo, 'until, deprived of the sound of its inhabitants, the ancient work of giants stood empty.'

I stared at him in surprise, not just since it was the most I had heard him say in a good many hours, but also because I hadn't known he could translate English so readily.

Ælfwold nodded solemnly. 'You are near enough. It is from a poem,' he explained to us. 'A poem of great sadness and loss, about things which were, but are no more.'

I dismounted, leaving my horse while I walked between the ruins of what must at one time have been houses. Not that there was any sign of those who had lived here; it was probably centuries since they had done so, and all their possessions would have long ago turned to dust.

Shards of slate were strewn across the grass, grey against green, but nestled among them I caught the tiniest glimpse of dull red. I crouched down to get a closer look. It was a stone, cut into a rough cube not much wider than my thumbnail: much like the

297

dice that Radulf owned. I prised it out from the mud and turned its rounded edges between my forefinger and thumb, wiping the dirt from its surface, searching for any hint of markings, though I could see none. One face was smooth, but the rest were rough, encrusted with flakes of something like mortar, which crumbled away at my touch.

Another of the stones caught my eye, less than an arm's length away from where the first had lain, and I picked it up. It was identical both in size and in shape, although this one was black rather than red. I turned the two of them carefully in my fingers, wondering what they could have been used for.

'This place, I believe, is what we know in the English tongue as Silcestre, but which the Romans used to call Calleva,' Ælfwold said. 'In its time it was a great city; since its fall, however, none have dared live here nor attempt to rebuild it.'

I tossed the two stones back on to the ground and stood back up. 'Why would God punish them?' I asked. 'I thought the Romans were a Christian people.' Though it was a long time since I had been at my studies, I was certain of that much.

'They were,' said Ælfwold, unblinking and unsmiling. 'But they were also a sinful race, proud and weak in morals, who spent more of their time in pleasure than they did pursuing God's work. Too concerned with preserving their worldly wealth, they cared little for the future of their souls.' He gestured all around him at the shattered stones, the broken tiles, the empty town. 'What you see is the result of His retribution: a warning to all men not to follow the same example.'

298

For a while no one said anything. The wind began to gust and I felt a drop of water strike the back of my neck, trickling down my spine and causing me to shiver. Overhead, the skies were darkening still further; around us the ground pattered as the rain began to fall.

'We should find shelter,' Wace said.

'A good idea,' I replied.

The most substantial remains were of a larger building a little to the south, and it was there that we led our animals. There was nothing to which we could tether them, but they were unlikely to roam far, so we left them to graze upon the grass. We huddled down within the walls, which rose here as far as waist-height, offering some protection at least from the chill of the wind at it swept amidst the shattered stonework. There was no roof to keep out the rain, however; instead we sat with the hoods of our cloaks up, eating in silence.

We could have set up our tents, but it would have taken some while, and I did not want us to tarry here any longer than we had to. At one point I imagined I heard a whisper—some words spoken, though I could not make them out—and thought that the ghosts of those who had lived here were trying to speak to us, before dismissing the idea. Such things existed only in the minds of children and the mad, and I was neither of those.

Even so, to shelter as we were doing within the houses of the dead made me uneasy. I was glad when all had finished and we were back in the saddle, and finally we left that place of ruin, that city of the condemned, that symbol of God's vengeance.

# CHAPTER TWENTY-THREE

The rain fell throughout the rest of the day, sweeping in from the south and the west, driven by a gusting wind which only grew stronger as the afternoon went on. Greyness hung like a sheet across the sky, the cloud veiling the tops of the hills in the distance. By the time we stopped for the night, in a village nestled at the bottom of a valley, known to the local folk as Ovretune, my cloak was soaked through and my tunic clinging to my skin.

Much to our relief there was already a fire roaring in the alehouse when we arrived. We huddled around it, warming our fingers by the flames while platters of smoked trout and boiled vegetables and pitchers of wine were brought out to us by the innkeeper's wife. She was a thin woman, about the same age as Lady Elise, with chestnut-brown hair and a timid demeanour. Perhaps it was because she recognised most of us for Frenchmen and knights, or perhaps she was merely uneasy around strangers, but she kept her head bowed whenever she approached, as if the slightest glance might incur our wrath.

She reminded me in a way of my mother, the little that I could recall of her at least. It was not that they looked alike; as much as I tried, I could never picture my mother clearly. But I did remember the manner with which she carried herself—quiet and humble, and somehow always afraid—and as I watched this woman now, I felt that I could almost see her again, though it was near twenty years since I had known her.

We ate in silence, content simply to be indoors at last and to have food in our bellies. Gradually the common room filled with men, many of whom seemed to have come straight from the fields, their trews and tunics caked with mud. They kept to small groups, huddled over their cups, occasionally turning their heads in our direction as they muttered to one another in their own tongue. I'd become so used to the company of Ælfwold in recent weeks that it was strange to see such men speaking without a single word of French. I was suddenly aware that we were the only ones in the room who were not English. My fingertips brushed against the cold hilt of my sword beneath my cloak; I pulled them away quickly. I did not want to have to use it tonight.

I turned my attention back to our table. 'All being well, we ought to reach Wiltune by sunset tomorrow,' Ælfwold said.

'How long will it take you to deliver your message?' Wace asked.

'Not long. I'd hope that we can be on our way the following morning.'

A roar erupted from across the room and I turned abruptly as a group of Englishmen slammed their cups down upon the table in front of them. One of them, a heavy-set man about the same age as myself, began to splutter, droplets spraying from his mouth, until a friend slapped him on the back. Red-faced and blinking as if in surprise, he wiped a sleeve over his dark moustache before joining the rest in their laughter. After a moment he noticed me watching and I returned to my wine.

'I need a piss,' Eudo announced to no one in particular. He stood up, resting a hand on the table to steady himself, and made, half stumbling, for the door. I didn't think he had drunk so much, but when I went to pour myself a fresh cup, I found the pitcher all but empty, with only the dregs left.

'How many cups has he had?' I asked.

Radulf pointed to the pitcher. 'Has he finished it?'

'We'll have to get another,' Philippe said as he looked about for the innkeeper.

'Maybe if we wait for him to return, he'll pay for it,' Godefroi added, grinning slyly.

I glanced at Wace, but he only shrugged. 'I should make sure he's all right,' I said, standing and wrapping my cloak around me. It was still damp, despite having been hanging beside the fire, but it was better than nothing.

The chill of the air struck me as I opened the door. It was still raining, though more lightly than before. I raised my hood over my head, gritted my teeth and ventured out. The ground was slick with mud, and I took care where I trod. Water dripped from the thatch; all about large puddles gleamed in the light from the doorway.

I found Eudo by the stables around the side of the alehouse. He had one arm extended in front of him, propping himself against the wall; even above the sound of the rain I could make out the steady trickle of water on to the sodden ground.

'Eudo,' I said.

He kept his back to me. 'What do you want?'

I shivered as the wind gusted again, its icy fingers grasping at my skin even through my cloak. 'I want to talk.'

He made a noise that was somewhere between a sigh and a groan, and I saw him fiddling with the

302

laces on his braies before at last he turned. His face lay in shadow; there was no moon and the only light came from inside the alehouse.

'There's nothing to talk about,' he slurred as he began to trudge unsteadily through the mud towards me.

'How much have you drunk?' I asked.

'What does it matter to you?' He wasn't wearing his cloak, I noticed. He stumbled forward, his dark hair damp and matted against his head, trying to make his way around me, but I stood in his path. 'Let me past.' His breath stank of wine.

'You've had enough,' I said.

'I'll do what I want,' he said with a snort. 'You're not my keeper.'

'You've been like this ever since Lundene,' I said, watching him carefully. 'What's wrong?'

'You pretend to be interested but I know you don't care.'

I felt myself tense. Whatever it was I had done, it had clearly upset him far more than I had thought. 'That's not true,' I said.

'I know you—don't think that I don't. I've known you longer than anyone. When you disappear in the middle of the night like you did in Lundene, I know there's something not right. I know when there are things you're not telling us.'

'Is that what this is about?' I asked, trying to keep the anger from my voice. Of course he was right; I hadn't told any of them the whole story about that night. But how could he have guessed that?

He shook his head, his mouth set in disgust. 'You've changed. Since Dunholm you've kept more and more to yourself. You talk to the priest but

303

never tell us anything. You never tell *me* anything.' He pointed at his chest and looked me straight in the eye. 'I've been your friend for all these years. After everything we've been through, you still don't trust me enough—'

'Do you think I've found it easy since Dunholm?' I burst out.

He glared at me. 'You think it's been any easier for me or for Wace? We were all there, all of us. Not just you.'

I'd opened my mouth when I stopped. So caught up had I been in my own grief that I had not understood how much Lord Robert's death had affected him too.

'What is it that you want?' I said, more quietly. I could hear voices and the sound of footfalls upon the mud by the front of the alehouse, and I was wary of attracting too much attention.

'I want to be in Eoferwic,' he said. 'I want to be killing the men who killed Lord Robert. Instead we're here, wandering the whole damned kingdom after this priest, and I'm tired of it.'

I remained quiet for a moment as I thought of Eadgar, remembered the promise I had made to him outside Eoferwic's walls. The promise that I would kill him. The fingers on my sword-hand itched even as I thought of it. And so I knew how Eudo felt. But I knew, too, that until we had fulfilled our service to the vicomte, vengeance would have to wait.

'It's our duty to Malet,' I said.

'No.' He jabbed a finger at my face. 'It's *your* duty, Tancred. Wace and I never swore any oath to him. He's promised to pay us and so we're here, but we owe him nothing.'

I waited in case there was more to come, but there was not. The night was quiet; the rain had eased and was now little more than a steady drizzle.

'Leave, then,' I said. 'Take your horse and ride back to Eoferwic, or wherever you want to go. Take Wace with you. If it's silver that you're after, there'll be plenty of lords willing to pay.'

He took a pace back. 'No one's leaving,' he replied. 'Maybe you think you don't need our help at the moment, but you will. Just try to trust us from now on.'

He shouldered his way past, back towards the common room, and this time I didn't attempt to stop or follow him. Probably he need 'd a while to gather himself, I decided. At the same ime I didn't want to see his face again so soon. I was angry with him, yes, but there was something else as well: something in what he'd said that had struck me, though I could not place it exactly.

I waited until he had gone back inside and then turned in the opposite direction, towards the stables. Within, my horse was gorging itself on a sack of grain which had been left hanging on the inside of the door, and which was now less than half full. I looked about for the stable-boy, but he was not to be seen. Cursing his carelessness, I lifted the sack down. If the horse overate then he was likely to develop colic, in which case I could well find myself having to find another mount come the morning, for this one would be dead.

I placed the sack on the ground outside the stall and rubbed his muzzle before bolting the door again and checking on the others, making sure that the stable-hand had not left any more feedbags

305

out, but he had not. I would mention it to the innkeeper, and if the boy got a beating as a result, it was no less than he deserved.

I crossed the yard back towards the common room, which was even more full than it had been when I had left. Every one of the men who lived in this village must have come here, I thought, all of them reeking of wine and ale, sweat and dirt.

Eudo was sitting with the rest of the party by the fire. As I approached, the innkeeper's wife was bringing them another two large pitchers of wine, each one full to the brim, to join the three which were already there. She set them down; Radulf held up a silver penny towards her, but as she held out her hand to receive it, he tossed it to the floor, where it fell amidst the rushes. A roar of laughter went up from Godefroi and Philippe, who began banging their fists on the table. The woman blushed deep red as she got on her knees to retrieve the coin.

Ælfwold rose suddenly. 'You heartless . . . *nithingas!*' he shouted at the knights. They looked back in confusion. I did not know what the word meant, but I had never before heard the chaplain speak so vehemently.

I rushed over and knelt down beside the woman. She tried to wave me away, speaking in English as she scrabbled around on the floor, and I saw her blink away a tear. In my mind I saw my mother weeping in much the same way.

'Let me help,' I said, but she did not seem to understand me, for she simply spoke more loudly as she began to sob. I spotted the penny resting next to the leg of the table, and picked it up to offer to her. She shook her head as water began to

306

trickle down her cheeks, and got quickly to her feet.

'*Hwæt gelimpth?*' a voice shouted from across the room. It was the innkeeper.

I stood and turned to the five knights. 'Have you forgotten yourselves?' I demanded, snatching up one of the wine-jugs and tipping its contents on to the floor, staining the rushes red.

'What are you doing?' Radulf asked, rising.

'We paid for that!' said Philippe.

'You've had enough,' I said, grabbing the next pitcher in line and doing the same. 'All of you.'

'Tancred—' Radulf began.

I thumped the empty vessel down upon the table so hard that it shook, and glared back at him, then turned to Ælfwold. 'I'm sorry, father,' I said.

The chaplain's cheeks were a bright scarlet, his face tight with anger. 'I'm not the one in need of an apology,' he said, and he pointed to the innkeeper, who was hustling over. He was a short man, but broad in the chest and well built for his size, with a large forehead and small eyes.

'*Ge bysmriath min wif,*' he said, sending spittle flying. He gestured towards his woman, who had scurried back to the other side of the room, and stared up at me, for I stood a whole head taller. '*Ge bysmriath me!*'

I stared back, uncertain what to do. I looked about for the chaplain, and saw him making his way through the crowd towards the stairs at the far side of the room.

'Ælfwold!' I called after him, but either he did not hear me or he chose to ignore me, for he did not turn around.

Hurriedly I reached for the coin-pouch at my

belt, tipping a stream of the pennies out into my palm. I held them out towards the innkeeper, hoping it would be enough to placate him.

He looked first at them, then at me, and half spoke, half spat some more words in his tongue. But the sight of so much silver was enough to cool his temper; he snatched at the coins, almost as if he thought I might take them back if he didn't accept straightaway. He grunted, whether in appreciation or as a warning I was not sure, and after a final glance at me he returned to his wife.

A few of the other Englishmen had turned to watch, but not many—only those who had been closest—and as I looked around at them they one by one returned to their drinks. For that I thanked God, for they looked like strong men, used to working hard in the fields. Full of ale as they were, it would not take much to incite them.

I turned to the rest of the knights. 'Do you want to get us killed? Because that's what'll happen if the rest of this alehouse turns on us.'

'It was but harmless fun,' said Wace, who I had thought the most sober of them all.

I stared at him, scarce believing what I heard. 'You think it amusing to mock an innocent peasant woman?'

'We meant nothing by it,' put in Radulf.

I spat on the floor. 'There'll be no more drinking tonight,' I said. 'I'm going to find the chaplain.'

Ælfwold had gone upstairs to his room. The door stood open, and I found him kneeling on the floor, his eyes closed and hands clasped as he murmured a prayer in Latin. I waited until he had finished, when he looked up and saw me standing beneath the doorframe. He rose as I entered.

'Father,' I said. 'I'm sorry—'

'You must keep better control of your men.' His voice was surprisingly calm; his anger, it seemed, already diminished.

'They are not my men,' I said. Wace and Eudo were my comrades, it was true, but only Eudo had ever ridden in my conroi before. I thought of Dunholm and faces rose up like spectres in my mind: Gérard, Fulcher, Ivo, Ernost and Mauger. Those were my men—not this group that Malet had burdened me with.

'Lord Guillaume has placed them under your command,' the priest said simply. 'Hence they are yours.'

'They don't respect me,' I said.

'Then you must make them respect you. Otherwise, sooner or later they will do someone real harm. The English are my people, Tancred. I will not stand them being treated in this way.'

'What about the ætheling and the Northumbrians in Eoferwic?' I countered. 'Are they not English too?'

'They are rebels against the lawfully crowned king, and so enemies of our Lord.' He spoke slowly, as if trying to contain his anger. 'But this is Wessex; this is different. You cannot just allow your men to do what they will.'

'What do you expect of me?' I asked. 'I can't govern everything they do.'

What he must have thought of me then, I didn't know. Doubtless he was coming to resent the way I was always challenging him. Perhaps he was even regretting Malet's decision to put me in charge of this party in the first place.

'You can teach them to restrain themselves,' said

309

Ælfwold.

'They are trained warriors,' I retorted, 'not boys but men fully grown.'

'Then perhaps they need reminding of that!'

So surprised was I by the force of his voice that I took a step back. And in any case, why was I defending the others? What they had done was wrong; I knew that and I had told them so. But I also saw that it was borne not out of malice or lack of respect, as the chaplain seemed to assume, but rather out of frustration. And I remembered what Eudo had said to me only a little earlier, and suddenly I understood.

Like myself, these were indeed trained warriors. Their role on this earth was to fight, and if they could not do that, then they grew restless. Because instead of being where they felt they ought to be, on the march to Eoferwic, they found themselves deep in the English countryside, far from anywhere, without any real notion of what they were doing, let alone why. Like me, except that I alone had some idea, for I had the name that Malet's son had given me—

'Who is Eadgyth?' I asked.

I hadn't intended to mention her then, but I realised I would get no better opportunity than this.

The priest stopped still. Outside, the wind buffeted against the thatch; above our heads, the roof-timbers creaked. The sound of men laughing sounded through from the common room below.

'How do you know that name?' Ælfwold asked.

'Who is she?'

'It's none of your concern.'

'I know that she's the one you're meeting in

Wiltune,' I said, feeling my heart begin to pound. It was more a guess than a lie: despite what Robert had said, I could not know for sure, though the chaplain's reaction suggested that I was right.

He stared at me, blinking, but said nothing.

'Do you deny it?' I asked.

'Who told you that name?'

I thought it unwise to mention Robert, and so changed tack. 'Is she a lover of Malet's?' I demanded. I was on unsteadier ground now, but my blood was rising and I wanted to press the advantage as long as I held it. Had she fled to the nunnery to escape him, perhaps?

'You dare to insult my lord?' he shouted. 'The man to whom you swore an oath of service?'

I had half expected him to say something like that, and was not about to be deflected. 'Is she?' I said again.

'Of course not!'

'Then who is she?'

'She used to be wife to the king,' Ælfwold said, with some impatience.

'To King Guillaume?' I asked, confused. As far as I knew, he had only ever been married to his present wife, Mathilda.

'To the usurper,' the priest said, his cheeks flushing red. 'Harold Godwineson.'

This was not at all what I had expected. 'And what business does Malet have with the usurper's wife?'

'What concern is it of yours?' he said, his voice rising to a screech. 'It is the vicomte's private business, which as his chaplain I am privy to. But you are not. You are just a knight, a sworn sword. You are nothing more than a servant!'

311

I was about to open my mouth to reply—to say that as leader of this party how could it not be my business too—but his last remark stirred a fury inside me, and it was all I could do to restrain myself.

'Leave me,' Ælfwold said, his face scarlet. 'Go and rejoin your men. We ride again tomorrow at dawn. I don't want to see any of you until then.'

I hesitated, searching for something to say, but I could find no words to convey my disgust at him. *Just a knight, a sworn sword. Nothing more than a servant—*

'Leave,' he repeated.

Casting a final glare at him, I turned, slamming the door behind me.

## CHAPTER TWENTY-FOUR

The following day passed in relative quiet. I did not speak to the chaplain and he did not speak to me, instead keeping his gaze on the way ahead as long as we were on the road. The few times that I met his eyes, they held only disdain. But if he expected me to offer him an apology, he would be disappointed, for I had said nothing that hadn't been deserved.

And yet I was still no closer to understanding what his business was with this nun Eadgyth; what was so important that Malet would send his men halfway across the kingdom? The fact that she was the widow of the usurper was significant, it seemed to me, though in what way I could not work out. At least I had managed to glean that much from the

312

priest, whose determination to tell us as little as possible was sorely testing my patience. There would be answers once we reached Wiltune; I would make sure of that.

I told the others none of this, for I was still angry with them. Angry with Eudo, who after his words to me about trust had only betrayed mine in him. Angry with Radulf, who had caused the commotion in the first place. Angry with Wace, whom I had thought would have had more sense. I did not see that they deserved to know what I had learnt. In any case, it would not be long before we were on our way back to Lundene, and thence on to Eoferwic. If it was battle that they wanted, then they would get their chance soon—so long as Malet still held out, I reminded myself.

Hills rose and fell before us like creases upon the fabric of the earth, each valley a tapestry of green and brown, interwoven with silver threads where streams wound their course. Once or twice we spotted deer amidst the trees in the distance, their bodies rigid as statues, watchful heads turned towards us, though most of the time we didn't see them until they came darting across the road in front of us: three or four, even five at a time, all in a line, bounding one after another.

And still the ancient way went on, stretching seemingly without end into the west. Such tremendous builders the Romans must have been, I thought, for their works to remain standing after so many centuries. And yet, as the chaplain had pointed out, even they were made to suffer God's wrath; even they had left this island in the end.

It was evening when we finally left the road, at a place Ælfwold called Searobyrg. Whatever his reason for meeting this nun, he was clearly anxious about it, for he kept looking at the position of the sun between the clouds, then back at us, telling us to keep up the pace, even though we'd been making good progress that day. That he was feeling the burden of our company was obvious, though probably like us he was simply eager for our journey to come to its end. It had been eleven days since Malet had sent us from Eoferwic, and apart from those two nights we had spent in Lundene, we had been travelling all that time. Of course it was nothing compared to the kinds of marches we had endured on campaign, but an army travels slowly, rarely more than fifteen miles from sunrise to sunset, whereas on some days we must have covered more than thirty miles. It was not a pace that could be sustained for long, especially for one unused to long periods in the saddle, as I suspected the priest was.

As the Roman road turned away to the south, then, we headed west, into the setting sun. The cart-track we followed was rutted and ill travelled, and it took us some time to make our way through the woods; by the time we emerged again the sun had gone completely. Amidst streaks of purple cloud the evening star shone brightly, and beneath it, rising out of the gloom in the depths of the valley, was a church, built of stone with three towers rising to the sky. Around it, a cluster of buildings formed a square cloister. One had smoke rising from it, and that was surely a kitchen; nearby stood a long two-storeyed hall which might have been a dormitory.

Wiltune. And so at long last we had arrived.

There was no wind, almost no sound at all. I

314

gazed down upon the church's towers, silhouetted against the fiery skies with the mist settling around their lower courses, and as I did so, something of the serenity of the sight touched me. It was a feeling I had known before, brought up from the very depths of my memory, more intimate than anything else in the world. The feeling that I was in the presence of God himself.

Only then did I realise how many years had passed since I'd last set foot in a monastery. Now I was to go there once more, except that this time I was no longer a boy, but rather a man who had knowingly fled that path, who had rejected the ideals of poverty, chastity and obedience which had been laid out before him.

A shiver ran through me. Yet I had served God with heart and mind in everything that I had done since I'd left. Why did I still feel guilty?

'Tancred,' Ælfwold called sharply. He was some way down the track, and I realised I had stopped, the other knights behind me, waiting.

'Come on,' I said to them as I followed the chaplain down the muddy hillside. My cross weighed heavy around my neck, the silver cold as it pressed against my chest.

I inhaled again, letting the earthy scent of the evening air fill my lungs as I tried to rid my mind of such thoughts. We were here with the priest, I reminded myself: here to make sure he delivered Malet's message, whatever that was. Until we returned to Lundene, I could not afford to be thinking about anything else.

I gritted my teeth, concentrating on the track before me. All that could be heard was the faint *kew-wick* of an owl somewhere off to our right. In

315

the distance, beyond the convent, fires were being lit, for I could see their smoke rising into the steadily darkening heavens.

The nunnery itself was ringed by a wide ditch and low wattle-work fence, both of which ran all the way down to the river to the south. The entrance was defended by a stout gatehouse of dressed stone, of the kind I might have expected to see at the manor of a lord, not at a house of God. From beneath its archway shone a single feeble light; a number of figures, all in dark vestments, were closing over two great oak doors.

'*Onbidath!*' Ælfwold called to them, waving his hand above his head as he pulled ahead of us. '*Onbidath!*'

The gates stopped and a woman's voice replied in English. I glanced at Eudo, in case he had managed to make anything out, but he only shrugged.

'*Ic bringe ærendgewrit sumre nunfæmnan,*' the chaplain said as he stopped his horse on the cobbles before them.

'He says he brings a message for one of the nuns,' Eudo murmured.

I rode forward, motioning for him to follow. Three nuns stood in the gateway, each dressed in a brown habit. The one Ælfwold was speaking to was holding a lantern, and the light flickered across her lined face. She was shaking her head, gesturing up towards the east, where the sky was turning an inky blue.

'*Tomorgen,*' the nun said. Then she saw us riding up behind him, and drew back inside the half-closed gates. She was a round woman, and short, with a gaze like a falcon's, watchful and sharp.

'*Ic wille hire cwethan nu*,' the chaplain said, in a stern tone.

'He wants to be allowed to enter now, I think,' Eudo said. 'She's telling us to return in the morning.'

The nun looked nervously up; the chaplain turned and saw us there, and straightaway raised his hands in what I took for a calming gesture. '*Ic eom preost; ic hatte Ælfwold*,' he said, producing a wooden cross from his cloak pocket. '*Me sende Willelm Malet, scirgerefa on Eoferwic.*'

There was a moment of silence, before the nun repeated, '*Willelm Malet*?' She turned to one of the other women, taller and more youthful in appearance. The two conversed in their own tongue before the younger one hurried away somewhere inside the compound.

'*Onbidath her*,' the round one said. She did not leave, but neither did she make any move to close the doors again, which I took for a good sign.

Ælfwold nodded and breathed out a sigh as he sat back in his saddle.

'What now?' I asked him.

'Now,' he said, 'we wait and see if they will let us in.'

As much as a quarter of the hour might have passed before the young nun returned. My horse began to grow restive, pawing the ground and tossing his head; I dismounted and paced about with reins in hand, rubbing his flank.

At last, however, the nun did come back. After exchanging a few words with the one bearing the lantern, the gates were drawn full open with a creaking of hinges, and slowly we led our mounts through.

'*Ne*,' the older one said, pointing towards the scabbard at my side. Her face was solemn. '*Ge sceolon læfan eower sweord her.*'

'You must leave your swords here,' the chaplain warned.

In any other situation I might have protested, for I did not like to go anywhere unarmed, but I didn't want to cause a stir here, in a place of God. At the very least, we would still have our knives, since they were as much for eating with as they were for fighting.

I nodded to the other knights as I unbuckled my sword-belt and held it out to her, and one by one they did the same. I watched closely as she carried them within the gatehouse. As she came out, she called to the other two who were behind us, and they began to close over the gates, before each taking an end of a long wooden bar and dropping it into place. For good or for ill, I was here now.

The older nun was already hustling ahead, waving for us to follow her across a gravelled yard to a stable building. We left our mounts there, together with our shields, and then she led us on foot up a wide cart-track towards the church and the long stone halls that I presumed were the living quarters. The fence and outer ditch enclosed a wide area, most of which was taken up with fields, from which even now sheep and cows were being herded. The smell of dung wafted on the breeze. Down by the riverbank, on the southern side of the enclosure, I saw the shadowy form of a mill with its wheel turning.

'Where do you think she's taking us?' Eudo murmured.

'Somewhere where there'll be lots of women,'

318

Radulf answered, glancing at a group of nuns passing us in the other direction. 'Young ones, too, with any luck.'

I stopped and turned on him. 'You keep quiet,' I said, pointing a gloved finger at his large nose. 'Do you understand?'

He stared back at me in surprise. But I'd already had enough of his remarks on this journey.

'This is a house of our Lord,' I said to all of them. 'As long as we're here, we show nothing but respect.'

As I pulled away, I noticed the chaplain watching me. He said nothing but, before he turned around, I thought I saw the slightest of nods—of approval, maybe, though I could not be sure.

What Radulf had said made me wonder, though, for the nuns of Wiltune were clearly used to men visiting, or they wouldn't have admitted us in the first place. Some houses were far stricter; in such places men would not be permitted to enter at all, except for pilgrims and the sick, and the priests who came to deliver Mass and hear confessions. Which meant the women here had decided to trust us, especially surprising considering that we were obviously men of war, and not of their own people either.

The sun disappeared below the tiled roof of the church ahead of us. Now that it was before us, it was all the more impressive. Each of its three towers were more than four storeys tall, while even the nave looked taller than six men. The glass in the windows was coloured with reds and greens, blues and even yellows, intricately arranged to show pictures of saints or angels, like nothing I'd ever seen.

319

Ælfwold took no interest in any of this, however, and I was beginning to wonder whether he'd been here before. But if so, did that mean he also knew Eadgyth?

We crossed the courtyard towards a large stone-built hall. The nun knocked at the door and then, though I couldn't make out any reply, entered. Ælfwold went next and I after him, ducking to avoid hitting my head on the low cross-beam. The inside of the hall was lit only by two candles, arranged either side of a slanted writing desk. There was a hearth at one end but no fire had yet been lit, and so there was a damp chill to the air. Beside the hearth, a door led through into the next room, from which a girl promptly appeared. Her hair was fair in colour and unbound. She looked no older than about eleven or twelve years. Her eyes were wide as she saw us all standing there, and I wondered what we must have looked like to her: seven strange men, six of us in mail hauberks and chausses, marked with the scars of battle. If she had grown up solely in the convent, she might never have seen so many men together in one place.

The nun said something to her; the girl nodded and, hardly taking her eyes from us, retreated through the doorway.

'Go back outside,' Ælfwold told me curtly. 'I wish to speak with the abbess alone.'

'The abbess?' I asked, surprised. I thought we'd been coming to see Eadgyth.

'Who else?' he said, with some impatience. 'I can't deliver my message without her permission. Now, go.'

I didn't move. 'We wait here,' I insisted.

'This is not your concern—'

He turned as the door opened again, and through it, a woman entered, dressed in a brown habit with a simple cross embroidered in white thread on each sleeve. Like the nun who had brought us from the gate, she was advanced in years, but there was wisdom in her eyes, which were the colour of burnished copper, and dignity in the way she walked towards us, as if every step held some divine purpose.

She gave a flick of her hand towards our nun, who nodded solemnly and then departed, leaving us alone in the candlelight.

'*Fæder Ælfwold*,' she said.

'*Abodesse Cynehild.*' The chaplain knelt down before her, taking her hand and kissing the silver ring which adorned it.

'You come with a full conroi this time, it seems,' she said, speaking suddenly in French as she looked about at the six of us. 'How times are changing.' But if she was trying to make a jest, it did not show in her face, which remained expressionless as before.

Ælfwold rose. 'The escort given to me by my lord,' he explained, replying likewise in French.

'Guillaume Malet,' she said, and I thought I detected a hint of scorn in her voice, though I was not sure.

If there was, the chaplain did not seem to notice. 'Indeed, my lady.'

The abbess looked pensive for a moment, then she turned her gaze towards the rest of us, as if inspecting us. 'You look surprised,' she said to me. 'Why is this?'

I hadn't realised it was so obvious. 'You speak

321

French well,' I said, not out of politeness but because it was the truth. In fact she spoke it remarkably well, as only someone who hailed from the country would. Or at least, one who had spent a good many years in French company.

'And that surprises you?' she asked.

'Only because I'm not used to hearing it from English lips,' I answered, choosing my words carefully.

'Yet Ælfwold here speaks it just as well as I.'

'His lord is a Norman,' I said with a shrug. That seemed to me plain; how could she not understand that?

'Then, by that same measure,' she said, with a smile that spoke of quiet victory, 'should not the whole of England be French-speaking, since we are all subjects of our liege-lord, King Guillaume?'

I felt my cheeks turn hot. It seemed to me that I was being put to the test, for some reason that I could not discern. 'Yes, my lady,' I replied, not knowing what else I could say.

She frowned, keeping her gaze upon me.

'My lady,' Ælfwold spoke up, and for once I was thankful for his interruption. 'I'm here—'

'—to speak with the lady Eadgyth,' she finished for him, turning her eyes away from me at last. 'Yes, I had thought as much.'

'To pass on a message from my lord, if you will allow,' the priest said, unperturbed.

The abbess nodded. 'It would be hard for me to deny you. Unfortunately at present she isn't here, but in Wincestre.'

'In Wincestre?' Ælfwold was silent for a moment, his eyes closed as if in thought. 'How long ago did she leave?'

322

'A week ago, perhaps.'

'But she will return soon?'

'Tomorrow or the day after, I should expect,' she said. 'You are welcome as always to stay here until she does.'

Her words gave me a jolt. I was right; the chaplain had been to Wiltune before.

'That's most kind,' Ælfwold said.

The abbess gave a thin smile that quickly retreated. 'It is no more than what's expected. You will, of course, remain in the guest house at all times,' she said, and she glanced around at all of us as she did so.

'I understand,' the chaplain replied.

I gave a start as suddenly bells began to ring: a deep, long tolling which seemed to come from all around. The door opened and the same nun who had greeted us on our arrival appeared again, making her way carefully to the abbess's side, where she whispered in her ear.

The abbess murmured something in reply, and then drew herself up. 'I am afraid I must leave you now for compline,' she said. 'However, if you would all follow Sister Burginda'—she gestured towards the nun—'she will lead you to your quarters. I will see to it that food and drink is brought to you once the service is over.'

'Thank you,' Ælfwold said, bowing.

'My lady,' I said, nodding respectfully towards the abbess, as I allowed the others to leave first.

She looked back, her eyes fixed without feeling upon me, until the rest had all filed out and I myself turned and followed, out into the blue twilight.

# CHAPTER TWENTY-FIVE

Night had settled quickly across the convent. Beyond the hills to the west there was only the faintest of glows, and even that was fading, while to the east the stars were already beginning to emerge.

A line of nuns, about twenty or so in number, proceeded in double file across the central cloister towards the church. Some of them held small lanterns and I could see their faces in the soft light. There were women of all ages: a few wrinkled and ancient, half shuffling, half stumbling on their way; and others, helping them along, who looked barely older than the girl who had met us in the abbess's house. We waited until they had gone by, before the one the abbess had called Burginda led us away from the cloister, towards an orchard.

The other knights were murmuring and grinning amongst themselves, I noticed.

'What is it?' I said, though I guessed who it was they were smirking at, after the way the abbess had managed to discomfit me.

To my right, Wace only smiled and shook his head, while behind me I thought I heard Radulf snigger. Another time, I might have found it amusing, but I was only too aware of where we were. Every one of the nuns I'd seen had her head bowed, and not one had been speaking.

I glared in warning. After what had happened the night before, I didn't want another argument with the priest. But he and Burginda were some way ahead of us, and the bells were chiming so loud that I doubted he could hear.

On the other side of the orchard stood a long hall, surrounded by a wattle-work fence—there to set it apart from the rest of the convent, I supposed. Burginda set down her lantern by the door and reached inside a leather pouch fastened to her belt, producing a key. It gleamed in the light of her lantern as she put it into the lock and gently twisted. The door swung open without a sound. Within, the hall was dark. The nun picked up her lantern and went inside, followed by the rest of us. Orange light played across the walls, revealing a long rectangular table, a hearth with copper cooking pots beside it, a set of stairs at the rear.

Hardly were we all inside before Ælfwold turned on me. 'When I speak with Eadgyth, I will do so alone,' he said in a low voice. 'I won't have you always watching over me.'

'Your lord made me swear an oath to protect you,' I replied. 'I am only following his instructions.' It was not much of an answer, and I knew it.

'I don't need your protection,' he snapped. 'This is a place of God. What possible harm do you think will befall us here?' He turned his back on me as he made for the stairs.

He was right, of course, though I didn't like to admit it. 'So what do we do now?' I called after him. 'Do we just wait here until she returns?'

'There is nothing else we can do.'

'We could ride on to Wincestre and see if we can find her there,' Wace suggested.

'And what if she's left by the time we arrive?' the priest asked.

Wace shrugged. 'Then we might meet her on the

325

road.'

Wincestre was not far, and it would take only a few hours to get there—a little longer by dark, perhaps, but even so, if we left now and rode hard we could surely get there before daybreak. Although that would mean even longer in the saddle.

'This isn't for you to decide,' the chaplain said.

'Wace is right,' I said.

'No,' the chaplain replied, fixing me with a stare. 'I won't be dictated to. I say that we stay. Whether we have to wait a day or a week for the lady Eadgyth, it doesn't matter.'

'The king's army will be leaving Lundene soon,' Eudo put in. 'If we delay here too long, we won't be able to join it.'

'I don't care about the king's army!' Ælfwold said, his face as scarlet as it had been the night before. 'This is the task that Lord Guillaume has sent us here for. Nothing else matters!'

The room fell silent. I realised that the nun was still with us, watching us as we argued. How much of what we'd been saying had she understood?

But before I could point this out, Wace asked, 'Who is this Lady Eadgyth, in any case?'

Ælfwold closed his eyes and lifted his hands to his face, his fingers like claws digging in to his brow as he muttered something in his own tongue: a curse, perhaps.

'She used to be the wife of Harold Godwineson,' I said, before he could answer. 'Harold the usurper.'

Wace looked at me in surprise, although I wasn't sure whether it was surprise at what I had said, or because I was the one who had said it. 'Is this

326

true?' he asked the chaplain.

'It doesn't matter who she is,' Ælfwold answered. He was staring at me, his eyes full of menace.

'It's true,' I said.

Wace frowned, and I could see the same question running through his mind as it had through mine. 'But why—?'

'It is not your business!' the priest said. He closed his eyes and took a deep breath, as if trying to calm himself, and murmured a short prayer in Latin. He spoke too quickly for me to follow all of it, but somewhere in the middle I heard the words for anger—*ira*—and forgiveness—*venia*.

'I will stand this no longer,' he said. 'You are insufferable, every one of you. I promise you, the vicomte will hear of this. He will hear of everything.' He shook his head as he stalked up the stairs.

'You knew?' Wace said once he'd gone. 'He told you?'

'I only learnt yesterday,' I replied. 'And only after I'd pressed him.' That wasn't strictly true, I realised, since I'd known the name of Eadgyth ever since we were in Lundene. But it was only yesterday that I found out who she was, and that was what was important.

'You knew, and you didn't tell us,' Eudo said.

I felt my temper rising. 'After what happened last night?' I asked, making sure that Radulf and the others could hear as well. 'Do you think I could have trusted any of you then?'

Eudo fell quiet.

Wace was the first to speak. 'We were wrong,' he said, glancing at Eudo and the others, as if seeking affirmation from them too. 'Wrong to act as we did. We forgot ourselves.'

'It was foolishness,' Philippe said sombrely, and beside him Godefroi nodded his agreement. But Radulf's expression did not change; his lips remained unmoved.

'It was more than that,' I said. 'What you did was reckless. But we're here now, and that's all that counts.'

Floorboards creaked and muffled footsteps sounded through from the room above—the chaplain moving about, I thought. My gaze fell once again upon the nun and, as my eyes met hers, she turned quickly, knocking over a stool behind her. It clattered to the floor.

'Why is she still here?' said Wace as the nun bent down to pick it up.

'Why worry?' Radulf asked. 'She won't have understood anything that we've said.'

'We don't know that,' Wace said as he approached her. 'The abbess spoke French well enough, remember. In these places they learn many tongues.'

The nun stood, regarding him with a look of defiance, though she was at least a head and a half shorter. Whether or not she understood exactly what was being said, I could not tell, though she clearly knew we were talking about her.

'Perhaps we should speak somewhere else,' Philippe suggested.

'It might be best,' I said. 'Though we've not said anything that she probably didn't know already.' She already knew that we were here to deliver a message to Eadgyth. And if she had lived here any length of time it was likely she already knew of the lady's connection to the usurper.

'Why is she here, though?' Eudo asked.

'It's just the custom,' I said. 'One member of the convent is appointed to stay with guests and watch over them. She's here for our care and, supposedly, our safety.'

Wace raised the eyebrow above his one good eye. 'Our safety?' he asked, a smile spreading across his face. He turned back to the nun, who remained standing where she was, unblinking, watchful.

'It's what happened where I grew up, at least,' I said with a shrug.

'What do you mean?' Radulf asked. 'How do you know so much?'

'I know', I said, 'because before I was a knight, I myself grew up in a monastery.'

He made a sound halfway between a snort and a laugh. 'You were a monk?'

'Only an oblate,' I said sharply as I stared him down. 'I was given to the Church when I was seven; I fled when I was thirteen. I never took the vows.'

Wace stepped back from the nun, though still he did not take his eyes off her.

'Let her alone, Wace,' Eudo said, yawning and grinning at the same time. 'What's she going to do? She's just an old woman.'

Now that Wace had retreated, Burginda set about making a fire. Next to the hearth stood a soot-blackened pail filled with sticks and logs, which she began to arrange across the grate.

I imagined fresh meat roasting over that hearth, and my stomach rumbled. Compline must soon be coming to an end; I hoped it wouldn't be long until food arrived. We'd bought fresh bread and sausage from the innkeeper when we left the alehouse that morning, but it was still in our saddlebags, and we

329

had left them together with our animals at the stables.

'Ask her when our packs are going to be brought to us,' I said to Eudo.

He paused for a moment, probably to think of the right words, then crouched down beside the round frame of the nun, who had lit one of the smallest twigs from the lantern and was now trying to get the rest to take flame. She didn't meet his eyes, instead kept concentrating on the hearth as he spoke to her and she mumbled something in return.

Eudo stood. 'They'll be bringing them after compline, she says.'

So my stomach would have to wait, although as it turned out, it wasn't long before the abbess arrived. She came with four nuns, who as Burginda had promised brought our packs, together with bread and jugs of water—clearly all that could be offered at this hour. It was hardly much of a feast, but it was welcome nonetheless. Ælfwold joined us for that meal, though he said nothing throughout, save for giving a simple thanks to God before we ate, and he was joined in his silence by the abbess and her sisters, who did nothing but sit and watch us from across the long table. Of course they'd have eaten before the service; there would be nothing more for them until sext the next day. I did my best to avoid meeting the abbess's gaze, but she kept her eyes trained on me, and I saw little warmth there.

At last they left, and Ælfwold retired upstairs. Only Burginda stayed with us, and for most of the evening she kept out of our way. She knelt by the fire, eyes closed in prayer, while we ate from our own provisions and diced upon the great oak table. I didn't know the rules on guests gambling, though of course it would be forbidden between the sisters themselves, but the aged nun did nothing to stop us and so we played for several hours. After a while Eudo took out his flute and started to play a few short passages, trying to recall a piece long forgotten; he kept stumbling over the same few notes until we all called for him to try something different: something we could at least sing to.

Eventually the flames in the hearth began to dwindle, and I could feel the cold of the night seeping back into the hall. Before too long the others were starting to yawn; first Godefroi and then Radulf retired upstairs, where there were private rooms enough for all of us. Clearly the nuns were used to receiving guests, and large numbers of them as well.

Philippe followed soon afterwards, leaving only myself, Wace and Eudo. There was Burginda too, still sitting on her stool by the fire. Now, though, her chin was resting against her slowly rising and falling chest, and I could hear her steady, sighing breaths.

'The usurper's wife,' Wace muttered. 'Why would Malet want to send a message to her?'

'I've been trying to work that out myself,' I said, keeping my voice down so as not to disturb the sleeping nun. 'At first I wondered if she might have been his lover, though Ælfwold denied it.'

Eudo looked at me in astonishment. 'You asked him if they were lovers?'

'It wasn't the wisest thing I have ever said, I know.'

'I'll admit I'd been thinking it too,' Wace said.

331

'To actually say it, though,' Eudo pointed out, 'and to the vicomte's own chaplain—'

'But why else would he go to such trouble?' Wace cut him off. 'To send men all this way when Eoferwic lies under siege, and to risk his own chaplain as well?'

I nodded. 'What message would be so important that he needs to send it now?'

'There is another possibility, of course,' said Wace, glancing at the nun and then at the stairway, as if one of the others might suddenly appear. 'Though I hesitate to say it when there's the smallest chance that someone could be listening.'

I met Wace's eyes, steely grey, across the table. The same thought had crossed my mind, but I had dismissed it just as soon as it appeared, for I didn't want to believe it. Could Malet be involved in some sort of conspiracy with Harold's wife?

'We can't know that,' I said to Wace. 'There is no proof, only supposition.'

'I know,' he replied. 'That's why I didn't want to say anything.'

'What?' asked Eudo.

I glanced at Wace, wondering which one of us should say it. He took a deep breath and lowered his voice to almost a whisper: 'Malet might be a traitor.'

Eudo frowned. 'A traitor?' he said, too loudly for my liking.

I waved him quiet and leant closer. 'There's one more thing which might be important,' I said, and stopped suddenly, unsure whether to go on. But they were watching me expectantly; they would know that I was hiding something if I didn't say it, and I needed their trust above all else.

'What is it?' said Wace.

I tried to recall everything Ælfwold had told me on the ship. 'In the years before the invasion it seems that Malet was a great friend of Harold Godwineson,' I said. 'He was granted land on these shores by the old king, Eadward, and used to spend much of his time in this country. That is, until the king died and Harold stole the crown, when he returned to Normandy to join Duke Guillaume.'

'He knew the usurper?' asked Wace.

'And of course he's half-English as well,' Eudo murmured.

'So now he sends word to Harold's widow,' Wace said. 'What does it mean?'

'It may mean nothing,' I said. 'For one thing, it seems that their friendship was broken when Harold assumed the kingship. Whatever sympathies Malet once had with the English, they were buried when he fought at Hæstinges.'

'Though even now he fills his household with Englishmen,' Eudo pointed out. 'Ælfwold and Wigod, and no doubt there are others too.'

This was true, and it was yet another part of the riddle. But an even bigger question hung in my mind: why would Ælfwold have revealed all this to me if he knew that his lord was a traitor? It didn't make sense. None of this did.

'If we knew what the message was, then we would know for sure,' I said. 'But the priest won't say.'

'He must have a letter on his person, or in his room,' Eudo said.

'Unless he carries the message in his head alone,' Wace put in. 'If so, we have no way of finding out.'

Then all of a sudden I remembered the scroll he had dropped that day we had left Lundene, how abruptly his manner had changed when I picked it up. 'No,' I said. 'There is a letter.'

'You're sure?' Wace asked.

The more I thought about it, the more I was convinced. What else could it be? 'I saw him drop it on our way here.'

'If we could only look at it before he delivers it to this Eadgyth,' Eudo said.

'He wouldn't leave it unguarded, I'm sure,' Wace said.

'But would you recognise it if you saw it?' asked Eudo.

'Probably,' I said, picturing it in my mind, with its rough edges and the leather cord tied around it. Otherwise there had been nothing especially distinctive about it. 'Why?'

'He's likely to be asleep by now,' Eudo said, keeping his voice low. 'We need only slip into his room and find it—'

'You'd have us steal it?' I asked. Angry as I was with Ælfwold, the thought filled me with distaste. Malet had placed his confidence in me, after all. I had sworn an oath to him, an oath to which God had been witness, and as such was not to be treated lightly.

Eudo shrugged.

'What if we're wrong about the priest, about Malet and everything?' For if we did as he suggested, and our suspicions turned out to be false, then I'd be breaking that confidence— breaking that oath. 'No, there must be another way.'

'Do the others know about Eadgyth, do you think?' Wace asked. 'Godefroi, Radulf and Philippe, I mean. Did you see if they reacted to her name?'

'I wasn't watching them,' I admitted.

'Neither was I,' said Eudo.

'I wonder,' Wace said. 'If they've served Malet for some time, it's possible they already know who she is, and of his connection to her. And if they know that, they might also have some idea what this message is about.'

'It's possible,' I agreed. 'But remember in Lundene they wanted only to get back on the road to Eoferwic. If they'd known that coming to Wiltune was in any way important, they wouldn't have said that.'

'That's true,' Eudo said. 'It was the chaplain who reminded them that we had this task to fulfil first.'

'And I,' I said.

'And you,' he added, with a smile. 'You and your sense of duty.'

Another time I might have laughed, but I didn't feel in good humour that night. A log shifted in the hearth and Burginda gave a snort as she moved on her stool; I saw her eyelids flutter as, with a great intake of breath, she began to stir.

'I just hope things become clear soon,' I said.


# CHAPTER TWENTY-SIX

Wiltune by dark lay silent and still. I stood leaning on one of the fenceposts outside the guest-hall. A thin sliver of moon protruded from behind wisps of cloud; the stars in their hundreds were scattered like seeds in a pale band across the sky.

The only other light came from the nuns'

dormitory, where a faint glow framed the doorway. It was another of the precepts that St Benedict had laid down in his Rule: that a fire be kept burning in the dormitory throughout the night, a symbol of the eternal light of our Lord. And to those who neglected their duty—who fell asleep when it was their turn to watch the hearth, and so allowed the flames to dwindle and die—were dealt the harshest punishments, as I knew only too well.

Still I recalled that frosty winter's morning as I stood before the two of them: the circator with his lantern, who was the one who had found me, and beside him the prior, his face dark as he delivered his words of condemnation. Still I could picture the crowd of monks gathering around, witnesses to my failure. And I remembered my own desperate pleas to mercy and to God as they struck and struck again, each time harder than the last, bringing their hazel rods to bear upon my exposed back—pain of a kind I had never before known—until at last I was left trembling, bloody and alone upon the hard earth.

It was not the first time I had been beaten for my sins, but I was determined it would be the last. And so I fled.

Of course I had to wait for the right opportunity. For the next day and night I was watched carefully, in case I made any more mistakes for which they could punish me, and so I had to bide my time. But on the following night, under the light of the full moon, I took my chance, treading lightly as I passed the other monks in their beds, making my way quickly across the yard, past the smith's workshop and the stables, hoping to avoid the circator as he made his nightly rounds. The gatehouse I knew was guarded; instead I made for the northern wall and the gnarled old tree that grew beside it—an oak which, it was rumoured, had stood there ever since the monastery was founded, two hundred years before.

I had reached the infirmary when I heard voices close by. I ducked around its corner, my heart pounding. Lantern-light glowed softly upon the ground, and I held my breath, determined not to be heard. The gruff tones of the circator carried across the yard as he conversed with one of the other monks, whose voice I did not recognise. The light grew brighter; they were coming closer.

What I should have done was wait until they had passed, and probably they wouldn't have noticed me. Instead I panicked. Thinking that they would find me and all would be lost, I decided to run.

Almost straightaway I heard cries behind me, demanding to know why I was about so late, but I didn't stop as I made for the old oak and quickly began to climb. I heard their feet running across the grass as I slid along one of the branches and scrambled over the wall, the stone grazing my palms and my knees as I dropped down the other side. And then I ran, down the hillside, towards the river and the town of Dinant below. They tried to come after me, of course, but I was fast and a boy of just thirteen years is easy to lose in the shadows, and before long their shouts had faded to nothing. As soon as I had made it into the woods, I collapsed. All my strength was gone and I was half-starved besides, but I knew at last that I had done it: I knew that I would never have to go back there.

A few days later, I met Robert de Commines, and my life's path was set.

This story I had told to few others. Of those who were still alive, none but Eudo and Wace knew it. Yet even when I considered everything that had happened, still a part of me felt ashamed for having left, for having forsaken that life, and I did not know why.

From far off came the sounds of cattle: one long, doleful cry that was answered by another, and then a third and a fourth, carrying clear across the convent. I was aware of Burginda behind me, watching me from the doorway. When she saw me putting on my cloak earlier, she'd tried to stop me from going out. Perhaps she thought I was planning on paying a visit to one of the younger nuns—although if I had, there was little she could have done to prevent it. But that was not why I had come out here. My mind was filled with so many different thoughts, like a hundred skeins of yarn, all twisted together, and I needed the space to tease them out.

Still, I did not blame her. Countless were the stories I had heard of nuns taken against their will, by men who had lusted after them before they'd taken their vows. Often such men would arrive at a convent feigning injury or some other affliction to gain entry; sometimes they would come alone, sometimes in bands. The details changed from tale to tale, but in each one they wasted no time in showing their true purpose once they were inside: marching straight to the chapter house, or wherever else the nuns might be gathered at that time of day, and then stealing away just as quickly.

And so I didn't resent Burginda for continuing to watch over me, though I did my best to ignore her. My thoughts, however, were not of any of the nuns here, but of Oswynn, and the dreams I'd had the other night. It troubled me, the way her face had been hidden from me; as if my memory of her were already fading.

I heard raised voices behind me. Over my shoulder I saw Wace trying to get by the nun, who was standing in his path.

'Let me past,' Wace said, and even in this faint light I could see the tiredness in his eyes.

I straightened and turned back towards the door. Burginda glanced at me, then back at Wace, before grudgingly moving aside, no doubt deciding that two of us was more than she could deal with.

'I thought you were asleep,' I said to him. I had waited until both he and Eudo had gone upstairs before venturing out, and had not expected to see either of them again until the morning.

'I came down for a piss,' he said. 'What are you doing out?'

'Thinking,' I said, and looked away again, towards the main part of the convent and the three dark towers of the abbey church, like giant pillars holding up the great vault of the heavens. 'Until today I hadn't set foot inside a monastery since I was thirteen. Being here brings so much from that time back to my mind.'

Wace said nothing. How much of this did he understand?

'I was just seven years old when my uncle gave me up to the monks,' I went on. 'He was the only family I had left, after my father's death.' Of course I had told Wace all this before, though it would have been long ago, and whether he would remember, I did not know. At any rate he did not stop me.

'It was probably the kindest thing he could do for you,' he said.

'Probably,' I agreed. 'Though it did not seem that way at the time.'

'Nor after what happened later, I'm sure.'

I nodded. 'You know the rest.'

'Why do you mention it now?'

'I've been thinking how much our lives are shaped by events beyond our control. My father's death, and everything that followed. What happened at Dunholm, and where that has brought us now.'

'What of it?'

'Is all of it just chance?' I asked, and I could hear the bitterness in my own voice. 'Or have all these things happened because that is God's will?'

He shot me an admonishing look. 'We must believe that it is,' he said. 'Otherwise what meaning is there to anything?'

I fingered the cross that hung around my neck. I knew that he was right. For everything on this earth there was a purpose ordained by God, difficult though it might be to comprehend what that was. From that at least I knew I ought to draw some comfort: the thought that He had a design for me, in spite of all that had happened.

'And He has brought me here,' I murmured. I looked up again across the orchard and towards the bell-tower, and hesitated, unsure whether I should say what I was about to. 'I've been wondering,' I said. 'Wondering what it would be like to go back.'

'You would give up your sword?' he asked, with a wry smile. 'You'd take the vows?'

He sounded like Radulf had only a few hours

ago, I thought. It was a mistake to have mentioned it. 'Someday, perhaps,' I said, trying not to let my irritation show. 'Not for many years, but someday, yes.'

The smile faded from his face. Maybe he had not known at first how seriously I was speaking, but now understood. I often found it hard with Wace to tell what he was thinking, and it was rare that he let anyone, even those closest to him, know his true feelings.

'I've been wondering as well,' he said after a while. He glanced behind him at Burginda, who was only a dozen paces away from us, and spoke more softly. 'About Malet and everything that we spoke of earlier. And I know that whatever friendship he might once have had with Harold Godwineson, he can't be a traitor.'

'What makes you say that?' I asked.

'Because if he were, he wouldn't at this moment be under siege by an English army in Eoferwic.'

Indeed in the midst of all our excitement earlier we had forgotten that. Of course it made no sense for Malet to be engaged in any kind of plot with Eadgyth when he himself was threatened by her own countrymen in Northumbria—when his own life was in peril. Had we been trying to make connections where there were none, where in fact there was a perfectly ordinary explanation?

Even if that were true, I could not help but still feel uneasy. There were so many things that we didn't yet understand.

'Have you spoken to Eudo?' I asked.

'Not yet,' he replied. 'I wonder if we owe the chaplain an apology.'

'Perhaps.' After what Ælfwold had said last

341

night, the idea was not a welcome one.

'He's not our enemy.'

'How do we know that?' I asked, and when I saw that Wace had no answer, said, 'The longer we travel in his company, the less I trust him.'

I was thinking of that night in Lundene, in the street outside St Eadmund's church. At the time I had been so sure that it was him; it was only later that I convinced myself I had been mistaken. But now I had seen how much the priest was hiding from us, I wondered if perhaps he had been lying about what he had been doing that night as well. What if my instincts had been right, and if they were, what did that mean? What did any of it mean?

'All we can do is what Malet has asked of us,' Wace said. 'After this, after we've driven the English from Eoferwic, any obligation we might have to him will be over. We'll be free to do what we want, and what Malet does then is his concern, not ours.'

'*If* we drive them from Eoferwic,' I muttered. I closed my eyes; my mind was full of possibilities and half-formed thoughts. Never had I been so completely uncertain of my life: not just of the business with Ælfwold and Malet, but also of what I was doing here, of where I was headed.

Sometimes I thought that if I could only wake myself from this dream then I'd find myself back in Northumbria, with Oswynn and Lord Robert and all the others, with everything just as it had been before. I felt like a ship cast adrift on the open sea, subject to the whims of the tide and the wind, riding each and every storm while always clinging to the hope that I would soon find a safe haven. A hope that seemed to be growing fainter by the day.

'Let's see what happens when Eadgyth arrives,' I said. 'Then we'll know what to do.'

Wace placed a hand briefly on my shoulder before he walked away, around the side of the hall.

I stood there a moment longer, gazing out across towards the dormitory and the thin tendrils of smoke rising from its chimney to the stars. Soon, however, the silence was broken by the sound of bells pealing out, this time for matins, I realised. I had not known it was so late.

I returned inside, back to my room. Shortly I heard footsteps on the stairs and on the landing beyond my door: Wace returning, I thought. The creak of hinges followed and then all was still. I shrugged off my cloak and lay down on the bed. The straw mattress was hard and offered little in the way of comfort, no matter how I positioned myself, and after several attempts, at last I stopped trying and sat up instead.

In the darkness I held my head in my hands as I mulled over everything. Amidst all the uncertainty, one thing was becoming ever clearer: I could not carry on not knowing the truth. Above all my conscience would not allow me to serve a man who was a traitor to his king and to his people. If there was some conspiracy between Malet and Harold's widow, I had to know. Despite what I had said to Wace, I knew there was no guarantee that we would have any answers even when she arrived. I could wait no longer.

And suddenly I knew what I had to do.

The bells had stopped ringing some time ago; if anyone in the house had been woken by them, they would surely now be settled again. I stood up and went to the door, opening it just enough to be able to look out on to the landing. A faint orange glow played across the stairs from the hearth-fire in the hall below.

For a moment I wondered again: what if we were wrong? But I knew that if I carried on thinking in that vein, then I would lose this chance. There was no other way. We had to know.

The landing ran almost the whole length of the up-floor. At the far end, furthest from the stairs, was the chamber in which Ælfwold was staying. Barefoot, I slipped out of the door, closing it gently behind me; the last thing I wanted was to wake anyone else. There was little wind that night, or anything else which might have helped mask my movements. The only noise I could hear was that of mice rustling in the thatch.

Breathing as lightly as I could, I made my way along the corridor, keeping close to the right-hand side: the outer wall of the house, where the boards were less likely to creak. A little way further along, I could hear snoring, and saw that the door to one of the other knights' rooms lay open. It was Philippe, his lanky frame stretched out, one arm hanging off the side of the mattress. A copper candlestick stood on the floor, the wax itself almost burnt down. He stirred, muttering to himself, though not in any words that made sense. I froze, thinking that he might have heard me, but thankfully he did not wake.

The next room belonged to the chaplain. This would be the main guest chamber, south-facing: usually reserved for visitors of the highest honour. Ours were mere retainers' quarters by comparison. For we were just knights, I thought grimly. Nothing

344

more than servants.

The door was sturdily built, with a great iron lock and handle. I pressed an ear up against the wood, stilling my breath as I tried to make out any sound of movement within, but all was quiet. I gripped the handle, hoping that it didn't turn out to be locked. The iron felt cold against my palm, which I now realised was sweating. I gritted my teeth and pushed: gently at first, gradually putting more force behind it, until I felt it begin to grind open—

I stopped, my heart beating fast as I waited for a sound, though what I was expecting I did not know. A rush of feet towards the door, perhaps; the chaplain's voice? I heard none of that, only silence.

There was the slightest crack between the door and the frame, and I peered into it, into the darkness. No candle or lantern was lit, and it took some time before I could make out any forms, but then I saw the windows on the far side, with the moonlight filtering through the shutters, the hangings upon the wall. And Ælfwold himself, a woollen blanket wrapped around him as he lay on the great bed, his paunch rising and falling in steady rhythm.

Again I pushed. The door met with some resistance as it grated against the floor, but I could not let it make a noise and so I had to move it slowly, all the time fearing that one of the others would come upon me and wonder what I was doing there.

Eventually the gap was wide enough that I was able to squeeze through sideways, pressing my back against the frame and ducking my head; the doorway had been built for men much shorter than I.

Then at last I was inside. Still the chaplain did not rouse, nor make any sound at all. I closed the door behind me; I didn't want anyone to see it lying ajar and think that there was something amiss.

I glanced about, taking in the whole of the chamber. The bed itself took up a large part of it: about six feet wide and almost as long, it was made for lords, with posts of a dark-coloured wood, intricately carved in a plant-like design, with leaves and stems and flowers all interwoven. In one corner of the room lay a small hearth; grey ash filled the grate. Another door led from this chamber, no doubt through to a private garderobe. Beneath the shuttered windows on the far side of the room stood a writing-desk, and there I saw what it was I had come for.

It was as I remembered it: the same size, with the same rough edges and bound with the same piece of leather. Lightly I stepped across to it, avoiding the chaplain's saddlebag, which he had left at the foot of the bed, looking about to make sure that I was not confusing it with any other scroll that he might have had with him. I could see none. A single white goose-quill protruded from a wooden stand, beside a small dish filled with ink. Otherwise there was nothing on the desk. This had to be it.

I heard a low grunt and cast a glance over my shoulder as the priest twisted in his blanket. For a moment I thought he was about to open his eyes, but he did not; he settled facing the opposite direction, towards the door.

My heartbeat seemed to resound through my whole body; I could feel it thumping in my hands, my feet, my ears. When was the last time I had

346

done something so reckless? But I wasn't going to leave until I had what I'd come for.

I picked the vellum up, holding its ends between my palms, feeling its lightness, its dry crispness. This was it.

I swallowed. I hadn't planned this far. Did I dare take it with me and return it later, or should I read it now? There was enough light here—as long as the moon did not go behind another cloud, at least—but the longer I stayed, the more of a risk I was taking. But at the same time, if I took it away, I had to be sure that I could get it back before the chaplain noticed. Which meant I would have to do all of this again.

I gave another glance towards the chaplain, but he appeared soundly asleep. Breathing slowly, I started to untie the leather string. It was fastened with a simple knot, and once I had worked free one strand, the rest came easily. Then, holding my breath, I began to unroll it.

And felt a lurch of despair in my stomach. For where I was expecting to find line after line of delicately scripted black letters, there was nothing. At the bottom of the page was Malet's seal in red wax—a delicately scripted initial 'M', with vines climbing and weaving between its legs—but above it, nothing.

Perhaps the chaplain had switched the scroll with another—but why would he have done that? Or else the one I was after was in this room somewhere. Yet it looked every bit the same; it had to be the one.

I squinted at the page, angling it into the faint slats of moonlight shining through the shutter, and as I unfurled the final few inches, a rush of

347

excitement came over me. I saw two simple words, written in Latin, in a shaky hand: one that I presumed must have been Malet's own, for no scribe could have prided himself on such work.

'Tutus est.'

That was all it said. I read it again, to make sure that I had understood it all, even turning it over to see if there was anything on the other side that I had missed. There wasn't. Those two words were all there were.

*Tutus est. It is safe.* But what did it mean? Perhaps he was writing about Eoferwic, but why then didn't he mention the city by name, and in any case how could he be so sure that it was safe?

The priest sighed deeply as he turned again, startling me. His face was pressed against the mattress, his grey hair hanging limp across his eyes. His body lay contorted like a hunchback's as he mumbled some words in English, his brow creased as if he were deep in concentration. Then he settled again, his breathing slow and even as before.

I kept as still as I could, watching him until I was satisfied that he was indeed asleep. But there was no advantage to be had in staying here any longer. I had what I wanted, even if I didn't yet understand it.

I rolled the vellum back into a scroll, tying it in the same way as it had been before, or as close to it as I could manage, then I replaced it as I had found it. An owl began to hoot outside and I took that as my sign to leave. I remembered Ælfwold's pack lying on the floor and took care to step around it.

At the door I paused, checking that I hadn't left

anything behind that might later betray that I had been here. Then, shutting it slowly behind me, I made my way across the landing, back to my room.

## CHAPTER TWENTY-SEVEN

I awoke late the next morning—later than I had done in a long while, in fact, for when I opened the shutters, the morning light spilt in and I saw that the sun was already high. I dressed as quickly as I could, tugging my tunic on over my shirt before pulling on my braies and heading down to the hall.

The others were gathered around the table, and they greeted me as I made my way over to them. More food had been brought to us: small loaves of bread and cheeses; as well as eels, salted and dried, perhaps caught from the river by the nuns themselves. It was a generous provision for guests, particularly since during these winter months they themselves would receive nothing until after the noon service.

I was about to sit down to eat, when I realised that the priest was not there.

'Where's Ælfwold?' I asked, looking about to make sure I had not missed him. Unless he was still abed, though at this hour that seemed unlikely.

'He went to speak with Eadgyth,' Wace said. 'She returned from Wincestre this morning, apparently. One of the nuns came to fetch him.'

At last she was here, then: the woman we had come all this way to see. 'When was this?'

Wace shrugged and glanced at the others. 'Not long ago,' he said. 'We heard you rousing a little while afterwards; we thought you might have heard him.'

'And you didn't think to go with him?' After everything we had been saying the night before, I would have expected them to keep a closer watch over him, and especially over his business with Eadgyth. *Tutus est*, I remembered—whatever it was supposed to mean. Only she and Malet would know.

'He said he wanted to speak with her alone,' Eudo put in. 'He wouldn't allow any of us to go with him.'

'Where has he gone?' At least he had only just left.

Eudo and Wace shook their heads, and inwardly I cursed. They ought to have woken me earlier; I would have made sure, somehow, that the priest was not left on his own. But then I spotted Philippe glancing uncertainly at his two comrades.

'You know, don't you?' I asked them, wondering at the same time what else they might have been withholding from me. 'Where has he gone?'

They exchanged looks, as if they did not know whether or not to tell me, but Philippe must have seen that I was not about to be swayed, for he spoke up.

'They'll have gone to Eadgyth's private chambers,' he said.

'And where are they?'

'The up-floor in the dormitory . . .' he began, but if he said anything else, I did not hear it as realisation dawned upon me. The three of them had been here before now. They must have known all along: about Eadgyth and who she was, who she had been. I felt suddenly foolish. Why hadn't I seen this?

'This isn't the first time that Malet has sent you here, is it?' I said. 'When were you going to tell me this?'

'We didn't think it was important,' Radulf said sullenly. I met his stare. Ever since we had met he'd been testing my patience, and I confess that I had even less liking for him at that moment.

I strode towards him; he rose from his stool to face me but before he could raise his hands to defend himself I had grabbed him by the collar of his tunic. I heard Philippe and Godefroi shout out in protest, heard the clatter of wood upon stone as they leapt up from their stools, but I ignored them.

'What do you know of the priest's business with Eadgyth?' I demanded.

Radulf had gone white; no doubt he had not been expecting this. The blood was roaring through my veins now. Before me stood a trained warrior, a man of the sword, a knight of Normandy, and he was afraid.

'Tell me!' I yelled, spittle flying, striking his cheek.

But Radulf was clearly too shocked to speak, for no words came out, and before I could say it again I felt hands on my shoulders, tearing me away from him. Desperately I tried to struggle, to flail my arms; all I wanted at that moment was to strike him, to punish him for his lies, but it was no use, for they had me pinned.

'Tancred,' someone shouted in my ear, and I recognised the voice as belonging to Wace. 'Tancred!'

The fury started to fade and I found myself breathing hard as my senses returned. I shook my

351

shoulders and felt the hands lift from them. The others were all staring at me, I realised, keeping their distance. None of them were speaking. The nun, Burginda, had risen from her chair, but she clearly did not know what to do, for she stood as if frozen to the floor. There was silence.

I felt the weight of their gazes pressing upon me. It was too much; I couldn't stand being in this place any longer, surrounded in this way. I turned and made for the door.

'Where are you going?' said Wace.

'To find Ælfwold,' I answered, neither looking back nor caring to close the door behind me as I marched outside.

It must have rained during the night, or earlier that morning, for all about lay bright and glistening in the sun. The grass was wet, the ground soft under my shoes. The scent of damp earth was all around me, and had the wind not been so piercing I might have thought that spring was almost upon us.

This was the first time I'd seen the nunnery in daylight, and for some reason it seemed smaller than when we had first arrived. The grounds seemed more confined, the walls pressing in. All was closer than it had appeared at first; the guest house in fact was hardly fifty paces from the cloister.

I passed through the orchard: through the row upon row of leafless trees, set apart at strict intervals, their branches barely touching. Beyond it lay the nuns' dormitory, where I would find Eadgyth's chambers. That any nun but the abbess herself should have her own quarters was unheard of, to my knowledge at least, but then perhaps it was not uncommon for a woman of her standing: a woman who, after all, had been wife to a king, even if it was to a false king such as Harold.

I heard Eudo's voice behind me, calling: 'Tancred!'

I did not answer but carried on until I heard footsteps and I glanced across my shoulder to see him running up. Further behind, the nun was following, lifting her skirts in ungainly fashion as she hustled across the grass. I knew that I wasn't supposed to venture anywhere in the convent grounds unescorted, but at that moment I did not care. Finding the priest was all that mattered.

Eudo fell into step beside me. 'Ælfwold won't be pleased,' he said.

'He isn't pleased with me anyway,' I replied. 'If he had the choice, he'd probably sooner be rid of me. But we have to know.'

'I thought we would wait—'

'—until Eadgyth arrived,' I finished for him. 'And she is here now.'

By now we'd entered the cloister, which ran around three sides of the courtyard between the church, the dormitory and what I guessed must be the refectory, from the smell of bread that was wafting from it. Ahead of us two nuns were walking, speaking to one another as they did so. They glanced over their shoulders as we came up. Both were fairly young—novices most probably— round of face and in stature, with wisps of brown hair trailing from beneath their wimples. They were alike enough, indeed, to be sisters, if not in fact twins. They shied away as we approached, letting us past.

'What are you going to do once you find him?'

Eudo asked.

'I'm not sure.' I stopped and leant closer to him, lowering my voice. 'I've seen Malet's letter.'

'What?' Eudo asked. 'When?'

'Last night,' I replied. 'While he was sleeping I went into his room and read it.'

'You—' he began, but didn't go on. No doubt he had been about to rebuke me for having done it alone, except that he had given me the idea in the first place. 'What did it say?'

I glanced about to make sure no one was listening. 'Nothing that I could make sense of. Just two words in Latin. *Tutus est.* "It is safe".'

'What does it mean?'

'I don't know,' I said. 'But Eadgyth will.'

The doors to the dormitory building lay open before us. Inside, a short hallway opened into a larger, vaulted chamber with plastered walls. To one side a flight of narrow stone steps led upwards. I checked to see if the two novices were still about, but they had gone, and there did not seem to be any other nuns near. At this time of morning they were probably out in the fields seeing to the animals, or else tending to the herb-garden, if they had one.

'This way,' I told Eudo as I went in, heading for the stairs. The sound of my footsteps echoed off the stonework, though at the same time I could make out voices, raised but nevertheless indistinct.

I began to climb, with Eudo close behind me. The voices grew louder as we ascended. There were two of them: one clearly belonging to the chaplain, for I recognised his gruff tone even though I could not make out his words; the other that of a woman. She sounded agitated, distressed even. It was then that I realised their voices were more than just raised. They were shouting at one another.

I exchanged a look with Eudo, and we hurried on up the stairs, into a wide room with low beams and a sloping roof. Its length was taken up by an oak table, while upon the floor lay richly embroidered rugs in threads of many colours. A private dining-chamber, I guessed, or else a place for receiving and entertaining guests.

There was a door at the far end, and the voices were coming from within. The floorboards creaked gently as we rounded the table towards it, and I hoped that we were not making too much noise, though above their shouting I doubted they'd be able to hear. I let Eudo in front—he was the only one who could understand what they were saying—and he crept up to the door, I behind him, taking care to step upon the rugs so as to muffle our footsteps. He pressed his ear against the door, although in truth he hardly needed to. Even from where I stood I was able to make out distinct words, even if I did not understand what they meant.

'Eadgyth—' I heard the chaplain say, in what sounded like a soothing tone. He was cut off.

'*He is min wer!*' Eadgyth said.

'"He is my husband,"' Eudo whispered, as a frown crossed his face.

'What?' I said, too loudly, and he waved me quiet. That wasn't what I had been expecting. *He is my husband.* Eadgyth's husband had been Harold, but what did the usurper have to do with this?

'*Hit is ma thonne twegra geara fæce,*' she shouted. '*For hwon wære he swa langsum?*'

355

'Two years,' Eudo murmured. 'Something about it being more than two years. The rest I'm not sure.'

It was more than two years since the invasion, I thought. Was that what she meant?

*'Thu bist nithing,'* she screamed, over what sounded like protests from Ælfwold. *'Thu and thin hlaford!'*

*Nithing.* That word, at least, was familiar. Had not the priest himself used it of us not so long ago?

'What is she saying now?' I asked Eudo.

He shook his head as he drew away from the door. On the other side I began to hear footsteps. 'Quickly,' he hissed. 'Let's go.'

I turned and made for the stairs, but in doing so forgot about the table behind me. I crashed into it, and it shuddered loudly against the floorboards. I stumbled forward, cursing my stupidity. Before I could recover, the door flew open.

Ælfwold stood there. 'Tancred,' he said. 'Eudo.' He looked confused for a moment, before his face turned to anger. 'I told you to stay behind.'

I was paying him little heed, however, for behind him was standing the oath-breaker's wife herself: a woman somewhere in her middle years, although she was not unattractive for that. Slight of build, her complexion was milky-pale, her neck long and graceful as a swan's. It was not hard to understand what one even such as Harold Godwineson might have seen in her. But her eyes were brimming with tears, her cheeks wet and glistening in the candlelight, and despite myself I felt a sudden stab of sympathy for her. What had the priest said that had driven her to such sadness?

Then I saw that she clutched to her breast a

356

sheet of parchment that curled at the edges, as if holding on to the memory of the scroll it had once been. The same parchment that I had found and read in the priest's room last night; it had to be. Was that what had distressed her?

'Why are you here?' Ælfwold demanded. 'Were you listening?'

I hesitated, trying to think of some reason I could give, but nothing came to mind. The silence grew, and I felt I had to say something, anything at all just to break it, when anxious shouts rose from the floor below. I looked down the stairs and met the aged eyes of the nun Burginda. She was pointing up at us, and beside her stood Cynehild, the abbess, her gaze fixed unflinchingly upon us.

'You,' she called up to us. She raised the skirts of her habit and climbed the steps, the hem just trailing upon the stone. Burginda followed close behind her. 'You're not allowed in here. These chambers are for the sisters of the convent alone.'

'My lady—' I began to protest, though in truth I could think of nothing to say. For I could hardly tell her why we were really here, and what good would it do in any case?

She reached the top and glanced about the room. 'Ælfwold,' she said, in French still, no doubt so that we too could be party to what she had to say. 'You know that men aren't allowed in the nuns' dormitory.'

'I told them not to come with me,' he said angrily, and he glared at me. 'I don't know what they are doing here.'

A number of other nuns were beginning to gather at the bottom of the stairs, and I spotted amongst them the two sisters we had passed beneath the cloister.

'I don't just mean them,' the abbess said, almost spitting the words. 'You cannot be here either. This is not a place for any man, even a priest.'

She walked past me and Eudo towards Eadgyth, whose face was streaming with tears, then looked back to us, placing an arm around the lady's shoulders.

'You dare to upset the nuns under my care,' she said, her voice rising. She was speaking to all of us now; her eyes, glinting as if aflame, settled first on the chaplain, then on Eudo, and finally on myself. 'You dare to come here and disturb the order of this house.'

'*Min hlæfdige*—' Ælfwold began, more gently, almost beseeching, I thought.

The abbess was not to be placated. 'There will be order in this house,' she said, raising her voice over the chaplain's, silencing him. 'As long as you are here, you will respect that order.'

I bowed my head. None spoke: not myself, nor Eudo or the chaplain, nor the nuns gathered outside the dormitory below.

'Now,' the abbess said. 'Return to the guest house while I decide what is to be done, and consider yourselves fortunate that I'm not expelling you from here forthwith.'

The priest bowed deeply to Eadgyth. Her face reddened, and I thought she might be about to cry once more, but she did not. Instead she clutched at the parchment, crumpling it in her hand, and threw it at the priest, her gaze defiant.

'Go,' the abbess said.

The day was not warm but suddenly it felt stifling in that chamber.

'My apologies, my lady,' I said to the abbess as I left. But I did not dare meet those fiery eyes again, nor witness the wrath of God contained therein.

## CHAPTER TWENTY-EIGHT

Throughout the rest of that day the priest said nothing to us. Towards evening one of the nuns arrived with news that the abbess wished to speak to him, and he went to her hall to meet with her. I wondered what they were discussing, for he was gone some time, and it was dark when at last he returned.

While he was gone I spoke with Malet's men, to see what else they knew, which turned out to be very little. As I had thought, this wasn't the first time that Malet had sent them here, nor was the name of Eadgyth unknown to them. On the other hand, it seemed that they hadn't known until now who she was—that this was the same Eadgyth who had been wife to the usurper—and so that at least had been a surprise to them. But still I did not trust them completely; the thought that they had been hiding things from us all this time made me more than a little uneasy.

All six of us were gathered at the long table when the priest came back in, bringing the cold air with him. It played at the hearth-fire and rustled the rushes that lay upon the floor.

'We're to leave tomorrow morning,' he announced, and made for the stairs.

'Tomorrow?' I asked. It seemed as though we had hardly arrived, though I supposed that, now we had done what we had come for, there was no reason for us to stay.

He paused for a moment, regarding me with tired eyes. 'Our business here is done,' he said. 'We leave for Lundene at first light, at the request of Abbess Cynehild. She has given us her grace and allowed us to stay this night, but no longer. Make sure that you are ready to leave on the stroke of prime.'

He carried on up the stairs; I watched him go. The abbess had decided, then, that we should leave after all. It didn't surprise me, for we had broken the rules of the convent, and though I was not proud of that, at the same time neither did I feel particularly ashamed. We had done only what we had to, though I was still unsure what we'd learnt. Nothing of what Eudo and I had heard seemed to have been of much consequence. Except, that was, for Eadgyth's mention of her husband, Harold. And what was it that she and the priest had been arguing about?

The rest of us retired not much after that. For a while I lay upon my bed, listening to the calls of the owls in the orchard. There had to be some way of finding out, though I could not see it. After I had seen how distressed Eadgyth had become earlier, I could hardly go back, for she would only raise the alarm. And I couldn't bring myself to force information from a nun.

Eventually I must have slept, for the next I was aware the moon was shining in through the shutters, throwing faint light across the wall. I blinked, trying to work out what had woken me. I lay still, taking shallow breaths.

Footsteps, light and quick. They came from

below: from the hall. Briefly I wondered if it could be Ælfwold, or one of the other knights, but I had grown used to the sounds of their movements by then, and I didn't think it was any of them.

I sat up, suddenly alert. I was still dressed; I had learnt last night how cold it could become in this house, especially with a draught blowing in. The wind was less blustery tonight, but even so, it was not warm beneath the blankets. I shook them off and rose, lifting my knife-sheath from the floor and buckling it to my belt. Then, barefoot, I ventured out on to the landing, towards the stairs.

The hearth-fire had long since burnt out, but whoever it was must have had a lantern with them, for a soft glow lit up the stairs and the hall below. But who would be about at this hour, and in this house? I placed my hand upon the hilt of my knife, and then, moving slowly so as not to make a sound, started down the stairs.

The lantern-light flickered and I heard a crash of metal, as loud, I thought, as the bells in the church. A muttered curse followed—a woman's voice. I edged further down the stairs, keeping as much as I could to the shadows, crouching low.

A figure dressed in brown cloak and habit knelt beside the hearth, hastily collecting the cooking pots she had knocked over, replacing them where they had stood. The copper gleamed in the light of the lantern, which rested on the table beside a vellum scroll. Another one, I thought.

She was turned towards the hearth, away from me, and so I could not see what she looked like. Even when she stood up and turned, still her face lay in shadow. She made for the door, pausing only to retrieve her lantern. The scroll she left on the table as the room fell into darkness.

I heard feet upon the landing and turned to see a shadow standing at the top of the stairs.

'Tancred,' it said, and I recognised the voice as belonging to Wace. I motioned for him to be quiet and he followed me as I went down into the hall, moving as quickly as I could, though it was dark and the steps were not even.

'What was that noise?' Wace asked, more softly this time. 'What are you doing down here?'

I glanced back up past him towards the landing. If any of the others had been woken by the noise, they had no sooner fallen asleep again. But I heard no further signs of movement.

'There was someone here just a moment ago,' I murmured. 'One of the nuns, I think.'

The table was in front of me, the scroll upon it. I picked it up. It was smaller than the one Ælfwold had carried, and sealed with a blob of dark-coloured wax, into which I could feel imprinted some sort of symbol, though it was too dark to make it out.

'She left this here,' I said. Yet another letter. But why come in the middle of the night to leave it here, rather than give it to us during the day? I tucked it into my belt and went to the door.

'Where are you going?'

'To follow her,' I said, and hurried outside.

A cloud had passed in front of the moon and the convent buildings lay in shadow. There was no sign of her. I shivered as cold gripped my bare feet; the grass was white with hoarfrost. Over my shirt I had only my tunic.

'She's gone, whoever she was,' Wace said, with a yawn. 'And it's too cold to be standing here.'

He went back inside, leaving me there. And then, amidst the trees in the orchard, I spotted the soft glow that could only come from a lantern and, holding it, a dark figure making for the cloister. If she reached it then she could easily lose me. There were too many buildings, too many doorways that one could slip into, and I didn't know my way around.

I ran after her, my feet pounding the hard earth. She was nearly at the other side of the orchard when she must have heard me, as she gave a glance over her shoulder, lifted her skirts and began running too. Stones, sharp and hard, dug into my soles, but I didn't care, for I was catching her, when she turned beneath the arch between the church and the chapter house. The arch that led into the cloister. She disappeared from sight and I willed myself faster, arriving just in time to see her duck into the church to my right, at the same time as on the other side of the courtyard another nun came into sight, swinging a lantern of her own. The circatrix, I realised, on her nightly rounds.

I shrank back behind a pillar, watching her even as I kept glancing at the church door. The stone was cold upon my fingers. I was breathing hard, the air from my lips turning to mist, and I tried to still it so as not to be seen.

The circatrix stopped by one of the doors on the southern range, sliding a large key from a ring at her belt into the lock. She gave the door a shove; it opened with a great creaking of hinges and she entered.

Without a moment's hesitation I made for the church entrance. The door was already slightly open—not by much, though if the circatrix had noticed it, she would have known that something was wrong. I went in, taking care to close it again.

Inside, the church lay in almost complete darkness. Only the moon gave any light, its milky gleam coming in shafts through the great glass windows that I had seen when we arrived, lending everything a grey, ghostly appearance. Columns rose up in two rows from the nave, decorated with plant-like designs in many shades, though it was too dim to see what they were. Nor did I have time to admire them: I didn't know how long it would be before the circatrix's rounds brought her here.

All was quiet, and I wondered if perhaps there was another way out of the church that I had not seen from the outside. I stepped forward across the stone floor, towards the centre of the nave, and looked around for any sign of the nun. Beyond the choir benches lay the chancel with its high altar, draped with white cloth trimmed with gold, upon which rested a gospel book. To either side were side altars, smaller and less grand in their decoration, but probably no less effective as hiding-places.

I tried the high altar first of all, approaching slowly, listening out for the slightest sound of movement that might give her away. But I could hear nothing, and when I reached it and searched behind it, there was no one there. I crouched down, lifting the cloth to reveal the cavity where relics were often kept, but it was barely large enough for a child to squeeze into, let alone a woman.

I heard footsteps behind me and turned as a shadow darted out from behind one of the columns in the nave, running towards the door. She had a start on me but I was faster, and before she had even reached the handle I had caught her, placing my hand on her outstretched arm and spinning her about to face me. She gave a stifled cry and tried to shake me off, but I held firm.

It took me a moment to recognise her, but then she looked up at me and I saw her face: her skin pale in the moonlight; the wrinkles about her eyes; the weary expression she wore, as if she had seen everything there was to see in the world, and wished only to be free of all its burdens.

Eadgyth.

She tried to tug her arm away, and I realised I still had hold of her wrist. I let it go. 'The circatrix is close by,' she said in strongly accented French. 'If I were to call out now, she would hear me, and you would face the abbess's wrath.'

If it was meant as a threat, then it was a poor attempt. 'And you would have to explain why you're not in your chambers,' I replied. 'What were you doing in the guest house?'

She looked back at me, lips pursed, unspeaking. I pulled the scroll that she had left out from my belt, brandishing it in front of me. 'What is this?' I asked her.

She eyed it carefully. 'It is meant for your lord.'

'What does it say?'

'Do you expect me to tell you?'

I ran my fingers towards the seal. 'I could read it for myself, and then I would know.'

She looked at me doubtfully, probably wondering if I were bluffing, since what reason would I, a knight, have for knowing my letters?

'I cannot stop you,' she said eventually. 'All I can do is give it to you in good faith, and hope that you will do the right thing.'

I placed the scroll back in the loop of my belt; I would return to it later. 'You were speaking with Ælfwold earlier,' I said. 'What were you saying?'

'I was telling him how worthless your lord is,' she said. 'How he is too free in making promises that he does not intend to keep.'

'Promises?' I asked. 'What promises has he made?'

She did not seem to hear me. 'It is amusing, I suppose, that it should be so, given that your people accused Harold of the same failing.'

Of course: several years ago, Harold had sworn an oath to be Duke Guillaume's man, to support his claim to the kingship. An oath made upon holy relics, which he had later broken when he had assumed the crown for himself. As a result he was now dead, killed on the field at Hæstinges.

'Your husband was a perjurer and a usurper,' I told her.

'He was a good man,' she said, and I saw tears forming in the corner of her eyes. 'He was kind and honest and truthful in all matters, and above all else loyal to his friends. Your lord used to be one of them, at least until his betrayal.'

'Malet betrayed him?' I asked. 'How?'

'First by joining your duke's invasion,' she said, almost spitting the words. 'And even now, after Harold's death, he continues to betray his memory. He and Ælfwold both.'

'Ælfwold? What do you mean?'

But again she appeared not to be listening. 'He is no better,' she said, shaking her head as anger entered her voice. 'But he is nothing but his lord's man; he merely does what he is told. He cares not

366

for what is right. I trusted Guillaume, and this is how he repays me?'

'I don't know,' I said, a little too harshly maybe, but I was tiring of the way she seemed to be speaking only in riddles. Clearly she thought that because I was one of Malet's men I knew more than I did. Although, I realised, as long as she thought that, I held the advantage.

'It has been more than two years since Harold died,' she said. 'Two years since I stood on that field after the battle and saw him lying there. Does he think that I do not grieve, that I do not deserve to be told?'

'Told what?' I asked her, but she had already turned away, her sobs echoing off the walls and the vaults of the church. A glimmer of orange light shone in through the windows. The circatrix, I thought, and froze, thinking that the door was about to open and she would come in. But she did not, and after a moment the light moved on. Even if she was not on her way straight to the church, she must be nearby.

I cursed under my breath. If we were caught together, the consequences would be severe, but particularly for Eadgyth. I recalled the beatings I had taken; I didn't know whether such punishments were prescribed here at Wiltune. More probably being caught with a man who was not of the church would mean her expulsion from the convent. I didn't wish that upon her, even if she were the usurper's widow. For, despite her riches and her private chambers, it was plain to me that she was a broken woman. This nun's life of humility and servitude was all she had. What else was there for her in this world?

'Come on,' I said to her. 'We can't stay here.'

I went to the door, opening it just enough that I could peer outside, into the cloister. A cloud had come across the moon, which was good, since it would make us less easily seen. Then I caught sight of the circatrix emerging from the dormitory, her lantern held beside her, iron keys dangling from her belt. There was one more door on that eastern range, which would belong to the chapter house, if I remembered the monastery at Dinant correctly. But after that the next place she'd check would surely be the church. We didn't have much time.

I watched as she walked along the cloister towards the chapter-house door, unlocked it and went inside. If we were to go, this was our chance.

'Come on,' I whispered, signalling for Eadgyth to follow me. The door opened smoothly, without a sound, and I hurried out and down the single step into the cloister, Eadgyth behind me. Beneath her habit she was wearing shoes, I noticed, but that could not be helped now.

'Quickly,' I said, and started making for the arch that we had come in through.

She caught my sleeve. 'This way,' she said, and headed off straight across the grass, towards the dormitory. I hesitated, but I knew that the longer we waited, the more likely it was that the circatrix would come out from the chapter house and see us.

I went after her, the frost upon the grass biting the soles of my feet. The doors to the dormitory were unlocked and we slipped inside, just as I heard the jangle of keys further down the cloister. But no shouts followed; we had made it. I looked to Eadgyth, but she was already climbing the first few steps up to her chambers.

'My lady—' I began, trying to keep my voice low. I was aware not just of the circatrix outside but also of the rest of the nuns in the next room.

'No,' she cut me off. 'I cannot risk being out any longer. I must go.'

'I would speak with you again later,' I said.

She shook her head. 'I will speak no more. There is nothing else I wish to say, to you or Ælfwold. But give the letter to your lord; he will know what it means. If nothing else I ask that you do this for me.'

She appeared so small and fragile, somehow, though I knew that she was neither old nor infirm. As I looked up at her, I could not help but feel sorry for her.

I felt a dryness in my throat, and swallowed. 'I cannot promise that.'

'I know,' she replied, and there was a resigned look upon her face. 'You are one of his men, after all.'

She turned and, neither making a sound nor looking back, ascended the rest of the stairs. And then she was gone, her dark habit vanishing, becoming one with the darkness. Eadgyth, Harold's widow.


## CHAPTER TWENTY-NINE

I had to wait until the circatrix was safely out of sight before I could pass through the cloister again. In all it might have been as much as half an hour from my leaving the house to coming back, though it felt like much longer. Wace and Eudo were both waiting in the hall when I returned.

'Where were you?' Wace asked.

'Let's go somewhere we can't be overheard first,' I told them. 'Then I'll tell you.' I wasn't sure that the walls or floors here were thick enough to stop anyone else from listening.

The mill was close by, and so that was where we went: far enough from the house or from the cloister that we could neither be seen nor heard. The door was unlocked and I pushed it open. Sacks lay piled along one wall, some of them split with grain spilling out. The dark forms of rats scurried away as we approached.

'Enough of this, Tancred,' Eudo said. 'Tell us what's going on.'

'It was Eadgyth,' I said. 'She was the one who left this.' And I brought the scroll out from my belt. 'I caught up with her in the church.'

'What did she say?' Wace asked.

'Nothing I could make much sense of,' I said. 'She kept talking about her husband. About Harold, and how Malet was betraying his memory.'

Eudo narrowed his eyes. 'What do you mean?'

'I don't know,' I said. 'It seems he made some promises to her some time ago, though she never explained properly. Promises which he hasn't kept, at any rate.'

'So we were right,' Wace muttered, raising an eyebrow. 'He has been conspiring with her.'

'Except that she seemed to want nothing more to do with him,' I said.

'Yesterday she called him *nithing*,' Eudo put in. 'It means someone who is worthless or depraved. It's one of the worst insults the English have.'

I had wondered what that meant. Ælfwold himself had used it of us the night before we had arrived here, I remembered now. Was that how he regarded us? I tried to put it from my mind; it wasn't important now.

'I don't see how Malet can be a traitor,' I said. 'Whatever pledges he might have made to her once, it's clear that they mean nothing to him now.'

At the very least his message hadn't given her the answer she wanted. What was it, then, that she believed she deserved to be told?

'Still,' Wace said, 'as long as they continue to pass secret letters between each other, how can we be sure?'

'There is one way,' Eudo replied, and he pointed to the letter in my hand. 'We have to open it.'

Wace nodded. 'It's the only way we can know for certain.'

'That's what we thought about Malet's letter,' I said. 'And we're no closer after that.'

It struck me as unusual, too, that Eadgyth would leave any important message in our hands, if she had any reason to worry it might be intercepted before it reached Malet. I'd made no assurances to her—as if I would to the widow of our enemy. And so whatever words were contained within this scroll, it seemed unlikely that they would tell us what we wanted to know.

But all the same I knew that Wace and Eudo were right. It was not the hardest decision I'd ever had to make.

'I need light,' I said. There were no windows in the mill-room, nor had we brought any torch or lantern, in case we should be seen. But I could hardly read in the darkness.

The moon was behind a cloud, but it was enough to see by as I stood in the doorway, with the other two gazing over my shoulder. I ran my finger over the seal, which I now saw bore the imprint of a dragon, or some other large winged beast, with the words 'HAROLDVS REX' around its edge. *King Harold*. Another mark left by the usurper. But Harold was long dead, and Eadgyth must surely possess a seal of her own. Why would she use his?

I pressed it between my fingers; it broke easily. I unfurled the parchment, and in the moonlight I saw neat lines of carefully rendered script, only this time it was not in Latin. Some of the letters I did not even recognise.

'What does it say?' Wace asked.

'I don't know,' I said. 'Whatever tongue it's written in, it's not one that I know.'

Latin was the one language in which I was lettered; even French and Breton I knew only how to speak, not read. I glanced down the sheet, hoping to find a word I might know. In the greeting on the first line was Malet's name, as I might have expected; a little further down I found Harold's, but otherwise there was nothing.

Of course it might be in English, I realised. That would make sense, since it was Eadgyth's first tongue. And though I had never heard him speak it, it seemed likely that Malet knew it too, given his parentage and the many years he had spent in England.

My eyes passed over a phrase from the middle of the letter. '*Ic gecnawe thone gylt the the geswencth, and hit mœg geweorthan thœt thu thone tholian wille*,' I said slowly, trying to pronounce the strange words. The writing was not as clear as the gospel books I had read when I was younger; the letters were smaller and harder to distinguish. I turned to Eudo. 'Do you know what that means?'

He shrugged. If it was English, I was evidently saying it wrongly.

'Is there anything at all you can make out?' Wace asked.

'Nothing of any use,' I said. 'Malet is mentioned, and Harold as well. That's as much as I can tell.'

'There's one man at least who might be able to tell us what it says,' Eudo said.

'Ælfwold,' I said grimly. Above all else one thing was becoming clear: sooner or later we had to speak with him. Short of Malet himself, who was two hundred miles away in Eoferwic, only he could have any idea of what all this meant. He had been to see Eadgyth before on this or similar business; we already knew that. And there was no one who was closer to the vicomte. If we were to find out what was really happening, he was the one we had to confront.

The only question was when.

*      *      *

We rode out from Wiltune at first light. Abbess Cynehild was there, stern-faced as ever, with half a dozen other nuns as well, huddled in their habits. Among them was Burginda, as well as the fair-haired girl who had met us in the abbess's house on our arrival. Eadgyth, though, was not there. Was that her choice, I wondered, or had the abbess told her to stay away?

Our horses and weapons were brought to us without a word, and it was likewise in silence that

373

we mounted up. It was good to have my sword by my side once more—not that I thought we were at any risk in the convent, but I was so used to its presence that without it I couldn't help but feel vulnerable.

I was relieved to be leaving Wiltune behind us, even though that meant another three days on the road, for at least we could be our own masters, rather than bound to the strictures of the nunnery and its abbess. Yet I was content to let Ælfwold continue to take charge for now, to let him make the decisions and for us to appear the servants, since perhaps then he would not suspect what was to come. For I knew that everything would change when we reached Lundene.

\*       \*       \*

As it had on our way to Wiltune, the rain continued to fall, bitter and unrelenting, each day coming down heavier than it had on the last. Down in the valleys the winterbournes were in full flow; some of the larger rivers had overspilled their banks and the fields all about lay in flood. In one place the waters had risen so high that it was impossible for us to cross, and we had to ride more than a mile upstream to find the next fording point before we could join the road again.

Our only respite came when we stopped for the night, but even then we kept hearing stories of fresh risings nearby. Norman traders had been set upon in the market at Reddinges; at Oxeneford a whole ship's crew had been killed in a tavern brawl when their Flemish speech was mistaken for French. And so shortly before Stanes we left the old road, deciding it was better instead to strike out across country and approach Lundene from the south, rather than risk running into trouble on the road. Even then we kept our hands by our sword-hilts. The paths that we followed were not the best travelled: the kind of way often frequented by robbers, who would lie in wait to ambush the unprepared. But if there were any, we did not see them, and it was past noon on the third day of March when the city came into sight, clinging to the northern shores of the grey Temes.

Of the encampment that had stood on the hill above Westmynstre, there was now not a single banner or tent to be seen. The king and his army were marching, just as we'd learnt in the alehouses and from other travellers we had passed on the way. They could not have been gone long, though, and I hoped we'd be able to catch them before they reached Eoferwic.

Wigod greeted us warmly on our arrival at Malet's house. Elise and Beatrice had gone to visit friends across the city and so weren't there, but the boy Osric was and he took the horses to the stables. I sent Malet's three men to help him, and gave the signal to Eudo and Wace, who accompanied the priest inside, while I went with the steward to fetch some food and drink.

The kitchens were modest in size, but then this was only a townhouse, not a great palace such as the one the vicomte had at Eoferwic. In the corner stood two large barrels; Wigod wrested the lid from one of them and filled a pitcher from it. Against the walls were long tables with pots filled with some kind of stew, while at one end of the room was a great fireplace with a spit over it, on which some kind of meat was roasting. My stomach rumbled, but it would have to wait a little longer.

'Your journey was pleasant, I hope,' Wigod said.

'Not particularly,' I replied. 'It was cold and wet. It rained all the way.'

He grinned. 'You'll be glad of some food inside you, then. Here, help me with these.' He pointed to some clay cups which rested on one of the tables.

I looked around to make sure that we were alone. 'You know your letters, don't you, Wigod?' I asked.

'Of course,' he said as he rested the pitcher upon one of the tables. 'Why?'

Being the steward of Malet's house I'd thought he must have to, if only to be able to receive his lord's writ when the vicomte was away from Lundene.

'I have something I thought you might be able to read for me,' I said, producing Eadgyth's letter from my cloak pocket. I had folded it to make it easier to carry, and opened it out before handing it to him. 'It's written in English, or so I think.'

He looked at me quizzically, and I suppose it was an odd request to make. But he took the parchment nonetheless, laying it out on the table where the light from the fire played across it.

'It is English,' he said. He frowned, then slowly began to read: '"To Guillaume Malet, vicomte of Eoferwic and lord of Graville across the sea, Lady Eadgyth, wife and widow to Harold Godwineson, rightful king of the English, sends her greetings—"' He broke off and drew back, turning away from the table. 'I cannot be reading this, Tancred. This is meant for my lord, not for me. If he were to

376

discover I had been doing this, he would expel me from his service, or worse.'

'I was the one who broke the seal,' I said. 'I will carry the blame, if anyone.'

'Where did you get this?' he asked.

'At Wiltune,' I said. 'From Lady Eadgyth herself. She was the one that Ælfwold was sent to meet. We think that your lord may be conspiring with her.'

'Conspiring?' Wigod said. 'No. That isn't possible. He is a loyal servant of the king.'

'And yet we know he was once a good friend of Harold,' I said.

'That was a long time ago.' I saw that there was sweat upon his brow, and his face had turned a shade of pink.

'So you knew of this?'

'It was never any secret,' he protested. 'In the years before he took the crown, Harold and his wife often stayed in this house when they came to Lundene. But he's dead now, and Eadgyth I haven't seen in years—I didn't even know she was still alive.'

'But Ælfwold did,' I said. 'He has met with her more than once, to pass on messages from your lord.'

'I know nothing of that, I swear,' Wigod said.

I had been given no reason to disbelieve the steward's word before now, and so perhaps he was telling the truth. I tried a different approach. 'Do you know anything about the promises Malet made to her?' I asked.

'Promises?'

There was no time to explain everything; I could not be too long in case suspicions were raised. In

377

any case, it was becoming clear to me that the steward knew nothing of Malet's business with Eadgyth. In one sense that was a good thing, for at least then I could rely on him to give me honest answers.

'Tell me what this says.'

'I cannot—'

'We need to know, Wigod,' I said. 'And one way or another, I will find out.' I rested my right hand upon my sword-hilt, so that he could see and understand my meaning. I'd hoped that he might offer his help freely, for I did not like resorting to threats, particularly to a man with whom I had no quarrel. But I knew that this was the only way.

For a moment he did nothing but stand there, his mouth agape. In shock, no doubt. But then he returned to the parchment, rolling it out across the table, for it had become creased again.

He cleared his throat and began, ' "To Guillaume Malet, vicomte of Eoferwic—" '

'I know that part,' I said impatiently. 'What comes next?'

'Of course,' he said, and I saw the lump in his throat as he swallowed. His trembling finger traced along the lines as he read, pausing at times, I assumed, so he could work out the right French word. ' "Every day I live I am consumed by grief. I cannot escape it, nor can I overcome it. In over two years while I have been here at Wiltune, you have given me nothing but false promises and false hope. I send this letter to beseech you, in the name of Christ our Lord and in the memory of the bonds of friendship which used to hold between us, to tell me where the body can be found—" '

I frowned. 'The body?'

378

'That's what it says,' Wigod replied. He carried on reading: ' "His blood is on your hands. I know the guilt that plagues you, and perhaps you are content to bear that. But I cannot live for ever without knowing. Otherwise, if you are unwilling to grant me this, then there is nothing more for me in this world, and my blood will be on your hands also." '

He stopped. 'That's all,' he said, as he looked up at me.

It sounded more like a plea for help than anything else, and a desperate one at that. But what did she mean about a body, and the blood that was on Malet's hands? Were the two things connected in some way; was he somehow responsible for someone's death? And how did his own message to her—*tutus est*—fit with that?

'You will say nothing of this to anyone,' I told the steward.

'No,' he said. His face had gone pale.

'Now, we ought to return to the others.' He nodded but did not move, and I placed a hand on his shoulder. 'I will find out what all this means, Wigod,' I said. 'I swear it.'

I did my best to sound confident, even though each time that we had sought answers so far, we had only found more questions. Yet I sensed that we were growing closer; that soon we would know. There was just one thing that we needed to do first.

\*     \*     \*

We waited until that night to speak to the priest, when we could be sure that he was alone and that

379

no one would interrupt us. The house was silent: Radulf, Godefroi and Philippe were asleep downstairs in the hall, while the ladies had long since retired to their chambers—almost as soon as they had returned, in fact, so I had not yet even seen them. It was probably a good thing, since I didn't think I could face them now, knowing what I did about Malet. If we were right and he was a traitor, how was I to tell them?

It was a blustery night; outside the wind was howling, the rain pattering upon the yard. We stood on the up-floor outside the door to the chaplain's room: Wace, Eudo and myself, swords by our sides. It was so dark that I could barely make out their faces, though each was standing not an arm's length away from me. Their lips were set and they did not speak. Neither of them wanted to do this, and nor in truth did I, but we did not have much choice.

I nodded to them and placed my hand on the handle. There was no lock on this door so far as I could see, and if there was any bolt on the inside, it had not been fastened, for the door opened easily and without a sound.

The room was small and sparsely furnished, not at all like the one in the guest house at Wiltune, which had been more akin to a royal bedchamber. Ælfwold lay asleep on his bed, his blankets twisted about him, his face pressed downwards into a pillow filled with straw. I entered slowly, taking care not to make too much noise. The walls were thin, and I didn't want to disturb the others in the house. Wigod's room was next to this one, and on the other side of that were the Malet family chambers.

I shook Ælfwold by the shoulder; he grunted and tried to roll on to his side, clutching at the blanket, but I wrenched it away. Beneath it he was dressed only in his undershirt.

'Wake up,' I said, shaking him again, more roughly this time.

He rolled back, hand still flailing for the blanket, and this time his eyes opened. 'Tancred,' he said, bleary-eyed and blinking. He looked up at Eudo and Wace, who were standing beside me. 'What's happening?'

'We know,' I said. 'About your lord and Eadgyth, and the promises he made to her.'

'What?' he asked, sitting up abruptly, glancing about at the three of us. 'What is this?'

'What promises did he make, Ælfwold?'

'Why should I tell you?' he retorted, and began to get up. 'I will not stand for this—'

'Stay where you are,' Eudo said, and I heard the scrape of steel as he drew his sword, pointing the tip towards the priest's throat. 'Otherwise I swear my blade will meet your neck.'

'You would not dare,' Ælfwold said, but he quickly sat back down as Eudo edged closer to him. 'I am a man of God; you kill me and your souls will burn for all eternity.'

I had not forgotten that, but then I had no desire to kill him. All I wanted was to frighten him enough that he would tell us what we needed to know.

'What do you know about a body?' I asked.

His face turned red. 'Who told you about that?'

I drew Eadgyth's letter out of my cloak pocket and tossed it to him. He caught it in his lap, unfolded it and, squinting closely, began to read.

'This is treachery,' he said after a moment. 'You swore an oath to the vicomte. You have no right to be meddling in his business, to betray his trust!'

'It is no more treacherous than what Malet has been doing,' Wace said. 'Conspiring with the widow of the usurper.'

'What are you talking about?' asked Ælfwold, growing angry all of a sudden. 'Lord Guillaume is no traitor. He will hear of this, I swear. He will hear of your disloyalty—'

'Don't play games with us,' I said. I was fast losing patience with him. 'What does she mean when she says Malet has blood on his hands? Whose is this body?'

'This is not your concern!'

'Tell us,' Eudo said as he advanced further, the point of his blade lightly touching the skin on the Englishman's neck, 'or I *will* kill you.'

I almost shot him a glance, but then thought better of it as Ælfwold stiffened and fell suddenly silent. If the chaplain had doubted our resolve before, he surely did not now.

'Whose is the body?' I asked again.

Outside the wind continued to howl; it rattled the shutters and rustled the thatch. I stepped towards the priest, the floorboards creaking beneath my feet; he tried to edge away but I reached forward and grabbed him by the collar of his undershirt. He stared back at me for what seemed an eternity, trembling in my grip, and I saw the fear in his eyes.

'It belongs . . .' he said, his voice starting to quiver. He broke off, and even in the dim light I saw drops of sweat forming upon his brow.

'To whom?' I demanded.

382

'It belongs', he said, speaking slowly, 'to the man who, three years ago, would have been king. To the oath-breaker and usurper, Harold Godwineson.'

## CHAPTER THIRTY

I stared at him for what seemed like an eternity. This wasn't what I had expected to hear. Harold Godwineson. His was the body that Eadgyth wanted to see.

I let go of Ælfwold's collar and stepped back; he sank back on to the bed. I glanced at the other two, and they back at me.

Wace frowned. 'Is this true?'

'It is the truth,' the chaplain answered, eyeing us nervously, as if unsure what to expect from us. As well he might, for this was far larger than any of us had been considering.

Eudo held his sword out once more, towards his face. 'If you are lying to us . . .'

'By God and the saints, I swear it is the truth!' Ælfwold said, his eyes wide, his voice trembling even more than before.

'But why should Malet know where Harold's body is?' I asked.

Wace frowned. 'I thought it had never been found. From what I heard no one could identify it among the fallen, so trampled and broken were all the corpses that day.'

I'd heard the same tale. We had all been there at Hæstinges, but there had been so much confusion that few had known exactly when the usurper had been killed and the field became ours. Some said that he was already maimed when an arrow had pierced his eye; others that it took the efforts of four mounted men, Duke Guillaume himself among them, to defeat him as he fought on alone, clinging to the vestiges of his power to the very end. The only thing we knew for certain was that it had been done.

Of his corpse, however, nothing had ever been said. Like most people, I assumed it had never been found: that he had simply been left to be eaten by the wolves and the crows, no different from the thousands of Englishmen who were slain that day. For as long as he was dead, it did not matter what became of his body. In the eyes of God he was a perjurer and a sinner, and even had he been recovered, no Christian burial could have been accorded him.

'That at least is the story as King Guillaume would wish it told,' Ælfwold said. 'But it is not what happened. The body *was* found—don't you see that it had to be? Without it, he couldn't be certain that Harold was truly dead. At first he called upon my lord to look for it amongst the slain, thinking he would be able to recognise him on account of the friendship he knew they had once shared. But when he was unable to do so . . .'

'He sent for Eadgyth,' I finished for him. Her words came back to me now, from that night when we had spoken in the church at Wiltune, and I understood what she had meant. She had been there after the battle, she had told me so herself. And she had seen her husband's battered corpse. 'That's right, isn't it?'

Ælfwold nodded, still watching us warily. 'They came to an understanding, that if she identified the body, in return she would be told where it was to be buried.'

'That was the promise Malet made to her, then,' I muttered. My heart beat faster; everything was beginning to make sense at last. 'And she upheld her part of the arrangement?'

'She did,' he said. 'She was able to recognise him by certain marks on his body: marks that only a wife could know. Though once she had done so, the resemblance soon became clear to the rest of us. His head had been severed, and was found some way from the rest of him, which even then was missing one leg, hacked off at the thigh. But it was him nonetheless.'

'You have seen the body?' I asked. 'You were there as well?' It was not unusual for chaplains to travel in their lords' companies, even to war, but I had not thought Ælfwold would have the disposition for it.

'I was,' he said with a touch of impatience. 'And I was on your side then, just as I am now.'

'Perhaps.' I wasn't sure that I yet believed him. 'What happened to Harold's body after that?'

'After that the duke entrusted it to Lord Guillaume's safe-keeping. He was told to see to its burial.'

'Except that he obviously went back on his word,' Wace pointed out. 'He didn't tell Eadgyth where he was burying it, or else she wouldn't be asking to see it still.'

'Where is it, then?' Eudo said. His sword was still in his hand, though it was no longer pointed towards the priest.

'I cannot say,' Ælfwold replied. 'It has been hidden these past two years. No one knows where

385

it is, save for the vicomte himself.'

'Hidden?' said Wace. 'What do you mean?'

'Don't you understand?' The priest rose to his feet, staring at each of us in turn. 'There are many who still support Harold, even this long after his death—many who now regard him as a martyr. If the place of his burial were to be made widely known, it could become the centre of a cult, a rallying point for rebellion. The king cannot allow that to happen. No one may know where the body is—not even Eadgyth.'

The priest was right, I realised. There were already many who wished to see us gone from these shores. I thought of the army that had attacked us at Dunholm, which even now was besieging the castle at Eoferwic—all those thousands of men. How many more might there be if King Guillaume had allowed the English to openly honour the usurper?

'Do you know?' I demanded of Ælfwold.

'No!' he said. 'I told you. Only the vicomte knows. Even I am not trusted with such knowledge.'

That hardly surprised me, but I did not say it. Certainly after all that had happened in the course of our travels, I would hardly trust him. Though Malet had felt secure enough at least to give him the letter in the first place. But then again, there had been nothing in it of any consequence, even if one knew what it was referring to—

And all of a sudden I understood how the pieces fitted together. 'So that was what he meant,' I said, turning to Eudo and Wace. 'He couldn't risk telling her where it was, in case word got out, and so that was all that he could say. *Tutus est.* "It is safe."'

'How do you know that?' Ælfwold said. Anger flashed across his face as he turned to look at me.

I opened my mouth to speak, but I had no answer. Silently I cursed myself for having let it slip.

'The vicomte will hear of this,' Ælfwold said, and it was not the first time that I had heard those words from him. 'You swore an oath to him!'

'We thought he was conspiring with Eadgyth against the king,' Wace said.

The chaplain gazed sternly at him. 'And so instead you betray the confidence which he placed in you. You are fools, all of you. You think you know what you're doing, but you're just interfering in matters that are beyond you. Lord Guillaume is no traitor, and never has been.'

I remained silent. Beside me, Eudo sheathed his sword.

'What about the other three?' Ælfwold asked. 'Have they had a part in this too?'

'No,' I said. 'They haven't.'

'Perhaps that is as well.' The chaplain sighed. 'Now, I've told you all that I know. You have what you wanted. Leave me, please.'

He closed his eyes as if in silent prayer. This was the man who had done so much for me after my injury at Dunholm. What had happened to our friendship to cause it to sour so quickly—to sow such distrust, such enmity?

I nodded to Wace and Eudo and we went, closing the door as he sat down upon the bed, his head bowed, hands clasped before him. We had what we had come for, which meant that we could now return to Eoferwic in good conscience. After everything, Malet was to be trusted.

And yet despite that, for some reason I could not help but feel uneasy, though at what I could not say exactly. Something in what the priest had said, perhaps: something that did not quite make sense. I no longer knew what to think. So far all my suspicions had been misplaced. We had held Ælfwold at sword-point; we had got all that we could from him. What else was there?

In any case we had other concerns now. The rebels awaited us in Eoferwic, and whether we fought for Malet, or in the name of Normandy or out of vengeance for Lord Robert, what was important was that we were there. For the army of King Guillaume was marching, and I meant to be with it when it struck.

*          *          *

We gathered at the stables the next morning as soon as we had broken our fast. Ælfwold was not to be seen, which I took to mean that he wouldn't be coming with us. In truth I was glad, for I had seen far more of him this past week than I would have wished, and my patience with him was all but spent.

Each of us took two mounts. Wigod had supplied us with destriers from Malet's own stables, and others he had managed to purchase while we had been away. He had a good eye for horseflesh, it turned out, for each one of them was in fine condition, strong and spirited as a knight's mount needed to be. As the leader of our small conroi, I assumed first choice—a brown with powerful hindquarters and a white diamond on his forehead—leaving the other knights to decide

388

between themselves.

I knew, though, that if we rode these horses north they would not be fresh when we needed them for the fighting, and so instead we saddled the rounceys we had bought in Suthferebi: the same ones that had also borne us to Wiltune and back. It meant we'd have twice the work, since we were not travelling in our lord's company and didn't have the retinue of servants who would usually care for the animals, but we had little choice.

I was leading my horses out into the yard when I spied Beatrice watching us from one of the windows on the up-floor. It was the first time I had seen either of the ladies since we had returned from Wiltune. Her eyes met mine, and she signalled to me, or so I thought, but it was only for a moment, for then she turned and was gone.

'I should go and tell the ladies we're to be on our way,' I said, leaving the others to see to the horses.

'Don't be long,' Wace called after me. 'We need to leave soon if we're to make best use of the day.'

There was no one in the hall. Wigod and Osric I knew were in the kitchens, mustering provisions for us to take on the road. I had seen little of the steward that morning; he had hardly spoken to me and in fact seemed to be avoiding me. I could hardly blame him for that.

'Your lord is a good man,' I had assured him when I'd met him in the yard earlier. 'I know it.'

I didn't feel that I could tell him yet what we had learnt. It was too soon, and still these doubts kept coming into my mind. There was something that we had overlooked, I was sure, though again I could not work out what.

'There is an explanation for all of this,' I told the steward. 'Whatever it is, I will find it.'

'I trust that you will,' he'd replied solemnly before hurrying away.

I ventured now up the stairs, towards the family chambers, which were at the far end of the up-floor. The door was fitted with a sturdy iron lock, while at either end of the lintel above it were carved the shapes of flowers with wide petals.

I knocked on the door; Beatrice opened it. Her face was drawn, as if she had not slept well. Her hair fell loosely across her shoulders, which took me slightly by surprise, but then she was in her own house, in her own chambers, where she had no need to keep it covered.

'Come in,' she said.

I remembered the last time we were together—the kiss she had laid upon my cheek—and suddenly I felt the same shiver running through me.

I tried to put it from my mind as I entered, finding myself in a small anteroom. A light breeze blew in through open shutters, and I could hear the rest of the men talking down in the yard. On one wall hung bright tapestries depicting a hunt in progress: men on horseback pursuing a tusked boar, with dogs running beside them, while other men waited with bows raised and arrows notched, waiting for the moment to let loose their fingers. An embroidered rug lay on the floor; at the other end of the chamber were two chairs, positioned either side of carved double doors.

'Is your mother here?' I asked.

'She is still abed,' Beatrice replied, glancing towards the doors. 'She worries for my father.'

'As do we all, my lady.' I did not like to think what she might say if she knew I had been accusing him first of consorting with Harold's widow, then of conspiring against the king.

'She has had stomach pains for several days. Since Robert left she has been hardly sleeping at night, and she is eating less and less during the day. Some days she barely goes beyond her room.'

'I'm sure Ælfwold will care for her, now that he's here.' The words did not come easily, and I had to force them out. I was no longer sure of anything when it came to the priest.

'I know,' she said.

'You've known him a long time, haven't you?'

'Almost all my life,' she replied. 'He came into my father's service when I was very young.'

'How young?'

'Five, perhaps six summers old,' she said. 'No more than that. Why?'

'What do you remember of him from then?'

She frowned at the question. 'I don't see what—'

'Please,' I said. 'I'd like to know.'

For a moment she hesitated, her brown eyes searching, but then she bowed her head. 'He often took care of me when I was small and my father was away on campaign,' she said. 'He liked to teach me things: how to speak English, to read Latin, to play chess. Even when I was older he was always ready to listen when I had something to say, always watching over me.'

'You trust him, then?' I asked.

She stared at me as if I were mad. 'There are few whom I trust more,' she retorted. 'Why do you ask?'

'Because he is English.'

'As are many of my father's men,' she snapped, her voice rising. 'And his own mother too; you must know that.' She continued to stare, but I said nothing, and eventually she turned away, towards the open window, looking out over the yard and the men and horses below. Her hair fluttered in the breeze, catching the light like threads of gold; her breasts rose and fell as she sighed.

'I see you're leaving again,' she said.

'We have to go if we're to meet with the king's army before it reaches Eoferwic.'

She drew away from the window, turning to face me again. 'You must promise that you will do all you can to aid my brother, and to rescue my father.'

'My lady, of course—'

'Listen to me,' she said sharply, cutting me off. Her cheeks flushed red, but she held my gaze as I watched her, waiting for her to go on. 'Robert is brave but he can also be foolhardy. He is a good horseman but he has few battles behind him. He will need your help. I want you to see that no harm comes to him.'

I wanted to explain to her that in the confusion of battle, with the enemy all around, it was impossible to keep watch over others. If her brother could not hold his own, there was little I could do to help him. But she would not understand that.

'I will try, my lady,' I said instead.

She did not look altogether pleased with that, but it was all the answer I was going to give her.

'In Eoferwic my father asked you to give us your protection,' she said. 'Now I ask that you do the same for him, and for Robert. I have seen with my own eyes your skill at arms. And I have heard from my father how you fought at Hæstinges, how you saved your lord's life there. I want you to serve them with the same conviction and honour as you served him.'

Honour, I thought bitterly. After what had happened these last few days, I had little enough of that left.

She was gazing at me expectantly. There was something of her father in that look, I thought: a confidence in the way she bore herself; a strength of will that I admired even as it frustrated me.

'Will you swear it?' she asked.

'What?' The question caught me by surprise and it took me a moment to recover my wits. 'My lady, I gave an oath to your father—an oath made upon the cross. I will do everything I can—'

'I want you to swear it to me,' she said. She came closer, holding out her right hand, slender and pale, towards me. Around her wrist a silver band shone in the light from the window.

'There is no need,' I protested.

'Swear it to me, Tancred a Dinant.'

I stared at her, trying to work out whether she was speaking seriously. But her eyes were steady, unflinching, as she drew herself to her full height before me.

Still she held out her hand, and I took her palm in mine. Her skin was soft and warm against mine, her fingers slender, her touch light. My heart quickened as I knelt down before her, clasping my other hand loosely over the back of hers.

'By solemn oath I swear that I will do my utmost to aid your father, and to bring him and your brother back safe to you.'

I looked up, waiting for her to say something, holding her hand between mine, our gazes locked together. I could feel the blood coursing through my veins, throbbing behind my eyes, which were suddenly hot, and growing hotter still for every beat of my heart. Soon I would have to look away, I thought, but I could not, for those eyes kept drawing me in, closer, closer.

Slowly I rose to my feet, reaching up to her temple, brushing her hair, like threads of silk, behind her ear. Her cheeks, usually milky-pale, were flushed pink, but she did not shy away at my touch, did not turn her eyes from me, and though she opened her mouth she made no protest. I could feel her breath, light but warm, upon my face, and suddenly my hand was sliding from her temple, running down the side of her neck, to the small of her back, feeling the curves of her body, so new and unfamiliar, and I was holding her to me as she placed her arms upon my hips, reached around to my back.

I leant towards her, and then at last our lips touched: softly, hesitantly at first; but the kiss quickly grew in intensity as I felt her breasts press against my chest and I held her tighter—

She broke off, wresting herself free of my embrace, twisting away. 'No,' she said. 'I can't.' She turned towards the wall, towards the tapestry, and I couldn't see her face, only her hair trailing across her shoulders and her back.

My heart was beating fast, my throat dry, and I swallowed. 'Beatrice,' I said, resting my hand upon her shoulder. It was the first time that I had called her by her name.

She shook my hand off. 'Go,' she said, her voice

raised as if in anger, though I wasn't sure what she could be angry about. She did not look at me.

'My lady—'

'Go,' she repeated, more forcefully this time, and this time I did as she asked, retreating across the chamber, watching her back, feeling an emptiness inside me, and I wished for her to turn, but she did not.

I closed the door behind me and, as I did so, I found myself determined that it would not be the last time I saw her. That whatever happened at Eoferwic, I would make it back alive.


## CHAPTER THIRTY-ONE

The skies were still heavy as we began our northwards journey. I did not see Beatrice again, and when I glanced towards the shutters on the up-floor as we left, they were all closed.

Just as we were readying to go, Wigod presented us with a bundle of cloth wrapped around a spear. It was mostly black, but as I unfurled it I saw that it had also stripes of yellow decorated with golden trim at regular intervals along its length.

'Lord Guillaume's banner,' the steward said. 'Take it. Use it. Bring it safely to him.'

'We will,' I replied. 'And when you see Ælfwold, tell him we're sorry.'

'For what?'

'Just tell him,' I said. 'He'll know what we mean.'

With that we had ridden away, leaving Malet's house behind us and climbing up the hill towards the Bisceopesgeat. We passed the place where I had been attacked that night, and the church of St Eadmund where I had seen the man I'd thought was the chaplain. Already it seemed so long ago, even though it was only a little over a week; the memory was growing hazy, as if I had but dreamt it. But all that was behind me now, I reminded myself, and so, soon, was the city itself.

It took us four full days to catch the king's army, by which time we had put, I thought, around a hundred miles between ourselves and Lundene. In every town we passed through, we heard stories of trouble out in the shires, of halls being burnt, of peasants rising against their lords. News of the northern rebellion was commonplace now, and everywhere the English were becoming restless, their confidence growing as they heard of their kinsmen's successes at Eoferwic.

The sun was dipping below the trees on the horizon when finally we came to the top of a ridge somewhere north of Stanford, and there looked down across the valley before us, and a sea of tents. There were hundreds of them arrayed there on the plain—not since the night before the great battle at Hæstinges had I seen so many men together in one place.

Truly it was a sight to behold. The wind was rising and by each fire flew the banner of the lord who camped there. Some had animals or fantastic beasts embroidered upon them—I saw amongst them boars and wolves, eagles and dragons—while others were simply divided into stripes with their owner's colours. And at the centre of the camp, by the tall pavilion that was the king's own tent, flew the largest banner of them all: the glistening gold embroidered on scarlet field that was the lion of

Normandy.

How many men there were I could not judge, though certainly their numbers had swelled since we had left for Wiltune. Two thousand men had accompanied Lord Robert to Northumbria, but it seemed to me that this host was even larger. Naturally not all of those who had gathered would be fighting men, for each of the lords would have their various retainers and servants: men to bring them food and wine, to look after the horses, to polish their mail. And there were craftsmen too, working at fires and at anvils, with hauberks hanging from posts outside their tents: armourers, I thought, working to repair broken mail. But it was, nonetheless, a significant host. I only hoped it would be enough.

I signalled to Eudo, who had been carrying the banner whilst we were on the road, and he passed it to me as I handed the reins of my destrier to him. Carefully I unfurled the cloth; then, holding the shaft in my right hand, I spurred my weary horse into a canter and rode along the ridge, giving the banner flight. The black and gold soared proudly in the wind, the bright threads glittering in the low sun. I waved for the rest to follow, then started along the stony track that led down the hill towards the camp.

Men looked up from their fires as we approached, and some even called greetings, but most took no notice of us. Indeed they had little reason to, for we could have been any number of things: scouts sent out to explore the country, or a foraging party, or messengers dispatched with the king's writ to the halls of nearby lords. But I had thought that the sight of the black and gold might

397

inspire some recognition at least, being as they were the colours of the man on whose behalf this whole army had been raised.

We wove in and out of the shadows of tents, past packhorses hitched to carts, along tracks that were already muddy with the passage of hundreds of feet. There were pits dug into the ground behind every tent, and the stench of shit filled my nose.

'Keep looking for the vicomte's son,' I told the others. 'He should be here.'

We rode past men carrying bundles of spears, and others rolling barrels that might have held ale, or else salted meat of some kind. In the shadow of a lone oak tree, knights practised with cudgels and shields, and a few with swords; their blades flashed in the low sun. Further ahead, a small stream ran through the camp, and men were collecting water in cups and pitchers, or else giving their animals drink.

Eventually we caught sight of the banner we had been looking for: the twin of the one I held. It flew high, not far from the king's pavilion, which meant that Robert Malet was held in high regard.

Of the king himself there was no sign; the flaps had been drawn across the entrance to his tent and there were two of his retainers posted outside, preventing anyone from entering. No doubt that meant he was in council with one or another of his barons. I'd never faced him in person, though I had often seen him from a distance: at his court in Westmynstre at Pentecost last year; and of course on the field at Hæstinges.

We made our way to the black and gold, beneath which six tents had been set up around a fire. Robert was indeed there, along with his men, who at first glance I guessed numbered around twenty, as well as his manservant: the thin one with the boil on his neck, who had been with him when we had first met.

Robert saw us approach, and he came over to greet us as we all dismounted. Again I noted he was clad all in black: an affectation that I hoped did not hinder his ability to fight, which was the reason we were here, after all.

'Your business at Wiltune went well?' he asked me after we had embraced.

'Well enough, lord,' I replied. For a moment I thought that he was about to enquire further, but he did not. How much did he know, I wondered, about the business with Eadgyth and Harold's body?

He introduced us to his men, and in particular to a burly, broad-shouldered man whose name he gave as Ansculf. He was the captain of Robert's household knights, and was evidently a man of few words, for he did little more than grunt when he saw us. He smelt of cattle dung and I noticed that he was missing two of the fingers from his shield hand, as well as part of his ear on his other side. But so far as I could tell he seemed experienced; there was a certain confidence about him that I recognised, for it was the kind that came only when a man had seen many hardships, many battles, and weathered all that could be thrown at him.

We left our horses with those of the rest of Robert's men, driving thick stakes into the earth between the tents and the stream and tying them to those. There was grass enough for the packhorses, but I made sure that mounds of grain were laid out for the destriers, and they stood around those, eating contentedly.

Robert's men were roasting what looked like a haunch of deer over the fire when we came back. It was a big slab of meat and the fire was yet small, but then one of them arrived with a bundle of sticks and began to build it up, and soon I could feel the warmth upon my face.

'What news is there from Eoferwic?' I asked Robert.

'Not much,' he said grimly. 'The castle still holds, so far as we know, but the rebels continue to press at its gates.'

'Any word on the enemy's numbers?' Wace put in.

Robert shrugged. 'Four, five thousand. Maybe even more. No one knows for sure. More are joining them every day, or so we hear. Men from all over the north: English, Scots, even some Danes as well.'

'Danes?' I repeated. I remembered what Malet had told me, about the invasion he believed was to come this summer. Was it possible they had arrived already, and we hadn't heard about it? 'You mean King Sweyn is with them?'

'Not him,' Robert said. 'Not yet, at least. These ones are adventurers, swords-for-hire, though there are certainly enough of them. We hear that half a dozen ships' crews have gathered beneath Eadgar's banner, some of them from as far afield as Orkaneya and Haltland.'

The Danes were fearsome fighters, wherever they came from. And even a mere six ships could mean anything between two and three hundred men.

'All the northern lords have allied with him, as

400

far as we've heard,' Robert went on. 'Gospatric of Bebbanburh, his cousin Waltheof Sigurdsson, and many more besides. The old families are uniting under Eadgar's banner, all of them proclaiming him king.'

Another usurper, I thought. As if the English had already forgotten the end that had befallen Harold. But this was not a thing to be taken lightly; since Hæstinges we had not faced a host of this size. Until now the risings we had encountered had all been local ones, and easily put down, the enemy weak and disorganised.

This was different. As I looked at Robert, I saw the unease in his eyes. He was thinking about his father, about whether we could save him. But I was uneasy for a different reason, for I had seen how well defended Eoferwic was, surrounded by its high walls and easily supplied both by land and by ship. Even if we laid counter-siege on one side of the river, the city as a whole could not be cut off. And so the only way we could break the English siege and save Malet was if we forced the enemy to do battle with us: for our host, led by King Guillaume, to face that of Eadgar, until only one remained.

And on that, I feared, hung not just our own fates, but that of England itself.

\*     \*     \*

For the next few days progress was slow—at least for those of us riding close to the vanguard, since every few hours we had to stop to allow the baggage train in the rear to catch up. Still, the country was easy and we must have made more than fifteen miles each day.

More of the king's vassals joined us as we marched, and each of them brought men: not just knights, but spearmen and archers too. They were not large bands—often as small as five men, sometimes as large as fifty—but they were all welcome. And so slowly the army grew, and I found my confidence returning, my anxieties subsiding. Not completely, for the fact was that most of these men had come fresh from their halls, from the comfort of their feasting-tables and the leisure of the hunt, ill prepared for the rigours of campaign. But as we came closer to Eoferwic, ever more of their time in camp was spent in training, and each evening the sound of steel upon steel rang out across the hills.

The land was slowly shaking off the grip of winter, and the days were noticeably warmer than they had been of late. The wind no longer held the same chill, and when we rose in the mornings there seemed to be less frost upon the ground: all of which helped to lift the mood while we were on the march. Even within our small group I found I was speaking more easily with Philippe and with Godefroi, the business at Wiltune almost forgotten, the tension that had once been there diminishing. Radulf alone remained distant, but at least he was no longer as hostile as before, and I was content with that. For in truth this was the first time in a long while that I found myself happy. I was at last where I belonged: not mired in suspicions of conspiracy, in talk of promises made and then broken. Not amidst men and women of the cloth, but here, among warriors, men of the sword. This had been my life since I was thirteen years old, and it was my life still. My lord might be dead, but I was not, and as long as I lived I knew it was my purpose to fight.

Of events ahead of us we heard little more, until on the fifth day after we had joined the army the king sent out his scouts to see what they could learn. They returned that evening with the news that Malet still held out, for they had seen the black and gold flying from the castle tower. But it was small relief, for the rebels' numbers were swelling still; it was said that more than five hundred from the fyrd of Lincoliascir had gone to join them. But if that was right, then they were the only Englishmen from south of the Humbre who had chosen to do so. The rest had refused to ride out for either side, unprepared on the one hand to march against men who were their kin, but on the other unwilling to defy a king who was their lawfully crowned liege-lord, chosen by God. Most of all I suspected they feared reprisal if they happened to choose the wrong side, and so by joining neither they hoped that they would escape punishment altogether. At the very least they were denying Eadgar men he might usefully employ, and that could only be a good thing.

The enemy had their own scouts, of course, and every so often we would spy the dark forms of horsemen upon the hills in the distance, watching us, though they quickly fled into the woods whenever a party was sent out to intercept them. The ætheling knew, then, that we were coming.

It was late on the sixth day when the order was passed down from the front to halt and to set up camp. I recognised the country here, for this was the same road we had taken on our way to

Dunholm not two months before, and I knew we couldn't be far from Eoferwic—no more, I thought, than half a day's march.

Towards sunset the king called all the leading nobles to his pavilion, no doubt to discuss with them how best to attack the city. Robert, as the son of the vicomte, was among them, and he took Ansculf and two other men with him. In their absence we sat on the ground outside our tents, sharpening our swords, cleaning our mail. A few ate; most drank. All knew that the fighting would soon be upon us: whether tomorrow or the day after, or the day after that, it would come, and so we had to enjoy this time while we could. Robert's men told stories of past battles they had fought, of foes they had killed, and in turn Eudo and Wace and I told them of Mayenne and of Varaville, and others we could think of.

By then the sun had set, and all across the camp fires burnt brightly in the gloom. Soon silence fell upon us; all that could be heard was the scraping of stone against steel and the crackling of the flames, when Eudo took up his flute and started to play.

His fingers stepped deftly along the length of the pipe as the song swept from soft to loud and back to soft, at first slow and almost mournful, before rushing into a furious cascade—like the clash of blades in the battle that was to come, I thought. And then just as suddenly it was falling away again, the rhythm slowing as it settled on one last sweet note which Eudo held, letting it draw out the last of his breath, until all about us was quiet once more.

'Where did you learn that?' I asked. Even though he had finished, still it seemed that note was there,

404

hanging in the air.

'It was passed on to me when I was a boy,' Eudo said. 'There was a wandering poet who came to play at our Easter feast. He always liked me, even gave me one of his whistles to practise with. Each year when he came back he'd teach me to play a different song, until my twelfth birthday when I left to serve Lord Robert. He was old then; I suppose he must be long dead now. That's the only one of his songs I remember.'

From somewhere not far off the sound of a harp floated on the breeze, following Eudo's example, perhaps. Men were singing drunkenly along to the tune, though it was not one that I recognised, at times even breaking out into laughter.

'We should be marching upon them now,' snarled one of Robert's knights, Urse by name. He was solidly built, with a stub of a nose and wide nostrils that gave him a piggish appearance. 'Why are we delaying here?'

'You'd prefer to attack now, after a day's march, rather than be fully rested?' Wace asked, rubbing at his injured eye.

'We'd have the advantage of surprise. We attack now and we can be upon them, inside the city before they even know it. The longer we wait, the longer the enemy will have to strengthen their defences.'

He was yet young, I saw, and like all youths he was impatient, eager for the bloodlust, for the joy of the kill. 'Have you ever been in an assault on a city?'

'No—'

I did not need to hear any more. 'Then you know nothing.'

405

He rose suddenly, cheeks flushed red with anger and with ale, and pointed a finger towards me. 'You dare to insult me?'

'Sit down, Urse,' one of his comrades said.

'No,' Urse barked as he stepped forward, almost stumbling over his shield, which lay at his feet. I didn't know how much he'd had to drink, but it was clearly too much. 'Who are these people, anyway? They join us from out of nowhere, and then think they can tell us what to do, what to think. We don't even know them, and we're expected to fight alongside them!'

'It's only the truth,' I said, not even troubling to get to my feet. The fire lay between us, preventing him from coming any closer, and he was more likely to hurt himself than me if he tried to do anything.

'Tancred is right,' Wace said. 'There's no sense rushing into an attack. Better to wait, to send out scouts and work out the enemy's weaknesses.'

'The king is not a stupid man,' I added. 'If he thought it was wise to attack now, then we would be doing so. But he doesn't, and so we wait. If you disagree with him, maybe you should tell him yourself.'

Urse looked at me, then at Wace, scowled at us and sat back down. Perhaps he saw the reason in what we were saying, though I doubted it. More probably he'd decided that two of us were more than he could handle on his own.

'Besides,' I said, 'more men are joining us by the day. By tomorrow we could have another two hundred swords.'

'Though so could the enemy,' Eudo put in.

I glared at him; he was not helping. At that

406

moment, though, I saw Robert returning, and alongside him Ansculf and the other two knights who had accompanied him. They all bore solemn expressions, and I understood what that meant. The plans had been decided, and all of a sudden the prospect of battle had become real to them. I knew the feeling well. It didn't matter how many years one had been campaigning, nor how many foes one had killed, for the fear was the same for every man: the fear that this fight might be his last.

'We attack tomorrow, before dawn,' Robert said. 'Rest now, gather your strength. You'll need it for the battle. We march when the moon reaches its highest.'

A murmur went up amongst the men. I glanced towards the west, where a glimmer of light was still visible above the line of the trees. I was relieved to see that the moon had not yet risen; we had a few hours, then, in which to sleep, and to ready ourselves. A chill came over me. It was happening, and it was happening tonight.

'Tancred,' Robert said.

'Yes, lord?' I replied.

'Come with me.'

I glanced at the others, wondering what this was about, then I got to my feet, buckling on my swordbelt. Robert turned away from the fire and the tents, towards the horses, and I followed him. His lips were set and he did not speak, nor did I press him. He saddled up his destrier, and I did the same, and then we rode out. The last light had faded and the camp was quiet now, save for the whinnying of horses in the distance and the occasional bout of laughter from around the fires. News of the impending attack could not have reached them yet.

Eventually we left the camp behind us altogether, striking out across the furrowed fields to the north and east, to where a clump of trees stood atop a small rise. All else was still. My breath misted before me. Though the days had been growing warmer, the night was yet cold.

We reached the top of the rise, where we dismounted. The branches formed a roof over our heads, blocking out the stars and the newly risen crescent moon. I looked back the way we had come, at the dots of firelight arrayed across the hillside. Not all had men by them; to fool any enemy scouts more had been lit on the fringes of the camp, to disguise our true numbers and make the army appear larger than it was.

'Why have you brought me here, lord?' I asked at last.

'Look,' he replied, pointing out into the distance. Beyond the trees the land fell away to a wide plain, beyond which, some miles away, wound a line of deepest black. It was a river—the Use, for it could be no other—and huddled on its shores was a town, ringed with walls and a palisade, in the midst of which rose a tall mound, with a castle tower set atop it, all in shadow.

'Eoferwic,' Robert said. 'That is where my father is. Where in only a few hours we will be too.'

'Yes, lord,' I replied, not knowing what he expected me to say. He couldn't have brought me all this way just to show me the city, surely?

'I have something I wish to ask of you, Tancred.'

His tone and his words brought me back to the morning I was summoned to see Malet at the castle, when he had first mentioned the task he had in mind for me. I glanced at Robert, and saw the same heavy eyebrows, the same pronounced nose and angular chin. Without a doubt he was his father's son.

'What is it?' I asked.

Robert's eyes were fixed on the city in the distance. 'Our scouts came back a few hours ago with further news of the enemy. It seems that while many of them are within the city, the rest have made their camp just outside the northern gates. In a few hours King Guillaume plans to send a thousand men to ride upriver to the next crossing. They will descend upon Eoferwic from the north and attack that camp before first light, hoping to draw the rest of the enemy out from the city. At the same time the rest of us, led by the king himself, are to attack from this side and capture the western quarter of the town, before crossing the bridge and taking the enemy in the rear.'

'And how does the king plan to get inside Eoferwic?' I asked. We had no siege weapons with us, so far as I had seen, and though we might try to break through the gates without them, it would mean the loss of many men, and I didn't think we had such numbers to spare.

'That's why I've brought you here,' Robert said. He took a deep breath. 'Before we can get inside, someone must first open the gates for us. Since it is my father we are fighting this campaign for, it has fallen upon me to find the men to do it.'

He looked at me then, his eyebrow raised, and I saw what he meant.

'You want me to do this,' I said.

'You and the rest of your companions. The king has asked for a small band of men, no more than half a dozen, to approach the city by river later this night, make its way through the streets unseen and to secure the gates.'

It would be dangerous, of that I had no doubt. All it took was for one person to see us, to raise the cry, and we would be dead men, for once we were inside it would be hard to get out again. And the only reason that Robert was asking us was because he didn't want to risk any of his own knights.

A sudden anger filled me. He was not my lord; I didn't have to do his bidding. While I was prepared to ride into battle with him, help him in what way I could, as I had promised Beatrice, I wasn't about to risk my life on some fool's errand for him, whom I barely knew.

I turned away, back to my horse. 'Find someone else, lord.'

'You know the city,' he called after me. 'My own men do not. I would not ask this otherwise.'

I ignored him as I swung up into the saddle and gripped the reins.

'I will see that you are well rewarded,' he said. 'I can give you silver, gold, horses, whatever you wish.'

I was about to dig my heels in and ride back to camp when I stopped. The wind blew; above my head the branches creaked.

'What about land?' I asked. In all the years that I had served his namesake, Robert de Commines, that was one thing he had never given me. A manor of my own, that I could call home, with a hall and a gatehouse and retainers to serve me as I served him. Since the day he had given me command of one of his conrois, that was what I had dreamt of, more than anything else. To

410

become a lord in my own right.

'If that is what you desire, I will see to it, for you and your comrades.'

I regarded him for a moment, wondering if he meant it seriously, and he watched me in turn. 'I have your word?' I asked.

'You have my word.'

'I will have to ask my men first.'

'Of course,' he replied. He mounted his horse; we rode back to the camp in silence. In truth I was somewhat disappointed in myself, as it dawned upon me how easily I had been bought. It was not that I thought I ought to have asked for more, but rather that I had given in at all. For land, to a great family such as the Malets, was like bread: they had enough that they could afford to give it freely.

But he had made the offer, and I could not deny that it was one worth fighting for. And all we had to do was make it through this night.

## CHAPTER THIRTY-TWO

The others took some convincing at first, most especially Wace, who like me was reluctant to risk his neck on Robert's behalf. But once I told them of the reward he had promised, it wasn't long before they agreed to the plan.

Thus it was that as the moon approached its highest we readied ourselves to ride out, donning mail and helmets, fastening our sword-belts to our waists, looping shield-straps over our heads. Around us the whole camp was rising; everywhere men were seeing to their horses, or kneeling in

411

private prayer. A priest was doing the rounds of the men, hearing confession from those who wished it, and I heard him murmur back in Latin as he absolved them of their sins.

How I wished for such consolation then, but I knew we didn't have the time. Already I could see gathering the men whom the king had chosen for the attack upon the rebels' camp, although it seemed to me it was far more than a thousand, for when all the spearmen and archers were added to the knights it looked as if nearly half our army was there. We were to go with them, and that meant we had to leave shortly. They had many miles yet to cover if they were to cross the river and reach Eoferwic before dawn, which by now could be but a few hours away.

Tiredness clutched at my eyes. I had not slept much, for every time I had tried, I saw only Dunholm and the faces of my comrades rising before me. My leg throbbed where I had taken that blow, though I had not thought about it in some time. While the wound had all but healed, the scar remained, and buried in it was the memory of my failure. This would be the first true battle I had fought since then.

We were leaving our destriers at the camp, since we had no need for them, and saddled the rounceys instead. They had done us good service so far; now they only had to take us a few miles more.

Robert came over just as we were about to leave. Like us he was dressed in his mail, and his helmet-strap was tied, though his ventail was open, the flap of mail hanging loose by his neck. Certainly he looked formidable, if not entirely comfortable. But

412

then not all men were born to be warriors. He was here not from a desire to fight but rather out of duty, to his father and to his king, and that was as much to be respected.

'We will bring your horses,' he said. 'As soon as the gates are open, look for us. There is a place for each of you in my conroi.'

I thanked him and he smiled, but it was a weak smile, and one that betrayed his anxiety. 'God be with you.'

'And with you,' I replied.

With that we spurred our mounts into action, riding out beyond the camp to where a mass of horses and men were assembling, under a banner which displayed a white wolf on a crimson background. I recognised it as belonging to Guillaume fitz Osbern, of all men in England and Normandy perhaps the closest to the king. I had met him more than once at the royal court, and knew how capable he was as a commander, for he had led the right wing of our army at Hæstinges: the very wing on which we had fought. He had a reputation as a hard man, though thankfully I'd never incurred his wrath.

He sat mounted on a grey horse at the head of the host, marshalling men, surrounded by other lords, and I knew them for such because their scabbards were inlaid with precious stones, their helmets rimmed with gold. Probably many of them had never faced a proper battle before, or at least if they had, then they had stayed some way back from the real fighting. Otherwise they ought to have known that such things only marked them out to the enemy and so made them easier to kill. Whatever wealth they had, it counted for nothing

413

on the field of slaughter.

I tried to force my way through the crowd, towards Fitz Osbern himself, hoping he might recognise either myself or Wace or Eudo, though the last time we had met with him we had been in the company of Earl Robert, and I was not sure whether he would recall our faces.

'Lord,' I called. Men on foot were in the way, but I kept riding forward and they soon moved aside, albeit not before cursing me.

He turned in his saddle, and his gaze fell upon me. 'What is it?'

'We are the men Robert Malet has sent,' I said.

He glanced at each of us in turn. 'You are the ones who will be opening the gates?'

'That's right.'

I gave him our names, though he did not appear to be interested. 'Six of you,' he said. 'I was given to believe that it would not be as many.' He sighed. 'It matters not. There is a boat waiting by the river for your use. It is a small craft, but it ought to be enough for your purposes—'

He turned suddenly as a call came from behind him and another man rode up, flanked by two knights on either side. Fitz Osbern headed towards them as if he had already forgotten us, leaping down from the saddle just as the other man did the same. The two embraced, and it was then that I saw the banner—the lion of Normandy—carried by one of the knights, and realised that the other man was no less than the king himself.

He was then about forty or so in years, tall and set like an ox, with a thick neck and a powerful sword-arm that I knew had sent many foes to their deaths. His eyes were shadows beneath stern eyebrows and his face was drawn, but he bore himself with confidence, as a king should. It was the first time I had seen him at close hand, and though I had stood before many nobles over the years, I could not help but feel awed by him. For this was the man who by his will and his vision had brought us here, to England, and won us this kingdom. The man who had gone against the usurper in battle, though the numbers had not favoured him, and who had defeated him.

Hurriedly I signalled to the others to dismount, for it was not right to remain mounted when the king himself was standing. The two broke off their embrace and strode towards us.

'My lord king, these are the men who will be opening the gates for you,' Fitz Osbern said.

I had enough presence of mind to kneel. King Guillaume towered over me, all six feet of him, and I met his eyes, glimpsing the fire contained within. Quickly I bowed my head. It was often said that the king was prone to anger, and I had no wish to see if that were true.

He walked around the six of us. 'You,' he said, his voice stern. I looked up, wondering if he meant me, but in fact he was speaking to Wace. 'What is your name?'

'Wace de Douvres, my king.' He, at least, did not appear perturbed.

'You have served your lord long?'

'I serve his father, the vicomte Guillaume Malet,' he replied, his crippled eye twitching slightly, which I took as a sign of nerves. 'Though before then I was sworn to the Earl of Northumbria, Robert de Commines.'

'Earl Robert,' the king said, more quietly. 'I knew

415

him well. He was a good man, and a good friend too. How long did you serve him?'

'Since I was a boy, lord. Fourteen years.'

The king nodded, as if in thought. 'Then no doubt you knew him far better than I,' he said at last. 'He met his end too soon, but I promise that you will have your vengeance upon the English who murdered him. We will fill the streets of Eoferwic with their blood.'

'I hope so, lord.'

The king placed a hand upon his shoulder. 'I know it.' Then he turned, marching back to his own knights and his banner, where he mounted up.

'Guillaume,' he called to Fitz Osbern. 'Show the enemy no mercy.' And then he and his men were gone, heading back towards the main part of the camp, their horses' hooves drumming against the earth as they disappeared into the night.

For a moment I stayed there, still kneeling, scarce daring to believe that I had come so close to the king himself. As I got to my feet I glanced at Wace; he seemed to be almost in shock.

'You did well,' I told him, but he merely nodded, and did not speak.

Fitz Osbern came over to us. He was mounted again, and had his helmet on and his lance in his hand, while a brown cloak covered his mail.

'Come,' he said. 'Ride with me. We're ready to leave.'

I glanced at the host assembled behind us: I could see now there were perhaps six hundred knights in all, with the rest comprising foot-warriors, and a few archers too. By itself it would not be enough to defeat the enemy, but it would certainly be enough to create a diversion, and that was all it had to do, until at least the king came from the south with his part of the army.

It was a couple of hours, and possibly more, before we came to the river Use. There was a bridge there, a simple wooden thing wide enough for two men on horseback to cross together. Fitz Osbern signalled for the host to keep moving—it would take some time before they were all gathered on the opposite shore—and took the six of us aside, down to the banks, where a small fishing boat had been drawn up beneath the drooping branches of a willow.

'Captured earlier by our scouts,' he explained. 'I trust it is sturdy enough. I am not sure that the man who built her had in mind six knights dressed in mail, but it should hold.'

Even in the dark I could see that it was not the grandest vessel I had ever sailed in. Nails protruded from her hull and it looked as though some of the top strakes were rotten. But it was dry inside and there was space aplenty for all of us, even with our shields and our weapons.

'It will be enough, lord,' I said.

'Then this is where we part. Once you are inside the city, wait until you hear us attack the camp. If nothing else you will surely hear the enemy's horns sounding. That will be the signal to open the gates and let the king and his army in. Do you understand?'

I nodded. The others murmured their agreement.

'We are trusting in you,' he said, his face stern, lit sharply in the light of the moon. 'I wish you good luck.'

He rode away and we were alone.

*     *     *

We pushed the boat out on to the river. I was pleased to see that it floated without letting in any water. Then we climbed in, placing our shields and our swords in the bows where it sat highest in the water. There were two benches and four oars, and so we took it in turns to row, while the other two rested and kept a watch over the river and the shores.

In truth there was not a lot to see. Under the stars and the crescent moon it was hard to see more than a few hundred paces, and harder still when the clouds came over. Of course if the enemy had scouts patrolling these banks, they would spot us far more easily than we would them, though it seemed unlikely, since what reason would they have to expect an approach by river, and especially one from upstream of the city? All the same, we wore dark cloaks to hide our mail and we tried to keep the splash of the oars as quiet as we could. Sometimes we would spy houses on the shores, and then we would haul the oars in, letting the boat drift on the current until we had passed. But most of the time we heard no movement save for the rustling of water voles amidst the reeds, and the occasional splashes as they entered the murky water.

The banks slid past and slowly the moon descended to the east, though there was no sign yet of day approaching. As far as I could judge we had made good time, but I also knew that Fitz Osbern and his men would be moving fast, and we had to be ready when they attacked. When I was not

418

rowing I was watching the sky, praying silently not to see the first glimmers of dawn. But then as we rounded a bend in the river, set against the starry heavens I suddenly saw the black forms of houses and walls, of the bridge and the minster church, and rising above it all, the shadow of the castle. Eoferwic.

The city lay still. I imagined the enemy asleep in their beds, oblivious to the slaughter that was shortly to be visited upon them. Only the sentries on the walls would still be awake, and I hoped they were watching the gates rather than the river. I tried to look out over the marshes and fields that lay to the south, wondering if the king and his host were there yet, lying in wait, but of course I could see nothing.

'Ship the oars,' I said. Now that we were so close, it was more important than ever that we did not attract attention, for it was not just victory that was at stake, but our own lives as well. I tried not to think of the fates that could befall us if we were caught.

The oars were pulled from the water and, dripping, laid down between the benches. The boat rocked gently from side to side, settling slowly as we drifted on the current.

'What now?' Wace asked, keeping his voice low.

'Now we have to find somewhere to moor,' I said.

'The wharves are the other side of the bridge,' Philippe pointed out.

I shook my head. 'We should land as soon as we can. Once we're in the streets we'll be safe, but the longer we stay out on the river, the greater the chance we'll be spotted.'

'And if there are any men waiting on those ships,

we're likely to wake them,' Eudo said, pointing downriver through the arches of the bridge.

He had better eyes than I did, and I had to squint to see them. But indeed there they were, huddled close to both shores. Their masts were down but I could see their hulls, high-sided and narrow in beam: shadows upon the moonlit water. Longships, and as many as a score of them. Perhaps some were the same ones that had chased us on the Use, or perhaps not, but either way Eudo was right. We could not use the wharves.

At the same time we needed somewhere we could keep the boat hidden from sight, since if someone saw it empty and suspected something then they might raise the alarm. But inside the city I could see nowhere that we might easily do so; the land along the banks all lay open.

'Where, then?' asked Godefroi.

I gazed ahead of us, scanning each side of the river, and it was then that I saw. From far away the walls looked as though they ran all the way down to the river, but from this vantage it was clear that there was in fact a gap between their end and the water's edge, where the rampart was crumbling away. It was not wide, nor did it look as if it would be easy to cross, as it was thick with reeds, and probably the ground underfoot would be marshy too. For any larger group it would surely prove impassable. But the boat could be easily concealed amidst the reeds, and besides, we were only six men, and difficult to spot. So long as we didn't make too much noise we could land this side of the walls and cover the rest of the way on foot, I was sure.

'There,' I said, pointing towards the gap.

'Between the walls and the river.'

'It'll be risky,' said Eudo, after a moment. 'If there are any sentries up there we'll be seen for certain.'

'But they won't be expecting it,' Wace put in, and I was grateful for his support. 'They'll be looking towards the south, watching for an army, not for a small band like us.'

I glanced at the others, to see what they thought.

'I agree,' Godefroi said.

Radulf shrugged, as if indifferent, and I wondered if he had been listening at all. He had better be concentrating, I thought, since otherwise he was likely to get himself killed here tonight, if not the rest of us as well.

'Philippe?' I asked.

'If the wharves are closed to us, I don't see we have any other choice,' he replied.

That was as much agreement as it seemed I was going to get.

'Very well,' I said, scrambling to the stern. On the way I picked up one of the oars, which I used as a paddle to steer us out of the midstream, closer to the southern shore, where the branches of low-hanging pine trees would offer us some cover. Then I let us drift once more, only using the oar when the current took us too close to the bank, or too far from the trees.

The city loomed closer with each passing moment. Somehow by night it appeared far larger than it had done by day. So forbidding were the shadows that I found it hard to believe that this was the same place where I had spent my recovery all those weeks ago.

Slowly, taking care not to make a sound, I

buckled my sword-belt to my waist, then made sure that my mail was hidden beneath my cloak as we approached the walls: banks of earth with a timber palisade running along the top. I looked up, but I could not see any men there. God was with us.

I steered the boat towards the reeds, breathing as lightly as I could, thinking with every slightest splash that we would be heard. The prow slid amongst the first of the tall stems, which rustled gently. By now I could see nothing beyond the clumps of reeds that were in front, behind, all around us. I wanted to get us as close in as I could, so that we had less ground to make on foot, and I steered us towards where I thought they seemed least dense. In the darkness, however, it was difficult to tell, and before long I could feel the bottom of the hull scraping against the riverbed, until, a few moments later, the boat gave a shudder as it ground to a halt. I tried to paddle further, in case this were merely a shallow patch with open water beyond it, but it was no use.

'We'll have to walk from here,' I said.

I got to my feet, keeping my head low until I could be sure that there was no one watching. Some twenty paces away the ramparts rose up. I stepped outside the hull, feeling my boots sink into the soft mud, and then held out a hand as Wace passed me my shield, which I hung around my neck, over my back.

The rest followed, and we set off. The mud sucked, squelched beneath me; it was impossible to tell which parts I could trust with my weight, and so I led them carefully, thinking only about one foot following the other, testing the ground as I went. I glanced up at the ramparts, still ten paces ahead, realising just how exposed we were. This was taking too long. If anyone were to see us—

There came a stifled yell, followed by a great splash behind me and I turned to see Philippe flailing in the muddy water. He was trying to stand up, but his mail was weighing him down and his cloak was tangled about him. He was spluttering, coughing so loudly that I thought the whole city might wake.

I reached out a hand, swearing under my breath. From close by came angry quacking, followed by a clatter of wings as a flock of birds shot up into the night.

'Philippe,' I said. 'Take my hand.'

It took a while for him to find it in the darkness, but at last he reached out and grabbed it. I tried to pull, but with his mail he was too heavy, and the mud and the river kept sucking him back.

'Help me,' I hissed to the others. 'Someone help me.'

Wace was the first there, kneeling down beside the pool in which Philippe had fallen. 'Your other hand,' he said. 'Give me your other hand.'

Together we managed to haul him out of the water and back to firmer ground, where he raised himself to his feet, still coughing up water.

'I'm sorry,' Philippe said, too loudly. He was dripping from his nose and his chin, and his cloak was soaked. 'I'm sorry.'

'Shut up,' I told him, looking again towards the palisade. 'Shut up and keep moving.'

We went as quickly as we could after that. Thankfully the closer we came to the remains of the rampart, the easier it became to find our footing. We scrambled across, drawing our cloaks over our heads so as to be less easily seen.

'Quickly,' I said. The sooner we could get away from the walls, the better. Ahead a narrow alley passed between two large storehouses, and beyond it lay the city, a maze of shadows.

With every beat of my heart I thought that I would hear cries behind us, but I did not, and it wasn't long before we had rounded those storehouses and found ourselves beneath the tower of a church. At this hour there ought to have been no one about, but nonetheless I made certain to check up and down the street before we laid down our shields and recovered our breath.

Philippe began to wring out his cloak by the corner of the tower. His mail and helmet were strewn with rotten leaves and mud, and other things he'd brought from the river.

'Take more care,' I said. 'Otherwise you're likely to get us all killed.'

But I knew that this was not the time to get angry with him. We had made it inside the city unseen, which was the first part of our task, but there was still much work to be done if we were to make Eoferwic ours.


## CHAPTER THIRTY-THREE

We did not stop there long. The gates were some way to the south from where we were, but how far I could not say for sure. Already as I looked towards the eastern horizon, the skies seemed lighter than before, and I knew we did not have much time. Day was approaching and soon Fitz Osbern would be leading his charge.

We set off, staying away from the main ways as much as we could, for if there was anyone about at this hour, that was where we would probably find them. In the distance, a dog barked, and its call was taken up by another. But of people there was no sign anywhere. A strange feeling came over me as we hurried through the silent streets, knowing that it would not be long before the rest of our army was here in force, before the sound of steel on steel was ringing out amidst the houses. My sword-arm itched even as I thought about it.

The moon was edging lower in the sky, almost touching the thatch of the houses by the time we saw the gatehouse ahead of us, its stonework lit by the soft glow of a brazier. In front of the gates were gathered several figures, all in shadow, all of them roaring with laughter, no doubt at some jest.

By the side of the street stood a stack of barrels, and I ducked behind them, raising a hand to the others, who were behind me. The barrels contained some kind of meat, only it seemed to have turned rancid, and some time ago as well. My nose filled with the stench of rotting carcasses, as bad as any battlefield I had known.

Breathing as lightly as I could, I crouched and peered through a gap between the barrels, towards the gatehouse. None of the Northumbrians there seemed to have heard or seen us, and for that I thanked God. There were five of them warming their hands around the brazier, but atop the gatehouse, facing the country to the south, stood two more, making seven in all. They were dressed in what looked like leather jerkins reinforced with metal studs, and each of them carried a spear, while one, who was in mail, carried a sword by his side as well, and I took him for their captain.

'What do we do?' Philippe asked as he wiped still more dirt from his face.

'Nothing yet,' I said. 'We wait for the signal.'

Again I looked to the east, and this time I was sure dawn was breaking: the blackness receding, turning to a deep blue. By now I was beginning to grow anxious. Had something gone awry? Had the attack been called off? If so, we had no way of knowing. All we could do was wait, and then if the attack did not come, try to get out the same way that we had entered the city. Except that as soon as it was light we would easily be spotted. At some point, then, we would have to decide: whether to stay or whether to go. It was not a choice I wanted to make, for if the whole plan failed because of us then we would have to bear the king's wrath.

My head was filled with all these thoughts when suddenly it came, blasting out from the north. The sound of war-horns. Fitz Osbern was attacking.

The Englishmen by the gate looked at one another; one of the two atop the parapet called down to the others. All looked confused; if they had been expecting any assault that night, they were probably expecting it to come from the south, not from the north. Then the guard-captain shouted at one of his men, who scurried off up the main street into the town.

That left just six: one for each of us. I placed my hand on my sword-hilt as my heart beat faster. I felt a thrill such as I had not known in weeks, but I held back, waiting while the enemy returned to their brazier, waiting for the right moment, waiting until they had let down their guard—

'Now!' I shouted, rushing from the shadows, roaring as I pulled my blade free of its scabbard.

The first of them turned, wide-eyed in surprise, his spear held before him, but I knocked it aside with my shield and ran him through before he even knew what had happened. Blood spurted forth as I wrenched the blade free, and he fell to the ground. My first kill of the night.

The one in mail had drawn his sword and he came at me now, wielding it in both hands, bringing it crashing down, but I lifted my shield in time and the blade glanced off its face as I stumbled back. He was stronger than he looked, but not quick, and as he tried to raise it for another blow I lunged forward, crashing my shield into his chest. He shouted out some words I did not understand, as, already off balance, he fell to the ground, and as he struggled to get up I stamped down on his chest and drove the point of my sword into his face.

Up on the parapet the other two Englishmen were shouting, hurling down spears at us, and I turned just in time to avoid one as it plunged into the ground, sticking in the mud. Another five men in leather jerkins were rushing towards us from one of the side streets, even as Wace, teeth gritted, finished the last of the gate guards on his sword.

'We'll hold out down here,' he shouted to me. 'You and Eudo go for the ones up there.'

On either side of the gatehouse was a doorway, inside each of which I knew would be a set of stairs leading up. I glanced at Eudo, then ran to one side while he went to the other. My cloak was slipping, threatening to get in the way of my shield-arm, and I cast it aside.

I started up the wooden steps, only to meet one of the sentries rushing at me, his spear aimed at my head. I ducked to one side, almost crashing against the wall, managing to stay on my feet as I swung at his leg, but my blade found only air. He had the advantage for he held the higher ground, and though I could defend myself against his blows, I could not get any closer than the length of his spear.

He came at me again, growing in confidence as he charged down the steps, his shield covering his chest as he tried to drive the spear towards my shoulder. I stepped back, encouraging him to press the attack even as I gave my sword-arm room. He fell for the ploy, thrusting further forward, but in doing so he had overstretched and left himself open. Before he could recover his balance, I lunged forward, driving my sword up beneath his round shield, towards his groin, twisting the blade as it went in. His eyes opened wide and a silent gasp escaped his lips, and as I stepped back he collapsed, his limp body tumbling towards the bottom of the stairs.

I left him there and hurried on up, coming out on to a wooden platform, as Eudo forced the other sentry back towards the outer parapet. The Englishman yelled as he was sent sprawling over, until he met the ground, and then his cries stopped.

From here I could see the whole of the city, from the bridge to the shadow of the distant minster. And I saw that Eoferwic was beginning to wake. Once more the enemy's horns blew out from the north, and in the streets now I could see men carrying torches, many of them running towards

428

the bridge, in the direction of that rallying call, others towards us. But in the fields and woods to the south I saw nothing but darkness, and I hoped the king and his army were out there, or else all this would have been for nothing.

'Come on,' I said to Eudo.

We sheathed our swords and hurried back down, taking care not to slip where the sentry I had killed had fallen. His bowels had emptied and the steps were slick with his blood and his shit.

The night was filled with the screams of the dying. Radulf sliced his blade across a Northumbrian's throat; Philippe kicked the brazier into the path of another man, and as it overturned, spilling hot coals across his lower half, he ran him through. The rest of the enemy had taken flight, for the moment at least, but there were shouts not far off and the torchlight was drawing closer. Godefroi seemed to be nursing a wound to his shield-arm, though it did not look serious, while Wace had turned his attention to moving the great oak bar that held the gates in place, and we joined him. It was far heavier than I had imagined and straightaway I felt the strain upon my shoulders, but together we managed to lift it, setting it down on the ground before turning our attention to the gates themselves.

Godefroi gave a shout and I glanced across my shoulder, down the street. Little more than a hundred paces away a horde of Englishmen were rushing at us with seaxes and spears and shields: more than I could count at first glance.

'Get these gates open!' I said, pulling harder on the iron rungs that were set into the timbers, but even with two of us on this door, and three on the other, it seemed that nothing was happening. I saw the enemy growing closer, and knew that if we did not do this now, then the battle would be lost before it had begun. At last with a great grinding noise, the gate began to move.

'Keep pulling,' Wace shouted. 'All the way!'

The grinding ceased and I felt the gate begin to swing open. Behind me I could hear the cries of the English growing louder, closer, but I did not dare turn my head as I concentrated all my strength. My arms burnt with pain, and I wanted to stop, but I knew that I could not. Gradually the gap grew wider, so that first one, then two men might pass through easily, and wider still, until we stepped aside and, with resounding crashes on both sides, the timbers struck against the walls of the gatehouse.

If ever the king needed a signal to begin his attack, that was surely it. We had done what was asked of us, and the gates to Eoferwic lay open.

But for now we had our own battle to fight, as the enemy in their dozens came like a torrent towards us, their faces white in the moonlight, the steel of their blades reflecting their fury.

'Shield-wall,' I shouted, gripping tightly the straps of my own shield. 'Hold the gates!'

I retreated until I stood just beneath the arch of the gatehouse itself. It was a narrow space, wide enough for only three men to fight alongside one another, or six men split into two ranks. At the very least we could not be out-flanked, although as I saw again the enemy's numbers, despair clutched at my stomach. I glanced over my shoulder, hoping to see mailed knights charging from out of the night, but there was nothing, only blackness. And so it was upon us to hold out here. We had no choice, if we were to succeed.

Wace and Eudo lined up on either side of me, shields overlapping, feet set to receive the charge, with Malet's three men behind: all of them so close that I could smell their sweat, the blood of the enemy soaking into their mail. The sound of their breathing filled my ears.

'Let's kill the bastards,' Eudo shouted as he banged his sword against his shield. 'Let's kill them!'

Not that we needed any encouragement, since they were upon us, the bosses of their shields crashing against our own. I staggered back under the force of the attack, but Radulf was behind me and our short line held firm.

Before me an Englishman bared his broken teeth, his breath reeking in my face as he tried to swing at my legs, but I met his blow on the point of my shield, trapping his seax, and brought my sword down upon the back of his bare head. He fell at my feet, though I had no time for celebration as another man stepped over his corpse to take his place in the wall. This one was taller, and had a helmet as well. He lifted his spear high and stabbed down, and I raised my shield to defend it, realising too late that I had left myself open from below as one of his friends thrust forward. I was lucky, for it was a weak strike which glanced off my chausses, but it could have been worse.

'We can't hold them,' Radulf said. 'There are too many!'

'Hold the line,' I shouted over him, drowning his voice out. 'Stand firm!'

But I knew he was right, as together the enemy

431

roared, and then all at once they began to push against our shields. We lacked the numbers behind us, and suddenly were being driven back, beneath the gatehouse.

'Stand firm!' I said again, but it was to no avail, for they had dozens of men and we did not have the strength to check them. I gritted my teeth, putting all my will into my shield arm, but even then it was not enough. We were losing ground, losing the gates, losing the battle—

The tall Englishman started to raise his spear, ready to stab down again, but this time I would not fall for the same trick, and kept my shield where it was, instead thrusting forward with my sword, up and into his face. He was not expecting it, and as I struck his helmet he staggered back, dazed, into the midst of his comrades, and the enemy halted for a moment.

Once more the horns sounded: two sharp blasts that were the signal to rally. By now the English would surely be gathering against Fitz Osbern, and whatever advantage he might have gained by the surprise attack would soon be lost. Sickness swelled in my stomach. We had failed.

It was then I noticed that some of the enemy, at least among the front ranks, had stopped driving forward, but were just standing there, as if unsure whether to keep attacking or whether to flee. The horns came yet again, and this time I realised they were not coming from inside the city, but from behind us.

I risked a glance over my shoulder, between the heads of Radulf and Godefroi. Mail and spearpoints gleamed in the moonlight, and there were pennons flying, horses galloping, and as I turned back to face the enemy, suddenly I found myself laughing, my arms filled with renewed vigour.

'Forwards!' I shouted.

The enemy wavered. Those in the shield-wall at the front had noticed what was happening and were hesitating, but those at the back could not see and they were still trying to push forward. In such moments of indecision did the fate of battles lie, and I knew that we had to take this chance.

I charged, hoping that Eudo and the others would follow, swinging my blade into the shield of the tall man before me. The blow shuddered through my arm as the edge cut through the leather rim, digging into the wood. He gave a cry as he stumbled back, still holding on to the shattered shield though it was now all but useless, and I pressed the attack, ramming the point of my blade towards his chest. He tried to block but it was in vain, as the steel broke through the wood and found his heart.

The sound of hooves could be heard now, drumming upon the earth, and it seemed that more of the enemy had spotted the danger, for some of those further back were abandoning their comrades, turning and running.

Their shield-wall was breaking, and even though we were but six men, we were amongst them, tearing into their ranks, exulting in the joy of the fight, the glory of the kill, challenging those who remained to stand against us, to meet their deaths on our sword-edges. Then, almost as one, they fled, making for the safety of the side streets, for the bridge, for anywhere they could hide.

The gates belonged to us, and through them now

came a column of horsemen, lances couched and ready to strike, riding at full gallop, kicking up dirt and stones as they went, and I saw on their pennons the familiar gold lion upon a scarlet field.

'For Normandy and King Guillaume!' I said, pointing my sword to the sky, and Eudo and Wace took up the cry, followed by Radulf and Godefroi and Philippe, all of us roaring as one.

I sheathed my sword and untied my helmet, pulling back my coif while I wiped the sweat from my brow. I looked for the king, or Robert, or any other lords I might have recognised, but they were not there, or at least not in the vanguard. For still the column of knights continued. I had forgotten how many men we had in our army, but they all came now: knights to begin with, then spearmen and archers. And then I saw King Guillaume, resplendent in his mail, his helmet-tail flying behind him, with one of his retainers alongside, bearing the same banner that just a few hours ago had been soaring over the camp. And not far behind him was the vicomte's son, alongside Ansculf and Urse and all the rest of his men, and with them they had brought six mounts without riders.

'Lord,' I called to him, waving to catch his attention. 'Robert!'

His gaze found me, and he rode to where we were standing by the side of the street, his men releasing the reins of our horses and handing them down to us. I looked for the white diamond on the forehead that marked mine out, and swung myself into the saddle.

'It's good to see you, Tancred,' Robert said.

'And you, lord.'

I noticed he was carrying two lances, one of which he tossed across to me. I caught it comfortably, before he gave a tug on his reins and rode to the head of the conroi. I understood: this was no time for conversation. The night was not over, the fight for Eoferwic not yet won. We had to get to the bridge before the enemy's leaders realised that we had entered the city and sent men to hold it against us.

Already other lords were passing us. We were at risk of being left behind, and I wanted to get as close as I could to the front of the charge when it met the enemy lines. For my heart was pounding, no longer with fear but rather with exhilaration. It was a long time since I had felt so free. Revenge and victory were at hand; I could sense it in the air.

'For Lord Robert,' Wace called out, and I knew he didn't mean Malet's son, but the man who had led us at Dunholm and through so many battles before. He was the one we were fighting for, as we had always fought: not for the vicomte, nor the king, nor anyone else.

Eudo hooked his ventail into place over his chin and neck. 'For Robert,' he said.

'For Robert,' I agreed. I pulled my coif over my head once more, retied my helmet-strap, then I turned and spurred my horse on.

'With me!' Malet's son shouted from the head of his conroi. His lance with its black-and-gold pennon was pointed towards the sky. 'With me!'

There was light on the horizon now, the stars fading as black gave way first to purple, then to blue. We rode down the curving main street as Englishmen fled in every direction. Houses and churches flashed past on either side, and then for the first time that night I heard the battle-thunder. For as we rounded the bend, there, marching in their dozens and their scores, came the enemy.

## CHAPTER THIRTY-FOUR

They beat their hafts and hilts against their shield-rims, filling the morning with their fury. Their banner displayed a black raven, a symbol much favoured by the Danes, and I saw that these must be the swords-for-hire that Robert had told us of. All were shouting, taunting us in their own tongue, inviting us to come and die on their blades.

Ahead, the king and his knights pulled to a halt, allowing some of the spearmen to rush forward through the ranks. They formed a line five deep across the road, standing shoulder to shoulder with shields overlapping to form a wall, and through the gaps in that wall they thrust out their spears, ready for the Danish charge.

'Robert,' the king shouted, and beneath his helmet his face was flushed. 'Take your men through the side streets; try to outflank them!'

Robert raised his banner in acknowledgement and then turned to the rest of us. 'Follow me!' he said, raising his lance with its pennon high for all to see. Flanked by Ansculf and Urse, he spurred his horse down one of the narrow alleyways between the houses.

I gripped the haft of my lance tightly. So long as I held that, my shield and my sword, nothing else mattered. I checked who was alongside me, and was relieved to find Wace and Eudo. There were none whose sword-arms I trusted more.

Behind us rode another hundred horsemen, as more lords joined us. The thunder of their hooves resounded in the narrow way. I glimpsed torchlight ahead, saw a band of ten or more Englishmen running from us, but we were a tide of mail and hooves and steel rolling in upon them, our lances couched under our arms, sharp and glinting in the dawn, ready to send them to their deaths. They were burdened with shields and spears, whereas we sat astride swift animals trained to the charge, and they had nowhere to go.

I heard Robert shout something, though what it was I never knew, as he thrust his lance through a man's shoulder, riding over him, and we were behind, cutting the enemy down. One caught his foot on a corpse while he ran and stumbled, falling to his knees, and as he tried to rise my sword-edge penetrated his skull. And then we were through, galloping on past grand timber halls and hovels of mud and straw. Dirt flew up from the hooves of those before me, landing on my cheek, my hauberk, my shield. The way turned sharply to the right, towards shouts and screams and crashes of steel, and as it opened out once more on to the main street, the Danish rear stood before us.

'For Normandy!' Robert shouted, and as one we returned the cry.

Some of the enemy heard our approach and were turning, their spears thrust out to try to deflect us. We were many, though, and they were few, and they had no time to come together—to form a shield-wall—before Robert and Ansculf and Urse were crashing into their first line, spearing into their midst, carving a space for the rest of us to follow.

We fell upon them without fear, without mercy. I was shouting, feeling the cold wind whip across my face. The first of the Danes stood before me, and my lance struck his shield, the force of the charge carrying it past the rim and into his chest. He crumpled and fell, face first, upon the mud, and I was pulling the point free, riding on, as we drove a wedge into the enemy ranks. Ansculf's lance glanced off the helmet of another man, and as he staggered back, dazed from the blow, I drove the point of my spear through his ribs, until it found his heart, and I left it there as I drew my sword instead, hacking down upon the next man's shield before backhanding a blow across his neck.

My mind was lost to the rhythm of the blade as it sliced across throats, pierced mail and cloth, the fuller flowing with blood. Another of the enemy charged at my right, swinging his axe, his face and hair spattered with mud, but Wace was beside me and he thrust his shield's iron boss into the man's nose, at the same time as I buried my sword in his chest. They moved so slowly, and I so fast, as I brought the blade down again and again and again. I leant back against the cantle as a spear jabbed towards my head, before slicing my sword-edge upon the hand of the one who held it.

But a conroi's strength lies in its charge, when it can bring its speed and its force and its weight of numbers to bear, and as our charge slowed, so the enemy began to rally. Before us rose a wall of shields, each with the raven emblazoned upon it, and all of a sudden the enemy were forcing us back. Even a mount trained to battle will hesitate to go against such a wall, against so many blades, and I saw Robert's horse rear up, tossing its mane from side to side. The enemy, recognising him as our leader, sensed their chance and suddenly surged forward, and for every one of them that he killed, it seemed that two more joined the wall.

'On!' I shouted, trusting in my horse not to falter. I saw Ansculf struggling to fend off those surrounding him, Urse's horse shying away, and I remembered my oath to Beatrice and knew I had to get to Robert.

So blinded were the enemy in their desire for glory, in their desire to be the ones who killed our lord and leader, that, despite our shouts and the noise of hooves and our naked blades shining in the glow of the morning, they didn't see us coming. I scythed my blade through leather and through flesh, tearing the point into one man's throat before turning and stabbing it down into the back of the next. Blood, hot and sticky, trickled down my arm, over my sword-hand.

I looked up and saw Robert, face clenched in desperation as he swung at the head of one of his attackers. He missed by a heartbeat: his foe ducked low and thrust his spear up, striking Robert low on his sword-arm, below the sleeve of his hauberk, and he yelled out in pain as his weapon slipped from his grasp. The Dane started to come at him again, jabbing the point towards his breast, but he had not seen me. I slammed my shield into the side of his helmet, and he lost his footing, falling under my mount's hooves.

'Back!' I shouted, hoping Robert would hear as the wind gusted from behind and I beat down upon the shields of the men before me. 'Get back!'

Robert's horse reared up and still the enemy

pressed forward. It only needed for one thrown spear to catch him in the chest, and he would be dead. I had to get him away from there.

'Lord,' I said, trying to rouse him from his pain. Blood was flowing freely, staining his sleeve, but there was nothing that could be done about it, and he would lose more than his sword if he stayed here any longer. The Danish line still held, while more knights were coming to join the fray. They would hold the enemy back for a moment, but not for ever.

I called to Wace, who had found himself in space. Eudo was with him, and Philippe, and several others I did not know but recognised from Robert's conroi.

'Hold them off,' I said, then without waiting for Wace to reply I turned, reaching over with my right hand and grabbing Robert's reins, tugging on them at the same time as I dug my heels in.

A spear thrust up at my flank but I managed to fend it off with my shield, willing my horse faster. Men streamed past us, their spears draped with pennons I did not recognise, so soaked were they with the blood of our foes.

'Hold the enemy off!' I shouted at them, glancing at Robert beside me. He was leaning forward in his saddle, his face creased in pain. His horse's eyes were white with fear.

I found the same alleyway we had emerged from, drawing to a halt by the gable end of a merchant's great hall, far enough from the enemy that we would be safe, for now at least. Others of his conroi had seen that he was injured and were riding to join us. I shoved my shield towards one of them; he took it without a word.

'Show me your arm, lord,' I said to Robert.

He shook his head. 'It's all right,' he replied through gritted teeth, but I knew it was not, or he would still be fighting.

I took hold of it, peeling back the sleeve of his tunic, thankful for the faint light of dawn. He had been struck on the forearm; a long cut ran most of the way between his elbow and his wrist. The wound did not look deep; certainly I had seen far worse. Had it been his shield-arm he might have been able to carry on, but it was his sword-arm, and that made all the difference.

Others from his conroi were beginning to gather round, and among them was Ansculf. He still had his cloak wrapped around his shoulders. 'Are you hurt, lord?' he asked.

'No,' said Robert, but the grimace on his face betrayed him. 'I need a sword. I need to fight.'

I turned to Ansculf. 'Give me your cloak,' I said.

'Why?'

I had neither the patience nor the time to explain. The screams of the dying echoed in my ears; the battle was still being fought, and we were needed there. 'Just do it,' I told him.

He unclasped it and handed it to me. It was not all that thick, but it would have to do. I drew my knife from its sheath and began to hack at the cloth, until I had a strip long enough that I could bind it around Robert's wound. He winced as I did so, and tried to draw his arm away, but I held firm until it was tied. A monk or a priest might have done better, but it would serve for now to stop the bleeding.

A great roar went up, and I turned, fearing the worst. I was expecting to see our knights in flight, the rebels surging forward, their confidence renewed by Robert's injury. Instead the Danish shield-wall was breaking and now they were in disarray, as our men and the king's pressed their advantage, driving into their midst.

'Stay with him,' I told Ansculf. I signalled for my shield, passed the long strap around my neck and worked my forearm through the leather brases. I cast my gaze quickly over Robert's conroi, or those at least who were there: more than twelve but fewer than a twenty. 'With me,' I shouted to them as I rode to their head.

'These aren't your men,' Ansculf shouted after me. 'You can't just—'

'Let me lead them,' I said, cutting him off. 'You make sure Robert's safe. Get him away from the battle.'

I knew I had no right to ask such a thing, but my mind was racing, the blood running hot in my veins, and I could not stop myself. This was the chance I had been waiting for ever since Dunholm: the chance to prove myself, to atone for my lord's death and make everything right.

Ansculf's cheeks flushed scarlet with anger as he stared at me, but he said nothing, no doubt stunned by my nerve. In any case we had no time to argue, and so before he could answer I lifted my sword to the sky, digging my spurs in as I called again, 'Conroi with me!'

'Tancred!' he yelled as I rode away, but I ignored his protests, glancing behind only to check that the rest of Robert's men were following.

I led them back through the narrow alley, on to the main street, where the Danes had realised the fight was turning against them and so were fleeing.

442

Of course they were paid warriors, not oath-sworn, and like all such men they were cowards: their only concern was for their purses and they had no wish to fight on till the last.

Beneath us the street lay thick with blood, thick with corpses. The stench of shit and vomit and fresh-spilt blood hung in the air. Not fifty paces away amidst the rush of men I glimpsed the raven banner, and beneath it the man whom I took to be the Danes' leader. He was built like a bear, with fair hair down past his shoulders, and a beard that was stained with blood. On his arms he wore silver rings, and he bore a long-handled axe. He was bellowing to his men, waving down the main street in the direction of the river.

Men scattered from our path, both Danes and Normans; our own spearmen had come out from their wall to give chase to the enemy. I lifted my sword high for all Robert's men to see, and spurred my horse into a gallop. There were barely a dozen men with me, whereas the Danish leader had more than thirty, but I knew it would be enough.

'Kill them!' I shouted. The street sloped down towards the river and I felt a fresh burst of speed. I found myself laughing as I saw the Danes in front of me, turning at last as they saw the danger coming from behind. Their leader roared in desperation as he rallied his men, but then they did something I did not expect, for all as one they came charging at us.

Whether the battle-rage had taken them, or whether they just wished for a noble death, I did not know; nor did it matter. One came at me, screaming, his face streaming with tears, and I raised my shield to fend off his spear, leaving him for Urse to finish as I arced my sword down into the path of another. And then I was turning, searching for the raven banner, for the Danes' leader.

I did not have to look far, for at that moment he came at my flank, wielding his axe in both hands, hacking down upon my shield. The force of the blow sent a shudder through my arm, but the blade slid off its face, and as he readied himself for another strike, I thrust my elbow out, bringing the point of my shield up and into the side of his face, sending him backwards. Blood streamed from beneath his nasal-guard, spilling across his beard and his thick moustache, dripping on to his mail hauberk, but he did not seem to care. His eyes were blue fire as he came at me again, and again, and again, each strike ringing off the boss of my shield, each one pressing me further back. His friends were gathering around him, but I knew that if I could kill him, the rest would break.

He lifted his axe for another assault and I saw my chance, pressing my left heel into my horse's flank. The animal turned sharply, bringing my undefended side to face him, and I saw the gleam in the Dane's eyes as he lifted for his next swing, but my sword was quicker, driving up and into his shoulder. He reeled back, and as he did so I plunged the blade into his chest, driving the point between the links of his mail into his breast. I twisted my sword and he let out a gasp, and as I pulled it free he fell forward, already dead.

To one side was the raven banner, smeared with scarlet, and I saw Urse as he ran its bearer through, driving his lance into the man's back. The banner fell to the ground under the hooves of

Urse's mount, and a roar erupted from the men behind me as it was trampled into the mud. The rest of the Danes were running.

'Fight us, you sons of whores,' someone shouted, and as I looked up I saw it was Eudo. He hacked at another of the enemy, his sword-edge ripping through the man's arm, just below the sleeve of his hauberk. The bloodlust was in his eyes. 'Fight us!'

Everywhere knights were giving chase: whole conrois darting down narrow ways, cutting the enemy down from behind, and I glimpsed the golden threads of the king's lion banner glimmering in the half-light as he and his knights rode down a group of Danes. Some of our spearmen had stopped to strip corpses of their helmets, their mail, their swords and even their boots, and others were fighting them for the same things.

'To arms,' I shouted to them as I rode past. 'To arms!' For if they thought that the battle was won, they were wrong. From the east I could hear the battle-thunder, more distant than before, but present still. The rest of the enemy were rallying.

I sheathed my sword while I retrieved a lance from the chest of a fallen Dane, checking first that the haft was still intact, the head still firmly fixed. I lifted it to the sky. 'Conroi with me!'

Eudo broke off from his pursuit to join us. His hands and the head of his lance were covered in blood, and his face bore a wide grin, which faded as he drew alongside me.

'Where's Robert?' he asked between breaths.

'He took a blow to the arm,' I said. 'He's with Ansculf.'

'Is he all right?'

445

'He'll live.' And so he would, as long as Ansculf kept him from the fray, at least.

With Eudo were Philippe and some half-dozen more of Robert's knights. Of Wace and Godefroi and Radulf there was no sign, and I could only trust that they were still fighting elsewhere.

As the ground began to fall away beneath my horse's feet, I could see the river, sparkling under the brightening skies, with the bridge spanning it. And upon the bridge were men in helmets and gleaming mail, marching towards us, under a banner of purple and yellow stripes, and their shields were painted in the same colours.

The colours of the ætheling.

My fist tightened around the haft of my lance. Eadgar. The man who called himself king; the leader of the rebels himself. The man who was responsible for the death of Lord Robert at Dunholm.

There he was, in the middle of the column, beneath the purple and yellow, with his gilded helmet that marked him out: a clear sign of his arrogance. Surrounding him were his huscarls, his household troops, with their axes slung across their backs, their scabbards swinging from their belts, their shields held before them.

I had pulled to a halt while the rest of my conroi gathered: almost twenty knights in all, including most of Robert's men, though a few others who had become separated from their own groups were now joining me. I glanced to either side, as always checking to see who would be with me in the charge. On my left was Eudo; on my right, Philippe, and beneath his helmet I saw the same solemn look I remembered from when I first met

446

him, though the youthful eagerness was gone now, replaced by a determination which I had not seen in him before.

The first of the enemy were almost across now, and following them was a column hundreds strong. I glanced over my shoulder; behind us all was confusion. By now some of the other lords had seen the ætheling marching, and they were hesitating, uncertain whether to rally around the royal banner or to attack straightaway. But I knew that if we were to head the enemy off, we could not afford to delay.

'For King Guillaume and Lord Robert!' I said, trying to catch the attention of as many of the other lords as possible as I spurred my horse into a gallop once more. 'For Malet, St Ouen and Normandy!'

And as the cry was taken up by those around me, I promised myself again that I would be the one who sent Eadgar to his death.

## CHAPTER THIRTY-FIVE

'With me!' I roared, lowering my lance so that it pointed towards the enemy as I rode knee to knee with Eudo and Philippe. 'Stay close; watch your flanks!'

We rode towards the dawn: some twenty knights and more, and I was at their head, leading them, leading the charge. Blood pounded in my ears, keeping rhythm with my horse's hooves. Around a hundred of the enemy had now crossed the bridge, but these ones were lightly armed, with only spears and shields and helmets, and many with even less than that. They saw us bearing down upon them, and straightaway came to a halt. My limbs, which had been starting to ache, suddenly felt fresh; my spear and shield were light in my hands. For I knew that these were not trained warriors, but men of the fyrd, the peasant levy.

'*Scildweall!*' I heard one of them cry. He alone was dressed in mail, and I took him for a thegn. The call was passed down their line as they brought their shields together: the faces painted in purple and yellow, the iron bosses shining, the rims overlapping. '*Scildweall! Scildweall!*'

They thrust their spears out towards us, the points shining silver in the dawn, as yet unbloodied. Above them, the sky was ablaze, the clouds lit with streaks of orange and yellow, and I thought of the mead-hall at Dunholm: of the flames rising up, engulfing the timbers and the thatch; of Lord Robert who had been inside; of the look of despair that had been on his face that last time I had seen him, branded forever in my mind.

I gritted my teeth, lifting my shield to protect my horse's flank. The shield-wall wavered, the men glancing at one another. Already I had sighted the first one that I would kill, and as we closed upon the enemy I met his eyes and saw the fear that lay within. He froze where he stood, his spear-haft falling limp in his hands as he stared at me, open-mouthed, and then I was upon him. Too late he raised his spearpoint to fend me off; too late he remembered to cover his head with his shield as I buried my lance in his neck.

Beside me hooves were battering down upon limewood, crushing legs and skulls, and the enemy line was crumbling as we forced them back. Their thegn bellowed to them, but whatever he was saying, it was in vain as they fell before us, our blades ringing with the song of battle. More men were coming to join us, pennons flying, adding their strength to the charge, and all of a sudden we were driving the enemy back towards the bridge.

From where came a wall of huscarls, their spears and their axes defiant, even as before them the ranks of the fyrd were failing.

'*Eadgar cyning,*' they shouted, all as one. '*Eadgar cyning!*'

Had I paused then, I would have seen how many they were and how well armed, and known that for us to ride towards their shining blades would be to invite death, for we had no hope of breaking them. But the battle-rage had taken me, and I saw victory at hand, knowing that if we could get to Eadgar and I could kill him, then we could win the battle there and then.

'On!' I said, willing my horse faster. Hooves clattered upon stone as we arrived five abreast upon the bridge. 'On! On!'

I lifted my lance above my head, drew my arm back and hurled it towards the first line of huscarls, as beside me Eudo and Philippe did the same. The enemy raised their shields to protect their heads, but in doing so they left themselves exposed from below, and at that same moment we came, swords drawn, riding hard, and I was thrusting my blade forward into their hauberks, cutting at their undefended legs. Some of our lances had sunk themselves into their shields, weighing them down, and as they tried to pull the shafts out we were cutting into them, bringing our sword-edges to

449

bear.

But for each one that I killed, another came to take his place. Just as before, once the impact of the charge began to fail, then they began to press us back, the first row bringing their spears to bear even as those behind reached over them with their long axes, the blades sharp enough, I knew, to sever a horse's neck in one blow.

'There are too many,' Eudo yelled, though I could barely hear him over the crash of steel, the screams of men and of horses. 'We need to fall back!'

A spear thrust up from my right, narrowly missing my mount's head, and I brought my sword down upon my foe's hand, slicing through the finger-bones before dragging the point up his ventail into his throat. I clenched my teeth and heaved my blade into the path of the next Englishman, missing by a hair's width as he ducked low. He lifted his head and then I saw his helmet with its gleaming cheek-plates, and the rim and nasal-guard, shining gold like the sun. It was Eadgar.

He charged, leading his men from the shield-wall, just as the bright disc of the sun broke above the houses on the far shore. The light glinted off the enemy's mail and off their blades, and for a moment I was blinded. Dark figures swarmed below; in desperation I slashed my sword at where I thought they were, and found only air.

'Tancred!' I heard Eudo shout, though I could not see him.

My mount screamed and rose up on its hind legs, kicking at the shadows darting about beneath. I leant forward in the saddle, trying to keep my

450

balance, to keep him under control, as there came a flash of steel from below. He screamed again, and this time he collapsed forward, and I was tossed from the saddle with my foot still caught in the stirrup.

Air rushed past me, but not for long as I came crashing to earth. The wind was knocked from my chest, and I tasted blood in my mouth as I looked up. A shadow towered above me, his sword and helmet glinting. I blinked, and as my eyes adjusted, I saw Eadgar's face: that familiar thin-lipped scowl that had tormented me ever since Eoferwic.

His eyes narrowed as he looked down at me. 'I remember you,' he said. 'You're Malet's dog. The one who made a fool of me.'

'You killed my lord,' I spat back at him. 'You killed Robert de Commines.'

Without warning he swung at me; I recovered my senses, raising my shield as I struggled to free my foot from beneath my mount's corpse. The blow struck the rim, inches from my neck, inches from killing me, but I had no time to dwell on it. The next stroke came, and the next, the force of each blow shuddering up through my arm, into my shoulder, pinning me down as the hide fell away from my shield, until I could feel the wood starting to splinter.

Eadgar raised his blade for another assault and I tried to scramble backwards, but my leg was still trapped and I could not get away. The ætheling's sword-edge ripped through my shield, through the mail at my shoulder, the point carving into the flesh.

I yelled out as pain seared through me. I saw the half-smile, half-sneer on Eadgar's face as he lifted

451

his weapon, ready to land the finishing blow. Desperately I jerked my leg again, feeling the blood pounding in my skull, the sweat stinging my eyes. Bile rose up, burning at my throat, and I found I could not breathe, and I knew that this was my final chance, when at last my foot came free.

Eadgar's blade came down, but not before I rolled to the side, shaking my arm from the straps of my now useless shield. His sword struck the place where I had lain just a moment before, sinking into the bridge-timbers. It stuck fast, and as he struggled to free it I glimpsed my own weapon lying beside me. I reached for it, clutching the hilt and turning on to my back, just in time to meet Eadgar's blade. Steel scraped against steel; he was strong and I could feel my muscles straining, but I held firm and managed to turn his blade to one side, forcing him off balance. In the time it took him to recover I rose to my feet, breathing hard, scarcely believing I was still alive.

'You murdered my woman,' I said as I clutched tight to my sword-hilt. The words almost stuck in my throat, but I forced them out. 'Oswynn is dead because of you. You killed her.'

'And I will kill you too,' Eadgar snarled, and thrust forward. The sun was in my eyes again, but I managed to parry his blow, gripping my hilt in two hands, using the strength of both my arms to force him back.

'Your mother was a whore,' I spat. 'Go back to her teat where you belong.'

He rushed at me, and this time I didn't wait for him to strike: instead I attacked first, swinging the point of my sword towards his neck, aiming for the gap between his helmet and his hauberk. It met his cheek-plate; he gave a yell and staggered back. There was blood streaming down his face, and I saw that I had cut him.

He screamed in anger and charged forward again, seeking revenge, and now his men were behind him, with their spears and their axes, and I realised that I was one man against half a dozen. Fear gripped my stomach and I steeled myself, praying to God as Eadgar rushed towards me—

A blur of brown and silver flashed past, and above a clatter of hooves and the crash of steel I heard Eudo's voice crying out: 'For Lord Robert!'

He drove his lance into the arm of the ætheling, who staggered back, blood streaming down the sleeve of his mail as the rest of his men closed around him, forming the shield-wall. Beside Eudo was Philippe, and after them came Urse and several others, with lances couched and swords drawn, and straightaway they were pushing the enemy back.

For a moment I could only stand there, dazed by what had happened, but then I recovered my wits.

'Kill them!' I shouted, and I was running to join Eudo and the others, pressing the attack, throwing myself into the fray, hacking down upon the purple-and-yellow shields before me, bringing the full weight of my blade to bear.

A spear struck the helmet of one of Robert's knights, the impact knocking him from the saddle, and he was pitched into the river below. There was a splash, followed by a cry for help as he struggled to keep his head above the water, but it did not last long as he was dragged down by his hauberk and chausses. His horse, now riderless, reared up, lashing out with its hooves at the heads of the

Englishmen in front.

And then horns were blasting out, cutting across the sound of the killing, and the enemy hesitated. For at the top of the hill to the east flew two new banners, with hundreds of mounted men gathered beneath them. The first was the white wolf on crimson that belonged to Fitz Osbern, while beside it, glistening in the dawn, was the black and gold that had become so familiar to me.

Malet.

Which meant that the castle garrison had sallied, and now the rebels were being attacked from two sides. His knights and Fitz Osbern's poured down from the east, and in that moment everything turned, as the English host, seeing the threat from behind, suddenly crumbled.

'For Lord Guillaume!' Philippe yelled, as he finished an Englishman on his lance. Eadgar had been dragged from the mêlée by a group of his huscarls and now they were retreating across the bridge, back towards the rest of their host. Some still remained, holding us off whilst their lord retreated, but they were few and we were many, streaming towards them on horse and on foot with sharpened steel in our hands. The bridge belonged to us, the enemy were in disarray, and I knew that victory was close at hand.

I ran to the horse that had lost its rider, vaulting up into the saddle, working my feet into the stirrups, pressing my spurs into his flank as I joined the pursuit, riding the enemy down. But though I saw my sword flash, saw it strike, for some reason I could not feel it, as if it were somehow without weight, with a mind that was all its own, and it were the one controlling me. Around me men were

454

dying on its edge and its point, breathing their last, and I was riding through them as the rest of the king's host followed: a tide of men rolling across the bridge.

Horns blew again—long forlorn blasts, like the dying wails of some monstrous beast—and suddenly everywhere in their dozens and their scores the English were turning, abandoning their shield-walls, abandoning the fight. Some were fleeing into the side streets while others were turning to the wharves, making for their ships, and among the latter I saw the ætheling with around fifty of his household warriors, his face and mail smeared crimson. In their attempt to reach the boats they were cutting down men on all sides, and they seemed not to care whether it was French or English that they killed, for all were falling to their blades.

'With me,' I said, raising my sword for all to see: not just my conroi but all the others were now joining us. I could feel my mount beginning to flag: every time I lifted the spurs he was slowing, but he had to keep going, and so I forced the steel points into his flesh as we chased the enemy on to the wharves. 'With me!'

The air whistled overhead as a flight of arrows soared across the river, spearing down into the ranks of the fleeing rebels. Some of the ships were already casting off from their moorings, though they were still only half full, and some even less than that. But in their haste to escape the enemy had cast down their shields in favour of oars, and now they were dying under a shower of steel.

'Eadgar,' I shouted over the din of battle as we closed on him and his men. 'Eadgar!'

My throat was raw, my voice hoarse, but they must have heard me, for some were rallying, turning to face us. We were on the wharves now, where the way was narrow and, just as on the bridge, it would only take a few men to hold us. I wondered where Fitz Osbern and Malet were, why they were not riding to close the rebels off from the other side, to prevent them from escaping. The ætheling wasn't far from his ships, and I knew that once he was out upon the river, we would be unable to catch him.

More arrows rained down, thicker than before, this time landing just a short way in front of us. Our archers were arrayed all along the length of the bridge. Together they raised their bows, drawing back their strings and letting fly, before notching fresh shafts as fast as they could draw them from their arrow-bags.

We were amongst the enemy now, and what had been a battle became a slaughter. I hefted my sword, summoning all the strength I had left, hacking it down upon them, using the full weight of the steel, and this time it was Oswynn's name that I was calling. Every man I slew was for her, and yet there was one I wanted to kill more than all the rest together.

Already he was climbing on to his longship, some of his men hacking through the ropes which bound them to the quayside, even as others leapt to take up the oars. But there were so many men before me that I could not break through, only watch as the ætheling's ship pushed off, surging forward with oars thrashing, its high prow cutting like a knife-blade through the water.

'Eadgar!' I roared as at last I found space for

myself. Wooden piers jutted out into the river and I rode down one of them. To either side corpses floated in water stained red with their blood. Feathered shafts protruded from their chests and their backs.

I untied my chin-strap, letting my helmet fall with a clatter to the pier below. I wanted the ætheling to see me clearly, so that he would remember the face of the man who had wounded him. The man who would one day send him to his death.

'Eadgar!'

Some of his men had spotted me, for they were pointing, directing their lord's attention. And then finally he turned, to gaze at me from beneath the golden rim of his helmet.

'I will kill you, Eadgar,' I shouted, hoping that he could hear. 'I swear I will kill you!'

He held my gaze for a while, but he said nothing in return, and then he turned his back and strode towards the bows. And I was left to watch as with every stroke the ship grew smaller and smaller. Behind me cries of victory rose up; men banged their weapons against their shield-rims, or else hammered the hafts of their spears against the earth, sending the battle-thunder back to the fleeing English. Eoferwic, at long last, was ours.

I shielded my eyes as I gazed into the rising sun, watching the ætheling's ship as it shrank to a black dot in the distance. The wind buffeted against my cheek, like icy teeth biting into my flesh, wounding deep. Inside I felt empty, as all strength fled from my limbs. My heart slowed as the battle-fury subsided.

And still I watched, until at last the ship slipped

away into the river-mist beyond the city, and I could no longer see it.

# CHAPTER THIRTY-SIX

I found Eudo and together we made our way back towards the bridge and the rest of the army. The sun had risen above the houses, above the mist, but I could not feel its warmth.

In the streets men were slapping each other upon the back, cheering, revelling in our rout of the rebels, in our capture of the city. Some, exhausted from the fighting, had collapsed upon the ground amidst the wounded and the slain. Others were grieving, offering prayers for their fallen comrades. A great press of men was gathered around the lion banner, and I sat tall in the saddle, straining my neck to see over their heads as we came closer.

'Normandy,' they chanted. 'King Guillaume!'

In the centre, under the golden lion, was the king himself, and before him knelt his namesake Fitz Osbern. Some of the other lords were there as well with their banners, but I could not see Robert or any of his men, and I only hoped that he had not been so foolish as to return to the fray.

'This way,' I said to Eudo as I tried to move around the edge of the crowd, retracing our path up the main street, up the rise. My shoulder throbbed with pain, though the bleeding had stopped. I was lucky, for Eadgar's blade had not penetrated all that deep, and yet had he struck me a fraction lower he might have found my heart. I shivered at the thought.

458

Most of the rebels who remained were fleeing through the side streets. A few fought on, but in vain, and they did not last long as, outnumbered, they were cut down or run through. One lay on his back, still alive, coughing up blood, shouting out in his own tongue for help that would not come, until a knife was drawn across his throat and he fell silent.

And then I spotted Wace. He was kneeling on the ground, his shield with its familiar black hawk resting against the trunk of a tall elm. He saw us and waved us over, a look of concern upon his face. Beside him was Godefroi, though it was from his build that I recognised him rather than his face, which was turned away from us, towards the ground and another man lying there.

My first thought was that it was Robert, and sickness swelled in my stomach as again I remembered the oath I had sworn to Beatrice. But none of his knights were there, and as we rode closer I saw that it was not him, but Radulf.

He lay unmoving upon his back, his head resting against the roots of the tree, facing the sky. His face was plastered with mud, and there was a bright gash along the line of his cheekbone. But I could see his chest slowly rising and falling; he was alive.

Hastily I dismounted and knelt down beside him. Godefroi was murmuring a prayer. Radulf's hand was pressed against the lower part of his chest. Blood covered his fingers, stained his tunic and indeed was coming still. In all the years I had been campaigning I had seen many injuries, some worse than others, and I knew at once that this one was bad. Whatever had struck him had gouged deep

459

into the flesh, perhaps piercing the gut: a spear most likely, to judge by the roundness and the depth of the wound, though it did not matter now.

'Radulf,' I said, and swallowed. I did not know what to say. 'I'm sorry.'

He turned his head to the side, not wishing to look at me. 'What do you care?' His voice was weak, hardly more than a whisper, but there was bitterness in it. 'You always hated me.'

I was about to say that it wasn't true, but I knew that he would not believe me. In any case this was not the time for arguments. 'You fought well,' I said instead.

'How would you know? You weren't even there.' He began to laugh, a thick rasp that was as painful to hear as no doubt it was for him to make. It descended into a cough, and then his whole body was shaking as he began to choke, and there was blood in his mouth, blood spilling on to the ground.

'Here, sit up,' Godefroi said. 'Tancred, help me.'

He took hold of one of Radulf's arms, and I the other, and together we dragged him closer to the tree, so that his back rested against the trunk. He shut his eyes and almost succeeded in biting back a yell, but not quite. I felt a stab of guilt, but at the same time knew that nothing we could do for him now would take that pain away.

Godefroi produced a wineskin from beside him and took out the stopper. He lifted the flask to Radulf's lips and he gulped at it, spluttering, groaning with every swallow. A flash of mail caught my eye and I turned to find a conroi of horsemen riding past. They were laughing, punching each other on the shoulder, raising their pennons to the sky.

'Normandy!' they shouted, all together. They sounded drunk, and perhaps they were, if not yet on ale and wine then certainly on the thrill of battle, on English blood.

'Can you hear that?' I asked. 'That's the sound of victory. The enemy have fled. The city is ours.'

'It is?' Radulf said. He had finished drinking and his eyes were closed once more, his breathing all of a sudden becoming shallower. He was not long for this life.

'It's true,' Godefroi put in. 'We showed them slaughter such as they had never seen.'

Radulf nodded, and there was for a moment a trace of a smile upon his lips, so slight as to be barely noticeable, but it quickly vanished as his face contorted in pain again.

'Where's Lord Guillaume?' he croaked.

I hadn't yet seen the vicomte; indeed in the midst of the battle and everything else I had almost forgotten that he was the reason we were here. I glanced at Godefroi, who looked blankly back at me, then at Wace and Eudo, who offered only a shrug.

'He'll be here,' I said. 'You served him well.'

Radulf nodded again, more vigorously, and now at last the tears began to flow, streaming down his cheeks as his breath came in stutters. He raised his bloodied hand to his face, as if trying to hide his sobs from us: his palm covering his mouth, his fingers splayed in front of his eyes.

'He will be proud of you,' I went on. 'Of everything you have done for him.'

He clenched his teeth, and his hand fell to his wound once more, leaving his face marked with

461

crimson streaks. The blood was flowing freely now, too much of it to be staunched. If the blow had been less deep, perhaps, or if it had struck his side rather than his chest . . . It was pointless to think that way, I knew, for nothing could change what was already done. But I could not help it. The same could have happened to me and yet I had survived. Why had I been spared but Radulf had not?

I felt moisture forming in the corners of my eyes, despite myself, and did my best to fight it back. Ever since we had first met I had thought him hot-headed, arrogant at the best of times, quick to take insult. Yet instead of goading him I might have tried harder to earn his trust, to gain his respect. And so in part at least I was responsible for him, and for what had happened.

'You did well,' I said again. 'And I am sorry. For everything.'

His eyelids opened, just a fraction, enough that he could look at me, and I hoped that he had heard. The colour had all but drained from his face, and his chest was barely moving, his breathing growing ever lighter, no longer misting in the morning air.

'Go with God, Radulf,' I told him.

He opened his mouth as if to speak, and I leant closer, straining to hear him above the roar of victory that was all around. Whatever he meant to say, though, he never had a chance to utter, as in one long sigh his final breath fled his lips. His eyes closed once more, and slowly he sank backwards, into the trunk of the tree, his head rolling to one side, his cheek falling against his shoulder.

'Go with God,' I murmured again. But I knew

that his soul had already fled this world, and he could hear me no longer.

*      *      *

Philippe found us not long after, and we left him together with Godefroi to stand vigil over Radulf. I did not know how long they had known him, or how well, but both seemed to take his death hard, and I thought it better to let them grieve by themselves while we sought out the vicomte. And someone had to stay with him, since now that the battle was over the time had come for plunder, and with his mail and helm and sword, the body of a knight held much that was of worth.

I rode with Wace and Eudo towards the minster, leaving the king and his assembled lords behind us. There was still no sign of Malet or his son, and I was beginning to grow worried when we turned up towards the market square and saw the black and gold flying before us. The vicomte was there, dressed in mail, though he had removed his helmet. Gilbert de Gand stood beside him, with the red fox upon his flag, and accompanying them both were some forty of their knights. Their spearpoints shone bright in the sun; their pennons were limp rags, soiled with the blood of the enemy.

We left our horses and made our way through the crowd. I was about to call out when I saw Malet embracing another man of around the same height: a man dressed all in black with a gilded scabbard on his sword-belt. Robert. Of course as far as the vicomte could have known, his son had been in Normandy all this while. How long must it have been since they had last seen one another?

463

I waited, not wanting to interrupt, but at last they stepped back, and Robert saw us. A grin broke across his face as he beckoned us over.

'This is the man who saved my life,' he said to his father. He was nursing his forearm where it had been wounded, I noticed; the cloth was bound tightly around it still. 'One of your knights, I believe. Tancred a Dinant. A fine warrior.'

Malet smiled. He looked somehow older than I remembered, his grey hair flecked with white, his face more gaunt, and I wondered what toll the siege had exacted upon him.

'Indeed he is,' he said, and extended a hand. 'It's been some time, Tancred.'

I took it, smiling back. His grip, at least, was as firm as always. 'It's good to see you too, my lord.'

'And Wace and Eudo as well, I see.' He smiled. 'Where are the others?'

'Radulf is dead, lord,' I said, bowing my head. 'He was injured in the battle; he died of his wounds. Philippe and Godefroi are with him now.'

'He fought bravely?'

'He did,' Wace said. 'I was with him. He sent many of the enemy to their deaths.'

Malet nodded, his expression sombre. 'He was a good man, loyal and determined. His death is regrettable, but he will not be forgotten.'

'No, lord.'

'Come,' said Robert. 'We will grieve for him in time, just as we'll mourn all those who have fallen. But this is an hour for rejoicing. Eoferwic is ours. The rebels are defeated—'

'Not defeated,' I interrupted him. For all the scores upon scores of Englishmen that had been slain, I remembered the hundreds more that had

464

filled the decks of their ships, that had managed to get away. I turned to face Malet. 'Eadgar managed to escape, lord. It was my fault. I had the chance to kill him, and I failed.'

'You wounded him,' Eudo said. 'You did more than any other man could manage.'

I shook my head. If my blow had struck him full in the face, rather than upon his cheek-plate, it might at least have dazed him enough that I could have cut him down. But it had not, and instead he lived.

'It doesn't matter,' Malet said. 'What's done is done and cannot now be changed. And Robert is right. Whatever battles there may be to come, it is this victory we must celebrate.'

'Lord,' someone called, and I turned to see Ansculf riding towards us, the black-and-gold banner raised in the three fingers of his shield-hand, a grin upon his face. Behind him rode the rest of Robert's conroi, their mail and their shields spattered with crimson.

'My men are waiting for me,' said Robert as he turned his horse about. 'No doubt we will meet again later.'

I watched as he mounted up and rode to join them, taking the banner from Ansculf, lifting it to the sky as his horse reared up, before he and his conroi galloped down the street.

'I hear my wife and daughter are safe in Lundene,' Malet said once he had gone.

'They are,' I said.

'That is good to hear. And my message has been delivered to Wiltune, as I instructed?'

I glanced at Eudo and Wace, unsure what to say. He had been bound to ask at some point, though I had hoped he wouldn't. But I could not lie to this man, to whom I had sworn my oath.

'Lord,' I said, lowering my voice as I drew closer. There were men all about us who might overhear, and I was sure Malet did not intend this for their ears. 'We saw your letter. We know about Eadgyth, your friendship with Harold, and the business with his body.'

If anything I had expected Malet to turn to rage, but instead his face seemed to go pale. Perhaps like us he was simply weary after the siege and the battle; the fire had gone out of him and he had not the will to be angry.

'You know?' he asked. His gaze fell on each of us in turn. 'I suppose it was always possible that you might find out. Ælfwold told you, I presume.'

'Not willingly, lord, but yes,' I said.

Malet glanced about. 'We can't talk of this here, surrounded by so many people. Come with me, back to the castle.'

\*　　　\*　　　\*

We passed through the bailey, past the tents and burnt-out campfires. There were men guarding the gates, but if they thought it strange to see their lord returning so soon, they did not question it.

Malet led us to the tower, to the same chamber where he had first spoken to me of his task all those weeks ago. It was much as I had remembered it: there was the same writing-desk, the same curtain hanging across the room, the same rug upon the floor.

'I would ask you to sit as well, but this is the only stool I have,' Malet said as he sat down. 'You will

466

forgive me, I am sure.'

None of us spoke, waiting as we were for him to begin, though he seemed in no rush to do so. An iron poker hung beside the hearth and he picked it up, prodding at the burnt logs in the fireplace. There were still some embers amidst the ash, and a faint tendril of smoke curled upwards as he disturbed them, but it was cold in the chamber nonetheless.

Eventually he turned back to us. 'So,' he said. 'You have read my letter to Eadgyth.'

I did not answer. He already knew that we had. There was nothing else to add.

'You cannot let this be known to anyone,' he said, a fearful look in his eyes. 'If the king were to find out that I had told her . . .'

He did not finish, but bowed his head as he wrung his hands. His lips moved without sound, and I wondered if he were whispering a prayer. The morning sun shone in through the window, causing the sweat upon his brow to glisten.

'You must understand why I did what I did,' he said. 'When I wrote that letter—when you swore to undertake this task for me—I did not think that Eoferwic would hold. And if the enemy managed to take the castle, I did not know whether I would survive.'

He had said something similar that evening when I had given my oath to him. Indeed I recalled how struck I had been by his honesty, how he had seemed almost resigned to the fact that his fate was bound with that of the city: that if Eoferwic were to fall to the English, then so too would he. But I did not see what that had to do with the business at hand.

Nor, it seemed, was I alone. 'What do you mean, lord?' asked Wace.

'I was the only one who knew the truth,' Malet said. 'Were I to have been killed, all knowledge of Harold's resting place would have been lost.' He sighed deeply, and there was a hint of sadness in his tone. 'I was only doing what in my mind was right. Eadgyth always saw me as having betrayed her husband, having betrayed our friendship. I thought that by doing this I might somehow atone for that—for all the hurt I had caused her.'

'I don't understand,' I said. Not for the first time, I thought.

'All she wanted was to mourn her husband properly,' he went on. 'I have lost count of the number of times she has sent letters to me, demanding to know where he was buried, and of the number of times I have sent word back, saying that I did not know. But when I heard that the English army was marching on Eoferwic, I knew I might not have another chance. The guilt upon my conscience was too great to bear.' He looked up from the floor, towards us. 'And that is why I had to tell her.'

'Tell her what?' I asked. He was not making sense.

Malet stared at me as if I were witless. 'Where Harold's body lies, of course.'

I glanced at Eudo and Wace, and they back at me, and I saw that they were thinking the same. For something was not right. I recalled Malet's message to Eadgyth: those two simple words. *Tutus est.* I had held the parchment in my hands, traced the inky forms of the letters with my own finger. There had been no clue there as to Harold's

468

resting place, unless somehow those words held some other, hidden meaning—one that we had not worked out.

'But you wrote that it was safe, nothing more,' said Eudo.

Malet's eyes narrowed. 'What are you talking about?'

'I saw the letter, lord,' I said. '*Tutus est.* There was nothing else on that scroll.'

'But that is not what I wrote.' The vicomte stood to face us now, and there was colour in his cheeks again as a puzzled look came across his face.

'I saw the letter.' My blood was still hot from the battle, but I tried not to show my frustration. 'Your seal was on it, lord.'

'I did not write those words,' Malet insisted. 'That was not the message I sent.'

'But if you didn't write them, then who did?' Wace asked.

So far as I could see, there was but one person who could have seen that scroll, apart from myself and Eadgyth. Indeed I remembered his anger when I let slip that I'd read it. He would not have reacted like that unless he himself had also known. Unless he himself were the one who had written those words. A shiver came over me.

'It was Ælfwold,' I said.

'The priest?' Eudo asked.

'He must have changed the letter.' It was not difficult: all it needed was for the original ink to be scraped away with a knife, which if done well meant that the parchment could then be used afresh. I had sometimes watched Brother Raimond doing it in the scriptorium, when I had been growing up in the monastery. More difficult would have been forging Malet's writing well enough to trick Eadgyth, and yet I did not doubt that the chaplain could have done it, for who else would be more familiar with the vicomte's hand?

'No,' Malet said, shaking his head. 'It is not possible. I know Ælfwold. He has given me and my family many years of loyal service. He would never do such a thing.'

'There is no one else it could be, lord,' I said. I felt almost sorry for him, discovering that someone whom he had trusted so closely, and for so long, could have deceived him thus. But I knew that this time I was right.

Malet turned away from us, towards the hearth, his fists clenched so tight I could see the whites of his knuckles. I had not known him to lose his temper before, but he did so now as he swore, over and over and over, before burying his face in his palms.

'Do you realise what this means?' he said. 'It means that he knows. Ælfwold knows where Harold's body lies.'

'But what good will that do him?' Wace asked.

'It depends what he means to do,' Malet replied. 'He wouldn't have acted without some purpose in mind, of that I'm sure.'

Silence filled the chamber. I thought back to that night we had burst in on Ælfwold, trying to remember what he had told us. There was only one reason that I could think of why the priest would do this.

'He means to take Harold's relics for himself,' I said. 'To establish them elsewhere and make him a saint, a martyr to the English.'

'To start a rebellion of his own,' Malet said, so

softly it was almost a whisper. He stared at me, as if he did not believe it could be true. But I did not see that there was any other explanation.

'How long ago did you leave Lundene?' Malet asked.

I counted back in my mind. We had spent four days riding to catch the king's army, and another six on the march before the attack on Eoferwic. 'Ten days,' I said.

'Then that is ten days in which he could already have carried out his plan.' He spoke quietly, his face reddening. 'If you're right and Ælfwold succeeds, this will be the ruin of me. He must be stopped.'

Not only the ruin of Malet, I thought, but of everything we had fought for since first we had sailed from Normandy more than two years before. For there were many among the English who had no love for Eadgar Ætheling and yet would march in Harold's name: men who if called upon would not hesitate in fighting under his old banner. If we let Ælfwold get away, it would not be long before the whole kingdom from Wessex to Northumbria was rising: before in every village men laid down their hoes, left their ploughs and their oxen to march against us; before halls and castles and towns were put to the torch, just as at Dunholm; before Normans in their hundreds were slaughtered across the land.

'How do we stop him?' I asked the vicomte. In ten days the priest could already have travelled far. So far that we might never find him, I realised with sinking heart.

The vicomte began to pace about. 'Have you heard of a place called Waltham?'

471

'Waltham?' I repeated. The name was not familiar. 'No, lord.'

'It lies half a day to the north of Lundene, not far from the Roman road,' Malet said. 'There is a minster church there—Harold's own foundation. That is where I had him buried; that is where Ælfwold will have gone. I want the three of you to ride there as swiftly as you are able. If he is still there, you must apprehend him and bring him to me. I will give you the fastest horses from my stables. Ride them to exhaustion if you have to; exchange them for fresh animals when you can, or else purchase new ones. The cost is not important. Do you still have the silver I gave you?'

'Some, yes.' The coin-pouch lay back at the camp, along with our packs and our tents and all the rest of our belongings.

'I will give you more,' Malet said. 'Do you understand what I am asking?'

'Yes, lord,' I replied.

'Then there is not a moment we can lose,' Malet said. 'I am relying on you all.'

## CHAPTER THIRTY-SEVEN

We rode hard, rising before dawn and travelling long into the nights, stopping only when we could no longer keep our eyes open, and even then not for long. For every hour that went by I knew that Ælfwold could be getting ever further away, and so we pressed on, pushing our horses as far and as fast as they could manage.

Hooves pounded in constant rhythm as hills and

472

forest, marsh and plains flew past. The skies were heavy with cloud, threatening rain which never came, while all the time the icy wind gusted at our backs. My eyes burnt with pain and every part of my body was clamouring for rest, but determination kept me awake, kept me going, until around noon on the fourth day, we arrived at Waltham.

It was a small village, set upon a hill above a brown, winding river. On the eastern side, looking down upon the valley, stood the minster in whitewashed stone: not quite as large nor as grand as the church at Wiltune, but then we had not come to admire its splendour or the tranquillity of its surroundings. At that time of day the gates to the minster precinct were open, and we rode up to them, where a greying, hunchbacked man leant heavily upon an oaken staff.

'Stop there,' he called out in our tongue, clearly recognising us for Frenchmen. He hobbled towards us, obstructing our path. 'What's your business here?'

'We've come on the orders of the vicomte of the shire of Eoferwic, Guillaume Malet,' I said. 'We're searching for a traitor. We think he might be here.'

'More of Malet's men?' he asked, his brow wrinkling as he eyed us suspiciously. 'You're not the ones who were here last night.'

I felt my sword-arm tense. 'What do you mean? Who was here last night?'

'Three of them there were: one a priest, the others men of the sword like yourselves. They left this morning, not long before dawn.'

After everything, then, we were too late. We had missed Ælfwold by less than a day. 'Where did they

473

go?' I asked.

'I don't know,' he said. 'You would have to ask Dean Wulfwin. There was some commotion, I can tell you that.' He shook his head sadly. 'Men rushing about in the middle of the night, all manner of crashing in the church, as if the last days of this world were upon us—'

'Where is this Wulfwin?' Wace said, interrupting him. 'We need to see him now.'

'He is in his hall at the moment, meeting with the rest of the canons, but if you would kindly wait I'm sure he will see you presently.'

'This matter won't wait,' I said. 'Stand aside.'

'My lords,' he said, drawing himself as tall as he could manage, which with his bent back was not all that much. 'This is a place of God. You cannot just come here and demand to be let in.'

'If you don't let us past,' Eudo said, 'you will have our swords to answer to.'

'Lord!' the man protested, his face turning pale. I fixed my eyes upon him, edging my horse forward. He began to step backwards, clinging to his staff, watching me as the animal snorted clouds of mist into his face.

'Let us past,' I said.

I saw the lump in his throat as he swallowed, and then at last he shuffled to one side. I did not wait a moment longer, spurring my mount on, past the hunchback, into the church precinct. We had no time to spare; as long as there remained the slightest chance of catching Ælfwold, we had to do whatever we could.

'Come on,' I called over my shoulder, and Wace and Eudo followed, leaving the gate guard shouting his protests to our backs. I knew that to

474

enter such a place armed was a grievous sin, but we were here for a greater purpose and I trusted that, when all was done, God would forgive us.

A cluster of some dozen high-gabled houses stood to the south of the church, with smoke rising from their thatch. They were surrounded by fields, where men and boys were sowing seed, or else tending to sheep and cattle. All stopped and stared at us as we passed: no doubt knights were a rare sight in the minster grounds.

One house was set apart from the rest. Standing on the northern side of the precinct, it was joined to the church by means of a cloister, and I guessed that this was where the dean lived. The recent rains had left the ground sodden, and the fishpool by the hall had flooded. We left our horses beside it and entered the cloister through a narrow archway. A row of stone pillars, painted white and red and yellow, ran all around, while in the middle a yew spread out its branches.

As we neared the door to the dean's hall, I began to make out a voice, intoning some words in Latin. It sounded like scripture, though I did not recognise the verse.

'This must be it,' I said to Wace and Eudo as we arrived before the doors. They were not barred or locked, and I flung them open. Both met the stone walls at the same time, sending a double crash resounding through the candlelit chamber.

At the far end a bald, round-faced man stood behind a lectern, with a thick-bound gospel book set upon it, its leaves open. His cheeks were ruddy, and his ears stuck out from the side of his head, and for some reason I thought he looked familiar, though I could not place him exactly.

He had stopped reading and his mouth hung agape. Another twelve canons, all of them dressed in black robes, sat upon wooden benches around the edge of the room. All looked up; a couple of them rose and were quickly seated again when they saw our mail and the scabbards swinging from our belts.

'Dean Wulfwin?' I asked.

'I-I am Wulfwin,' the man at the end said, his voice trembling as he stepped back from the gospel book. 'Who are you? What is going on?'

And suddenly I remembered where I knew him from. He was the priest I had seen in Lundene, that night I had been attacked—so long ago, it seemed, that until this moment it had all but faded from my mind. The bald head, the red cheeks, the prominent ears: it all came back to me now, as clear as if I were standing there still.

Which meant that the one he had been speaking with had to have been Ælfwold. Nothing else made sense; it was too much of a coincidence otherwise. I saw now how stupid I had been. If I had but trusted my own eyes, rather than let myself be tricked by him, then we might have saved ourselves all this trouble. But of course I hadn't known then everything we did now about Eadgyth and Harold. I only hoped that it was not too late to make amends.

I stared at the dean. 'You,' I said. 'You were in Lundene four weeks ago.'

Perhaps he was too afraid, or perhaps he simply had no answer to that, for he did not speak.

I advanced across the tiled floor towards him. 'Do you deny it?'

'H-h-how . . .' Wulfwin began, faltering over his

476

words as he stepped away. 'How did you know that?'

'I saw you by St Eadmund's church. You were speaking with the priest Ælfwold, conspiring with him against the vicomte of Eoferwic, Guillaume Malet, and against the king.'

A murmur rose up amongst the assembled canons, who until then had been silent, and out of the corner of my eye I saw them exchanging glances with one another. They did not concern me; I was interested only in finding the truth.

'No,' the dean said as he backed against the wall. 'It's not true. I would n-never speak against the king, I swear!'

'The dean is a loyal servant of King Guillaume,' another of the canons spoke up. 'You have no right to come in here and address him in this way, to accuse him of such things.'

I turned to the one who had spoken: a wiry man not much older than myself. He shrank back under my stare. 'We won't leave until we have the answers we're looking for,' I said, and then to the rest of them: 'Go. We will speak with the dean alone.'

He glanced at me, then at Eudo and Wace, whose hands rested upon their sword-hilts in warning.

'Go, Æthelric,' Wulfwin said. 'The Lord will protect me.'

The man called Æthelric hesitated, but at last his better judgement prevailed and he signalled to the rest of the canons. I watched as they filed out of the chamber. Wace closed the doors after the last had left and then set the bar across. I thought it unlikely that any of them would try to disturb us,

477

especially since they knew we all carried swords, but I did not like to have to resort to such threats if I could help it.

Throughout all of this the dean had not moved, as if his feet had somehow taken root where he stood. He watched me with wide eyes as I marched up to him.

'Tell me, then,' I said. 'If you weren't conspiring, what were you doing?'

'I w-was only receiving the instructions that Malet had sent me, through his chaplain, Ælfwold. He wanted Harold's relics removed to another place of his choosing.'

'He wanted them moved?' Eudo asked, but I waved him quiet. I would take care of this.

'P-please,' the dean said. 'I have merely been doing as the vicomte asked. I swear I have done nothing wrong.'

'Where is the usurper's body now?' I said. 'Is it still here?'

Wulfwin shook his head. 'They took it. The chaplain and two of Malet's knights came for it last night. I had to arrange for the high altar to be moved, the church floor to be pulled up. The coffin was buried beneath it—'

'Wait,' I said, as a memory long buried came suddenly to mind. 'These two knights. Describe them to me.'

A look of bewilderment crossed his face. 'Describe them?'

'We don't have time for this, Tancred,' Wace said. 'What does it matter what they looked like?'

The dean glanced at him, then back at me, uncertain what to do. I glared at Wace. We had been on the road for four days; I had not slept properly since before the battle, and I was not prepared to stand here arguing while Ælfwold put ever more miles between us and him.

'Think,' I told Wulfwin. 'What did they look like?'

The dean swallowed. 'One was tall, about the same height as him—' he pointed at Eudo '—while the other was short. I remember the tall one's eyes, of the kind that you imagine could see right into a man's soul, with an ugly scar above one of them—'

'He had a scar?' I interrupted. That was what I had been waiting to hear. 'Which eye was it?'

'Which eye?' There was a note of despair in the dean's voice. He hesitated for a moment, and then said, 'The right one, as you would look at him.'

'To him it would be his left, then,' I murmured.

'How is this important?' asked Eudo.

'It's important because the man who attacked me, that night we arrived in Lundene, had a scar above his eye. His left eye.'

'There could be hundreds of men with a mark like that,' Wace pointed out. 'How can you be sure it's the same one?'

'This man,' I said to the dean. 'He was unshaven, with a large chin?'

He looked at me in surprise. 'That's right,' he replied.

'It was him,' I said, turning to Eudo and Wace. 'Which means those men were serving Ælfwold all along.'

To have hired them he must have been planning this for some time, I realised. Since before we set off from Eoferwic, at least, and perhaps longer ago than that: since before we'd even met him. Which meant that all this time he had been deceiving us.

At last I was beginning to see how everything fitted together. My fingers tightened around my sword-hilt. Not only had the priest lied to me, but his own hired swords had tried to kill me.

I cursed aloud, filling the chamber with my anger. The dean withdrew towards the far wall, his face even paler than before. He was trembling now, his breath coming in stutters, and I wondered if he thought we meant to kill him now that we had our answers.

'P-please,' said Wulfwin. 'I have t-told you all that I know. By God and all his saints I swear it.'

'It's all right,' Wace told him. 'Our quarrel is not with you.'

Indeed I knew that for all the dean's squirming, he was not at fault. He was merely unlucky to have been caught up in this business.

'You were deceived,' Eudo said. 'Those weren't Malet's knights who came to take Harold's body away, but sell-swords. And the instructions you received came not from the vicomte but from Ælfwold himself. He is a traitor; we're trying to stop him.'

'A traitor?' A little colour was returning to the dean's cheeks, but he nevertheless kept his distance. 'Who, then, are you?'

'We've been sent by Malet from Eoferwic,' I said, though even as I did so I was aware of how feeble it sounded. 'We are knights of his household.'

Wulfwin glanced about at each of us. 'How do I know that you're speaking the truth?'

'You don't,' I said, no longer caring to keep the ire from my voice. The longer we delayed, the less chance we had of catching Ælfwold. 'Now tell us: where did they go from here?'

'I don't know,' the dean wailed. 'I swear I've told you everything.'

'Did they leave by road?' Wace said.

Wulfwin shook his head. 'B-by river. We had the coffin carried down to the village, where it was loaded on to a barge they had hired for the purpose. They sailed downstream, but they didn't say where they were bound.'

'Where does the river lead?' I asked.

'It flows into the Temes, a short way east of Lundene.'

'And they left this morning?'

The dean nodded hesitantly, as if afraid he might give the wrong answer. 'It was still dark, an hour or so before first light.'

'Which means they have only half a day's start on us,' Eudo muttered. 'If we ride hard, we might catch them before they reach the Temes.'

'If that's where they're headed,' Wace said, his expression grim.

'I don't see what choice we have,' I said. We had but a few hours until night fell, after which time it would be all but impossible to track them. I turned to the dean, still cowering in the corner. 'We will need your fastest horses.'

'Of c-course,' Wulfwin said. 'Whatever you need.'

I glanced first at Wace, then at Eudo, and saw the resolve in their eyes. Both knew, as did I, that this was our last chance. More than the battle for Eoferwic, more than anything that we had done since Hæstinges itself, this was what mattered. For if we failed to catch Ælfwold, if we couldn't recover Harold's body—

I drove such doubts from my head; now was not the time for them. 'Let's go,' I said.

# CHAPTER THIRTY-EIGHT

The river wound south through the hills, a brown ribbon showing us the way. We did not stop, did not eat, did not speak, but pushed our horses ever harder, pressing our heels in, drawing all the speed that we could from their legs, and more besides.

We galloped across the hills, through fields recently ploughed, skirting woods and villages, all the time keeping the river in sight, watching for the barge that might be Ælfwold's. But all we saw were small ferries and fishermen's boats, and as the sun descended towards the west and the shadows lengthened, and still there was no sign, sickness grew in my stomach. In one town we tried to ask some of the peasants who lived there if they had seen anything, but their speech was not of a kind that Eudo could understand, and so we had no choice but to keep going.

Slowly the river grew wider, bounded on either side by wide flats of mud and reeds where waterbirds had made their nests. The sun sank beneath the horizon and the last light of day was upon us when, just a few miles away to the south, I glimpsed the river-mist settling over the broad, black waters of the Temes.

I glanced at Eudo and at Wace, and they back at me. Neither of them said anything; defeat was heavy in their eyes. We had failed.

We carried on nonetheless, to the top of the next rise: the last before the land fell away towards the water. From here we could look down upon the river as it wound its way through the mudflats out into the Temes. The tide was on its way in, slowly flooding across the marshes, working its way into the many inlets that lay along the shore. At our backs the wind was rising, howling through the woods and down the valley. Streaks of cloud, black as charcoal, were drawing across the sky. The light had all but gone, and with it, our hopes.

All I could think about was how we were to tell Malet what had happened, what his response would be. We had done our utmost, and yet even that had not been enough to stop Ælfwold.

'What now?' asked Wace after what seemed like an eternity.

'I don't know,' I said. The wind gusted, buffeting my cheek. 'I don't know.'

I gazed out upon the Temes. For the first time I noticed there was a ship there, out in the midstream. It was yet some way off—a mile or so perhaps, barely visible through the river-mist—and heading upriver, but even so I could see that it was too big to be the barge that Wulfwin had spoken of. A trader, probably, from Normandy or Denmark, though it was late to still be out on the river, especially when there were ports further downstream where they might easily have put in for the night. I did not know how far exactly Lundene lay from here, but night was falling so fast that it seemed to me they had little chance of reaching the city before dark.

I watched it for a few moments. Certainly it seemed in no rush to make port this evening, for I saw that the vessel's sail was furled. Instead it seemed to be drifting on the swell of the incoming tide, its oars hardly moving, almost as if it were waiting for something—

'Look,' Eudo said, pointing out towards the south. 'Over there.'

I followed the direction of his finger, out to a sheltered cove perhaps a quarter of a mile away, close to the mudflats where our river joined the Temes. There, almost hidden behind a line of trees, was an orange light as might come from a campfire, around which were gathered several figures. I could not say how many and we were too far away to make out anything more, but I did not doubt that one of them was Ælfwold.

'That's him,' I said. 'It has to be.'

From thinking that all had been lost, suddenly my doubts fell away. My heart pounded and I tugged upon the reins, spurring my mount into a gallop one last time.

'Come on,' I shouted. I gritted my teeth, clutching the brases of my shield so tightly that my nails dug into my palm. A row of stunted, wind-blasted trees flashed past as the land fell away. Through the gaps in their branches I could see down towards the cove, where a low-sided barge had been drawn up on the stones. Beside it the campfire burnt brightly; a glint of mail caught my eye, but it was quickly lost amidst the trees.

I glanced out into the Temes, where the ship was closer than before. For it seemed to me that it was not there by accident, but was somehow connected with Ælfwold. And if so, that meant we had to get to him before they did. My blood was running hot, but even so I knew that the three of us could not fight a whole ship's crew alone.

I willed my horse faster, cursing under my breath. At last the line of trees came to an end and we were racing down the slope towards the cove, past shrubs and rocks. A stream lay ahead and I splashed on through it. Water sprayed up and into my face, but I did not care. I heard the crunch of stones beneath my mount's hooves as they pounded the ground; grass gave way to gravel as we arrived upon the beach. I looked up and there, directly ahead, lay the fire.

Men were running in all directions, scrambling to reach their spears and their knives. I was shouting, letting the battle-rage fill me. My sword slid cleanly from the scabbard and I flourished it high above my head, roaring to the sky as I did so.

'For Malet,' I called, and I heard Eudo and Wace doing the same as they drew alongside me: 'For Malet!'

In front of the fire stood the two knights, the one short and the other tall, just as the dean at Waltham had said. Their swords were drawn, their shields held firm before them.

And then behind them, next to the barge itself, I saw the chaplain, Ælfwold. He did not move. His eyes were fixed upon us, his feet frozen to the ground as if in shock. As well he might be, for he could not have thought he would ever see us again, and yet here we were.

'No mercy!' I yelled as I crashed my sword into the shield of the tall knight. It struck the boss and slid harmlessly off its face, and I was riding onwards, turning as an Englishman rushed from the barge, screaming in his own tongue. He raised his axe above his head, but I had seen him coming and my blade was the quicker, slicing across his hand before he had finished the stroke, taking three of his fingers before finding his throat. Blood gushed forth as he fell first to his knees, clutching

485

at his neck, then collapsed face down upon the ground.

But I could not pause even for a heartbeat as the tall knight came at me, raining blows upon my shield. Below the rim of his helmet, above his eye, I saw the scar that Wulfwin had spoken of, that I remembered from all those weeks ago.

His eyes met mine and a flicker of recognition crossed his face. 'You're the one who was there in Lundene,' he said between breaths. 'Fulcher fitz Jean.'

'My name is Tancred,' I spat back. 'Tancred a Dinant.' And I heaved my sword down towards his helmet, faster than he could raise his shield, and the steel rang out as it struck his nasal-guard. His head wrenched back under the force of the strike and he staggered backwards.

'Bastard,' he gasped, as a stream of crimson flowed from his nostrils, dripping on to his hauberk. 'Bastard, bastard.'

All around us the bargemen were shouting. Most had at least a knife in their hands, but only a few were daring to attack us; the rest had seen the fury of our blades and were running up the beach for the cover of the trees. I looked for Ælfwold, but amidst the confusion I could not see him.

The knight with the scar howled as he charged again, the light of the fire reflected in his eyes, but he had let his anger overtake him and there was no skill in his assault. His strokes were wild, lacking in control and grace, and I fended them off with ease.

The fire was at my flank: twisting tongues of orange and yellow writhing up towards the sky. Flames danced upon my blade, reflected in the steel, and I concentrated all my strength in my sword-arm, bringing the full weight of the weapon to bear as I slashed towards his neck.

His shield was out of position, ready for the low strike to the thigh that no doubt he had been expecting, and instead he raised his blade to try to parry. For the briefest moment our blades clashed, but he could not match the force in my blow, and suddenly with a great shriek of steel his sword shattered, shearing clean through above the crossguard, leaving him with just the hilt in his hand.

A look of surprise mixed with fear came across his face, and now at last he tried to lift his shield, but it was too late. Already I was following through the stroke, cutting through the links of his mail into the flesh beneath, driving the point through his ribs, deep into his chest. I twisted it, thrusting it deeper, and he let out a gasp, his eyes glazing over; then as I wrenched it free his legs gave way and he toppled backwards into the fire. A cloud of sparks lifted up into the night, as the flames began to consume his body.

I wheeled about, searching for my next kill, but few of the enemy remained. Those who did were either turning to flee or were soon finished on Wace and Eudo's swords; already the second knight lay dead upon the stones. Once more I looked out towards the Temes, looking for any sign of the ship. Now that we were on the beach I could not see it; the inlet was sheltered by two ridges of higher ground which blocked my view. But as soon as the ship rounded the first of those ridges, those aboard would see the light from the campfire, and when they did, all would be lost.

'The fire,' I shouted to Wace and Eudo. 'Put it

out! Put it out!'

My attention was elsewhere, as I had seen Ælfwold on the barge. He stared at me, his eyes wide, his face pale in the firelight, his countenance one of desperation. No longer was this the generous, kind-hearted man I had first met in Eoferwic, nor would he ever be again. Behind those eyes, I now knew, lay a mind capable of deceit and treachery of the highest order. An enemy of my lord.

I left my horse and ran towards him, vaulting over the side of the barge and on to the deck. The Englishman stood on the other side of a great iron-bound chest, more than six feet in length, and two in both width and depth.

A coffin, I realised, and not merely any coffin, but that of the usurper himself. Of Harold Godwineson, breaker of oaths and enemy of God. There was no inscription that I could see, but that was only to be expected, if he had been buried in secret, with the knowledge of just a few men.

'It's over, Ælfwold,' I said. 'We know all about your plan.'

He did not speak, nor take his eyes from me. With hardly a murmur of steel he drew a seax from a scabbard beneath his cloak, holding it before him in both hands, as if warning me not to come any closer.

'You would fight me?' I asked, more in surprise than in scorn. I had never seen the Englishman so much as handle a blade, let alone use one in anger, yet here he was, unafraid to stand before me.

The edge of his seax, polished and sharp, gleamed in what remained of the firelight. Out of the corner of my eye I could see Eudo and Wace stamping down on the flames, which were dwindling rapidly.

'You will not have him,' Ælfwold said, and there was hatred in his eyes. 'He is my king!'

'Harold was no king,' I said as I began to advance, one step at a time, towards him. 'He was a usurper and an oath-breaker.'

'It is your bastard duke, Guillaume, who is the usurper,' he spat back. He stepped away, keeping his distance, circling about the coffin. 'He stole this realm by fire and sword, by murder and rape and pillage.'

'That's a lie—' I began, my blood rising.

'He wears the crown and sits upon the royal throne,' Ælfwold went on, shouting me down, 'but as long as the English refuse to submit to him—as long as we continue to fight—he shall never be king.'

'Liar!' I said as I leapt up on top of the coffin and lunged towards him.

Ælfwold swung his seax, but it was with the clumsiness of one unused to arms, and he succeeded only in cutting my cloak. My shield slammed into his chest, and the blade tumbled from his grasp as he fell on to his back.

Straightaway he was trying to get up, reaching out for his seax, which lay just beyond his fingers, but I was quicker, kicking it away before he could get hold of it. I levelled my sword at his throat.

He gazed up at me and swallowed, eyes flicking between me and the point of my blade just beyond his chin. 'You wouldn't dare kill me.'

'Give me one reason why I shouldn't.'

'I am a priest,' he said. 'A man of God.'

Not so long ago I had spoken similar words in his

489

defence. Yet now he threw them back at me, mocking me. My hand tightened around my sword-hilt, but somehow I managed to restrain myself.

'You are no man of God,' I said. 'You are a traitor to your lord, to your king.'

'My king is Harold—'

I kicked him hard in the side and he broke off. I didn't have to listen to this. After everything, it seemed he was little different from all the other Englishmen we had been fighting since first we arrived upon these shores.

'Malet trusted you,' I said. 'You betrayed him.'

'No,' he replied, almost spitting the words. 'For two years and more I have stood by and done nothing while my kinsmen have suffered at your hands, been slaughtered on your swords. That was my only betrayal. All I wanted was to make that right.'

'You broke your oath to him.'

'Do you think I did so lightly?' he countered. 'Do you think it is so easy? Yes, I swore myself to him, and I gave him and his family my loyal service for as long as I was able. He is a good lord, a good man. But I have a duty more sacred than any oath, and that is to my people.'

He was trying to confuse me with his words, but I was not to be moved. 'You are a traitor,' I repeated, and pressed my blade closer to his neck, almost touching the skin.

Ælfwold stared at me, and I at him. 'Kill me, then, if that's what you're here to do,' he said.

'Don't tempt me.' My skull was pounding, almost drowning out my thoughts. Of course Malet wanted him brought back to Eoferwic alive, but at the same time I realised how easy it would be for

490

my sword to slip, for me to pierce the Englishman's throat and leave him here to die. I could tell the vicomte that he had fought on to the last, that we had had no choice but to kill him, and he would have to accept our word, never knowing the truth.

All around us lay in darkness. The skies were black, lit only by a few stars, the moon hidden behind the cloud. The fire was out; across the ashes were laid two cloaks, dripping with water, and Wace and Eudo were stamping down upon them, stifling the last tendrils of smoke. And just in time, for as I glanced out upon the black reaches of the Temes, there, edging past the first of the two ridges of land, a shadow amongst shadows, came the high prow, the tall mast, the long hull of the ship.

The point of my blade quivered as I held it before Ælfwold's neck, held his fate in my own sword-hand.

'That boat,' I said. 'It was supposed to meet with you, to take Harold's body away, wasn't it?'

He did not answer, but I knew from his silence that I was right. He was shivering, though whether from the cold or out of fear I could not tell. His eyes were wide, and I thought I saw tears forming in their corners.

And all of a sudden I realised that I could not do it. Despite his lies, despite his treachery, I could not bring myself to kill such a wretch of a man. I was holding my breath, I realised, and I let it out, at the same time sliding my bloodied sword back into its scabbard.

'Tancred,' Eudo said. He was pointing out into the river, towards the vessel. A point of orange light shone across the water, like the flame from a lantern. It lasted but a few heartbeats, and then was gone. A signal, I thought.

I turned back to face Ælfwold, about to open my mouth to speak, but at that moment he sprung at me, his face red and full of anger. He crashed into my middle, pressing at me with all his weight. Almost before I knew what was happening my feet were slipping on the wet deck, my ankle twisting, and I was falling. My back slammed into the wooden planks, the breath knocked from my chest.

But Ælfwold had no intention of finishing me, for already he was jumping down from the barge, running across the stones, making for higher ground. I rose to my feet, struggling under the weight of my mail. I loosened my arm from the straps of the shield, letting it fall to the deck as I leapt down and gave chase. Gravel crunched beneath my shoes, digging through the leather, into my soles. I heard Wace and Eudo shouting, but I did not know if they were behind me; all I cared about was catching the Englishman.

Already he had a start of some thirty paces and more as he scrambled up the grassy slope, through bushes, over outcrops of rock. Branches clattered against my helmet as I followed; thorns scratched my face and my hands. For a moment I lost him amidst a clump of trees, but I kept on going, and as I came out the other side I saw his cloak whipping in the wind.

He was running along the top of the ridge, towards the Temes, waving his arms at the same time as he yelled out in English—trying to catch the attention of those on the ship, I realised. Again the orange light came, glinting off the water, and again it disappeared, the signal unanswered.

'*Onbidath*,' Ælfwold screamed. '*Onbidath!*' But the wind was blowing more strongly now, and whatever he was saying, it was surely lost.

I was gaining on him with every stride now, despite my mail and the scabbard hanging from my sword-belt. Not much further ahead, the ridge came to a sudden end; instead of a steady slope down to the river, there was a steep drop on to the rocks where the land had fallen away. The priest was trapped, and he knew it too as he came to a halt.

'It's finished,' I said again, having to shout to make myself heard above the wind. 'There's no sense in fighting any longer.'

For the ship, I saw, was turning against the tide, its oars heaving as it began to make its way back downstream. For a third time the orange light shone, but it was fainter than before.

'You can't get away,' I said, and now at last he turned to face me. His eyes were wild, his face twisted in a mixture of despair and hatred, as though the Devil were inside him. I laid a hand upon my sword-hilt, ready.

'England will never belong to you,' he spat, and pointed a finger at me. 'This is our land, our home—it is not yours!'

He was raving now, driven to madness by the realisation of his defeat. Slowly I advanced, keeping my eyes fixed upon him.

'You will not take me,' he said, shaking his head as he took a step back. 'Kill me if you have to, but you will not take me.' He was fewer than five paces from the edge now, and I wondered if he knew.

I lifted my hands away from my body, away from my sword. 'I'm not going to kill you.'

493

The wind gusted again, pressing at my back, like icy hands laid upon my skin, digging into the flesh. The priest stepped backwards but the ground was muddy and he lost his footing, falling to his hands and knees. Behind him was nothing but air.

'Ælfwold!' I cried. I started forward, holding out my hand towards him.

He clasped it, his palm cold but his grip strong. Too strong, I realised, as he wrenched me from my feet. I met the ground hard, the brink no more than an arm's length away. My heart was pounding as I rolled on to my back and reached for my sword, but I was not quick enough. The priest flung himself at me, his face red, his cheeks streaming with tears.

He landed on top of me, his hands flying to my throat, and it was all I could do to swing my fist into the side of his head. The blow connected and he reeled back, and in that moment I saw my chance, throwing him off. I struggled to my feet, and he to his, wiping blood from his cheek.

Except that now I was the one with the cliff at my back. I pulled my blade free of its sheath, and held it before me in warning.

'Stay back,' I said.

But he was not listening. Screeching like some beast from the caverns of Hell, he charged.

Whether he hoped to catch me off guard and off balance, whether he planned to take us both over, I do not know, and never will. I recovered my wits just in time, waiting until he was almost upon me before dancing to one side, lifting my sword, turning and thrusting the blade out. A moment sooner and he would have seen what I was doing; a moment later and I would have been pitched, with

494

him, on to the rocks below.

My sword flashed silver in the night, striking only air, but Ælfwold was coming so fast that it did not matter. He flew past me, past the point of my blade, and in a single moment his expression turned from rage to fear when he saw the cliff-edge before him and found that he could not stop.

His cloak billowed all about him as, screaming, he tumbled forward, disappearing from sight. Dropping my sword, I rushed to the edge, gazing down towards the rocks. The priest lay on his back, unmoving, his arms and legs spread wide.

'Ælfwold,' I called, but he did not reply.

His eyes were open, the whites glistening in what little light there was, but he did not see me. His mouth hung agape, his chest was still and he was no longer breathing. His forehead was spattered with blood, his hair matted where his skull had cracked.

The chaplain was dead.

# EPILOGUE

The sun shone brightly upon Eoferwic. It was still early but the morning was warm, as Malet and I rode through a city blossoming with colour.

Hardly three weeks had passed since the battle, yet already traders were returning, farmers driving their livestock to market once more. Butchers' and fishmongers' stalls lined the streets, which were thronged with English and French alike. Everywhere the trees were in leaf, while in the fields the first green shoots were bursting above the soil. The scent of moist earth drifted on the breeze. After the long winter we had endured, it seemed that spring had at last arrived.

'It was on a morning like this, some fifteen years ago, that I first saw this city,' said Malet. 'I find it remarkable how little it has changed, despite all the troubles of recent times.'

We were alone. I had left Eudo and Wace at the alehouse where we were staying; neither were up when the summons had arrived for me from the vicomte. Exactly why he had called for me he had not yet said.

'My mother had died not long before,' he went on. 'I'd come to England to take up the estates she'd held here. It was only a few months later that I took a young priest into my household as my chaplain.'

'Ælfwold,' I said.

Malet's face was grim. 'I still find it hard to believe that he was capable of such deceit.'

With that I could only agree. We had told Malet

everything when we returned to his hall the night before: everything from our arrival at Waltham and our meeting with Dean Wulfwin, to the fight upon the shore, the ship waiting out on the Temes, my struggle with Ælfwold by the cliff's edge, and his eventual death. Through all of it Malet had hardly spoken as he sat, pensive and still.

We'd brought Harold's coffin with us, which had proven no easy task. First we'd had to find a cart to carry it, and of course there'd been the matter of how to raise it from the barge, but with the help of some local folk and generous offerings of silver we had managed. It had taken us many days after that to return to Eoferwic; far longer than it should. But we hadn't wanted to bring too much attention upon ourselves and so had tried to keep to country tracks, staying away from the old road as much as we could.

'Where will you bury Harold now?' I asked. 'Will you return his body to Waltham?'

Before us a man was driving a flock of geese through the mud. We plodded behind them until he came to a pen at the side of the street and, aided by some of the other townsmen, herded them through its gate, out of our way.

'Not Waltham, no,' said Malet. 'After this, I know I cannot rely on Wulfwin to keep such a secret safe.'

'Where, then?'

He glared at me, as if in warning, but I held his gaze and he soon turned away. 'I will find somewhere fitting,' he answered quietly. 'By the sea, perhaps, so that in death he may still watch over the shores he tried in life to protect.'

I wondered what he meant by that, whether he

was speaking in jest. But he was not smiling and there was no humour in his eyes. He had told me as much as he was prepared to, and it was clear I would get nothing more from him.

For a while we rode on in silence. Pedlars approached us, trying to sell rolls of cloth, wooden pots and all manner of trinkets, but when they saw that we were ignoring them they quickly moved on.

'What about Eadgyth?' I asked, recalling the letter that Wigod had translated for me. 'Will you send word to her now?'

Malet nodded. 'I'm leaving for Wiltune tomorrow to meet with her in person. At the very least she deserves an explanation for all that has happened.'

'You'll tell her the truth?' I asked, surprised.

'Or else I will think of some other story to placate her,' he said. 'That the body was lost, or something similar. Perhaps it would be better that way.'

I shot him a glance, but said nothing. A group of children darted about our horses' legs, chasing each other in some game I did not understand. I held the reins steady, slowing my mount to a halt until they had passed.

'I suppose I should thank you and your companions for everything you have done in my service,' Malet went on. 'I wouldn't have known of Ælfwold's deceit had it not been for you.'

He did not look at me while he spoke. I sensed he was testing me, and not for the first time, I thought. By now of course he must have realised that it was only our own treachery that had led us to the answer. For if I hadn't tried to read his letter in the first place, we could never have known the priest's plan.

'We did only what we thought was right, lord,' I said, picking my words with care.

He remained tight-lipped, concentrating on the road ahead. I wondered what was going through his mind, whether he was angry. But how could he be? He was indebted to us, whether or not he cared to admit it.

Not far off I spied the gaunt figure of Gilbert de Gand, laughing together with a half-dozen of his knights. The king had handed him the permanent role of castellan, I had learnt, with Malet returning to his duties as vicomte. Gilbert saw us, and waved in greeting. Certainly he seemed to be enjoying the new honour he had been granted, for I had rarely seen him in better humour.

Malet was clearly in no mood to speak with him then, however, as he pulled sharply on the reins, turning off the main street, his expression sour.

We passed the blackened remains of timbers strewn across a field of ash, where houses had once stood. In the wake of the battle there had been much looting, I had learnt, and many parts of the city had been burnt, including several of the churches. This was surely one of them, for amidst the ruins I glimpsed a figure dressed in brown robes kneeling upon the ground, eyes shut and palms together in prayer: a Mass-priest. I shivered, shifting uncomfortably in the saddle as I was reminded of Ælfwold, but soon the priest was lost from sight.

Overhanging the street was the great elm under which Radulf had died, its branches now dotted with purple-grey buds where new leaves were soon to emerge. He had been buried while we were

500

gone, in the grounds of the chapel attached to Malet's palace, as befitted a knight of his household. Others had been less fortunate, their broken bodies left to rot in great ditches dug outside the walls, where they were picked at by the dogs and the crows; we had smelt them on our approach to the city.

'I release you from your oath, Tancred,' Malet said as we left the crowds behind us. 'You may consider yourself no longer bound to me. Henceforth you may take your sword where you will.'

He had not asked whether I might extend my oath to him, nor had I expected him to. Instead he was making it clear that there was no further place for me in his household. As much as I had helped him, he couldn't afford to have among his retainers men whom he could not trust implicitly. The business with Ælfwold would have taught him that, if nothing else.

To tell the truth I was relieved to be leaving his employ, after all that had taken place these past couple of months. So much talk of intrigues and betrayals had tired me. I was a knight, a man of the sword, and I would be glad simply to return to that life once more.

'I hear my son offered each of you land in return for your part in the battle,' Malet said.

'Yes, lord.'

'Of course it isn't for me to say what men Robert chooses to keep around him.' His cold gaze fell upon me. 'But he clearly trusts in your ability. I only hope that you will serve him well, should you choose to follow him.'

Better than we had served Malet himself, was

what I took him to mean from that remark. The barb was not hard to miss.

'We will, lord,' I said. In all honesty I hadn't given much thought to what lay ahead or to where we might go: whether we would stay here in England, or return instead to France or Italy, where there were many lords to whom we might pledge our swords. Though I suspected that few of them would be able to offer as much as Robert.

For it wasn't just silver or land that I was thinking of; there was Beatrice too. The kiss we had shared remained fresh in my mind, even though many weeks had passed since then. I could sense her delicate touch still, the feeling of her lips upon mine. Unless I gave my oath to her brother, what chance did I have of ever seeing her again?

We drew to a halt by the bridge. Upon the river, sails of all colours billowed in the breeze. Drums beat in steady rhythm as shipmasters leant upon their tillers, bellowing orders to their oarsmen.

Across the waters a second castle was being built, opposite from the first. Already the ramparts and palisade had been erected, and a mound was under way, although no tower yet stood upon it. Even from this distance I could see men at work: sawing timbers, pushing barrows full of earth. In the centre of it all flew the wolf banner of Guillaume fitz Osbern, whom the king had placed in charge of the construction. For a long while Malet gazed at it, and I wondered what he was thinking. Overlooked for the command of not just one but two castles: a clear sign that he had fallen from the king's favour. It did not surprise me. After all, he was the man who had allowed Eoferwic to fall to the rebels in the first place, the dishonour of which would, I imagined, remain with him for some time.

As for the king himself, it seemed he had departed some days before we had arrived back. In his absence he had left Fitz Osbern with more than a thousand men to hold the city in case the enemy should try another attack. Not that many thought they would, at least not for some time. The rebels were divided, our scouts said, for while the ætheling himself had retreated to Dunholm, many of his followers had left him to go back to their halls. His Danish swords-for-hire had sailed back to Orkaneya and wherever else they had come from, and there were rumours of discontent among the old Northumbrian families.

Nevertheless, I knew that the year was long, the campaigning season barely begun. And as long as Eadgar lived, the English had a leader around whom they might rally. The pain of this rout would be felt for some while, but given time he could easily raise another host. I sensed that the battle for the kingdom was far from over.

'They will return,' Malet said, as if reading my thoughts. 'No matter how many castles we build, how many defeats they suffer, they will not stop until they have taken England back from us.'

I shrugged. 'In that case we must be ready for them when they come.'

A flock of gulls wheeled overhead, screeching in chorus. At the dock a sack had fallen from a cart, bursting along its seam, spilling grain on to the ground. The birds descended upon it in their scores, pecking and flapping, squabbling over every last speck of seed as deck-hands vainly tried to chase them away.

'Indeed,' Malet said, sighing. 'We must be ready.'

My horse snorted impatiently and I patted his neck. We would not stay here long; soon we would be moving on to places new. That was how it was, when one lived by the sword as I did. And I knew, besides, that somewhere out there was Eadgar, the man who had murdered Lord Robert, who had murdered Oswynn, and I was determined that I would find him: that before long I would take my vengeance upon him.

I looked out across the river a moment longer, listening to the bells ringing out from the minster behind me, feeling the warmth of the sun upon my face, until a cloud came over and a shadow fell upon us. Malet did not seem to notice when I tugged on the reins, leaving him there to gaze upon the half-built castle alone.

Nor did I look back as, under darkening skies, I rode to join my friends.

# HISTORICAL NOTE

The Norman Conquest is one of the defining turning points in English history, the date 1066 ingrained into popular consciousness. But whereas the events of that fateful year have been told many times, the story of what happened afterwards is less well known.

The Conquest did not happen all at once on the battlefield at Hastings, but in fact took several years to achieve. The years following 1066 were turbulent ones, as the conquered English slowly came to terms with their new, foreign overlords. England at the beginning of 1069 was still a kingdom divided. The south and the midlands had submitted relatively quickly—within weeks of King Harold's defeat at Hastings—and by this point had probably come to accept the invaders' presence as a fact of life, even if they did not accept the Normans themselves. By the summer of 1068, King Guillaume's armies had advanced as far north as York, where he built a castle and installed his namesake Guillaume Malet as *vicomte*.

This, however, was the limit of his authority, as the Northumbrians still refused to swear allegiance to him. Several attempts had been made through 1067 and 1068 to install in the region an English earl who was both loyal to King Guillaume and who would be accepted by the Northumbrian people. Each of these attempts, however, met with failure. Finally—probably around Christmas 1068—the king appointed Robert de Commines as earl, sending him north to take the province by force. It is this episode and its aftermath which form the focus of *Sworn Sword*.

In writing the novel I have tried for the most part to remain true to historical events. The Northumbrian rising—including the battle at Durham, the death of Earl Robert de Commines, the siege of York and its relief by King Guillaume—did indeed all take place in the early months of 1069 and on the timescale portrayed. Similarly, although Tancred and his companions are all fictional, many of the other characters are based on real historical persons, including Malet, his wife Elise (known in some sources as Hesilia) and their children, Guillaume fitz Osbern, Gilbert de Gand, the Northumbrian leader Eadgar Ætheling, Harold's handfast wife Eadgyth (popularly known by the more familiar name of Edith Swan-neck), and Dean Wulfwin. The original castellan at York, Lord Richard, is also based on a historical person, whose real name was Robert fitz Richard. However, since the novel contains two other Roberts—de Commines and Malet—I decided to change his name to avoid confusing the reader.

So far as possible, then, I have tried to stay close to the agreed facts. On some occasions, however, I have diverged from the agreed history to meet the demands of the story. For example, it is recorded that in the hours prior to the real battle at Durham, Æthelwine, the bishop of the town, actually warned Earl Robert of an impending attack, but that the latter did not believe him. Why the bishop would have betrayed his people in this way, and why the earl ignored him, are questions which I felt I could not satisfactorily answer, and which in any case did nothing to advance the plot. The true location of Earl Robert's death—burnt to death in the bishop's own house—only complicated matters further. Since I had no further role for Æthelwine in the novel, I chose to omit this episode entirely from the opening chapters, and to change the place of Earl Robert's death to the mead-hall in the fastness.

There are also many places where the true details are disputed or impossible to ascertain, and in these cases I have felt free to speculate. For example, although the Normans were known to decorate their shields and banners with their devices and colours, Earl Robert's hawk and Malet's black and gold—as well as those belonging to the other lords—are by and large my invention. The two exceptions are the gold lion on a red field that was the symbol of Normandy, and the purple and yellow which was the traditional banner of Northumbria.

The precise movements of individuals in the medieval period are often difficult to trace, and in this respect too I have engaged in some speculation. Whether Robert de Commines really fought in the battles at Varaville (1057) and Mayenne (1063), or campaigned in Italy—as I have suggested—is not known, although it is by no means impossible. The same applies to Robert Malet's journey from Normandy and participation in the relief of York, for which there is no evidence.

Whether Eadgyth was in fact even still alive by the time of the Conquest—and if she was, what happened to her—cannot be said for certain.

However, her second daughter by Harold, Gunnhild, is known to have been educated in the convent at Wilton (much later, in *c.* 1093, she was abducted from there by the lord of Richmond, Alan the Red). Thus it is not unreasonable to suppose that Eadgyth, if she lived, could have accompanied her in taking refuge there following the Norman victory and her husband's death at Hastings. If she did, she is likely to have enjoyed a comfortable existence. Ian W. Walker makes a strong case in his book *Harold: The Last Anglo-Saxon King* (Sutton, 1997) for identifying her with the Edith 'the Fair' and the Edith 'the Beautiful' who are named in Domesday Book. If he is right, then it is clear that she was a wealthy woman by the time of the Conquest, with large holdings of land worth more than £520, a significant sum at the time.

Guillaume Malet is another shadowy figure. For a start, there is no concrete evidence that he was in England prior to the Conquest, although for the purposes of this book I have followed the traditional belief that he was. There was certainly a significant influx of Normans during the early years of King Eadward's reign (1042–66). Eadward had grown up in exile in Normandy and so when he returned to England to take the throne, a number of prominent positions were filled with his Norman supporters. If Malet was in England before 1066, he could have come over at this time, or else might later have inherited land from his English mother. It is true that he held a manor at Alkborough in 1069, although its destruction by Northumbrian rebels *en route* to York is again my own invention.

Regarding the rest of Malet's family we know

surprisingly little for certain. There is no consensus on the number of the children that Malet had with Elise, their relative ages, or even (remarkably) on all their names. For the purposes of this novel, however, I have followed the family tree outlined by Cyril Hart in his article, 'William Malet and his Family' (*Anglo-Norman Studies*, vol. 19, 1996). Robert Malet is certainly known to have existed, as is Beatrice, although I have altered some of the details of her life.

The exact nature of Malet's relationship with Harold Godwineson is also open to debate. He is described by one source as Harold's *compater*, which historians have usually taken to mean that the two were co-sponsors at a baptism, although whose baptism, and when, is impossible to determine. Whether this acquaintance ever developed into full friendship is another matter. At the very least we know that when events came to a head in 1066, it was on the Norman side that Malet fought, so if any friendship did exist between him and Harold, it could not have lasted long.

The story of Malet's involvement with Eadgyth, and his role in Harold's burial, is based on a combination of two historical traditions. The first comes from our earliest account of the Conquest, the *Carmen de Hastingae Proelio* (*Song of the Battle of Hastings*), which mentions a man half-English, half-Norman whom the Norman duke made responsible for the burial. The same story is told by the chronicler William of Poitiers, who identifies this man as Guillaume Malet.

The second tradition is much later, originating with the twelfth-century *Waltham Chronicle*, which records that it was Eadgyth who was called upon to identify Harold amid the corpses on the battlefield at Hastings. This she was able to do because of her intimate knowledge of 'certain marks' on his body, which historians have usually presumed to mean old battle-scars, or else birthmarks.

Many other, often contradictory tales regarding Harold's death and burial emerged in the generations following the Conquest. As a result Harold's final resting place is unknown even today. One contender is Waltham Abbey, which Harold himself refounded in 1060, and which is named by both the historian William of Malmesbury and the canonry's own *Waltham Chronicle*. But the *Carmen* tells an entirely different story, in which instead of being accorded a Christian burial, Harold is interred in pagan fashion beneath a stone tumulus, overlooking the sea. According to this version of events, a tombstone was erected by his grave, on which was inscribed the message: 'You rest here, Harold, by order of the duke, so that you may still be guardian of the sea and the shore.' However, the author of the *Carmen* neglects to reveal the actual location of this tumulus—if, indeed, there ever was one.

More recently a claim for Harold's resting place has been put forward by John Pollock in his pamphlet *Harold: Rex* (Penny Royal, 1996) for Bosham, Sussex, the home of the Godwine family, after a stone coffin was uncovered beneath the chancel arch of Holy Trinity Church during repair work in 1954. Inside this coffin were the partial skeletal remains of a man, the condition of which Pollock contends matches the description of the injuries sustained by Harold at Hastings, as related in the *Carmen* and depicted in part on the Bayeux

Tapestry. The fact that no contemporary account makes any mention of Bosham is a problem, admittedly, though at the same time it is entirely consistent with the notion that King Guillaume might have wanted to keep the location of Harold's tomb a secret to prevent it becoming a focus for rebellion. Unfortunately, while Pollock presents a compelling argument, it is difficult to prove for certain. The true fate of Harold's body, now as in 1069, remains a mystery.

As a final note, the poetry recited by Ælfwold and translated by Eudo in chapter twenty-two is excerpted from an actual Anglo-Saxon text known to scholars as 'The Wanderer'. Perhaps appropriately, the poem tells the tale of a warrior whose lord and comrades have been killed in battle, and deals with his sorrow and his struggle to find redemption.

*Sworn Sword* reaches its climax with King Guillaume's successful relief of York in March 1069. But as will soon become clear, this is only the beginning of the unrest that the Normans will face, and so Tancred's fight will continue.

# ACKNOWLEDGEMENTS

Writing a novel can at times seem like a solitary affair, but the truth is that I could not have managed without the help and support of a great many people.

I first became fascinated by the period surrounding the Norman Conquest while I was an undergraduate at Cambridge, and my particular thanks go to Dr Elisabeth van Houts of Emmanuel College for helping to nurture that interest, which continues to this day.

For assistance with the various passages of Old English that occur in the novel, I am grateful to Dr Richard Dance of St Catherine's College, Cambridge, to Olivia Mills and Cherry Muckle.

Thanks also go to Tricia Wastvedt and Dr Colin Edwards, my tutors on the MA programme at Bath Spa University. Early readers Beverly Stark, Gordon Egginton, Liz Pile, Jules Stanbridge, Michelle Burton and Manda Rigby all gave feedback on the novel at various stages in its development. Their observations and detailed advice proved invaluable as I worked to hone the manuscript, and I am indebted to them.

I would also like to take the opportunity to thank my editor, Rosie de Courcy, together with Nicola Taplin and everyone else at Preface, and my copy-editor, Richenda Todd, all of whom have been instrumental in bringing this novel to publication.

Finally, and most especially, heartfelt thanks to my family and to Laura, without whose support and belief this novel would not have been possible.

# CHIVERS LARGE PRINT
## *–direct–*

If you have enjoyed this Large Print book and would like to build up your own collection of Large Print books, please contact

## Chivers Large Print Direct

Chivers Large Print Direct offers you a full service:

• Prompt mail order service

• Easy-to-read type

• The very best authors

• Special low prices

For further details either call
Customer Services on (01225) 336552
or write to us at Chivers Large Print Direct,
**FREEPOST**, Bath BA1 3ZZ

Telephone Orders:
**FREEPHONE** 08081 72 74 75